D1075094

Moonshine Light,
Moonshine Bright

By the Same Author

Southern Fried
Doctor Golf

A NOVEL

Moonshine Light, Moonshine Bright

WILLIAM PRICE FOX

J. B. LIPPINCOTT COMPANY

PHILADELPHIA AND NEW YORK

Portions of this novel have appeared in a different form in *The Saturday Evening Post, Harper's,* and the author's short story collection, *Southern Fried.*

For Mom, Dad, Bobby, Dicky, Jimmy and Buster

"Mm, Mm. And don't that sun feel good."
Lonnie Register

CONTENTS

PART I

June

Chapter 1

The Grove Chill Tonic sign thermometer on the drugstore door read 81 degrees when Doc Daniels opened up. After switching the overhead and exhaust fans on high to clear out the cigarette smoke and the stale beer smell from the night before, he made himself a double Bromo-Seltzer. He drank it fast. He frowned as he tasted his teeth and, tucking his bird-dog and rising-quail necktie under his apron, he began running water into the twin sinks.

The telephone rang. "Morning, Mrs. Osborne." Doc had a soft nasal voice. "I'm sorry to hear that. That's too bad." He yawned and looked up at the Pabst Blue Ribbon Beer clock, which read 8:35, as Mrs. Osborne complained about her lower back and described how the pains were settling in her legs. Doc had a round red face, and while he was only fifty-one his bushy hair and eyebrows were as white as the long marble fountain counter that ran half the length of the store. He nodded. "Yes, ma'am. I know exactly how it is." Today was Saturday and he figured he would go through a gallon of chicken salad, four cases of Pepsi-Cola, three cases of Dr. Pepper, and at least twenty cases of beer and ale.

Holding the phone with his shoulder, he slid back the top of the combination beer and soft drink box. He was low on Miller High Life. "Don't you worry, Mrs. Osborne. I'll make the pills up and you can have them the minute Bo-Bo comes in. Sorry, but I got to hang up now. Customer just came in and says he's in a hurry."

Doc rinsed the Coke glasses, the beer mugs and the ice cream dishes he was washing in hot water and then cold and began lining them up on the towel-covered back bar. In the yard Lonnie Register's retriever, Midnight, circled and sniffed the mailbox post and then moved over to the bicycle rack. When the big dog saw Doc watching him through the plate glass he turned and loped across the street toward the red front of the A & P store. In the distance a bicycle was coming down the long Bee Street Hill.

Cowboy Strickland coasted across the intersection of Mulberry Avenue and Bee Street and eased into the bicycle rack. He was tall, over six feet one, and when he moved off the seat and onto the bicycle frame his feet touched the ground easily. Cowboy was forty-one years old and had been on the Mulberry area paper route since he was seventeen. He crossed the small clay yard in four easy strides.

"Morning, Doc."

"Morning, Cowboy."

Cowboy wouldn't answer to any other name. His real name was Elroy Billy Strickland, but only his mother ever called him by it. He was wearing a white ten-gallon hat and blinding white boots with the initials C.S. set in red glass stones in the sides. There were over forty buttons down the front and on the sleeves of his dark blue shirt, and each scalloped and leather-trimmed pocket was embossed with a white cow's skull. He wore brown and white chaps of heavy horse hide with leather fringed full wrist gloves, two guns slung low and loose in open holsters, and forty or fifty rounds of silver plastic ammunition. Cowboy jutted his jaw and tipped his hat back. "Doc, you want me to fix the awnings?"

"Yeah, Cowboy. Let's get the sun out of here."

Outside, Cowboy released the knot on the awning rope and slowly lowered the big green and white canvas. The shaded glass in front of the White Owl Cigar display and the full rack of Dr. Scholl's shoe liners and corn removers mirrored the flat clay yard and the thin edge of iron grass and sour weed growing near the curb. Doc had painted the drugstore Coca-Cola red the year before, but the paint had been primed wrong, and after it had blistered in the summer heat it had peeled off, leaving the two-story building bright red with long shreds and shapes of undercoat green.

"Thanks, Cowboy, that'll keep it cooler for a while."

Doc emptied three fourths of a gallon of mayonnaise into a big salad bowl. "That a new necktie?"

Cowboy smiled. "Yessir, you like it?"

"Sharp, real sharp."

Wound firmly around Cowboy's thin erect neck was a tightly tied white silk scarf with a four-color rendering of the map of Texas, the Alamo, the ghost of Davy Crockett, and a small herd of grinning, long-horned steers. "That's all hand painted, every lick of it. Cost me four dollars."

Doc folded strips of chicken and cut-up celery into the salad and chopped up a bell pepper. He poured himself a glass of soda water and took four aspirins at once.

Cowboy looked at him hard. "You got a hangover, Doc?"

Doc nodded.

Cowboy drank a Pepsi-Cola and, leaning on the fountain as if it were a western bar, cocked his hat over his right eye and squinted up Bee Street. "Here comes M.L."

Doc mixed the bell pepper into the salad. "Why don't you go out and see him? Ask him if he wants a Bromo."

"O.K." Cowboy pushed his hat to the back of his head, shifted his gun belt, and went outside.

Martin Luther Anderson had a hangover. He crossed the intersection slowly, walking smoothly, trying to keep his throbbing head level and balanced. His right hand was raised in a half salute, cupped over his eyes, shading them from the sun. The bus stop bench was in the shade, and he sat down and opened his morning paper to the sports section. While M.L. could drink beer with Doc Daniels all night, bourbon always left him dried out and miserable in the morning. He and Doc had spent the night arguing baseball and drinking Old Crow.

M.L. was the same age as Doc. His hair was still dark, but it was receding in broad wings that threatened to come together at the top of his head. He never wore a hat, and the hairless wings were sunburned and peeling. M.L. worked on commission selling kerosene lamps, chenille bedspreads, comb-and-brush sets, and hair straightener to the poor whites, the mill hands, and the colored people that lived in the Bottom. The Bottom began one block west of the drugstore and stretched an entire mile to Pickett Street and the State Penitentiary and the muddy waters of the Cooper River. Since he had to demonstrate his lamps when it was dark, M.L. worked only at night. In the summer he worked from nine until eleven, but in the winter, when there was more money around, he put in an extra hour. Last night he hadn't worked at all.

14

Cowboy shifted his guns forward out of the way and sat down next to M.L. Stretching his long legs out to the curb, he wagged his white boots back and forth. "Doc wants to know if you want a Bromo-Seltzer."

M.L. didn't look up. "No."

M.L. read every word and number in the sports section of the newspaper every morning. He knew all the ball-players, their weights, their heights, ages, and home towns. He knew their salaries, how many children they had, and what they did in the winter. He kept a black notebook, and information that he couldn't remember—like batting and fielding averages, lengths of slumps, or consecutive games played—he marked down and kept current day by day. The Saturday paper listed all the batting, fielding, and pitching averages for both the American and National Leagues, and he was transferring the new information into his book.

M.L. snapped the paper down. "Boy, for God's sake why you want to go and dress up like that for? Just sitting next to you makes me itch. Jesus! Don't you get hot under that thick stuff?"

"No sir, I don't think so. Besides, I always like to dress up on Collection Day."

M.L. folded the paper over to page one and pointed his nose at the weather square. "Listen at this. Now listen. 'Temperature for Columbia, South Carolina, and vicinity to be in the high nineties, humidity sixty-five to seventy per cent.' That means it's going to be hot today. Damn hot."

Cowboy looked puzzled. "Heat don't bother me none, M.L."

"Seventy per cent humidity. Hell, you'll be able to squeeze it out of that fool shirt. Looks to me like you could at least loosen up on that infernal scarf. That's what holds the heat in."

"That's the way John Wayne wears it."

"Boy." M.L.'s head was pounding. He lowered his voice to keep it even. "When you going to learn that John Wayne is a rich man? Any time he puts on a scarf that tight, you can bet your ass there's a man standing next to him with an electric fan going. Besides, he's got all them stand-ins that do all the heavy work."

"No sir, no sir. I'm sorry, M.L., but that just ain't so. Other day Earl read me from a movie magazine how John Wayne does all his own stunts. Every one of them. Said so right there in that magazine from Hollywood, California. Said he wouldn't have no man do nothing he couldn't do himself. I swear he said that. There was a picture of him and he was standing there saying it. You ask Earl if you don't believe me."

"Earl might read you anything." M.L. changed the subject. "Where's your dog?"

"Not too good this morning. Got the croup or something and can't shake it. Ma was up with him all night."

"That's too bad."

Cowboy stood up and, grinding his right fist into his left gloved hand, frowned. "I gotta be going now. He's probably beginning to worry about me."

"So long, Cowboy."

Doc took the telephone off the hook and went outside. He sat down and leaned his neck back on the cool cement of the bench. "Don't you want a Bromo?"

"I had one at home."

Doc pressed his thumbs against the sides of his head. "They don't do a thing for me any more. I feel like I've been clubbed." He laced his fingers behind his head and closed his eyes.

The sun had cleared the chinaberry trees along Bee Street and was filtering through the tall sweet gums and the magnolias. The Chill Tonic thermometer had passed 85.

M.L. folded his paper around the crossword puzzle and looked down Mulberry. Two bicycles were tacking up the hill from the Bottom. "Bad news, old boy. Here come your buddies."

"I knew it was too quiet around here." Doc pushed his hands down hard on his knees and rose wearily. "I've got to get back on in. If I give them a minute alone they'll strip me clean."

Earl Edge and Coley Simms jumped their bicycles over the curb and coasted into the rack. Coley had a high-pitched voice, and he spoke as fast as he could. "How about the Cubs, M.L.? They win or lose? What about the Cubs? What do you think?" Coley would ask nine questions at once, hoping that maybe one would be answered.

M.L. didn't look up. He didn't want to get trapped in a flood of Chicago Cub history. "They lost."

"Awwwww, hell." Coley leaned into M.L.'s face. "But they're hitting, M.L., they're hitting fine. They hit Boston and they hit the Giants. They're hitting fine, M.L. You got to admit that." His bright blue fourteen-year-old eyes caught and held M.L.'s tired brown.

"Don't stand so close. Listen, everybody's hitting now. But the Cubs ain't got nothing in the bull pen, you understand that? They ain't going to make it. Be lucky if they finish sixth."

Earl moved in between them. "How about my Yankees? What happened?"

"Rained out."

Earl and Coley went inside and bought salted peanuts and Pepsi-Colas. Doc opened the bottles by touch, keeping both eyes fixed on the potato chip rack and on the boxes of Hershey bars and Butterfingers on the counter. He flinched as he watched Earl funnel his hand over the mouth of his Pepsi-Cola, pour in the peanuts, and begin shaking them up. Earl licked the salt from each of his fingers. "Looks like you and M.L. had a few too many."

Doc ignored him and, picking up the telephone, called the beer distributor and ordered four cases of Miller High Life.

Earl put a penny in the weighing machine, and the sweep hand rose and stopped at 111 pounds. "Jesus, look! I gained another pound. How 'bout that, two pounds in two weeks."

"Move over." Coley climbed on behind and Earl got off. The scale stopped at 109. "Damn! I lost one. A whole pound. Damn. What's the fortune say?"

Earl read loudly: "Weight: one hundred and eleven pounds. Fortune: you are generous and creative and have many friends." He chewed his peanuts and, studying himself in the mirror behind the fountain, he pulled out his ten-inch comb.

Earl's long broomstraw-yellow hair was dark and slick with Vaseline. He combed it down smoothly and tilted a high pompadour forward with the heel of his hand. At the sides the hair clung together in the thick grease, but the back was already drying and springing out at sharp angles. He pressed the sides down flat. Gaining a full pound a week for two weeks in a row made him feel good. He figured quickly. If he could keep gaining a pound a week he would weigh 125 or 126 when football practice started in September. He wondered if he looked bigger.

Coley picked at the paper label of his Pepsi-Cola, trying to remember what he had been wearing when he weighed the Saturday before. Maybe the scale was wrong. But even if it was, Earl still weighed two pounds more than he did. Maybe he had something heavy in his pockets. Coley put his Pepsi-Cola bottle in the crate by the door. "Come on, Earl. Can't you hurry with that stupid hair. The bus is coming." Coley's short curly red hair needed no attention. He pulled his Chicago Cubs baseball cap he had bought at Woolworth's from his back pocket and jammed it on.

The red and white Woodland Hills bus rolled up at the side of the drugstore and Earl and Coley jumped on. Earl leaned out and slapped the side of the bus. "Hey, M.L.! You ain't going nowhere, how 'bout keeping an eye on our wheels?"

M.L. looked up. "Wheels! You two still pushing wheels around? What happened to that car you were getting? Last I heard, you had everything picked out except the color."

Earl crossed his eyes, put a thumb in each side of his mouth, and belched loudly.

Claude Henry Hutto, the driver, glared back in the rearview mirror. "Cut that out! Where you think you are?"

The bus moved forward. Earl nudged Coley's arm and cut his eyes down. "Looka here."

Coley looked at the seat and smiled. There were two Hershey bars and two Butterfingers in Earl's right hand.

Chapter 2

At Monroe Avenue Earl and Coley got off the bus and trotted down the block to Paine Street and the Y.M.C.A. The lobby was jammed with the big Saturday morning fourteen- and fifteen-year-old gym-and-swim class. They were smoking, shouting, cursing, wrestling. Some were walking Yo-yos and tops across the floor; others were pitching pennies to the wall and playing jack-in-the-box with peanuts. The window seats were filled with readers hunched over comic books and thick stacks of baseball cards from gum packages. Henry Erby and Charley Polk were on top of one of the ping-pong tables, crouched back to back and jeering anyone into king-of-the-mountain. Under the other table two boys with headlocks and leg locks on each other were straining and cursing to a draw, while above them two more were trying to volley for serve.

The gym class bell rang and the room cleared. Earl and Coley were among the first down the hall and into the locker room. They stripped down to their shorts, and after wetting their socks in the drinking fountain so they could get a better grip on the slick waxed floor they went to the gym.

The class was too big for basketball or soccer. It was even too big for tug-of-war. Five instructors counted and lined the 120 boys into ten lines for relay races. The races began. There were hopping races, three-legged races, horseback races; there were crab walks, back crab walks, and complicated hopping, leaping runs with one hand on one ankle and one hand high in the air that would leave them gasping for breath and groaning on the wrestling mats under the parallel bars at the side of the gym. Every race was designed to tire them out and keep the noise and the fights down.

After the races the sweating class tossed their shorts and socks in their lockers and piled into the shower room. The pool door was unlocked and the instructors began indian-rubbing each boy's ankles and ears, checking for dirt. Earl and Coley and over half of the class were turned down and made to wash again. They pushed back through the steaming crowd and began scrubbing their ankles with a strong, chlorine-smelling solvent that stood in the corner of the room. Finally they were all in the pool.

It was a small pool ten yards wide and twenty yards long with a one-meter hemp-covered diving board at one end. Across the ceiling of the room were heavy plumbing pipes. The instructors began shouting that the first one to climb up on the pipes would be kicked out.

In two minutes the tile around the pool was soaked. Leo Morrison and Ray Barnes ran down the length and tried hook slides around the slippery corners. Leo cracked into the wall by the diving board but he wasn't hurt.

Bert Moore was the first to swing from the overhead

pipes, and when the instructors shouted he looked the other way and swung higher. He swung until he was parallel to the water and then laid out a perfect half gainer. Bert's dive was the signal, and in the next instant every foot of every pipe was covered with swinging, screaming, nude white bodies. The instructors couldn't be heard.

At the deep end of the pool Earl and Coley dove for Gene Demos' St. Christopher medal, and Ambrose Fogel lay on his back on the bottom and pretended he was an octopus. The diving board sagged low under the weight of four divers, while three more hung on grinning underneath, trying to trip them. At the eight-foot section the underwater swimmers raced back and forth. And at the shallow end the slow fats and the nonswimmers and the small kids who had said they were fourteen and were only twelve were gasping and crying into the spit drain that ran around the perimeter of the pool.

Luke Dubose shouted that he was going to try a one-and-a-half flip from the board. Bert told him he would need a lot of height and then stomped on the fingers of the boys hanging on underneath. The board was ready. Luke pushed off and got up to top speed. He hit the end of the board hard and soared up with good elevation. But he didn't use it fast enough and came down hard on his back. The sound was like a pistol shot, and he came limping in to the steel ladder with tears in his eyes and his back on fire.

Coley rammed someone under the water and came up with a nosebleed, while Earl wove back and forth through the churning water practicing and perfecting his Australian crawl.

And then it was time to go.

At eleven o'clock Earl, Coley, Luke, Ray, and Ambrose

and the rest of the class came leaping down the steps of the Y.M.C.A. into the Saturday-morning farmer traffic. Horns blew and men cursed as they zigzagged through the cars and pickup trucks and raced up Franklin Street Alley toward Broad and the Palace Theatre. Luke knew someone near the head of the long line, and rushing up the stairs to the seats in the front of the balcony next to the projection catwalk they claimed the five seats looking over the rail. The feature starred Bob Steele, and the fifteen-part serial was *The Green Hornet.*

Earl and Coley had brought June bugs with black thread tied to their back legs. They had been carefully prepared that morning and placed in penny matchboxes with the long thread professionally wound around the outside of the box. During a love scene Coley pulled his June bug out and lowered him down into the crowd. Nothing happened. He passed it to Ray and then to Earl and finally to Ambrose. Ambrose jiggled the thread. An electric scream of a girl's voice shot out. The lights came on and Ambrose quickly reeled the bug in. The manager and three ushers rushed to the girl. They searched the floor and shone their flashlights up at the balcony and the ceiling. Finally they left and the lights went off.

The June bug was lowered and passed to Luke. He felt the thread sag, and when he pulled it up the June bug was gone. Someone had snapped it off. They waited and removed the second bug from its box. This time it was slower. It went from Ray to Ambrose to Luke and finally back to Coley. Coley drew it up to make sure the bug was still alive. He felt the bug's buzzing wings and lowered it again.

A terrifying scream filled the theatre. "It was a black

widow! I tell you it was a black widow! It was on my face!"

Coley quickly pulled the thread but it was broken. The lights came on. The manager, the ushers, and a policeman pounded up to the balcony and came to the front row. "All right, which one of you is lowering spiders?"

There was no answer.

The policeman rapped his night stick on the balcony rail. "All right, now, this is the last warning. Anything else and I'm clearing this whole section out."

Someone on the other side of the balcony booed, and downstairs the audience started whistling and clapping. The show began, and when the theatre was quiet the lights were turned down.

Coley leaned out into the projection beam and, making a shadow with his hand, raced a biting dog down the leading lady's neck. The crowd laughed, and, leaning out further, Coley hooked his thumbs together and made a butterfly flap near her breast. The crowd applauded. The applause was too much for him, and he leaped over the low wall and stood in the catwalk and did a dance. The crowd went wild. He raised his arms like a giant bird and did an even wilder dance that appeared thirty feet tall on the big screen. The crowd cheered and whistled. Coley went into a vulgar hootch dance, and some cheered and some gasped and the lights came on once more. An usher on each side of the balcony closed in on him, dragged him away, and kicked him out of the theatre.

The movie started again and this time it was completed. During *The Green Hornet* a sudden noise of running feet was heard and three flashlights stung into the front row. A heavy voice shouted, "That's him! That one on the end. Right there on the end."

"That one?"

"Yeah, that's him all right. He's been spitting on us."

The three lights were on Earl. They grabbed him from both sides and pulled him into the aisle and up the steps. The policeman had him by the back of his collar. "What's your name, boy?"

"Earl."

"Earl what?"

"Edge. My name's Earl Edge."

"You any kin to Leroy?"

"Yessir."

"How much?"

"He's my father."

Chapter 3

Judge Charles Lee Monroe dangled his glasses in his left hand and gazed waterily out into the big courtroom. Without his glasses on, the world was in a white shifting fog. The American flag on his right and the Palmetto State flag of South Carolina on his left were a red blur and a blue blur. He couldn't see the brass eagles on top of the flag standards, nor could he see the outline of the oak-vaulted courtroom where he had been serving and presiding for over forty-three years. Leroy, Maude, and Earl Edge, sitting stiffly in the front row of the thirty-six rows of empty seats, looked like three shadows. Judge Monroe nodded in the direction of the clerk.

The clerk read aloud, "Earl Leroy Edge, son of Leroy Edge, Jr., and Maude Hall Edge of six-nineteen Cherry Street, Columbia, South Carolina, accused of expectorating from the balcony onto the audience of the Palace Theatre." He turned a page. "The manager of the theatre, Mr. Harvey Stone, claims that this is an infraction of . . ."

"Never mind about that," the judge interrupted. "Step up here, Earl. Let me have a look at you."

Earl glanced at Leroy and moved up to the bench. Leroy

and Maude came with him. The judge hooked his wire-framed glasses over one ear and then the other. He cocked his head down so he could see through the top half of the heavy bifocals. "How old are you, boy?"

"Fourteen, going on fifteen."

"And you're guilty of this?"

"Yessir, I'm guilty." Leroy had appeared before Charles Lee Monroe himself and had told Earl that he was an easy judge and to plead guilty and then pay attention when he lectured him. Leroy had said he would handle all the fine points.

Leroy stepped forward. "Judge, I'd like to say . . ."

Judge Monroe rapped his gavel once. "Now you just keep quiet."

"But, Your Honor. We don't have no lawyer."

Maude tugged at his sleeve. "Hush, Leroy, do like he says."

The judge looked at Maude, then frowned at Leroy. "You listen to your wife, Leroy. Sounds like she's got the only sense in the family." He went back to reading Earl's record. "You been pretty busy for a boy just going on fifteen. Reckless driving, speeding, fighting, insulting an officer of the law. From the way you're traveling here, looks like you might not make it." He looked down at Earl. "Judge Tabor claims you been selling whiskey bottles and being a lookout for Clyde Peevy."

Leroy was getting nervous. He started to speak but Maude reached out and put her hand on his arm.

The judge continued. "You appeared before Judge Tabor twice. Is that right?"

Earl slouched onto his right foot, copying Leroy's stance. "Whatever it says there."

"Don't get smart with me, young man. Now answer me straight."

Earl hitched his mouth to one side and looked at the floor. The words had come out harder than he had intended. "Yessir."

The judge drummed all ten fingers on his blotter. "I guess you figure you're kind of lucky getting old, blind, deaf, and senile Charley Monroe. Isn't that about right?"

"No sir. No sir. I ain't lucky."

Judge Monroe sighed twice, once high, once low. "Leroy, you ought to be ashamed. Look at him. Go on and look at him. He hasn't even got his first growth, and here he is with a record as long as my arm. You ought to be taken out and horsewhipped. You're the one that should be on trial here. You're a positive disgrace."

"But, Your Honor, I swear I'm doing my best to give him every advantage. I'm trying to . . ."

The judge raised his voice. "Will you keep quiet? I don't want to hear another word out of you."

Judge Monroe removed his glasses, and the white fog moved in again. He was getting too old for shouting. He closed his eyes and with his thumb and forefinger began rubbing his nose and the corners of his eyes. In the shadow of his mind he realized that he was indeed old and that he had been trying Edges for a long time, for forty years, through three wars and four full generations. Four generations of Edges. He wondered if it meant anything and decided that it didn't. But he could remember them, every one of them: Leroy's father, Leroy Senior; Leroy Senior's father, Justice. He remembered the courtroom joke about Justice Edge shouting that there was no justice when they dragged him away to do two years for buying a sheriff and owning five steam stills up in Kershaw County. He had been a young lawyer then, only a few years out of school. Yes, he remembered them all. They had all been lean, hard-faced men who could stare any man down even when they were lying like dogs. They had never been tall, but they weren't short. They all had had the same hemp-yellow hair and bushy eyebrows framing the same cold blue eyes. And none of them could keep his mouth shut. But there was something else about the Edges, something else they had in common which he had never quite been able to pin down. A fine feeling tickled over the judge, and he realized he had been thinking about this mystery for a long time. He put his glasses on to look at Leroy and Earl together, and then as the white fog parted he suddenly saw it. It was firmly planted and etched on Leroy's face. He could also see it in Earl. It was harder to see, but it was there. It was in the slight downturning at the corner of his mouth and in the loose way he held his body, springing his hips sideways and forward at the same time. It was a sneer and yet it wasn't, for there was more control than that; it was an expression of a delicate contempt.

The judge was pleased with himself. "Well, Earl, you're the spitting image of your granddaddy and you're starting off the same wild way he did. Boy, don't you have anything better to do with your time than this fool stuff?"

Earl said, "Yessir."

Leroy raised his hand as if the question had been asked of him, but the judge ignored him.

"Son, I been sitting here a long time, and I don't like the way things are going. You got a long summer coming up and I can almost smell trouble. You're bound to mess up. Maybe you'd do better out at the Correction Home until school starts. A whiskey house isn't any place for a boy to grow up in."

Earl's unblinking eyes showed nothing, but the judge saw the color drain from his face and his lips tighten.

He leaned forward on his elbows. "Now out at this home I got in mind, you can learn cabinetmaking. Always a lot of nice jobs around for cabinetmakers. Then there's electrical repair work and metal work and a whole shop just set up for welding. And something else, auto mechanics. Earl, they got the finest auto mechanic shop in the country out there. A boy like you ought to know all he can about that. That's something you can always use. Now how does that sound?"

"I don't want to go to no home, Your Honor."

The judge looked at Leroy. "All right, Leroy, you got a pretty good head on your shoulders. You tell him. Tell him it's a good chance to improve himself and stay out of trouble. I bet if you were his age you'd snap it up."

Leroy was quick. He shook his head. "Lord. Lord, no, Your Honor. What I was trying to tell you before was about me being out of the whiskey business. I'm in another field. I'm doing plumbing and appliance repair work."

"When did you start all this?"

"Pretty good spell now. A year or so, maybe more."

"Couldn't have been too long ago. You haven't been out of jail that long."

"I learned plumbing while I was doing that time, Your Honor. I've been going straight ever since, I swear it. And what I'm doing now is teaching Earl, here, the business. He's good, he catches on fast, real fast. Got himself a nice pair of hands, and he knows how to use his head."

The judge pulled away from Leroy's eyes and looked at Maude.

Maude stood with her feet together, scraping the red polish on her thumbnail. She wore a blue cotton dress with white shoes and a white purse. There were light touches of gray in her dark curly hair and she wore it in a short pageboy fashion. Maude was thirty-six, four years younger than Leroy, and she had married him sixteen years before when they were both working at Woolworth's. She had been on the cosmetic and notion counter and Leroy had worked on the grill and fountain until he and the manager had quarreled. Leroy had quit and, renting a house in the Bottom on Cherry Street, had followed two generations of Edges into the corn whiskey business.

The big courtroom was quiet except for the roller shade at the top of one of the windows, fluttering softly in the hot morning breeze from the river. The judge cleared his throat and nodded at Earl's record. "What do you think, Mrs. Edge?"

Maude gripped her purse strap. "Every word Leroy says is the truth, Your Honor."

"How about his school? Says here he failed everything last year. How do you explain that?"

"Leroy wasn't around, Your Honor, and I had to go to work and I just couldn't keep track of him. That's the first grade he ever failed. He always did so well in school until then."

The judge watched Earl carefully. "You have anything to say?"

"I'll do better, I swear I will."

The judge read back over his notes as if he had forgotten

31

something. "And you'll leave Clyde Peevy and that whiskey crowd alone?"

"Yessir."

Judge Monroe made a notation on the sheet before him and signed it. "I'm putting you on probation for ninety days, and you're in your parents' custody. You understand what that means?"

"Yessir, it means I have to do what they say."

"Is that all it means?"

"No sir, it means I have to go to the Correction Home if I get in any trouble."

"All right, then. Mrs. Edge, Leroy, I'm releasing him in your custody."

Maude put her arm around Earl's shoulders and smiled. "Thank you, Your Honor."

Leroy reached over and patted Earl on the back. He grinned up at the judge. "Thanks, Judge, I'll take good care of him. Thank you, sir."

"Case dismissed." Judge Charles Lee Monroe pounded the gavel once and waved the Edges away. He watched them go down the empty aisle together. Leroy had his arm around Earl's shoulders and was whispering to him. Maude walked ahead of them. The judge shook his head and removed his glasses. The white fog rolled in again over the big room.

In front of the marble-columned police station, jail, and courthouse, Leroy climbed into the right-hand seat of his Ford pickup truck. Ever since he had been caught speeding down the Charleston Highway and had had his driver's license suspended he had been letting Maude and Earl do the driving. He still had a week of the suspension left. "That old buzzard was all primed up to get rough."

Maude pulled her dress down over her knees and began looking for the car keys. "I thought he was right nice. He was certainly right about Earl."

Leroy propped his elbow on the window sill and spat out onto the red clay. "Right, my ass. What in the hell does he know about anything? All he knows is how to pound that gavel and say thirty days." He tapped Earl on the knee. "All the same, you're getting too old to be messing around like that. Spitting! Jesus Christ!" He glanced at Maude. "Can't you find the keys? Or is that a dumb question?"

Maude checked the folds in her red wallet. "They were right here a minute ago."

Earl sat back in the seat out of the way.

"They're always right there, and we're always sitting out here sweating like butchers while you look for them. Here." He reached across Earl. "Give me that damn thing."

She jerked it back. "Will you stop!"

Maude found the keys, but now she had another problem. They were parked facing up the Pine Street hill, and she dreaded having to shift gears so quickly. Sliding forward so she could reach the clutch, she held her breath and started the engine. She timed the clutch wrong. The car leaped forward, bucked, and stopped.

"Good Christ Almighty!" Leroy shouted. "Slower, release the damn thing slower."

"I'm trying! I'm trying!" She shifted into neutral and started over again. Earl watched her foot on the clutch. Leroy put both hands on the dashboard to brace himself.

This time she timed the clutch right and they climbed the hill smoothly and turned onto Franklin Street. The Monday morning traffic was thin and she sighed, concentrating on the lights ahead. If she could make the green lights she wouldn't have to shift gears again.

Leroy spoke around his cigarette. "Let us off at the Carolina. We'll be in on the bus."

Maude kept her eyes on the light. "Are you eating uptown?"

"Yeah, we might as well."

A bicycle flashed by, barely missing the front bumper. Cowboy had cut in front of them and was heading up Franklin.

Earl said, "It's Cowboy. Look at that fool."

Cowboy was coasting, waiting for them, riding side-saddle and looking back with his hand on the rack as if he were on a horse. Small American flags fluttered from the front and the rear fenders, and trailing out from each handle-bar grip and the rear of the chrome-plated saddle rack were three enormous brown and white raccoon tails. Playing cards were snugged with clothespins into the spokes of each wheel, and a rapid machine-gun noise filled the air.

The red light at Spruce caught Maude and she stopped. Cowboy pulled in close. "Morning, Mrs. Edge. Mr. Edge. Hi, Earl. How'd you make out?"

Earl said, "O.K., Cowboy."

The light changed to yellow, and Cowboy came down hard on his left pedal and streaked out. He was about thirty feet ahead of them when he leaned the bicycle over in a wide almost foot-dragging turn and cut down Spruce Street. He waved without looking back and went sailing away with his flags and raccoon tails flying.

Maude couldn't stand the idea of another leaping start. She decided to start the car in second. The car chattered,

then strained forward smoothly. To keep Leroy from cursing about wearing the clutch out, she spoke quickly. "How
about bringing some ice cream home for supper?"

At Cherry she stopped. Leroy pulled his tool kit out
from under the seat. "O.K." He shifted his hat to keep the
sun out of his eyes. "What kind you want?"

"Strawberry Ripple, if they got it. If they ain't got that,
get Butter Pecan."

Chapter 4

At the Carolina Double Dip Ice Cream Parlor, Leroy checked the ice cream box and told the owner, Nick Drege-apolis, that the four-horse compressor might last another month but no more.

"How much you asking for a new one?"

"Seventy dollars, including labor."

"My God, Leroy. I can't afford no seventy dollars. Maybe you could patch up the old one."

"No, Nick. It's shot. It's worn out. Face it, it's fifteen years old and now it's shot."

Nick poured himself a half a glass of seltzer water. Two aprons were tied together around his huge waist, and he wore them up high under his armpits. He had a thick heavy mustache that made his dark eyes look darker, and when he opened them wide he looked trapped and martyred. "Well, I can't go affording no seventy dollars. I just don't have it."

"Listen, Nick, I'm a plumber, I ain't no refrigeration man. If you think that's high, check around. Hell, call a refrigeration mechanic, he'll soak your ass twenty dollars just for sticking his head in the door."

"I know you'll give me a good price, Leroy, but you got to understand I'm not a rich man. I'm getting insomnia with all the bills I got. I got tax bills and the curb girls want raises or they say they're going to quit. Can you imagine that? My girls leaving me after all I've done for them."

"O.K., Nick. Go on, sweat it out. That's the way you like it, ain't it?"

"What are you talking about?"

"Don't you like being under the gun? Don't you like it when you hear that compressor start knocking and you think about that two hundred gallons of ice cream being poured down the sink?"

"No! I don't like that. You think I'm crazy?"

"You sure as hell act it."

"Well, what can I do? I can't raise seventy dollars now."

"You can pay me five dollars for the service call, that's what."

Nick handed Leroy three dollars. "Listen, how about stopping back in a couple hours and I'll give you the other two. It's been slow this morning."

"No, Nick, I ain't stopping back for no lousy two dollars. Give me a carton of Camels."

"Aw, come on, Leroy, I need those for the trade. I'll give you five packs and I'll owe you a dollar."

Leroy slammed his toolbox shut. "No. I got a better idea. Take the three back and we'll forget the whole damn deal."

Nick pulled a carton of Camels from under the counter. "O.K. I don't want no hard feelings. If I get in trouble I'm going to need you in a hurry."

37

Leroy jammed the carton into his back pocket.

"No hard feelings, are there, Leroy?"

"No, Nick, no hard feelings."

Earl picked up the toolbox and followed Leroy outside.

Leroy was mad and walking fast. "Boy, this is really low-life. It's bad enough working on their sorry units, but fighting with trash like that for two lousy bucks is the damn limit. I hope that compressor goes and he loses every drop of cream he's got."

He squinted down Broad Street as if he were looking for someone. "I'm starved. You getting hungry?"

"Yessir."

"Wonder if Buck's got anything good on the steam table." He pulled his hat down over his right eye. "Let's give it a look."

At Buck Pendleton's Silver Dipper Cafe and Pool Room, Leroy and Earl ate stew beef and rice with side orders of succotash. Leroy ate with his hat pushed back on his head. When he finished, he folded a piece of light bread and wiped his plate clean. "Give us a couple slices of that plain cake there, Buck, and put on a tad of that chocolate sauce. Yeah, that'll do it."

Earl ate his dessert and read the inscriptions on Buck's baseball trophies that were lined up on a blue cloth on each side of the cash register. Buck was a big powerful man with hard arms, thick wrists, and a flat rigid stomach. In high school he had been one of the hardest-throwing pitchers in the South. After he graduated he'd pitched for Chattanooga and Memphis and had finally become a starter for the Atlanta Crackers.

Earl spun his counter stool around and looked back at the

four pool tables lined up end to end into the light of the dusty screen door at the rear of the long room. Only the big ten-foot snooker table under the sunbathing and smiling nudes of the Golden Lion Towel and Linen Service calendar was in use. He whispered to Leroy, "How 'bout asking if I can practice on the back table?"

"O.K." Leroy pushed his coffee forward for a refill. "Hey, Buck, any chance of Earl here trying a few shots in the back?"

" 'Fraid not. Police been giving me a fit about minors lately."

Earl said, "Please, Buck, I don't need no lights. If the Law comes I'll beat it out the back." His eyes held Buck's until Buck laughed.

"Boy, you can't see your hand in front of your face back there. How you figure on seeing the balls?" He paused. "Aw, hell, take him back, Roy. I remember when the pool bug bit me it like to drove me crazy."

Earl pulled down a 22-ounce cue stick from the rack and dusted it with April Showers dusting powder. The black eight ball, the dark greens and blues, were almost invisible, but by playing with the light stripes and the bright yellow of the number one ball he was able to make a few simple short shots. He played from one end of the table, with the balls between himself and the faint light from the screen door.

Leroy sat in one of the big chairs that lined the wall. "I can't see a thing, but they're sounding good."

Earl liked the feeling of the firm high bridge he had copied from Leroy, and the sweet, flowery smell of the powder made goose flesh run up his arms. He hit the cue ball low and hard at the one ball and held the cue stick firm. The ball struck the one solidly, dug in, and came back to nuzzle against the waiting cue stick.

Buck came back and turned on the lights. "Go on, you two, play a rack. I'll keep an eye out."

Leroy slipped a stick out and twisted chalk on the tip.

Earl racked the balls. They rolled the cue ball for the break and Leroy won. He broke hard, and the thirteen and the five balls dropped. The cue ball was locked to the rail. Leroy tried a difficult bank shot on the one ball. He missed and left the table spread for Earl. Earl made the one and sucked the cue ball into good position. He ran three balls and then tied himself up.

Leroy knew that Earl was hot, and he played his next shot safe, leaving him frozen in the corner.

Earl tried to hide the fact that he knew what Leroy was doing and shot quickly, almost carelessly, scattering the wrong balls and tying the cue ball up again. Leroy saw the move and tightened up more. He played steadily and took no chances.

Buck said, "Just a little friendly game, right?" He laughed. "You two kill me."

The game went slowly with each watching the other and neither taking any complicated shots. And then Earl tried a combination on the fifteen. It missed; the table was open. Leroy smiled and smoothed chalk on the end of his cue. He ran the six, seven, and eight. On the nine ball he tried to cut it too fine and hung it on the side of the pocket.

Buck said, "Go get him, Earl."

Earl was ready. He drove the nine ball in and rolled the cue ball to the end of the table. He dropped the fourteen on

40

a ten-ball combination and then pushed in the ten. The three remaining balls were scattered and open, and he finished the rack.

Buck laughed. "Well, by God, Leroy, I never thought I'd see you being hustled by your own boy."

Leroy's face was drawn. He didn't like losing to anyone. "Rack them up again."

Earl reached for the wooden triangle under the table.

Someone shouted from the front, "Motorcycle, Buck. Looks like Hog." Buck pulled the light cord. Leroy and Earl shoved their sticks under the table and started to the front. They sat down quickly and Buck served them Pepsi-Colas as Patrolman Hog Wallace came in. Hog was almost a full head taller than Buck. He had a round moon face, pale eyes, and a full head of curly blond hair. He looked into the back and then at Earl. Earl kept his hands below the counter. He didn't want Hog to see the blue chalk or smell the dusting powder.

"You haven't been playing pool?"

"No sir."

"Weren't you in court this morning?"

"Yessir."

Leroy turned to Hog. "I've been playing, Hog. As a matter of fact, weren't you and me supposed to play a little game one day?"

"Don't give me any lip, Edge. You ain't been driving that pickup around, have you?"

"Sure, big boy. It's out front. Didn't you see it when you came in?"

"Listen, Edge." Hog had his left glove off and was carrying it in his right hand. He slapped it across his palm. "Listen, you just keep messing around. Just keep it up, you hear? I'm going to have your ass yet." He went to the door. "And you keep your nose clean, Buck."

Buck twisted his counter towel tight. "One night, I'm going to catch him out of that damn uniform and it's going to be me and him." Buck's wrists bulged as he jammed his shirt in under his apron.

Leroy said, "I'll bet the only time the bastard takes that badge off is when he goes to bed."

Buck pushed himself up on the back bar. "Big bastard, ain't he? He ever play any ball?"

Leroy laughed. "Hog Wallace play ball? Are you kidding? Maybe a little medicine ball. He's built like a tub of suet. You could take him with no sweat." He hitchhiked his finger at Earl. "How about my boy here's game? Ain't that something?"

Buck said, "He's going to be trouble, all right. Earl, you got yourself a good stroke there, just don't go tightening up. Couple years from now and you'll have yourself a nice steady income if you work it right."

Leroy picked a piece of beef from between his teeth with the corner of a matchbook cover. "I got better plans for him than being a pool hustler."

Buck said, "Too bad you ain't a couple years older. I could use another rack boy." He nodded at Earl's hands. "You still squeezing those rubber balls like I told you?"

"Sure am. I think it's doing some good, too. How old you have to be to get the job?"

"Seventeen. You keep working on those wrists. That's the secret. You got to stay with it."

Leroy stood up and paid for the pool and the two Pepsi-Colas.

Buck said, "Where you heading?"

"Miller Osborne's. The old lady says her sink drain's plugged up."

"Mabel Osborne! Roy, she'll talk your arm clean off."

Leroy picked up his toolbox. "Not a chance. I've been over that route before. I squirt a little sulphur in the room and she keeps pretty scarce."

Buck smiled. "Hell, that's the stuff you ought to be selling. You could put me down for some of that." He pushed the dime for the pool back to Leroy. "That's on the house."

Chapter 5

Lonnie Register's dog, Midnight, crossed Mulberry and began sniffing the drugstore bicycle rack. From the rack he loped across to the mailbox, circled it twice, and headed for the door. As he raised his leg on the screen door jamb, Doc came rushing out with a broom. "Get! Get! Get the hell out of here, you mangy bastard!" The big black dog ran a few yards, stopped, and then slowly walked off down Bee Street.

Dan Jackson's Chrysler was parked at the corner. Earl and Coley were sitting in the back seat. Earl had his cap pulled down low over his eyes and was listening to Coley read a *Captain Marvel* comic book to Dan.

Dan laughed. "Look at that old dog move. He knows exactly how many steps Doc's going to run, and that's exactly how many he takes."

Coley finished the last page of *Captain Marvel*. "That's it, Dan. That's all there is."

Dan opened the door. "You all want a Pepsi?"

Coley said, "Sure thing. Thanks."

Earl sat up and squinted out. "Could you squeeze out a bag of chips?"

"Yeah, I might could arrange that."

Dan was a tall, slow-moving colored fellow. Someone had said when he was younger he had played ball and had caught for Satchel Paige, but now he was almost fifty, and he made his living doing sheet-metal work out in West Columbia, near the Charleston Highway. Dan's 1939 Chrysler was his pride and joy. He kept it in perfect condition. Every time he got out of the car, he'd pull a soft chamois cloth out of his back pocket and buff and polish the hubcaps and the long strips of chrome edging on the grille. He always kept the Chrysler freshly waxed. In the evening when the wind would come up from the west, he'd curse and mumble and, wetting his finger tips, he'd pick off the fine lint blown over from the cotton mills.

Dan returned with three Pepsis and three bags of Jake's Potato Chips. He slid across the front seat until his back was resting on the door. "Boys, I got a little piece of news for you. Remember how I told you about all that racket those new high-speed reamers are making?"

Earl nodded and tore open his potato chip bag with his teeth.

"Well, yesterday I was watching a Dr. Pepper bottle sitting on the window sill, and that thing was trembling and carrying on like it had the tremins. So I said to myself, I said, 'Dan, you ain't getting any younger and that's the truth about that. If them machines and vibrations can do that to a Dr. Pepper bottle, what in the world are they doing to your insides?'" Dan took a drink from his Pepsi-Cola. "Yessir, that's exactly what I said. Then I reached

45

over and just as pretty as you please I turned my rig off for the last time."

Coley said, "You saying you quit?"

"That's right. The shop foreman came over, and he started in to telling me some story about how we all got to get used to the new noise. He said pretty soon we'd be getting so we didn't even hear it."

Coley leaned forward. "Damn, Dan, what're you going to do? There's not much call for ex-sheet-metal workmen around Columbia."

Earl swallowed a handful of potato chips. "Wait a minute! I know where there's a job. Good job! I tried to get it but they wanted somebody older. They want a rack boy up at the Silver Dipper. Man, I'd give my eye teeth for a job like that. Not much to do and you can play all the pool you want."

"No, boy, I'm all set."

"But Dan!" The thought of Dan racking balls and allowing him to come in the back door and play on the back table charged through Earl's mind. He sat forward, talking rapidly. "You at least ought to try it out. I know for a fact there ain't no better life than hustling pool. You look at Madison Creel. You look how he dresses and how he keeps his fingernails sharp and polished. I swear there ain't no one in town that lives as high as Madison, and he makes it all on that front table."

"Slow down, slow down, Earl. I already decided what I'm going to do. I'm going into the taxicab business. Besides, you ought to know I ain't cut out to be no pool hustler. I can't hustle nobody out of a Pepsi-Cola and a barbecue sandwich, let alone somebody's take-home pay."

Coley said, "Funny, Dan, I never thought about you as a

cab driver. Hell, you going to be making some good money."

"Shore I am." Dan was stroking the dashboard and the trim around the windshield with his chamois cloth. "There ain't a cab rolling that can touch my Chrysler, and there ain't a dog in Georgia if I don't know the streets in this old town."

Earl rolled his comic book into a tight tube and peered through it at the White Owl sign in the drugstore window. "Dan, me and Coley have sorta bogged down on getting that car we've been talking about. You ain't seen anything cheap sitting around, have you?"

Dan began blowing on the rearview mirror and polishing it. "You ought to be checking the lots, there's plenty cars up there."

Earl shifted the tube to his left eye and closed his right. "What do you think of Lonnie's Hudson?"

"I'd be afraid of that old bucket. Ain't no telling what all's wrong with it."

Coley spoke quickly. "But he works on it all the time. How you going to judge a car 'less you see it in action? How you going to tell anything unless you get it out on the road?"

Dan straightened the mirror. "That car just ain't right, and I don't care if Lonnie keeps working on it till the Resurrection. It ain't going to be right then, either."

Coley said, "But I've heard it run, Dan. It sounds like a sewing machine. I swear it does."

"Listen Coley, Earl. I been around cars a heap longer than you have. I know what I'm talking about. You buy that thing and you might as well be strapping a cancer to your pocket."

At the front of the Mason-Dixon Used Car Lot, Earl climbed into a 1948 Buick marked $1500, hiked the deep seat forward, and pumped the brake. "Look, Coley, only twenty-one thousand miles. It's practically new!"

"Come on, Earl, get out of there. Quit messing around."

They went back to the rear fence where two 1938 Fords and a dusty cement-colored Pontiac were parked under a string of blue- and orange-colored banners spelling out "Low Priced Specials."

Earl squatted down and looked at the tires on the Pontiac. "Good rubber! Real good."

Coley opened the hood. "She's clean. Clean as a whistle."

The salesman came back, and in a happy singsong voice he told them they had a sharp eye and, slapping the metal roof, he explained how the Pontiac had had only two owners. They were both women with daytime jobs at the Veterans Administration whom he knew personally. He opened the door for Earl, then slammed it solidly, then opened it again. "Go on, crank her up."

Earl started the engine. "Not bad. How about it, Coley?"

Coley looked in at the speedometer. "Sounds good."

The salesman sat next to Earl and told him he'd take an oath that it hadn't been driven any more than the indicated 41,000 miles.

Earl chewed his gum faster and let the engine idle.

"Go on, turn the radio on. It's got two speakers. Last gal said she got over twenty-two miles on a gallon of regular gasoline and she didn't know when she'd ever put any oil in her." The price was $250 with only $10 down. Earl gunned the engine and turned the radio on loud. The salesman

48

slapped him on the back. "Ten dollars keeps you under that wheel, Sport, and no problems on financing. I can absolutely guarantee that."

Coley got down on his knees and, laying his face in the gravel, he watched a black trail of oil smoke seeping out of the crankcase. He shouted, "Cut her off!"

Earl got out. "All he wants is ten dollars down, Cole. We can swing that. And no sweat on the credit."

"She's throwing oil." Coley pulled the oil stick out and rubbed it on his fingers. "Feel it. That's why she's quiet. He's got it packed with axle grease. The engine's shot, probably driven to death."

Earl rubbed the grease between his fingers and wiped it off on the seat cover. "Two women from the Veterans Administration. Boy, what a line of bull."

The salesman was heading toward the front of the lot.

They tried Piedmont Motors, Carolina Sales, Big Ben's Bargains, Zuck's New and Used Cars, and Honest Henry Loganberry's. There was a 1937 Ford marked "$105 As Is" at Piedmont, but the salesman said it might need a new engine. At Carolina Sales a Nash with no windshield that had recently been in a wreck and was so out of line it tilted forward was tagged "Make Me An Offer." A Chevrolet at Big Ben's for $80 had to be started by connecting a hot wire to a cold wire, and when a cloud of black graphite-smelling smoke belched up through the floor boards they almost choked. At Zuck's a '40 Ford with brand-new tires and leopard skin upholstery was marked $120, but when it started the engine sounded like ten tons of coal sliding down a steel chute.

Honest Henry Loganberry, with one hand on Earl's shoulder and one on Coley's, steered them to the back of his lot. "Boys, I swear before God, this is the cleanest, finest car I've seen all year. I'm telling you a man could eat right off of that engine." A long twelve-cylinder 1927 Buick with a brand new robin's-egg-blue paint job gleamed before them for $99.

Coley whistled. "Jesus, it's long as a hearse."

Honest Henry finished the sentence. "And it's quieter, boy. Much quieter. And ride, it rides like a Beautyrest Mattress. Here"—he tossed Coley the keys—"try her out. You got a license, haven't you?"

They showed him their permits.

"O.K., take her for a spin, and take your time and listen at that engine. Get back before one. I got somebody coming in to see her then."

Coley drove ten blocks, then Earl drove ten. "It handles nice, Coley. Real nice. Let's get it."

Coley crouched over listening to the transmission. "She sounds good. Pull into Gus's. I want to look underneath."

Earl straddled the Buick over the grease pit at Gus Haskell's Crescent Gas Station and cut the switch. Gus came over. "What's going on?"

Coley said, "We're thinking about buying it. Can we use the pit a second?"

Gus put his foot on the wide running board and looked over the blue hood at the crouched and gleaming eagle on the radiator cap. He was a short, wiry, pale-faced mechanic with red hair, red eyebrows, and a flat nose shaped like a bent spoon. At forty-five, he had one of the best-equipped service stations in Columbia. He specialized in automatic transmission work and engine overhauling and sold headlights, bumper guards, decorated gear shift knobs, motorcycle mud flaps, and a hundred other accessories. His prices were lower than Sears Roebuck's and every few weeks he'd run a special discount sale on three-toned horns or foglights that someone had stolen from the slow freights that moved through the Bottom.

"I guess so, but hurry up. I got paying customers coming in here every minute."

"O.K." Coley went down into the grease pit under the car. "All right, Earl, turn her over. And gun it!"

The racing, pounding engine sounded good and the exhaust was clean. Coley shouted up, "Cut her off!" He began checking the transmission and the U joint.

Gus crouched on the top step of the pit just below the Buick's gas tank. He tapped a pair of pliers on the springs. "Hey, Coley, listen here a minute. This car's too big for you boys. Let me give you a good deal on Jethro's Hup."

Coley looked up. "You got a crescent wrench?"

"Sure." Gus dropped it down. "That Hupmobile would be a nice cheap car to operate, I happen to know that for a fact. This thing here's going to drink gas like a tractor."

Coley unscrewed the rear end cap, checking to see if it was packed with sawdust or graphite. "I'll have to talk to Earl."

Gus said, "Come on inside when you get through. I'll buy the Cokes."

Coley joined Earl. "She's in great shape. Wonder what Loganberry will take for a down payment?"

Earl tightened the big blue and white fist-sized marble on the end of the gear shift stick. "Probably ten. We can borrow that. Hell, maybe we can get it for nothing down."

Coley nodded back behind him. "Gus wants to try and

talk us into Jethro's Hup."

Earl started the engine. "That'll be the day. Reckon he knows anything?"

"Hell, no. Who'd tell him?"

Almost everyone in the Mulberry area except Gus knew that the 1926 Hupmobile that Jethro Truesdale had left him as payment for a $150 debt had split a piston and that Jethro had replaced it with a wooden piston he had turned down on a lathe in Manual Training. The night before he had shipped out for Marine Boot Camp in Quantico, Virginia, Jethro had left the Hupmobile in Gus's station yard, telling him in a note under the windshield wiper that he could sell the car and anything over $150 they would split. Gus had been furious. He had called his lawyer, his accountant, and finally the sheriff. After finding out there was nothing he could do to collect his money, he had washed and Simonized the gray box-framed car and across the windshield he had soaped "Excellent Car $150." No one was interested. As the weeks went by and the car got dustier, Gus moved it to the back of his lot where he wouldn't have to look at it all day. He lowered the price to $135.

Earl backed the Buick up as Gus came out, smiling and pointing at the Coke machine. Coley shook his head and shouted, "No thanks, Gus. See you later."

Earl swung the long blue car around and headed for Mulberry. "Let's see what Lonnie thinks of her."

"Good idea."

Thelma Register, Lonnie's wife, was sitting in the rocking chair on her front porch snapping string beans. The radio in the living room was on full blast and she was rocking back and forth, keeping time to the hillbilly music of the Aristocratic Pigs from Greenville. Midnight lay panting in the striped shade of the porch swing.

"Morning, Mrs. Resister."

"Morning, Mrs. Register."

"Hello, Earl, Coley."

Coley leaned on the porch post. Earl dropped down on the top step and began scratching Midnight's head. "Is Lonnie around? We want his opinion on this car we got here."

Thelma was a tidy, matronly woman who wore her short, graying brown hair in a loose wave. She raised up so she could see the Buick behind the low hedge and slowly shook her head. "Cars, cars, cars. I declare it ain't bad enough the men spending every dime they can rattle on them, now you boys got to be getting into it." She snapped three beans in her wide lap. "Lord, it's gotten so bad around here Lonnie brings those filthy old parts right up to the supper table."

Coley said, "Is he out back?"

Thelma pushed a loose piece of hair back behind her ear. "No, he's up in Winnsboro on a job. He'll be home Friday. You can come by then, but it seems to me you could be coming up with something a little more interesting than sticking your head under some old greasy hood." Midnight sat up quickly and began scratching fleas. The porch boards rattled under the heavy thudding of his back leg. "Now when I was your age boys spent more time helping out at home. You take a few years back, why you never saw . . ."

Earl eased down the steps. "We gotta go, Mrs. Register. Thanks, anyhow."

Coley said, "Bye now, Mrs. Register."

They crossed the yard and Earl whispered, "Winnsboro

my foot! Dollar to a doughnut he's in the clink."

Coley started the Buick. "She must really think we're dopes!"

They pulled into the curb at the drugstore. M. L. Anderson came over. "Great God in the morning! Where'd you get that?"

Coley said, "Up at Loganberry's. We're trying it out. What do you think?"

M.L. pulled the two spring latches up on the hood and peered in at the long twelve-cylinder engine. "That's an engine, all right. No doubt about that. Enough there to pull four sawmills." He wiggled the ignition wires and the battery cables. "Somebody's taken good care of her. I'll say that."

Earl said, "But if you were us would you buy it?"

M.L. rocked the carburetor arm back and forth. "If I were you I'd go all the way. I'd go out to Fort Jackson and get me a Sherman tank. You any idea how hard it's going to be to find parts for this boat? Hell, you'll have to make forty calls to get a tire."

Doc came out of the drugstore drying his hands and squinting in the bright sunlight. He leaned in under the engine hood with M.L. "Twelve cylinders! Will you study that."

Coley said, "What do you think of her?"

Doc relit his cigar. "I wouldn't touch her with a ten-foot pole. You get any more than three miles out of a gallon and I'll drink what's left over."

Earl and Coley left the Buick at Loganberry's and rode the bus back to the drugstore. They had decided to wait and talk to Lonnie about his Hudson. Coley put a penny in the weighing machine and watched the sweep hand settle down at 109. He hated being two pounds lighter than Earl, but he refused to wear his pullover shirt on the outside of his pants to hide his waist the way Earl did. Earl kept saying it was cooler that way and less binding, but Coley knew it was because Bo-Bo Joyner, Doc's fountain boy, had told him he was as skinny as a snake and twice as slippery. Coley kept his shirt inside and tight and wore his pants as low on his hips as he could. He had bought a wide leather World War II garrison belt from the Army Surplus store and, not wanting to cut it off, he wore it wound one and a half times around his waist. Coley leaned on the fountain counter. "Hey, Doc, can I see your paper?"

"O.K., but don't mess it up. I'm not through with it yet."

Coley pulled the back section out. "You ain't heard of any jobs floating around, have you?"

The bass and rockfish had been running a week at the Santee River, and Doc had been telephoning all morning trying to find a pharmacist to relieve him. "Too bad you can't fill a prescription. What I need me is a pharmacist who isn't too proud to dip up a little ice cream."

Coley slid in the back booth opposite Earl and spread the classifieds out on the table. Earl scanned down the page. "Listen here: 'Nineteen forty DeSoto, less than twenty-five thousand miles, one owner, must be seen to be believed, will sacrifice at two hundred dollars.' How does that sound?"

"Sounds like two hundred dollars, that's what it sounds like. Besides, I wouldn't be caught dead in a DeSoto." Coley walked his fingers down the MALE HELP column. "Here's something. 'Carpenter helpers, no experience, Colonial Heights, a dollar an hour.' How about that?"

"That ad's a come-on. That's where Clarence Moody worked. They had him carrying hundred-pound kegs of roofing nails all day. He's lucky he didn't pick up a couple hernias."

Coley said, "Damn, I wish old Holly would hurry up and get back. He's bound to be needing some help."

M. L. Anderson came in, and after opening a beer he drifted back and leaned on the booth. "Hope this ain't a post-mortem on that deep breather."

Coley said, "Nah, that old thing was just too big."

Earl kept his place in the ads with his finger. "M.L., you seen Lonnie around? Thelma gave us some bull about him being in Winnsboro."

"No telling where he is. I ain't seen him."

Coley said, "Listen, M.L., say old Lonnie wanted to get shed of his Hudson. What do you think it's worth?"

M.L. looked into the mouth of the beer bottle as if the answer were there. "Worth's one thing. What he'd sell it for is another."

Earl said, "Come on, just supposing he would, take a stab at it."

M.L. touched the bottle top to the tip of his chin. "Oh, seventy-five, maybe a hundred, not any more than that. But you won't be catching Lonnie Register selling that Hudson."

Earl said, "Money talks, M.L."

M.L. laughed. "You two kill me with all this car talk. Five will get you ten if either one of you can rub four dimes together."

Earl looked back down at the ads. "We'll be getting some money in pretty soon; we're seeing about a job right now."

M.L. slid his empty Atlantic ale bottle into the rack, and after opening another he walked outside. The Woodland Hills bus pulled up to the corner, and a colored woman with a pile of wash balanced on her head stepped off and headed down Mulberry. Doc had just finished raising the window awnings to catch the last of the light and was talking to Claude Henry Hutto about the bass run. M.L. caught himself looking for Lonnie on the bus and wondering how Earl and Coley had come up with the notion that he would sell his car.

For the Hudson was more than just a car to Lonnie Register. Every day after supper he would rise from the table, change into his greasy blue coveralls, and picking up his drop cord and light he would go whistling out to his back yard and try to solve the mystery of his ten-year-old sedan.

Lonnie hadn't driven his Hudson in over a year. If someone asked him why, he would rub his hands together and tell them about the new ring job he had just completed, or how he had just finished installing a set of hand-ground valves. Then he would smile and say, "Couple more weeks, that's all she needs. You'll need a stethoscope to hear her then." But a couple of weeks would come, and a couple would go, and still he worked on the Hudson. He pulled the rear end, relined the brakes, overhauled the transmission, rebuilt the entire engine, everything. Every part of the Hudson had been taken out, washed in gasoline, dried, expertly greased, and carefully placed back in. But still the car remained jacked up on Coca-Cola crates, with the four wheels, the spare tire, the floor boards, and the seats stored under the back porch. There was always something wrong with the Hudson. Despite the new parts, and the months of slow and careful labor, the car never sounded exactly right. For if the Hudson ran and needed no work, Lonnie would have no place to go in the evening. If he didn't have the car to work on he would have to sit in the living room and talk with Thelma, and M.L. knew that Lonnie could never do that for long.

Coley turned the classified page over. "Looka here, looka here! John Wayne's at the Magnolia. Now that's what I want to do. How much money you got?"

Earl laid twenty-seven cents on the table. "That's it."

Coley had bought the Pepsi-Colas and had fourteen cents left. "Got any at home?"

"Nope. You?"

"Maybe ten or fifteen cents in pennies."

Judge Monroe's warning about selling whiskey bottles buzzed in Earl's ear. He knew there would be plenty at the Silver Dipper, and they hadn't been to James Brothers' in over a week. "How about some bottles?"

"Might as well." Coley folded Doc's paper up. "Here comes the Doc. He looks mad."

Claude Henry Hutto had told Doc that they were catching four-pound bass and channel cats down on the Santee. "Boys, dammit, I don't want you sitting back here all the time. I got paying customers that want to use these booths. You all squat back here nursing a Pepsi-Cola along for three hours and dog-earing my comic books until they're not fit to be touched, and I have to watch my beer and fountain crowd walk right on by 'cause there's no place to sit."

Earl rose. "All right, Doc. We were just leaving."

Doc yanked at his apron, straightening it out. "Aren't you forgetting something?"

Coley said, "The Pepsi bottles."

"That's it, the Pepsi bottles. I'm not going to tell you boys any more; I'm not running a café and smoking club here. You make a mess, you clean it up."

JUNE

Earl and Coley picked up two crokersacks at Coley's house and headed uptown. At the Silver Dipper they found fourteen half pints and six pints in the men's room. Buck let them go into the ladies' rest room, where they pulled six half pints out of the wastebasket and two from behind the toilet. At the James Brothers' Pool Room there were ten half pints and eight pints in the garbage. They went into the alleys behind the Dixie Bee, the Casablanca, and Ed White's. In the garbage behind the American Bar and Grill they found two fifths that would bring a nickel apiece.

Coley said, "You want to try Holly's?"

"No, we got enough. Besides, we don't want anyone telling him we're this hard up."

They headed back toward the Bottom and Clyde Peevy's.

Clyde was a short, nervous, spidery man who wore his pants too full at the waist and too deep in the seat. He claimed he was a quarter Cherokee and always tucked his long black knitted necktie down under his Indian beaded belt. Clyde sold half pints, pints, quarts, and short half-gallon Mason jars of corn whiskey from a thirty-five-gallon industrial mop sink in the kitchen that Leroy had installed for him. Single shots for a dime and doubles for fifteen cents were served from a five-gallon bucket sitting on a table in the middle of the room. A jukebox, which Clyde kept playing every evening at no charge, stood in the corner.

Clyde's whiskey came from all over the three counties of Richland, Calhoun, and Kershaw, but lately, with the Law watching the main roads, most of it was produced by the local moonshiners running in the swamp. Clyde hated selling unaged swamp whiskey which he knew had been run from straight sugar, and he kept a standing offer of fifty dollars open to any driver who would bring him in fifty gallons of year-old corn whiskey from his uncle L. J. Peevy up in Camden or from Tucker Wallace out near Augusta. Leroy had been broke one night two years before and had tried to run a load in on the Leesville Road. He had been caught near Batesburg and, in the fall term of court, he had been given a year and a day down the hill at the State Penitentiary. It was Clyde's ambition to own his own still in town and not have to depend on the whiskey drivers or the swamp runners. But Leroy, who was the only still maker whom he could trust, kept putting the job off, claiming that he wanted to wait until elections were over and the Law had eased off.

Clyde paid two cents for unwashed pint bottles, one cent for halves, and a nickel for fifths. He bought his caps new from the Triple A Cap and Seal Company on Pine Street, and he used no labels. He gave Earl and Coley $1.40 without even counting their bottles. "Listen, if either you fellows want to lookout for me, there's a dollar an hour in it for you."

Earl counted the money and handed Coley seventy cents. He had sat for Clyde on week ends while school was in session. "Can't, Clyde, I'm on probation."

Coley tucked his money into his watch pocket. "Me neither. Dad would kill me."

"Well, I need me a boy for the daytime. If you know one that's sharp, send him around."

Clyde slid the five-foot two-by-four wooden bolt back from the screen door and looked out to see if anyone was watching the house. "And tell Leroy not to make himself so scarce."

JUNE

It was dark by the time Earl and Coley had gone home for supper and met at the drugstore. Both wore their baseball caps pulled down low and square for the ride uptown.

Earl said, "Listen, we're getting too old to be making money like this. What if some gal from school seen us tipping around the Silver Dipper with those damn sacks slung over our backs? What could we say?"

Coley sat back on his seat. They were coasting down the last block of Mulberry. "Never thought about it like that. Boy, we must really be sights."

They turned the corner at Broad.

"O.K., Coley, tomorrow no more bottles. This is the last night. I don't care how much we need the money, no more bottles. Tomorrow, we find a better way."

They pumped hard to get up speed and climbed the short hill to Spruce Street. Broad Street and the city lay out before them, and in the summer night, that would with luck drop to 80 degrees, the tall cascade of white and blue lights of the movie house looked like Niagara Falls. They caught the green light at Maple, and ducking their heads to cut the wind resistance down they pedaled as fast as they could toward John Wayne in "Tall in the Saddle" and the great air-conditioning plant of the Magnolia Theatre.

Chapter 6

Earl sat down next to M.L. and fingered a stone out of the side of his tennis shoe. "Can I borrow the sports section? I want to see what the Yankees did." He bounced the stone out into the street. It was morning and the cotton mill whistle had just blown nine o'clock. Earl read quickly. "Damn! Twelve games out, and they lose both games to the stupid Indians. DiMaggio didn't even get a hit! Six—no, seven—pitchers. Who are they going to start tomorrow? M.L., you think they got a chance?"

M.L. said, "I been telling you right along they don't have a prayer. Yankees will be lucky to finish fourth." He creased the paper down the obituary page and began studying the names.

Earl dug his hands into his empty pockets and slumped down on the seat until his feet were touching the curb. "You wouldn't loan me a dime for a Pepsi and a Snickers, would you? I can pay you back first thing in the morning."

"Not a chance."

Earl sat up. The bus was pulling into the curb across the

street, and standing in the big front window next to the driver was Lonnie Register. Lonnie got off, carrying his dropcloths and a bucket of paintbrushes, and started across the wide intersection. He walked with his head cocked to one side. He seemed to be limping. Halfway across the street he stopped and, after clearing his throat with a sharp rasping hack that sounded like a dog trying to cough up a bone, he spat twice and came on.

M.L. sighed. "Oh, oh. Wonder what he's been drinking."

Lonnie stood before them squinting as if he were looking through a narrow crack. He hadn't shaved or changed coveralls in three or four days, and green paint was streaked and spattered over his face and clothes.

"Move over, Earl. I feel a little shaky." He hacked and spat again, and propping his elbows on his knees he leaned forward, cradling his head in his hands.

Earl said, "You been drinking Rub again?"

Lonnie was about the same age as Doc and M.L., but he seemed much younger. His arms and legs were hard from painting and plastering and his waistline was slim and flat. The top of his head was bald, but a thick trail of black hair, the same color as his heavy eyebrows, horseshoed around the back. "Hell, no! I ain't been drinking nothin'." He stared at the ground between his feet. "You got a smoke? I'm about to have a nicotine fit."

Earl offered him a Kool.

"That all you got?" He reached over and took a Chesterfield from M.L. "Thanks."

Lonnie's lips trembled as Earl lit his cigarette.

"Where you been?"

"Been in jail." He smoked as if he were in a hurry to finish.

M.L. said, "What they get you for, Drunk and Disorderly?"

"Nothing. No charge. Not a damn thing!" His face flushed. He snatched his painter's cap off and slapped it viciously against his leg. "They didn't have me on nothing. Not one damn thing." There were small dots of paint across his bald spot and on the tips of his ears. "They had me down there painting that lousy cheap-assed cell block." He spat out into the street and looked at M.L. "You know a little something about the law. Ain't there something saying a man can't be picked up from his house and taken to no jail without any warning? Ain't there some law about that?"

M.L. said, "You look terrible, like you got the death sweat or something. Go in and get Doc to give you something."

"I'm all right, I just ain't been eating. How 'bout it? Can they do that to me whenever they want?"

M.L. shaded his eyes so he could look at him. "They can do anything they want with you and you better believe it. You're just damn lucky they like your paint work and don't make you serve all the time you owe them."

"Lucky, hell! Here I was sitting on my porch with a bottle of beer and my dog, minding my own damn business and not bothering no one, when they come driving up and take me down to Pine Street. No search warrant, no summons, no nothing. Hell, they didn't even come up to the porch. Just parked in front of the house and blew their goddamn horn. Everybody on the block heard them."

Lonnie's mood changed. He got up, ground his cigarette out with his heel, and began cracking his knuckles. He squinted into the sun, sucked on his teeth, and rubbed the back of his paint-streaked hand against his four-day beard.

Earl balanced the heel of his left shoe on the toe of his right. "I think he wants you to buy him a beer."

M.L. said, "I know he does. Well, if you people think I'm going to sit out here and set up a charity association, you got another think coming."

Lonnie was glad that Earl had opened the subject. "Aw, come on, Martin, I ain't touched one in four days. You know me. You know I ain't ever hit you with any straight beg. Listen, you set me up with a couple now and I'll pay you back tonight. I ain't lying."

"You got a job?"

"All lined up. Nick wants his place done and some window lettering as soon as I can get there." He moved in close. "Just three dollars."

M.L. winced. "Jesus, you got a breath like a cat."

"Sorry." Lonnie backed up, talking rapidly, holding out three fingers. "Just three, Martin. That way we can keep track of it with no strain. And don't go worrying about me collecting from old Nick. That lettering work is all union, and they won't go near him. He ain't got no choice but me." He nodded at Earl. "I'll take Earl here along to help me out."

M.L. said, "Fancy lettering? Your hands good enough for that now?"

Lonnie held his hands out gingerly. They were trembling and twitching. The veins seemed to be moving around.

"Boy, you can't go doing no lettering work with hands like that."

"Sure I can. The minute I get a brush in my hands I settle right down. No lie, Martin."

Earl chipped in. "He's right, M.L. I swear he is. I saw him up at Holly's once. He came in so drunk I thought he was going to walk through the neon, but the minute he started in to lettering he was O.K."

M.L. said, "All right, Earl, ease off."

Lonnie said, "That's the way I am, Martin, you ought to know that. Earl's telling you the cold gospel truth."

M.L. pulled out his black book and carefully wrote in *Lonnie Register, three dollars* under the day's date—*June 14th, 1949.*

"You won't be sorry, Martin. I swear you won't."

Inside, Lonnie opened two bottles of Miller High Life for himself and a Pepsi-Cola for Earl. "Get yourself some chips." Earl reached for the potato chip rack but Bo-Bo Joyner's long arm snaked out first.

Earl laughed once, "You really trust me, don't you, Rabbit?"

Bo-Bo's name was Jones Junior Joyner, but he had two nicknames. Bo-Bo was for being slow in school; at sixteen he was still in the ninth grade, and he sat hunched at the back of the classroom with his coat-hanger knees sticking out into the narrow aisles. Rabbit was because of his four front teeth, which jutted out so far he looked as if he were trying to scrape peanut butter from the roof of his mouth. He had a flat crew haircut that was too long on top and shaved down to the skin at the back, and his long sideburns came down to within an inch of his pointed jawbones. He wore a wide red cloth belt with matching suspenders and kept his collar and shirt cuffs buttoned. He wore no necktie. "I trust you about as far as I can throw you. Want to make something out of it?"

Earl bucked his teeth out like a rabbit and made a quick

dog-paddling motion. "You haven't been getting enough carrots, Rab."

"Go to hell."

Lonnie and Earl sat down on the curb near the mailbox. Lonnie had one Miller's in his hand and one balanced in the gutter. He drank deeply, smacked his lips, and sighed. "Just ex-actly what I needed. Mm, mm. And don't that sun feel good."

A black and white hound came out of the alley by the drugstore. He smelled the potato chips and came over walking low to the ground, smiling and wagging his tail. Earl gave him a few chips and told him to go away. The long dog walked to the edge of the sidewalk and lay down facing him and the bag of potato chips.

Lonnie took another drink, gazed fondly at the label, and leaned back on his elbow in the short grass. "Man, that first one is sweet. Sweet, that's what it is." He sighed again. "How'd I ever stand it for three days?" He drank again. "Earl?"

"Yeah, Lon."

"Don't let me drink more than four."

"O.K. Give me the money. That way, I won't have to watch you every minute."

"Good deal." Lonnie pulled the money out of the top pocket of his coveralls and handed it to him. "Listen, you're coming along to Nick's, ain't you? I'll pay a dollar an hour."

"You sure you can get the money out of him?"

Lonnie was on his second bottle of Miller's. "Positive."

After four beers, Lonnie's eyes were bright and shining

and the color had returned to his face. When he stood up he weaved sideways as if he were on board a ship. Earl wondered if it was time to bring up the Hudson, but he decided Lonnie wasn't quite right.

It was eleven o'clock when Lonnie and Earl got off the bus at the Carolina Double Dip carrying paintbrushes, dropcloths, and coveralls. Nick greeted them at the door, smiling and drying his thick hands on the front of his apron. Nick's smile faded as he shook hands with Lonnie. "You've been drinking."

"Don't worry about it." Lonnie unfolded his wooden painter's ruler and began measuring the big plate glass window. "Listen, Nick, I'd like to get the lettering started while the light's strong. It might be cloudy tomorrow."

Nick opened an old Bible to the title page and laid it before Lonnie. "Lonnie, how much you charge me for this kind of lettering?"

Lonnie and Earl looked down at the complicated, curling illuminated lettering. Lonnie said flatly, "What do you think I am? Some damn fool monk spent four lives working on that. Christ, he's got nine or ten colors in it."

Nick's face fell into his thick mustache. "It's like the old country. I didn't think you would understand."

Lonnie squinted down. "Ain't nothing to understand. I just can't do that kind of work." He looked hard at the rich reds and golds and the vine-strewn letters. "I bet three or four of them old-timers worked on the 'H,' by itself. Look how those vines whip in there. Hell, I couldn't touch that." He peered closer and pointed carefully. "Here, take those leaves. See how small he got them? Now you know some fool must have had a hell of a lot to do with his time to work that hard."

Nick's stomach creased against the counter. "It's very important to me, Lonnie. If it's a question of—" he continued carefully. "If it's a question of money, I'd be glad to pay well."

"I can't do it, Nick. I ain't that good."

"Can you maybe come close? Can you do it so it looks like this from a distance?"

"How far a distance?"

Nick shrugged his heavy shoulders. "From the street. Like you were driving by real slow. Say, eight or ten feet?"

"Maybe. You want 'The Carolina Double Dip' in this monk script?"

"No. Just my name. Carolina stays the way it is. I want my name, my full name—Nicholas Dimetra Dregeapolis. Just that."

Earl said, "What if someone throws a brick bat at it?"

"Why would they do that?"

"It looks pretty foreign, Nick. You got to admit that. Maybe it's too foreign for around here."

"No, you're wrong, boy. I been in this town too long. No one cares where you're from as long as you keep a clean place and mind your own business."

Lonnie sat up on the counter and fanned his fingers through a four-inch brush. "I'll do it, Nick. I'll do it, but I want the money in advance. I don't want to be sweating over this job and worrying about collecting from you later."

Nick clasped his hands together and smiled. "I appreciate this, Lonnie. I want you to know that. How much you asking for the lettering and the walls?"

Lonnie said, "Lettering will be seventy dollars. Room will cost you another hundred, that's including the ceiling. I furnish the paints."

Nick said quickly, "Forget it."

"The room or the lettering?"

"Both. I'll do it myself. My boy will help me when he comes home from camp." He grabbed Lonnie's arm in a fierce grip. His voice dipped low. "Do you have any idea how much ice cream I have to sell, how many hours I have to put in, to make a hundred and seventy dollars?"

"No. And I don't want to know." Lonnie stuck his brush in his back pocket and slid down from the counter.

"Lonnie! Lonnie, please. Please give me a better price. I got troubles these days that would make your hair turn white. My curb girls are threatening to quit. I caught my fountain boy stealing on me. Besides, I got medical bills."

"Not a nickel, Nick. Not a nickel. That monk script would have probably ruined my eyes anyway."

Earl spoke. "Nick, one-seventy's so far under union scale it ain't even funny. You better grab him while you can."

Nick walked over to the cash register and punched No Sale. "Lonnie, I'll give you twenty-five dollars for supplies, and the balance when you finish. I still ain't sure you can do the work."

Lonnie shook his head. "Make it seventy-five. I got to pay Earl here, and we need special paints."

With fifty dollars in advance Lonnie and Earl left to buy paints on Spruce Street. Lonnie squinted up Broad. The sun was high and hot and the white buildings glistened. "I feel like another beer."

Earl said, "You already had your four."

"Yeah, but that was some time ago. Besides, I used them up arguing with Nick."

As Lonnie poured his second Miller's into a frosted mug at the Silver Dipper, Earl saw that the back pool table was open. Buck nodded. "O.K. But keep the light off."

Lonnie followed Earl to the end table and sat back in the shadows drinking his beer.

Earl finished three racks of balls. "How you doing, Lonnie?"

Lonnie smiled but didn't answer.

Earl laid his stick on the table and went over to him. "You all right?"

"I'm fine. Absolutely perfect. Never better." He was stone drunk.

Earl said, "God Almighty, Lonnie. I didn't know they hit you that fast."

Lonnie smiled. "I got no resistance. Happens every time I come out. How many I had?"

"Seven."

"That's too many. I'm probably drunk, then."

"You told me the others didn't matter. Damn, I asked you about that, Lonnie, you remember?"

"I know, Earl. I lied to you. You gotta watch me. That's my pattern. But don't worry, I won't let you down. I'll lie to you but I won't let you down. I won't let you down, or Nick Dregeapop—or whatever that fool name is—down. I won't let the Carolina Double Dip down, and I won't let them goddamn, dead, blind little monks down."

"But you ain't had no sleep, and now seven beers. I don't know, Lon."

"Don't worry about the mule, little buddy. You just load the wagon. That's what the man on the radio says. Don't you go worrying about that old mule, you just load that little old red wagon." He took a drink and smiled. "And I'll tell you something else. You think you've seen some painting in your life. Well, I'm here to tell you, you ain't seen nothing yet. Wait till old Lonnie gets on that fine work, you wait. You going to see a touch you ain't ever going to forget."

Earl hung his cue stick up and sat in the dark next to Lonnie. Now was the time. If Lonnie got any drunker he would be too drunk. He kept mumbling about monks and touching his finger tips together.

Earl cleared his throat. He sat closer and pitched his voice low. "Lonnie, I guess you heard about how me and Coley been looking around for a car. Well, we were kinda thinking about your Hudson. I mean we got some money coming in and all."

Lonnie began humming. "No. No, thanks, Earl. I like you, boy, you know that. And me and you are going to put old Nick's tit through the wringer. But I don't want to get shed of my Hudson. I swear I don't. There ain't no flies on that Hudson. No sir, not a one. Earl, that's the finest, sweetest, smoothest car that ever came out of Detroit, Michigan, and you better believe that thing. And one of these days . . ."

Earl interrupted. "Listen, Lon, you'd sell it to us if we came up with the right price, wouldn't you?"

"No, boy, not a prayer."

The noon whistle at the Griffin Cotton Mill sounded as Earl led Lonnie out of the Silver Dipper and back toward Nick's. The sun had softened the tar streets, and his tennis shoes made a sticking, sucking noise as they crossed Cherry.

He kept Lonnie balanced and moving and kept talking into his ear, trying to sober him up. Nick opened the door. He was furious at Lonnie. "I want my money back."

Lonnie said, "What's eating you now?"

"How're you going to paint? You can't even walk."

Lonnie blinked at Nick and pushed his cap back. "I ain't getting paid to walk. Let me tell you something, old buddy." He rubbed his hands together. "I'm going to show you a piece of talent that all the money in the world can't buy. Hand me that Bible."

Earl opened the Bible on the counter near the big window. "He'll be O.K., Nick. He works best like this."

"No one works best when they're drunk. If he wrecks my neon I'm suing."

Earl copied Nick's full name out so Lonnie could read it easily.

Lonnie began. His hand was firm and steady. He worked rapidly with six brushes, one for each color, and held a fine hairline so none of the colors bled together. He leaned in close to his work with the tip of his tongue running across his lips as he made his careful strokes. Slowly a great, curling, crawling letter "N" emerged on the plate glass.

Nick moved in close with his hands behind his back. He was almost breathing down Lonnie's collar. He stared at the big letter and crossed his mustache, praying that Lonnie would maintain the beautiful medieval touch.

Nick lost track of time, of incoming and outgoing orders, even of the curb girls. The girls made their own sandwiches and milk shakes, and made change on the marble shelf of the cash register. Gladys Hightower, who was captain of the curb, was sitting with her boy friend, Cecil Laslow, in his car. They were necking.

Lonnie finished the letter "a" in Dimetra. He added an extra flurry of gold leaves at the bottom and moved in with his gold brush to the "D" in Dregeapolis.

Nick was afraid to talk to him. He walked outside and stood blinking in the sun, watching Gladys and Cecil coiling and uncoiling in the back seat. He came back inside. He winked at Earl and crept up behind Lonnie. The "p" in Dregeapolis was being trimmed in gold. Nick began humming a Greek folk song. His eyes were misted and in his mind he framed a picture of his heavily mustached forefathers standing solidly in the olive groves. He thought of Troy.

The "s" in Dregeapolis was finished, and Lonnie began cleaning his brushes in a can of gasoline. Nick seized him carefully and, after pulling him away from the paint, hugged him close. He longed to kiss Lonnie on each cheek but he knew Lonnie would never stand for it. He held him closer. "Lonnie, Lonnie, Lonnie. You make me live again."

The screen door at the Edges' house squeaked open and then slammed shut. Maude called out from the kitchen, her voice rising above the sound of the hillbilly song on the radio, "That you, Earl?"

Earl sprawled out on the red sofa in the living room with one foot on an armrest and the other slung over the back. "Yessum."

Maude stood in the doorway drying her hands on her apron. "Get your foot down from there."

Earl dropped his foot onto the armrest.

The low-ceilinged room was small and covered with a faded blue and orange linoleum that had been mended near the door with black electrical tape. A clock with no glass

and no minute hand, flanked by red and green plumed
Kewpie dolls on each side, sat in the center of the mantelpiece. Above it hung a gold-bordered calendar from the
Mulberry Drugstore showing an Indian maiden and a deer
kneeling by a moonlit pool. Except for the dark and swirl-
ing knots in the unpainted pine, the rest of the walls were
bare. The sofa, a green and black easy chair with a broken
arm, and four ladderback cane chairs all faced a cinder-
colored trash burner which stood propped up on four
brickbats. A hump of six-inch stovepipe led into a sheet-
metal-protected fireplace.

Maude sat down in the easy chair. "Where you been?"

"Nowhere, just messing around."

A breeze riffled the roller shade at the window and
swung the rabbit's foot at the end of the light cord back
and forth. Maude drew on her cigarette and studied him
carefully. "You weren't over at Clyde's, were you? I hear
they raided him."

"They catch anything?"

"Answer me, young man. Were you there or not?"

"I wasn't there, honest, I swear I wasn't. I been helping
Lonnie paint. Go on, call him up if you don't believe me."

"Oh, Earl, what in the world am I going to do with you?
I can't believe a word you say any more."

Earl sat up and stuck his hands out. "Ma, look at my
hands! That's paint, blue paint! Good Lord, what do you
want?"

Maude said, "I want the truth, that's what I want. The
next time you get in trouble they'll be putting you in that
home the judge was talking about. Maybe you'd like it better there." She rose. "I've got to watch the hash. Come on
back with me."

Earl followed her to the kitchen. "They catch anything at Clyde's?"

Maude said, "No, nothing."

"Good." He sat down at the oilcloth-covered table. While Maude stirred the barbecue hash he picked at the blistered paint on the window sill and gazed out at the mulberry tree which hung over the driveway and scraped against the house. In another two weeks the catawba caterpillars would be feeding on the big leaves. "We're going to have catawbas pretty soon now."

Maude shuddered. "Ugh. I can't stand those things. Don't you go bringing them in here."

Earl remembered how she had screamed when Leroy had shown her how to use them for fish bait by turning them inside out and fastening a hook into the yellow slime. She hadn't been fishing with them since.

The noise of Leroy's truck crunching on the gravel came from the driveway. Leroy and Charley Carruthers were in the cab, and strapped to the back was a five-foot-high 1948 Westinghouse air conditioner.

Earl said, "I'll go give them a hand."

"I guess you'll have to. Now try and keep clean."

Earl helped Charley and Leroy lower the big cooler onto a dolly and wheel it back to the garage.

Charley was a short colored man with wide shoulders and big arms. He parted his dark hair down the center of his head with a straightedge and a pair of tweezers and kept it soaked in Joe Louis Pomade. He and his mother Rose, who sold fresh vegetables from her garden, and his eight-year-old son Little Bit lived directly across the street in a four-room tin-roofed house divided in half by a wide dog trot. On one side Rose lived and raised Little Bit; on the other Charley lived with his new common-law wife Ruth Ellen. His first wife, Ruby, had run off with a sawmill operator from Monck's Corners.

Leroy gave Charley two dollars. "I'll holler if I need you."

"Yes, sir, Mr. Leroy. If you don't see me on the porch, blow your horn. I ain't got no plans for tonight." He snubbed his cigarette out on the palm of his hand and tucked it behind his ear. "I'll be going now."

After Leroy finished washing his hands in Lava soap and gasoline he dried them carefully and began skinning out the rinds of grease from under his fingernails with a matchbook cover. "What's for supper?"

"Barbecue hash and potatoes. I think she said okra, too." Earl squatted down and looked at the air-conditioner motor. "What's wrong with it?"

Leroy sloshed the dirty gasoline into the yard. "Needs a valve gasket, leaking gas. How much Freon we got?"

There were four cylinders of gas in the wooden rack alongside the wall. Green was methyl, white was Karene, blue was sulphur dioxide, and orange was Freon. Earl picked up the orange tank. "Feels like fifteen, maybe twenty pounds."

"That'll be plenty." Leroy took his black hat off and ran his fingers through his long hair. "Let's eat."

Leroy ate with his hat on. He ate quickly, holding his fork like a trowel, and had three helpings of hash and five slices of light bread. Between helpings he spoke. "Any mail today?"

Maude served him from the stove. "Nothing but bills. Earl helped Lonnie on a paint job. Says he's getting paid a dollar an hour."

Leroy hunched back over his plate. "That's great, right when I needed you. How many times I have to tell you not to go on these jack-rabbit jobs? I could have used you all day today and you might have learned something."

Earl stabbed a potato with his fork. "God Almighty! I catch hell for doing nothing, then I get it for getting a job. A dollar an hour's good money."

Leroy leveled his fork at him. Maude interrupted. "Tom Bennet raided Clyde today. You hear about that?"

Leroy lowered his fork and folding a piece of bread he wiped it around his plate. "I'll be damn. They get any whiskey?"

Maude said, "I don't think so."

"Tom's going to have to get up early in the morning if he's planning on catching old Clyde. Was Hog there?"

Maude took the plates away. "Thelma didn't say. She heard it from Alma."

Leroy took his hat off and hung it on the back of his chair. "Got any dessert?"

"Apple pie and blackberries. How does that sound?"

"Fine, that'll do it."

It was dark when Leroy and Earl went out to the garage and pulled the Westinghouse unit apart. After Leroy sealed a new gasket onto the compressor pump head, Earl began balancing the Freon in the cooling system. They sat on up-turned beer cases and watched the needles on the gauges. Earl smoothed the kinks out of the brass connecting hoses and told Leroy about Lonnie doing the Greek script at Nick's.

Leroy said quietly, "You won't find a nicer pair of hands in the county than Lonnie's, drunk or sober."

They stopped talking and watched the gauges. Bull bats streaked and dipped around the street lamp at the corner, and in the next yard a mockingbird was trying a combination quail and redbird's song. Across the street Rose sat on a nail keg on the porch smoking a pipe while Little Bit with a flashlight was playing with a new litter of puppies in a whiskey carton.

"Dad?"

"Yeah."

"Catawbas are going to be ready in a couple more weeks."

Leroy had been promising since early spring that when the catawbas were right he would take a week off and they would go to the Edisto River. The valve gauge seemed to be binding and Leroy tapped it gently with the handle of his Phillips Head screwdriver. "I ain't forgetting. You just keep your nose clean." He put two cigarettes in his mouth and lit them together. He handed one to Earl.

They smoked and watched the gauges. The tangerine-colored moon rolled up on top of Charley's tin roof like a state fair balloon, and the mockingbird hammered away on his new song. Leroy turned the Freon off and began tightening the valve lugs. "I want you next Sunday night. Right after supper."

"O.K."

"And listen, this is the one I don't want your Ma to be knowing about. That goes for Coley, too. You understand?"

"I understand."

There had been no relief from the heat during the night, and at eight-thirty when Earl met Lonnie at the drugstore it was already 84 degrees. Lonnie was sitting on the bus stop bench dressed in a pair of clean white coveralls and a brand new Sherwin-Williams paint company painter's cap, drinking his first Miller High Life of the day. Three gallons of sky-blue paint stood before him on the curb with a heavy bundle of dropcloths, and leaning against the mailbox was his eleven-foot aluminum ladder.

"Morning, Earl."

"Morning, Lonnie. How we going to get all that stuff on the bus?"

"Claude Henry will take care of us."

A bus pulled into the curb but it wasn't Claude's.

Earl said, "It's almost full. We're going to be catching all that shopping crowd."

"Take it easy, Earl. Just take it easy. I'll handle it." Lonnie crossed his feet on the buckets of paint and flipped him a fifty-cent piece. "Here, get me a pack of Luckies."

Claude's bus stopped before them. Lonnie got on, and after dropping two dimes in the money meter he crouched over and began talking to him. Claude kept looking out at the long ladder and back at his crowded bus and shaking his head. Lonnie kept talking. Finally, Claude gave up and sagged forward on his big steering wheel. Lonnie stuck his head out a window. "All right, Earl, let me have her in the middle." He grabbed the ladder as Earl lifted it up. "Easy now, easy. That's it."

Earl got on the bus four seats behind Lonnie and, leaning out the window, began working the ladder back. Claude watched them in the rearview mirror. "Be careful there, Lonnie. I don't want her getting all scratched up."

Lonnie grinned. "She's riding like a baby. No pain, no strain."

JUNE

They finished painting the ceiling in the early afternoon and started on the back wall. Earl worked on the baseboards and the trim, while Lonnie stayed on the ladder and touched up the molding around the top of the room.

Nick came back, swinging his key chain around his finger and smoking a black cigar. He offered one to Lonnie, who shook his head and stroked up into the corner smoothly, leaving no brush strokes or dripping paint. Nick blew a cloud of smoke up. "My wife's sister came by last night and saw your work, Lonnie. Said it was beautiful. Absolutely beautiful. She does a little painting herself, oil painting. She said you must be a genius to hold a hairline like that. Those were her exact words."

Lonnie picked a brush hair from the wall and wiped it on his pants leg. "I always try to do a nice job, Nick."

Earl stopped. He didn't like the way Nick was studying his cigar.

A soft rubbery half smile pulled Nick's lips back over his big front teeth. His eyes were half closed. "Lonnie." His voice changed. It was slow and precise. "There's something I want to tell you."

Lonnie balanced his four-inch brush on his paint can and began wiping his fingers on a piece of cloth soaked in turpentine.

"I won't be able to pay you the balance until later. Something came up."

Lonnie's voice was even and controlled. "You sure as hell hummed a different tune when you wanted that lettering done."

"I know we agreed." Nick raised his sad hooded eyes to Lonnie. "I feel terrible, Lonnie. Terrible. I'm not denying

81

anything, but something came up. My wife's younger brother is coming to America. Three hundred and ninety-two dollars, that's what it costs just to get him here. Can you imagine that? And then I have to get him a room and a job. Maybe you could help me out there? You got good connections, Lonnie. Everybody likes you. You think maybe you could get a job for a strong boy? He's fifteen. He wouldn't mind starting at the bottom."

"Nick, dammit, I need the money. I ain't studying your wife's brother." Lonnie's voice picked up a sharp edge. "Listen, I damn near went blind doing that lettering. You forgotten that already? Jesus H. Christ!"

There were no tears in Nick's eyes, but he dried them anyway. "I'm very emotional about my country, Lonnie. Last night after we looked at the lettering I told my wife to send for her little brother Stephanos. That's how carried away I got."

"And that's right where I lost that hundred and twenty dollars."

"You haven't lost anything. I intend paying you every dime. Here, I'll give you five dollars now, and you drop in tomorrow or the next day and I'll pay you some more. You'll see, it won't take long."

Nick went out front and shouted at Gladys, who was sitting in a car with her boy friend Cecil. "I catch you doing that one more time and I'm taking a day's pay out of your envelope."

Gladys began putting lipstick on. She pursed her lips like a suck fish and blotted them with a napkin. "You pay me for last week's work and I'll give you a day's pay."

Earl finished the back wall. "You want to start in on the trim?"

"Hell, yeah, we'll do it now." Lonnie handed him two dollars. "Go get me a couple Miller's and then stop by Fletcher's and pick up a half pint of kerosene. I'm going to fix this bastard's paint so it'll never dry."

It was Monday, two days after the painting. Earl and Coley were eating banana splits in the back booth at the drugstore and reading the used car ads. Lonnie was thumbing through a *Mandrake the Magician* comic book and drinking a beer.

"How does this sound, Lonnie?" Coley read, " 'Nineteen thirty-nine Ford, twenty-two thousand miles, new engine job, runs like new, only a hundred and seventy-five dollars.' "

Lonnie said, "Everything sounds good in print. I'd have to see it."

Earl had twelve of the fifteen dollars Lonnie had paid him. "Listen, Lonnie, why don't you let us give you ten dollars on the Hudson? Then you can sort of think about it."

Lonnie thumped his beer bottle on the table. "Will you leave me alone about that car? I done said no and I mean it. It ain't for sale."

Coley tipped his banana split dish up and drank off the chocolate and strawberry syrups.

Suddenly Earl stood up. "Here comes Nick. He just parked his car and he's heading for M.L."

Lonnie finished his beer and raised his empty bottle to Bo-Bo for another. "Why don't you mosey out there and see what you can pick up? Tell him I'm out of town."

M.L. watched Nick climb out of his new black Cadillac and walk toward him. Nick didn't come around much. He had on black wool slacks and a short-sleeved silk shirt with the initials N.D.D. over the pocket. He seemed to have put on weight, but the slacks were so full in the front with the wide double pleats that it was hard to tell. "Hello, M.L. How've you been?"

"Hello, Nick. Pretty good. You been a real stranger around here."

"I know. I know. I never get a chance to go anywhere any more. I been having a lot of trouble lately." He sat down. "You seen Lonnie Register? Something's wrong with the paint job. My woodwork isn't dry yet, and the girls keep leaning against it and ruining their uniforms." He examined the dark hair on the back of his hands. "I think Lonnie screwed me."

"That's funny, wonder why it won't dry? Shouldn't take more than a couple hours."

"Funny, hell. A couple of customers got themselves covered with it. On top of everything else all I need now is a couple lawsuits. Listen to this, M.L." He held up his hand and began counting. "My curb girls are threatening to quit, my wife's younger brother Stephanos is coming over from Greece and there's another mouth to feed, my refrigerator compressor is beginning to knock again, and now this." He closed his eyes and wheezed.

"You worry too much, Nick."

"I guess I do, but if that paint doesn't dry clean out God knows what they'll claim the clothes cost. Once the lawyers get into it, I'm as good as through. If you own your own business they think you're made out of money."

"That's too bad, Nick."

"M.L., you got the right idea. Work for someone else. Let them take the risk and do all the worrying. When you go home at night you can take your shoes off and your day is over. But not me. My day never ends. Never. You know the only thing that doesn't give me any trouble in my place? The cigarette machine. I make less than three cents on a carton of cigarettes, but it doesn't give me any trouble. None. If I made a nickel, I bet you a hundred dollars I'd have trouble with it. Probably electrocute some kid, or some old lady would break her hand in the coin return slot, and then more lawsuits. It's a fact: any item I got where there's a decent living in it, I got trouble." He wheezed again and looked up Bee and out Muberry. He seemed to be talking to himself. "With luck I can make out good on ice cream milk shakes. There I can put in a little sherbet and no one's the wiser. There's a nice percentage in milk shakes, but listen to this. If my compressor goes out, I lose everything. Ice cream, sherbet, milk, butter, everything goes down the drain." He paused and took a long breath. "Every morning, I unlock the door with my heart in my mouth. Every morning, I turn the key, I say to myself, 'Nick. Nick, old boy, maybe today you lose your ass. Maybe during the night the compressor stopped compressing and everything is melted.' It ain't worth it, M.L. Life's too short."

Nick stood up quickly. Earl was standing by the bicycle rack squaring his cap.

Nick shouted, "Earl! Earl! Come here."

Earl pushed his bicycle over to the bench.

"You seen your friend Lonnie?"

"I hear he was out drinking again. He's sore about you not paying him."

"Pay him? Pay him? When I catch him I'm going to sue him! The paint won't dry and all my girls' uniforms are ruined. I got customers that are going to sue me and you talk about paying him."

"You put up a sign saying 'Wet Paint'?"

"I put up ten signs, fifteen signs. I put signs everywhere, but still they lean against it."

Earl said, "I got to go."

Nick grabbed the handle bars. "Wait a minute. You can't leave me here like this. You got to find Lonnie and make him fix that paint!"

"If I find him, will you pay him?"

"If he dries the paint, I'll pay him."

"In advance?"

"In advance."

"O.K. I'll bring him by." Earl swung onto his bicycle and headed down Mulberry. He circled the block slowly, waiting for Nick to leave.

Nick looked at M.L. "You know who is a very clever man? I mean a very clever man as well as a very fine artist?"

M.L. said, "Lonnie?"

Nick nodded. "In the old country we like to bargain. You know, back and forth. We shout and scream and lie; sometimes we threaten. Over there it's part of the business. You don't see that in this country. No, you don't see that in this country. Over here, they are clever, ver-ry, ver-ry clever."

In the morning, Lonnie and Earl walked into the Carolina Double Dip. Lonnie had a hangover, and he wore his painter's cap low over his eyes to keep out the sun. They stood in the middle of the big blue room. Wet paint signs were Scotch-taped down the entire length of the plate glass windows. Another series of signs framed the door, and a bigger sign was hanging from the back of the National cash register announcing "CAUTION—WET PAINT—THE MANAGE-MENT NOT RESPONSIBLE FOR DAMAGES OF ANY KIND—CAUTION." Blue paint was spotted and streaked on the jukebox selection stations on the counter. It was on the windows, and one funnel-shaped smudge was dangerously close to the gold leaves under the letter "s" in Nicholas. It was on the neon, on the Wet Paint signs, and three long sky-blue finger marks ran across the dark black hair, above the dark sad eyes, of Nicholas Dimetra Dregeapolis.

Earl said, "You got the money?"

Nick said, "I got it ready. Can he fix it?"

Earl nodded. "He can handle it."

Nick counted out the $115.

Lonnie counted it again, with Earl watching, and shoved it into his coveralls pocket. When the dropcloths were ready, he pulled a can of paint remover from his back pocket and began shaking it. He stopped and handed it to Earl. "Here, you shake it. My head's about to come off."

Lonnie took the can back from Earl and pried it open with his screwdriver. He winced and frowned at the strong solvent smell. "How about hopping down to Buck's and picking me up a couple of Miller's? Better make it three. And get yourself something. But for Christ's sake, hurry."

Chapter 7

By Sunday the men in the Bottom who had been drunk on Friday and Saturday nights had sobered up and gone to church. They came home tight-lipped and serious and filled with furious resolutions to straighten out. Porches, roofs, stoves, and furniture were fixed and painted, and some of the more ambitious, armed with simple mechanic's tools, would try to stop the flush mechanisms in their toilets from leaking. Before the day was over they would call Leroy to get them out of trouble.

Sunday was Leroy's busiest day, and Maude always fixed a light dinner and then a big supper. This evening it had been fried chicken and cream gravy, rice and giblet gravy, sweet potatoes with marshmallows, string beans, hot biscuits, and iced tea. For dessert she had served hot blackberry pie.

Earl sat on the porch swing trying to suck a piece of chicken from his back teeth and wondering what kind of job Leroy was taking him on and how much he would pay him. As the sun dropped behind the trees and a thick slice began framing itself in Charley's dog trot, the glare flooded the Edges' porch. Earl closed his eyes.

Leroy was lying on the living room sofa with his belt open from the big fried chicken supper. His feet were crossed up on the armrest and over his face lay the sports section of the Columbia *Record*. His shoes and black hat lay on the floor within easy reach.

In the kitchen Maude turned the radio dial until she found a hillbilly music program, and after stubbing her cigarette out and putting her wedding ring in the soap dish she began washing the dishes.

Little Bit, Charley's eight-year-old son, came whistling down the sidewalk rolling an automobile tire. He wore no shirt or shoes, and balanced on his head for a hat was a big chrome Cadillac hubcap. "Hey, Earl, how you?"

"O.K., Little Bit. Where'd you get the hat?"

"My daddy gave it to me. Brought it home from uptown and gave it to me."

The chicken came loose and Earl flicked it into the weeds. "Looks sharp. Don't it hurt your head?"

Little Bit balanced his chin on top of the white-wall tire and shook his head. "No, it don't hurt. I got it crammed up with an old piece of shirt. You ought to see it when the sun hits it. Shines up in the trees and on the roofs and anywhere I wants to shine it."

"It's something, all right. How's your ma?"

"She's all right."

"Tell her hello for me. O.K.?"

"O.K., Earl, I'll tell her." He pushed the tire off and trotted across the street.

Leroy mumbled and sat up. He came to the door yawning and fastening his belt. "Who you talking to?"

"Little Bit."

Leroy sat down on the top step and leaned back on the porch post. "Feels like rain."

A frog flopped out of the weeds and onto the brick path. Leroy let out a long sigh with a low yodel on the end. Earl knew what it meant, but he knew Leroy wanted him to ask. "What's the matter?"

Leroy stared at the frog, who took another short jump, stopped, and began panting. "Money, money, money. Goddammit, it's always money. Sometimes I wonder if there's anything else." He spat at the frog. "I worked like a plow mule this month, and I'm still in the hole. Truck needs two tires now."

Earl had his own problems. He spoke to himself. "Well, Coley owes me six." He ticked his teeth together six times.

Leroy lit a cigarette. "You hear what I said?"

"Yessir, about the two tires you need. They go fast, don't they?"

"It ain't only the tires, it's the whole damn mess. The little man ain't got a chance in this country any more. Those big Detroit and Chicago outfits, they don't want part of the money; they want it all. They want to wipe us repair men right out. That way they can sell refrigerators and cars and radios like they sell socks. Wear them out, then throw them away." He studied his cigarette. "Boy, I'll tell you something. When the little man goes, I mean the handyman like me who's good with his hands and his head, when there ain't no place around for us, this country's going right down the old rathole." Leroy spat a piece of tobacco from his tongue. "Every time I look at one of those sealed units and it says 'Return to Factory' I damn near puke. You want me to tell you something sad?"

Earl was wondering if they had been wrong about the Buick at Loganberry's. He nodded to keep Leroy talking.

"You know that spider wrench I got for working on switches? I spent two weeks making that scutter, and you know I ain't picked it up five times this year. Hell, I was all set to enter a patent on it. Now it's obsolete, and it just hangs in there and gets in the way. Boy, you listening at what I'm telling you?"

"Yessir, I'm listening."

"I give this country five more years. Five more, and half the country will be working for Ford and General Motors, and the other half will be out repossessing. That'll be it. Half making cars and selling them, and half out collecting and taking them back. That'll be the goddamn day!"

Across the street Rose came out on the porch and sat down on her nail keg. Little Bit dragged his carton of puppies down the dog trot and joined her. She called out, "Evening, Mr. Leroy. How you, Earl?"

"O.K., Rose."

Leroy called back, "Hello, Rose. How's the puppies?"

"They fine. Eyes are open and they fighting like they all bitches. Lemme give you a couple."

"No, thanks. I got enough mouths to feed right now."

"Don't we all, though." Rose fanned herself with a funeral parlor fan. "Lord, I tell you this heat is something else."

Leroy shouted across, "Rose, you getting too big for that nail keg."

She waved her fan. "Hee, hee. Ain't that the truth? What you take for a piece of one of those old Coca-Cola barrels you got laying around?"

"What you got?"

"Got some late field peas. Give you two quarts, fresh picked."

"Hell, it'll take me an hour to saw one down."

Rose grinned. "And two quarts of blackberries."

"O.K. You got yourself a deal. I'll bring it over tomorrow."

Rose said, "It feels better already."

Leroy flipped his cigarette over the sunflowers and into the drain ditch. He spoke to Earl. "I'll tell you how rough things are. Other night me and Charley worked three hours on a gas range for a Baptist preacher, and the son of a bitch paid us off in side meat. Boy, if that didn't grab me; fifteen dollars right down the sewer." A green lizard ran along the bottom two-by-four of the fence and vanished into the waist-high weeds in the yard. "Next time I work for any preacher it's going to be cash on the barrelhead. I'll be damn if I'm going over that side meat route again."

The soapy wedding ring slipped easily over Maude's finger, and she turned it up so the three small diamond chips were on top. Looking at the ring always pleased her, and she remembered the night Leroy had proposed. They had been dancing all night at the Red Apple Inn out on the Charleston Highway. They were soaking wet. Leroy had always loved to dance, and together they had won the Shag contest at the big Christmas party for the Woolworth employees. The jukebox was playing a slow version of "The Tennessee Waltz" and the lights were flashing on and off. It was the last dance. Leroy had danced her over into a dark corner and, putting both arms around her, had said, "Maude, baby, why don't you and me take a ride down to Charleston and get married?" She remembered putting her hands in his back pockets when he kissed her.

Maude dried her hands and turned the radio off. Leroy heard the music stop. He spoke fast. "Take off, Earl. I don't want your ma knowing you're going with me."

"O.K." Earl quickly tied one of his tennis shoestrings.

"I'll meet you in front of the Governor's Mansion. Hurry up now, get out of here."

Earl took the seven steps in two jumps and began running up the street.

Maude came to the door brushing her hair. "Where's Earl?"

Leroy shifted around. "Said something about going over to Coley's."

Maude kept brushing as she sat down on the swing. "Weatherman says it's going to hit a hundred tomorrow. My hair feels like I got glue in it." She began pulling hair from the brush. "You got plans for tonight?"

" 'Fraid so. I'm due out in Dentsville in an hour. What you have in mind?"

"Oh, I kinda felt like a movie. I thought we could go uptown and window-shop and maybe see a show."

Leroy said, "Honey, you know how it is. If I don't go out on this call, they'll just call somebody else. We'll try it pretty soon, though. Give me a couple more days to get straightened out."

"O.K., Roy." She began brushing again. "Ain't it a nice night to be so hot."

"Yeah, nice colors. Felt like rain a while ago but not now."

Four blocks from the Edges' house stood the Governor's Mansion. In contrast to the gray shotgun houses of the Bottom that were jammed so close together a cat could walk from porch rail to porch rail and circle a block without touching the ground, the Mansion stood alone in the center of an entire block. It was flanked and surrounded by one-hundred-year-old magnolia and chestnut trees and almost invisible from the street.

Earl sat on one of the low river-stone gateposts in front of the Mansion, smoking a Kool and watching down the hill for the truck lights. Maybe Leroy was taking him on a big money job. Maybe he would give him five or ten dollars. It had to be a still or a hauling job, or he wouldn't have been so secret.

A door slammed in the Mansion, but Earl couldn't see anything. He smiled as he thought how funny it would be if the Governor went along on the job.

He had never seen the Governor. Even though they lived only four short blocks away, all he had ever seen were the servants and the garbage and the groceries going in and out the white wooden gate on Spruce Street. He wondered what the Governor did during the night when he was through with his work. He wondered what he would do at night if he were the Governor. Earl didn't know how to inhale. He held the cigarette smoke in his mouth and let it drift out slowly. He would dress up in old clothes and walk through the Bottom, that's what he'd do. He would stand in the shadows and listen to the people talking. Maybe they would be talking about him. Maybe they would be talking about why he didn't see to it that the streets were paved in the Bottom so people wouldn't have to spend so much money on new tires all the time. Maybe they would be saying how hard he worked and how much money he gave out of his own pocket to the Community Chest and all. Supposing he wore a mustache or a big straw hat and disguised his voice and people invited him up on their porches to drink iced tea

or beer. He would sit on the swing and watch the lightning
bugs, and all the time he would be listening to them talking
about him. He heard Leroy's truck whining up the hill in
second gear. It sounded as if it needed a new muffler.

Leroy pulled into the curb and Earl climbed in. They
drove without speaking; Leroy was in a hurry. At Hoover
Street he turned the pickup into a driveway, crossed a big
yard, and entered a long dark garage. A door closed behind
them and the lights came on. Lonnie was on the light
switch, Charley was working the door. Copper tubing and
sheet stock were everywhere. A heavy metal bender, a drill
press, and two vises were anchored to a workbench that ran
the length of the room. Earl whistled two notes: one high
and one low. A complete steam still was being built. It was
almost finished.

Earl stuck his head out the pickup window. "Hey,
Lonnie!"

Leroy clamped down on his arm. "Quit that hollering!"

Leroy put on a welder's mask and gloves and fired the
acetylene torch. He adjusted the flame until it pinpointed
and moved in on the bench to run a seam down the big
copper cooking kettle. The flame made a strong whistling
sound and turned blue. Leroy played it down the side
slowly. The light hurt Earl's eyes and he looked away.

At the end of the bench Lonnie and Charley were building a waterproof wooden box around the coiled copper
condenser pipe. They were working fast, squaring the pine
boards and pounding in ten-penny nails. Earl put a block of
wood in the bench vise and tightened it up. "We sure fixed
old Nick's ass, didn't we, Lon?"

Lonnie grinned around his mouthful of nails.

Charley started a nail in, then stopped. "I'd of shore

loved to seen the face on old Greek when that paint started in to run. That rascal owes me three dollars from a cleaning job I did for him over a year ago." He hammered the nail in. "Man, he is one tough bird to part with that dollar."

Leroy finished his welding seam. He turned the flame off and tossed his mask and gloves onto the bench. The big sixty-gallon copper kettle was ready.

Earl whispered to Charley, "That's some piece of equipment. All I've ever seen is little pot stills, never nothing like this."

Charley grinned. "Hell, what you talking about, that's like putting a pair of roller skates up aside a brand new Cadillac. Mr. Leroy says it's exactly like the kind them bottled-in-bond operations use up around Louisville."

Leroy stepped back from the bench. "O.K., you two, let's get this gear in the truck. Run that fire hose in there first, that'll give us more room."

Earl and Charley pulled out the hose. It measured over forty feet long and the diameter was four inches. Earl dropped his end and spat on his hands. "Jesus, this thing weighs a ton. You ready?"

"Ready." They dragged the hose across the dirt floor and, lowering the tail gate, they coiled it on the truck bed. When the still was loaded, a canvas tarpaulin was spread over the back of the truck. Earl crawled in under it and sat with his back to the cooker to keep it from sliding, and Charley crouched between the condenser and the heavy Detroit gas burner and kept them from bumping together.

It was pitch dark under the tarpaulin and red hot. Earl opened a hole at the side to let some air in. They were near the Governor's Mansion. At Pope Street they turned left and went down the sharp hill to the Jewish cemetery. Leroy turned his lights and engine off and coasted up in front of the two-story house at 906 Pope Street.

They worked in the dark, carrying the still into the bottom floor of the empty house. Upstairs, Leroy checked the double-hung black shades at the windows with his flashlight. They were all drawn and two-inch strips of Bull Dog tape secured them to the window jambs and sills. When he was satisfied that no light could escape, he turned the overhead lights on. The room was filled with equipment and supplies. Three square wooden 250-gallon-capacity mash vats were lined up against the far wall. Earl realized they were too big to get through the doors; they had been built right there in the room. A preheater equipped with an electrically driven force pump to automatically suck up the mash slurry from the vats stood on an eight-foot-high scaffold of two-by-fours in the center of the room, and stacked around it as high as Earl's chin were hundred-pound sacks of Jack Frost sugar and sixty-pound sacks of Red Eel meal.

Leroy snapped his fingers at Earl and Charley. "All right now, I want this stuff cleared out of here. I need all the room I can get." Leroy had chalked in on the floor where he would put the burner, the cooker, the doubler, the condenser, and the blending tub.

Earl and Charley dragged the sugar and meal into the next room while Leroy and Lonnie carried the still upstairs. In the storeroom two gray-striped mattresses were rolled up and leaning against the wall. On a table, which was the only piece of furniture in the whole house, were stacked sheets, canned goods, flashlights, a box of tools, a big electric fan, and two cartons of cigarettes.

Leroy and Lonnie connected the wiring to the motor-driven force pump, the gas pipe from the burner to the outlet, and secured and doped and tightened the plumbing connections for the water supply from the sink. The still parts were placed on the green chalk outline, and the steam operation began rising almost as high as the fourteen-foot ceiling. The entire setup extended in a straight line from the mash vats at one end of the room to the sink at the other. Next to the mash vats were the copper cooker and the gas burner with pipes running up to the preheater above. The doubler for redistilling was next to the cooker. The big condenser was next, and after that was a fifty-five gallon copper-lined Coca-Cola barrel sawed in half and converted into a blending tub. Steam pipes crisscrossed and honeycombed in and out of the units. A length of garden hose ran from the water tap to the condenser, and running from the bottom of the cooker to take away the mash slop was the forty-foot fire hose. It crossed the room like a dead snake, plunged straight down the stair well, angled across the small back room at six feet high, and tapered off quickly, for maximum flow, into the toilet on the first floor.

The steam still was finished.

After Leroy let Lonnie and Charley off at Clyde Peevy's to get a drink, Earl climbed in the cab of the truck. He slipped down low in the seat and lit a Kool. "I never thought I'd see a setup like that! That thing's practically automatic."

"Yeah, that's a good rig. It worked out all right. Give me a drag off that."

Earl said, "Can I give you a hand when you break her in?"

"It's all Clyde's. I'm washing my hands of it."

"Man, that'll make him the biggest thing in the county! When's he figuring on running?"

"Soon as he gets some more sugar and meal in. I told him to wait until things cool off, but the damn fool won't listen." Leroy turned into the driveway and stopped. "I'm bushed."

"Me too."

"You want a soft drink or something?"

"Nope. I'm really tired. I'm going to bed."

"Wait a second." Leroy opened his wallet and handed Earl two five-dollar bills.

"Thanks, I can sure use it."

"You earned it. And listen, you remember about keeping your mouth shut on this."

"I'll keep quiet. Dad, where's Clyde aiming on storing all that whiskey?"

Leroy grinned. "Right next door in the Jew cemetery. He can stash a couple thousand gallons in those grave vaults."

Earl yawned as he crossed the yard and began taking his shirt off. "That was your idea, wasn't it?"

"What do you think?"

PART II

July

Chapter 8

Coley stood up from the drugstore curb and paced out into the street. "Fifteen! Fifteen feet! Come on, Earl, try it."

Earl snapped his neck and spat hard between his teeth but it fell short. Coley opened his knife and began prying the washer cork out of the back of a Coca-Cola cap. "Funny how you can spit farther after you have a milk shake. Wonder why it is." The cork came loose, and he stuck the cap on his T shirt and secured the cloth from underneath with the cork.

Earl picked up a popsicle stick from the gutter and scraped at a wad of chewing gum that had smeared across the bottom of his shoe. At the top of the Bee Street hill he could see Dan Jackson's stove-black Chrysler.

Dan eased the car into the curb and climbed out smiling. Across the back windows that were now painted black was printed FAST DAN. Along the trim below the window it read *Owner, Proprietor, and Operator, Dan Jackson.* And then, in square brackets, his new name: FAST DAN.

Earl said, "Where'd you get the name?"

Dan straightened his new, short-billed motorcycle cap. "That's what they used to call me."

The Mulberry Drugstore became Dan's cabstand during the day; at night he cruised back and forth between the Greyhound bus station and the Atlantic Coast Line depot. A passenger, drunk or sober, would get in at the drugstore. "How much to Irmo?" Irmo is fifteen miles from Columbia, and the last six miles are over dirt roads.

Dan would say, "Whereabouts in Irmo?"

"Al's Place."

Dan would pretend he was doing a complicated mathematical problem behind his eyes. Then he would shake his head. "I suspect whatever you think it's worth."

"Let's say three dollars."

"That sounds fine. But I'll want me a dollar an hour extra if I have to wait around all night to bring you back."

Dan couldn't read or write, so Earl and Coley agreed to keep his books in a Blue Ribbon tablet. They kept track of the miles he drove and the gas he used and the money he collected and the money he spent at Gus's. On the following Saturday, Dan bought a half a case of Pepsi-Colas, six beers for himself, and a box of sandwiches and potato chips and drove them down to the river to the Little Eddy.

The Little Eddy was their favorite swimming place. The water was too muddy to see through, but the hole was deep enough for diving from the big rocks that jutted out into the stream and, unlike the Big Eddy a mile away, there was no undertow. Earl and Coley played follow-the-leader from every tree and rock they could climb and dive from while Dan, with his cap on and a beer in his hand, calmly floated in the middle of the Eddy on an inner tube. When

Dan got tired of the water he returned to the Chrysler and began polishing it, and when he tired of that he opened another beer, unwrapped another sandwich, and stretched out on one of the big flat rocks.

The picnic was Earl and Coley's payment for doing the bookkeeping and advising Dan to quit spending so much money on his car. He had bought a pair of searchlights for twelve dollars, a pair of foglights for twenty-two dollars, new front and rear bumper guards, a three-toned brass-barreled horn for seventeen dollars that sounded like a trombone, and announced that he had seen a radiator ornament that he had to have of a silver winged angel with trailing flags and leaping deer for twenty-four dollars. He had given Gus two dollars to hold it for him, and he was convinced it would be good for his business.

Earl and Coley decided it was hopeless talking to him. They tried reasoning with Gus. They told him that he was taking advantage of Dan.

Coley said, "Jesus, Gus, he doesn't need any old twenty-four-dollar radiator angel!"

Gus fingered the screwdriver he carried in his pencil pocket. "What do you think I run this business on, peanuts? I got bills to pay."

Earl cracked a gum ball on his back teeth. "And that's why you keep loading old Dan up?"

Gus said, "O.K., I've heard enough. How about clearing out of here. I got work to do."

In the doorway Coley said, "We were talking about the Hupmobile last night, Gus." He leaned on the door jamb with his hands in his pockets, trying hard to keep from laughing. "You still wanting a hundred and thirty-five for her?"

Gus's face went blank. Then he flushed. "Listen, you freckled-face little twerp! You get the hell out of here, you hear?"

"We were just leaving."

On Wednesday morning when Gus opened up, Dan was there with the twenty-two dollars, waiting for him. Gus mounted the silver angel on the front of the car, and Dan began polishing it with his chamois cloth. He buffed it softly, blew on it, buffed it again, and stepped back to admire it.

Gus said, "It looks good, Dan, real good."

Dan's eyes softened and almost disappeared in his small head. He smiled like a weary hound being scratched behind his ears. "Don't it, though. Oh, but don't it, though." He picked a fleck of dust from one of the deer that flanked the angel, buffed it again, and put his cloth back in his pocket.

Gus hooked his thumbs under his overall straps. "I got a nice buy on some seat covers. They got some new sharp colors that'll knock you down. Come on inside, let me show you a few samples. There won't be no obligation."

Two days later Dan handed Earl a letter from his sister, printed on a piece of brown wrapping paper. Earl read it out loud.

Dear Dan,

How are you? I am in terrible trouble. I need $67.50 at once. My address is 606½ Fortune Alley, Valdosta, Georgia.

Your sister,
Eulalia

P.S. If you ain't got $67.50, $25 will be fine.

Dan took his cap off and wiped the sweatband down. He sucked in. "Oh Lord, she needs another abortion."

Coley said, "How they do that, anyway?"

"Well it's like a ring job or a valve job only it's more serious." Dan folded the letter back up and then traced it across his lips. "Now where in the world am I going to be coming up with twenty-five dollars?"

Earl said, "But she said sixty-seven fifty."

"She always does that. Always adds the month's rent on." Dan turned the radio on, then off. "I need me something to drink." He handed Coley a dollar. "Get me a bottle of Budweiser and you all get some Pepsis."

Coley slid the soft drink box top back. "Hey, Doc, how much would you say an abortion would cost?"

Doc said, "Keep your voice down. How come you want to know?"

Coley said, "Oh, just general information."

Doc poured himself a glass of soda water. "Right around three hundred dollars, I'd say."

Earl pulled a bag of potato chips from the rack. "What do you think of one that's going for twenty-five?"

Doc held his hand up. "Hold it. I don't want to hear another word about this."

Earl said, "O.K., Doc, whatever you say."

Dan was silent. He sat slumped down low in his seat, tapping his beer bottle on the steering wheel.

Coley said, "You want to hear some *Captain Marvel?*"

Earl propped his arms on the back of Dan's seat. "It might sorta take your mind off things for a while."

Dan spoke. "Yeah, let me hear a little of that."

Coley opened the comic book. "Billy is talking to Professor Clark in his laboratory. 'Gosh, Dr. Clark, this is serious. If that formula falls into their hands we're doomed.' The doctor says, 'I'm afraid you're right, Billy. But what can we do?' "

Dan barked a short bitter laugh. "All that Billy's got to say is 'Shazam,' that's all. That's all he's got to say and there ain't no problem. I can sit here and 'Shazam, Shazam, Shazam' until my jaw drops off, and it ain't going to change things one bit. If I only hadn't gone and bought them foglights."

Earl said, "Maybe Gus will take them back."

Coley said, "That'll be the day. We could get some bottles."

Earl closed his eyes and divided and multiplied. If they found all pints, they would need 1,250; if all half pints, 2,500. "It'd take a month to do it."

"Maybe Doc would loan it to him."

"Not a chance."

"Lonnie?"

"Naw, he's broke again." Earl sat forward. "Listen, Clyde's dying for some whiskey. He'll pay fifty dollars for a load in from Camden, and I know the roads like I know my name."

Dan didn't even turn around. "No, man, I ain't hauling no whiskey. If I lose my Chrysler I am through, and there ain't no mistake about that. That Law would catch me in a minute. Probably shoot my car full of holes and then where would I be?" Suddenly Dan snapped his fingers. "I got it! I got it! Small Loans, that's it. Up there on Franklin Street. Hell, I had me a buddy over at the shop who went there every week, they used to call him 'Small Loans.' "

Coley said, "That ain't a bad idea. Wait a second, I'll check the phone book."

The Mason-Dixon Finance Company on Franklin Street agreed that a twenty-five-dollar loan could be arranged and that even if Dan couldn't sign his name his mark would be fine.

Everything was set until the assistant manager explained that Dan would have to use his car for collateral. Dan looked puzzled. The man explained that it was really only a formality that the State of South Carolina required. Dan shook his head and pulling his hands away from the desk he put them in his pocket. "No sir, I ain't signing no paper mentioning nothing about my Chrysler."

The manager came out of the back and explained it all over again.

Dan said, "No sir, no sir. I appreciate it and I know you gentlemen will treat me right, but no sir. I just couldn't sign nothing that had to do with my car."

Later, parked in front of the drugstore, Dan sipped on another bottle of Budweiser. "That's what happened to old Small Loans. He signed some crazy fool paper, and next thing they took his Buick away. Man, that really messed him up."

As the last slice of sun turned the tin roofs gold and the tar roofs red, Dan began polishing his winged angel. He was moving too fast, and Earl and Coley could tell he was tense. He polished the grille and the front bumper and moved back to the door handles. His voice sounded as if he was strangling. "How much whiskey Mr. Clyde want hauled?"

Earl was blowing a spit bubble. He swallowed it. "Fifty gallons up and fifty back. It's a snap, Dan. You know how easy that Camden Road is."

"The Law ain't watching his house, are they?"

Earl shook his head.

Dan moistened his lips. "Boys, I could use some help on this one. How 'bout if you'd come along? I'd be splitting the money with you."

Coley said, "I don't know, Dan. My dad would skin me alive if I did something like that. Besides, Earl's on probation."

Earl glared. "How's your old man going to know anything unless you tell him?" He heel-and-toe-walked down the curb. Suddenly he pounded his fist into his palm. "I've got it! I've got it! Tomorrow's the damn Fourth. We'll do it then! Every cop in town will be down at the Fairgrounds."

Coley shook his head, "I still ain't going."

Earl said, "We'll do it alone, Dan. I'll go tell Clyde. Maybe I can get half the money in advance."

"That shore would help out."

Clyde Peevy tightened his lips and frowned at Earl. "Boy, I can't go letting you run no whiskey in here for me. Leroy would kill me quicker than a train." They stood on Clyde's back porch. The kitchen was crowded with drinkers, and the jukebox was playing "There's a New Moon Over My Shoulder."

"It ain't me, Clyde. Dan's going to handle the whole thing himself, I swear he is. I ain't getting messed up with anything like that, I'm still on probation."

Clyde stuck his head in the kitchen door. "Help yourself there, Julius. I'll be with you in a minute." He tucked his tie in under his belt and smoothed it down. "Well, as long as I got your word, I guess it's O.K. I sure as hell need that whiskey. You swear you ain't lying?"

"I swear."

Clyde explained how he wanted fifty gallons of unaged sugar whiskey carried to the Peevy Brothers' Feed Store Warehouse in Camden and how the fifty gallons of aged corn whiskey he wanted brought back would be waiting there. He figured the safest delivery time would be toward the end of the fireworks display, and he decided that Dan was to come down the Sycamore Street hill between eleven-thirty and midnight. If the porch light was off it meant it was safe and the Law wasn't around. If it was on, Dan was to keep on driving and hide out until the next day.

Earl snapped his fingers. "I knew there was something I forgot. Dan wanted me to ask you if maybe you'd let him have twenty-five dollars in advance. He needs some gas and he's got a tire that looks bad."

"No, sorry, Earl. You tell him I can't do that. I've been bitten on that one before. He brings the whiskey here, he gets fifty dollars. That's the way I do business." Clyde broke a kitchen match in half and burred it around in his ear. "Something else, you tell Dan I don't want any phone calls coming in here. I think they got me tapped."

Earl felt the short hair on the back of his neck cool and the skin tighten. "O.K., I'll tell him."

It was almost dark that evening when Earl coasted into Coley's yard. He leaned his bicycle against the chinaberry tree and knocked on the door. "Hey, Coley!"

"I'm coming!"

The Simmses lived in a low five-room clapboard house set close to the sidewalk on the corner of Stewart Street and Silver Meteor Alley. The house had never been painted and was the gray color of a wasp's nest. A thick pea vine growing from a sawed-off wooden barrel by the side of the two porch steps screened half of the porch in deep shade. From the same barrel a bright trail of Cherokee roses climbed through the dark green pea vine and crisscrossed the ceiling on a network of copper wires that Coley's father, Harlis, had laced from the porch posts to the front wall.

Coley opened the screen door. "We're finishing supper, come on in."

Coley's parents, Harlis and Mary Simms, sat on one side of the dining room table. His sister Helen and a tall policeman were on the other. Harlis said, "Hello, Earl, how you been?"

"Fine, sir."

Coley introduced Earl to the policeman. "This is Roy Jarvis. He's Helen's sweetheart."

Helen looked stricken.

"This is my buddy, Earl Edge."

Roy reached up and shook hands with Earl. He was thin and stoop-shouldered, and he cocked his head over his plate as if he were tuning a guitar. He had pale blond hair and almost no eyebrows.

Earl said, "How come I've never seen you around?"

"I'm out on the highway most of the time."

Earl pushed his hair back from his face and leaned against the wall. "You drive a patrol car?"

"No, got a cycle. Harley-Davidson Number Seven. You ever ride a Number Seven?"

"Nope, never did."

Mary Simms said, "Come on, Earl, sit down. How about some iced tea?"

"No ma'am, no, thank you."

Roy said, "Next time I'm around I'll give you a spin. Harley Number Seven will hit a hundred and forty if you open her up. You know that?"

Helen's hair was as red as Coley's, and light freckles covered most of her face. "I wish you would hush up about driving so fast."

Roy shifted his fork to his left hand and touched her arm. "You know I never ride that fast. A boy that age likes to know what a motorcycle will do. That's the kind of information they like to keep track of."

Mary spoke to Earl. "Is your ma coming over?"

"Yessum. Right after she gets through with the dishes."

Harlis twisted around. "How about Leroy?"

"I don't think so."

Harlis pushed his chair back. "Well, that's enough for me. I got me a ball game I want to hear."

After supper Earl and Coley sat on the bottom porch step. Helen and Roy were on the combination swing and sofa, whispering.

Coley said, "You two want to be alone?"

Roy put his hands behind his head and cracked his knuckles. "Makes no never mind to me. We're catching the movie at nine."

Earl whispered to Coley. "You changed your mind yet?"

"No."

"Listen, Coley, if we get fifty dollars out of Clyde, you and me can keep twenty-five. That's a lot of money on the car."

"No, I said no. Now leave me alone."

"What if I said I'd forget the six you owe me? That way

you'd be making eighteen-fifty instead of twelve-fifty."

Helen giggled on the swing. Roy said, "Stop that."

Maude came up to the porch. "Hello, Coley. What you and Earl up to now?"

"Nothing, ma'am. We're just sitting here."

Maude pushed Earl's hair back. "If you don't get a haircut soon they're going to be putting a dog tag on you."

Helen said, "Evening, Mrs. Edge. I'd like you to meet Roy Jarvis. Roy, this is Mrs. Edge, Earl's mother."

Maude said, "Pleased to meet you, Roy."

"Thank you, ma'am."

Mary came out. "Evening, Maude." She sat down on the wooden bench.

Maude said, "Ain't this weather terrible? I bet we went through a gallon of iced tea today."

Mary shook her head. "It's the same thing here. I can't make it fast enough. It wouldn't be so bad if the nights would only cool off. How come Leroy didn't come?"

Maude lit a cigarette. "He's tied up on something. He said to tell you all he's sorry."

"That's too bad." Mary spoke down the porch. "Coley, you and Earl want some sugar cane?"

"Yes ma'am."

Mary raised her voice to Harlis, who was in the living room listening to the ball game on the radio. "Harlis, where'd you put that cane?"

"On the back porch. I'll bring it out when the inning's over."

In a few minutes, Harlis came outside with a three-foot stalk of sugar cane and a long bread knife. "Here you go. Now don't whack yourselves up." He sat on the top step directly behind Coley.

Harlis had the same kinky red hair and blue eyes as Coley and Helen, but where their faces were covered with freckles he had only a few pale ones running across the bridge of his nose. He had two tattoos curling around his right forearm. One was a dark falcon over the inscription *The 101st Airborne* and the other was a small rose with the word MARY printed in simple block letters. Cotton lint from the weaving room at the Griffin Cotton Mill clung to his socks and shoestrings, and a faint odor of cottonseed oil was on his hands.

Coley began sawing on the joint. "Who's playing?"

"Giants and Dodgers. Sorriest game I heard all year." He spoke to Mary. "M.L. and Lonnie are dropping by for a beer. I told them we might have some moonflowers blooming tonight."

Mary touched one of the heavy pods. "They look ready. You better slide some more chairs out."

Harlis rassled Coley's hair. "Son, when you going to start putting on some weight? You two running around here looking like a couple lizards."

Coley laughed. "Earl says he's been gaining. Says he's going out for the B squad."

"He's a little taller, both of you are, but you going to have to put some beef on those shoulders. Maybe you'll fatten up when it cools off. You go on out, Earl. Do you good. They could use some fast men. Always plenty of heavy men around but they never get enough fast ones." He laced his fingers together and put a slight pressure on Coley's head. "How about you? You going out with him?"

"I will if he does."

"Well, let me know when you decide to start practicing. Maybe I'll show you a few tricks." He stood up. "Let me go hear the rest of this mess."

Helen and Roy told everyone good night and left for the movies.

A whirlwind sucked up the red dust under the street lamp at the corner, and in the chinaberry tree the dry noise of the locusts sounded like a Prince Albert can being dragged down a long wire. Coley sawed through the first sugar cane joint and handed it to Earl. Earl tore the stiff purple shell off with his teeth. "You hear that? Lonnie's coming by. If we had any damn money we could hit him on the Hudson again."

"Don't hand me that static."

"I think you're just yellow." Earl sucked on his white cane bolt. "It wouldn't take more than a couple hours. That's twelve-fifty an hour."

Coley sat closer. "You swear you know the roads?"

"I'll swear on a Bible."

Coley laid the long cane stalk on the top step and sawed on it. "Well, O.K. I'll go. But Dan does the driving, right?"

"Right."

Lonnie and M.L. came by from the drugstore. M.L. handed Harlis twelve bottles of beer in a paper sack. "You'd better get them in the Frigidaire. They're getting warm already." Harlis pulled the cane chairs out from the kitchen and began telling them how the Giants threw the game away.

The women drank iced tea, the men beer, and Earl and Coley crouched close together on the bottom step, chewing and sucking on fresh white bolts of sugar cane and whispering about Clyde Peevy's whiskey, Lonnie and his Hudson, and the twenty-five dollars they would soon have.

Mary said, "Lonnie, how's Thelma these days?"

"She's fine, Mary. Just fine."

Maude said, "I saw her at the A and P the other day and she looked real good."

Midnight came loping up to the porch. He put his head in Lonnie's lap and Lonnie scratched him behind his ears. "Where you been all day?"

Maude and Mary were giggling, Earl and Coley were still whispering, and Harlis laughed at a joke M.L. told him.

A dog crossed under the street lamp, and Midnight pulled away from Lonnie and trotted into the shadows.

Harlis laughed. "That dog's got more sense than all of us put together."

Lonnie took a long pull on his beer. "It sure keeps him busy." He took out his harmonica and began playing the "Freight Train Blues." It was the only song he knew besides "Taps."

Eugene Huckabee, the Clovis Cab man from next door, came over with his guitar, carrying his own beer. He began tuning up and Harlis got him a chair and a fresh beer.

Lonnie slapped his harmonica in his hand to clear it and put it back in his pocket. He spoke to Mary. "Harlis says you might get a couple moonflowers tonight."

"I hope so, Lonnie. It's certainly hot enough."

He took another pull on his beer. "I sure wouldn't mind seeing me a couple. Yeah, I'd like that."

Eugene's guitar was ready and he played "Sweet Kentucky Rose."

Maude asked him if he knew "Juanita."

He did. He played "Beautiful Dreamer" and "Greensleeves" and "Come Where My Love Lies Dreaming" and the songs he had learned in junior high school. He played slow and faraway songs, as if a fast song or a loud song wouldn't be in keeping with the evening. Maude and Mary sang most of the songs. Harlis and M.L. would occasionally hum, while Lonnie kept going for more beer and walking up and down the porch, looking at the moonflower buds.

It was about eleven when Harlis said, "Here you go, Lon. Here's one now."

They all gathered around the bud. The stem was jutting out thicker than a pencil and almost as long. It was straight out with no support, and at the very end a heavy, green folded ball was pulsing. They were quiet, as if listening for a sound, a green sound. Eugene leaned his guitar against the wall, and the tight A and B strings made a faint buzzing sound. They watched. The bulb began throbbing and straining, and they held their breath and almost prayed that it would come. And it did. A liquid, muted pop sounded and the white bloom as big as a saucer and as white as snow burst before them.

In the morning the flower would be dead. It would die when the full moon set. But now it lived, and, quivering in its moving juices and listening to the mysterious sounds it heard, it arched and turned and began following the moon's short and somber flight across the night. A fragrance sweeter than honeysuckle and stronger than lilac swept down the porch. No one said anything. Finally Lonnie spoke and said what he always said. "Now ain't that something."

Chapter 9

The light from the street lamp shone through Earl's open window. He lay awake in the damp heat, a clammy sheet pulled up to his waist; he wore only his jockey shorts. He thought about how in talking Coley into the whiskey run he had almost talked himself out of it. It would be easy going to Camden. The back roads would be deserted, and no one would suspect a cab of carrying whiskey. And it would be easy coming back. But how would they deliver it? If the Law was watching one house in all of Columbia on the Fourth of July it would be Clyde Peevy's. Earl's pillow was wet. He pushed it to the wall. He rolled over on his stomach and kicked the sheet off and then, like a dog scratching away the hot topsoil, he burrowed and searched for a cool spot. There was none.

Only one wall of Earl's yellow cull-pine room had been painted white; the three others and the ceiling except for the knotholes and the nailheads were bare. The roof had leaked the winter before, and two big brown water stains that looked like dancing bears had appeared on the wall near the foot of the bed. When the wind blew the branches of the dead peach tree alongside the house and the twigs scraped at the window screen, the stains changed into fields, clouds, lakes, and the map of Alaska and Japan.

Tonight there was no wind, but the marks looked leaner than bears. They were more like panthers, black panthers. Earl lay rigid, sweating and staring at the looming black shapes. He closed his eyes. If they got caught they would make a run for it. No one could catch them if they got under the houses. He and Coley would lead Dan through their old pirate trails that they had explored and mapped when they were smaller. Earl remembered how with red bandannas over their heads, one or two teeth blackened out with tar or Black Jack chewing gum, lead pipes in their back pockets, and kitchen knives clenched in their teeth they had crawled under every house in the five-block area. He felt better. They could even slide through the sewer grating at Stewart Street and drop down into the six-foot sewerage pipe that led to the river. No policeman would ever look for them there.

Earl opened his eyes. The panthers were gone. Now the marks looked much bigger than bears. He was beginning to go to sleep. Through half-closed eyes he made the water-marks slide together. In the pale moonlight the knotholes and the nailheads became the waiting crowd; the large dark shape was Yankee Stadium. He could hear his fans scream as he came out of the dugout. DiMaggio was on second. He strode toward the batter's box, waving three bats; then, dropping two and tipping his hat to quiet the roaring crowd, he dug in and stared into the eyes of the lean pitcher from Chicago.

The next evening Dan went to the rear of Clyde's place for the pickup. The sugar whiskey was packed in ten five-gallon wooden kegs. Each keg weighed over sixty pounds. Clyde helped load the whiskey into the trunk of the Chrysler and then gave Dan the key to the Peevy Brothers' Warehouse. He was afraid that Dan might change his mind, so he avoided any talk about the porch light signal and the tapped telephone.

Dan picked up Earl and Coley two blocks away and they headed for Camden. The car began fish-tailing, and every bump felt as if they were driving over a railroad crosstie.

Dan stopped. "I'm going to ruin my car like this."

The rear of the car was down on the chassis and looked as if the back springs had been removed. The taillights were almost touching the ground.

They took five kegs out of the trunk and put them on the front seat and on the front floor boards. Earl and Coley crouched on top of the kegs to keep the weight forward. They started again. They went out the Asylum Road and cut through Sugar Hill until they came to the back dirt road that paralleled the Two-Notch Road. The washboard road made them bounce, and Earl tucked his head down to keep from hitting the ceiling. The slow coolness that had touched the back of his neck at Clyde's was now moving down his spine. What if the Law was waiting in the dark, waiting to spring a trap? He sighed.

Coley said, "What's the matter?"

"Nothing, my neck's getting stiff."

At the Peevy Brothers' Feed Store Warehouse they unlocked the door, unloaded the whiskey, and began looking around for the ten kegs that were to go back to Columbia.

Coley played his flashlight over the floor and around the walls. "Where in the hell is it?"

Earl had climbed up on the loading platform. "Shine it up here, Coley, up here." Earl's eyes followed the light beam across the platform.

Suddenly Dan groaned. "Oh, Lord! Oh, Lord! Will you come look at this! Oh, Lord, we are through."

Coley's light crossed the room and stopped. At the side of the room, standing up on one end, was a huge fifty-five-gallon Coca-Cola barrel. It looked like an enormous stove.

Dan's voice seemed to come from far away. "They must've figured we had a panel truck. We can't carry that thing."

Earl pushed at it with his shoulder. It didn't budge. "Jesus, it must weigh a ton."

Coley circled it quickly as if there was some secret way of picking it up, some handle he could grab. He shook his head, kicked it, and sliding down the barrel with his back against it he sat down and spat. "We can't even move it, let alone get it in the trunk." He spat again. "What a rotten goddamn trick."

Dan ran his finger around the top of the barrel. "I knew that trip was going too good." He talked aimlessly. "Too good, I knew it. I knew it. I should have stopped back there before we even crossed the Two-Notch and called this whole thing off."

Earl shoved his hands deep into his pockets and walked toward the big sliding door at the front. He wanted to be alone for a minute. He had to think. The strong smell of fertilizer and creosote was heavy in the dark room. Outside the night was quiet and there were no cars on the road. He was confused. Two feelings crisscrossed in his mind, and he tried to watch them both at the same time. One was a strange relief; the whole burden and the risk had been miraculously taken out of his hands. The other was the absolute terror of driving through town with the huge barrel sticking up in the trunk.

Coley joined him. "This is crazy, Earl! Clyde knows Dan's car. Let's go call him."

Earl said, "We can't, I told you he won't talk whiskey on the phone. Besides, I gave him my word about not coming along."

"That doesn't make sense." Coley was so mad he was almost stuttering. "This is an emergency! An emergency!"

"Well, I can't help it."

Coley jerked his cap bill down and stalked back toward Dan, who was sitting silently in the dark.

Earl leaned against the door jamb. He felt hemmed in. The relief had faded, and the thought of the huge barrel riding in the trunk made his palms and the bottom of his feet sweat.

A lightning bug had lost its way and was blinking in the corner of the room where coils of rope and guano were stored. In the distance the red neon of a honky-tonk winked off and on, and a dog barked twice and then began howling.

Finally Dan spoke. "I'm lost, boys, I don't know what we're going to do."

Earl was fast. "Let's go back, Dan. We'll make Clyde pay us half the money. He knew what kind of car you got, and he knew damn well you couldn't haul this."

Dan's face was resting in the palms of his long hands. "No, that ain't no good. If he don't get his whiskey he ain't going to be giving us doodle-e-squat."

Coley was still mad. He spat between his teeth at the barrel. "Boy, Edge, you sure backed down from last night, didn't you. Old Mr. Know-it-all." Coley's voice skittered up to a sharp falsetto. "No trouble, Coley. No trouble at all. Ain't nothing to worry about."

Earl said, "Shut your damn mouth!"

Coley sneered. "You want to try doing it?"

Dan said, "Easy, boys, easy. We got enough problems already."

Coley laughed. "No problems the mighty Captain Earl Edge can't handle. That right, Captain?"

Earl jumped up and cut a piece of rope from one of the coils. He quickly measured across the diameter of the barrel. He measured the car trunk lid clearance and then checked the barrel's girth. He was furious at Coley and himself and was determined to jam the barrel in or lash it to the roof or drag it behind. "Take a look."

They laid two timber skids from the ground to the trunk and tipped the barrel over on its side. The barrel weighed over six hundred pounds, and Dan began pushing the back while Earl and Coley strained at the sides. Slowly it rose up the skids.

Dan said, "That's it. Watch your fingers now." The barrel thumped hard on the trunk bottom.

Earl looped the rope under the bumper and pulled on the trunk lid. It came down only five or six inches and stuck up in the air on a 45-degree angle.

Dan moaned. "No question about what we're hauling. How do my springs look?"

Coley tried to shine the flashlight under the rear end but he couldn't. The mud flaps were dragging the ground and the taillights seemed to be resting on the floor. He whistled.

"She's right down on the frame. I can't even see the wheels."

Dan sighed and stepped back. The Chrysler's front end was pitched so high it looked as if it was climbing a steep hill.

They locked the warehouse and started off. As they got up speed, the rear end suddenly swerved toward the ditch. Dan stopped and went back to check the barrel. "She's still in the middle. It's sloshing; that's making her snatch and grab like that."

They started again, but this time Dan drove much slower.

Earl began checking the dashboard. They had plenty of gas, the oil pressure was normal, the ammeter was positive, and the car wasn't overheating. The enthusiasm of measuring and loading and being angry at Coley had worn off, and now there was nothing to do except sit and wait and watch the roads and sweat. He stared into the darkness, trying to see out beyond the range of the headlights. The low dark trees looked like the black Fords of the Law, and he caught himself bracing for the blinding searchlight and listening for the bone-chilling siren.

Below fifteen miles an hour the car held the road, but above fifteen the fish-tailing increased until the back end was almost jumping. On downhill grades Dan rode the brake and kept the car in low, trying to hold the speedometer needle on fifteen. When they went up a hill or down a hill, the exhaust pipe and the gas tank scraped along the roadbed, and every time the car went around a curve it would lurch toward the ditch. Dan had to stop and start over and over again. His feet were either on the brakes or the clutch, and his right arm was kept busy changing from low to high and back to low. The car groaned and coughed and the valves began clattering; it was overheating. The thirty-two miles that had taken fifty-five minutes earlier took two hours and forty-one minutes to return.

The dashboard clock read 11:14 when they started up Spider Hill, overlooking southwest Columbia, the State Fairgrounds, and all of the Bottom. Earl's throat was dry. The sweat in his armpits had run down and made his arms slick, and to keep from breathing too loudly he breathed through his mouth. He thought quickly and frantically rehearsed what he would say if Clyde's light was on. Maybe he should tell them about the signal now. But maybe the light would be off. Maybe there wouldn't be any trouble.

The silver angel pointed at the stars as the Chrysler slowly climbed the hill. The car leveled off, and in the bright distance to the south they could see the Fourth of July fireworks display at the Fairgrounds. Earl located the drugstore and, counting the street lights up two blocks to Sycamore and then down three to Stewart, he saw Clyde Peevy's house. It was dark. It was safe. Now he could keep quiet. He sighed through his teeth and dried his palms on the side of his pants. "Pretty good timing, Dan. We got fifteen minutes to burn."

Dan raised the hood to cool the engine. He whistled one note softly when he sat back down and, resting his chin on the top of the steering wheel, he watched the fireworks. He shifted gears in his mind and glided over his fear of the Law, of the dark streets, and of the six hundred pounds of aged corn whiskey that had flattened the rear springs and had probably twisted the Chrysler's chassis out of line. In this new magical overdrive, his troubles, like a winter-weary snake shedding his old skin, slipped away, and for the next full two minutes, while the sky blazed with a series of three-stage star bursts and then a thumping Sky King bomb that rattled the window glass, he was relaxed and free.

Coley was scared. He followed a long high skyrocket that exploded and re-exploded and then exploded again. Each stage was a different color—red, then green, and finally a burning, sulphurous yellow—and each color was followed by a louder blast. His thoughts raced from the sky to Clyde Peevy's and then back to the Fairgrounds. Maybe the police were all down there. Maybe Earl was right about that. Somebody had to keep the crowd in line. There would be pickpockets and parking problems and drunks. But there was bound to be a cop at Maple and Harris, and he'd have to be drunk or asleep not to see that the Chrysler that looked more like a street sweeper than a car was carrying whiskey. The fury swept back over him, and he swore that when the night was over he was going to hit Earl in his bragging mouth.

Earl watched the fireworks, too. But in the pause that followed the blast of a Dago-red Roman candle, he remembered the nights he and Leroy had sat on Spider Hill watching for the signals from Clyde Peevy or Wing Miller or Jeep Rogers to let them know if it was safe to bring the whiskey in. He and Leroy had carried whiskey back from Charleston and Augusta and Camden, and Earl had learned most of the back roads before he was twelve. Leroy had made it a practice to take him along to confuse the police. On the night that he was caught, Earl had been with him. He remembered the car suddenly stopping for the roadblock, and Leroy leaning over and opening his door and pushing him out. It had been raining, and he had slid down into the drain ditch that ran alongside the Batesburg–Leesville Road. He had lain in the shallow water, looking up at the flashlights and listening to the hard voice of an officer shouting into his radio. "Caught Edge, Sheriff! Leroy Edge! Near Batesburg. 'Bout a mile out. Loaded to the windows. Looks like thirty cases. Yeah, all alone."

Earl had lain in the ditch, scared and shaking with the cold, hoping the flashlights wouldn't spot him and, at the same time, hoping they would. He wanted to be with Leroy. But he had promised he would stay hidden if they ever got caught. The rain had begun to come down harder, and as he pulled his leather jacket up over his head and chewed on his woolen cuff he had begun to cry. The thought had taken shape in his mind that, if he hadn't been along, Leroy might have been able to jump out of the car and run for the woods.

It was the same fear that was now racing through him. Only this time it was different; this time it really was his fault. He tried to decide to tell them that Clyde might wave them off but he couldn't.

Coley spoke. "It's eleven twenty-eight."

Dan said, "I reckon it's time to go."

Earl said, "Yes."

Dan turned the key. "I shore wish my hands would stop trembling."

A wet panic seized Earl as the engine turned over, and a pair of ice-cold claws began kneading his stomach. The fear came flooding back. He had to speak or explode. "You'll have that money in no time now, Dan." There was a shrill, metallic quality in his voice. His teeth felt strange; they were soft and seemed to cling together as if they were covered with tin foil. "Maybe a bonus for all this extra risk." The words "extra risk" echoed in his head and he tried to take them back. He kept quiet, and as the car turned onto Sycamore he tried to see into the shadows. He couldn't tell who or what was parked on Franklin Street or Haygood.

Dan stopped a block from the Governor's Mansion. "O.K., you boys hop out here. I'll take her on in."

Coley said, "Hell, no, Dan. We're in this together."

Earl said, "Right. Come on, Dan, keep rolling."

Dan didn't argue; he started the car again.

A block beyond the Governor's Mansion the pavement ended, and Dan slowed down to go over the deep clay ruts. The car windows began rattling and the tail pipe banged against the gas tank. The vibration felt familiar and good to Earl. He leaned forward with both elbows on the dashboard. Kerosene lamps were burning in the front rooms of some of the houses on Sycamore and in the kitchens of others, but Clyde's house two blocks ahead looked like a black cave. He pressed his face against the windshield. They were less than a half a block away.

Suddenly Clyde's two-hundred-watt porch light came on flashing. It lighted the porch, the stairs, the yard, the street.

Earl jumped. "Jesus! Keep driving! Keep driving! Don't slow down! God Almighty!"

Coley said, "Oh, God."

Dan groaned.

Parked across from Clyde's were two dark cars. They looked like Fords. Earl could see the burning cigarettes of the Law. He braced for the searchlight. It didn't come. They were in front of Clyde's. They passed it. Dan drove stiffly and sat erect as if he had been struck dead at the wheel.

Earl wanted to turn around to see if they were being followed, but he was too afraid. His shoulders were trembling.

"Keep going, Dan! Keep going!" He could barely speak. "Little Eddy! We can go there." As they turned the corner at Jackson he looked back. The Law wasn't following.

Coley finally spoke. "You lying bastard. You knew about that signal." They were on the weed-covered path to the Little Eddy. "I figured there was something wrong."

Dan said, "Leave him alone, let's get shed of this stuff. Oh Lord, I should have never got messed up with this." He pulled the car up to within six feet of the water and jumped out. "Come on, boys! Hurry! My car's as good as gone." He cut the rope, and he and Coley began trying to roll the barrel down into the river.

Coley grunted. "It ain't moving!" He climbed up on the bumper and strained backwards. "Damn you, Earl, we're going to wind up in the Reformatory."

Dan said, "They going to take my car, I just know it." He tried to rock the barrel back and forth to start it moving. "We need some timbers or some wood or something. Let me see something here." He wedged the car jack between the barrel and the back of the trunk and began winding the long handle.

The barrel creaked and began rising.

"Almost, Dan." Coley edged over to the end of the bumper. "Keep her coming."

Earl said, "You're going to smash it."

Coley kept pulling. "You go to hell!"

Dan cranked the jack; the barrel rose up to the level of the bumper.

Suddenly Earl grabbed Dan's arm. "Wait! Wait a damn minute! This is crazy! There ain't no Law coming. We got plenty time."

Coley said, "Oh, yeah."

Dan was breathing heavily. "What you got in mind?"

"The Law ain't coming or we'd of seen them. Let me take a crack at Clyde. We got to try him, we just got to."

Dan said, "Mr. Clyde won't be bothering with us now. That Law's covering him like a blanket."

"But Dan, this is perfect! Anyone comes you can dump her."

Coley dropped down. "Let him go! He gets caught, it's his funeral."

Earl said, "I'd be back in no time."

Dan backed the jack off half a turn. "All right, but any lights or any noise, she's going in."

"Great. I'll come back through the canebrake. When I hit the sand bed I'll whistle 'Shave and a Haircut, Two Bits.'"

Dan leaned on the barrel. "Well, you be careful, boy, and hurry back."

Earl scrambled up the path through the heavy blackberry bushes and the sand bed. Out in the open, he began running. At the corner of Sycamore and Silver Meteor Alley he crawled under the first house. He worked his way under the next three and finally under Clyde's. After lying still a minute to catch his breath, he crawled from under the back porch and knocked on the screen door. Clyde came to the door but didn't unlock it. He whispered, "Who's there?"

"Me, Earl. Dan's got the whiskey."

"Get the hell out of here! The Law's crawling all over me."

Earl said, "Dan says he wants his money now. He says it

ain't his fault the Law's here. Besides that, he says they packed it in a fifty-five-gallon barrel and he almost killed himself."

Clyde counted out twenty-five dollars and opened the door. "Here's half now. Where's he got it?"

Earl had the money. "And Dan told me to tell you that a job like that's worth more than any fifty dollars."

Clyde handed him another five-dollar bill. "O.K., O.K. I'll give him an extra ten. Now, where's he stashing it?"

"The Little Eddy. Just the other side of the sand bed."

"All right. Tell him to stay with it till I get a truck down. And listen, for Christ's sake be careful coming out of here."

Earl went home, picked up a jacket, and told Maude he was spending the night at Coley's. He headed back for the river on the dead run. At the Little Eddy, Dan counted the money and kept twenty-five dollars, saying that he wanted to wire it to Eulalia right away. Coley had to go home. Earl agreed to stay with the whiskey until it was picked up.

They piled leaves and twigs up as high as the bumper and inched the barrel out. It sank into the pile, made a deep gurgling sound, and was quiet.

Earl poured dirt out of his shoes, and sitting with his back against the barrel he turned his socks inside out. "You all go on now. I can take care of this."

Coley said, "I'll try and sneak back out if I can. Same whistle, O.K.?"

Earl zipped his jacket up to his chin and pulled his cap bill down low. "O.K., but you don't have to if you don't want."

Earl's knees and elbows were scraped and sore from crawling under the houses. He was tired. His eyelids felt thick and grainy and he yawned heavily. He watched the dark Chrysler until it vanished in the canebrake and then heard Dan shift into low gear to get through the sand bed. The stars were bright and pulsing above the spiked tops of the pine trees, and he traced the Big Dipper and followed the handle out to the North Star. The strong corn whiskey smell cleared his head, and he thought of the thirty dollars that Clyde owed them. Maybe Lonnie would take it as a down payment. The swamp was filled with the crickety call of peepers and the watery thumps of bull-frogs. A low fog was spreading over the Eddy. Earl closed his eyes and saw himself and Coley coasting up to the drug-store in the black shiny Hudson. He was driving.

An hour passed and Coley returned alone. "I told Dan to go on home. He has to work in the morning." He had on a sweater and a jacket and he was carrying a paper bag. "You hungry?"

"Starving. What'd you get?"

Coley pulled out a half a loaf of bread, his pocketknife, and almost a full quart of peanut butter.

They made thick sandwiches and leaned back on the bar-rel with the peanut butter and the bread between them. The moon was high and, against the smoky background of the river fog, the rocks and the willow trees had the ghost-like coloring of a photograph negative.

Earl said, "Got any cigarettes?"

"Almost a half a pack."

"Perfect, perfect."

It wasn't until six-fifteen that Clyde's panel truck arrived for the whiskey. The driver gave Earl and Coley the thirty dollars, and when they had finished helping him load the barrel he drove them up to the bus stop on Maple Street.

They had grits and eggs and bacon and coffee at the Midtown Restaurant on Broad, and after playing the pinball
machines at the Broadway Arcade for an hour they went to
the first movie at the Palace Theatre. They saw it once and
then shifted over to the side and slept through the next two
showings.

When Dan showed up at the drugstore that afternoon,
Earl gave him his half of the extra ten dollars. Dan bought
himself two bottles of beer and sat down on his back
bumper. He didn't want to talk. He didn't even want to
hear Coley read from his new *Captain Marvel* comic book.
He just wanted to sit and drink beer and watch the traffic
go by.

It was almost first dark, and the mockingbird that had
been hanging around the transformer at the corner was imi-
tating a combination whippoorwill and meadowlark when
he finally got up. Slowly, for he had just finished his seventh
bottle of Budweiser beer, he took his chamois cloth from his
pocket and began stroking softly, softly stroking, the searchlights and the foglights, the angel and the deer, the grille-
work and the hubcaps and all of the chrome on his 1939
Deluxe four-door Chrysler.

Chapter 10

Earl lay flat in the rabbit tobacco at the side of Silver Meteor Alley, watching the eleven o'clock freight train go by and wondering why Lonnie had turned down their thirty dollars. He sucked on a sour ball. "We got to raise more cash, Coley. We can't get nothing but junk with thirty dollars."

Coley nodded at the train. He was counting the cars.

Earl said, "How many?"

"Eighty-three, eighty-four. . . ."

Earl rolled over on his back. The night wind was from the west and low rain clouds were drifting up from the river. "Let me know when she hits a hundred."

The hammering noise of couplings whacking coming together ran down the train. It was slowing down.

Coley shot up. "Come on! The coal cars are loaded!"

They slid down the bank and jumped the drain ditch. The street lamp lighted the steel ladders and the black gondolas and, swinging on, they climbed up and began tossing off coal.

Earl worked furiously, scratching, scraping, and shoving

135

it over the side. The train bucked twice, made a screeching metal-on-metal sound, and came to a stop. They scrambled to the top of the coal and began pushing with their feet. Coley kicked, and a long string of pieces bounced over the bulkhead and pounded on the ground. "I'll bet we hit a thousand pounds."

"Hell, we'll do better than that. I'm looking for a ton."

Suddenly a sharp beam from a flashlight crossed the car. They dropped. It missed them and began playing on a red Atcheson, Topeka & Santa Fe boxcar in front of them. The guard was on the far side of the car. Earl pressed himself down hard. He buried his face in the oil-smelling coal and pushed his hips down as low as he could.

Coley had frozen on a mound of coal at the top. He wanted to move off of a jagged piece that was hurting his ribs, but he was afraid the pile might start slipping.

The light swept slowly over the boxcar. They lay still. Then the light swung back and the guard left.

Earl raised his head. The guard's light was skimming over the freight cars far ahead of them. He sighed and sat up. "I thought he had us."

Coley wiped his forehead with the inside of his sleeve. "Me too."

A voice came from within the boxcar. "Is that guard gone?"

Earl looked at Coley and then back at the car. "Yeah, he's gone." They climbed down and stood in the gravel path at the side of the crossties.

The sliding boxcar door opened and a long figure dropped down onto the path. He was a tall fellow dressed in a wrinkled pin-striped suit. He carried a small zipper bag, and set in the side of his narrow face was a bright white cigarette holder that looked to be about four inches too long. "Either of you boys got a cigarette?"

Coley pulled out a package of Kools. "Sure. Help yourself, my hands are dirty."

"Good, that's what I need." His cigarette lighter was made of the same white bone as his holder. It worked on the first try. He inhaled deeply, closed his eyes, opened them, sighed, and smiled. He had a long pleasant face and narrow eyes. "That's better. Much better. Haven't had a smoke for a week." He looked around at the dark streets. "This is Columbia, right?"

Earl said, "Yeah."

"That's what I figured." Smoking the cigarette seemed to relax him, and he smiled again and looked back at the train. "How 'bout that for service? Getting let out right where I wanted to go. Maybe I'll write the Coast Line people a note. You boys get much coal?"

"Did pretty good." Earl looked up at him. "How long you been traveling?"

"Long time, boy. Long time. Seven nights and six days. All the way from Detroit, Michigan, in that car right there." He made a long slow motion toward the car, as if he were giving a lecture about it.

Coley whistled. "What's she carrying?"

The stranger ran his thumbs over the long blond hair that was curling over his ears. He needed a haircut. "Can't you tell? Can't you smell it?"

Earl said, "Smells like peat moss."

"Boy, you never smelled peat moss like that before. That's fertilizer. Good old yellow fertilizer."

Coley said, "Yeah, yeah, I smell it now. How'd you stand that in there for seven days? I get near fertilizer and I get the rash."

The man smoothed his hand down the long lapel of his one-button suit coat and looked toward Franklin Street. "You get so you get used to it." He studied the short cigarette in the end of his holder. "Mind if I hit you for another one of those Kools?"

Coley gave him their last one.

He lit the second cigarette with the butt of the first and grinned. "Hell, fertilizer wagons are a cinch. I used to ride refrigerator cars. Used to get myself a couple blankets, a few bottles of whiskey, and that's the only way I'd travel. None of those guards figure a man can stand it, so once you're in ain't nobody going to bother you."

The clouds were lower and a fine rain began blowing over them.

Coley said, "What you doing in Columbia?"

"I used to be an officer out at the Fort during the war, and I kinda took a liking to the town. I just thought I'd drift back down here and look her over again. Tell me something. Is the St. Louis Cafe still operating?"

Earl said, "Sure, it's still there."

"And how about the old Jewel Hotel?"

"She's still right up there on Chestnut."

"Good, that's where I'm staying then. Can I get a cab there?"

Coley said, "No need for that. You can walk up to Broad and get a bus. They go right by it."

"No, I don't want nothing to do with no bus. I need me a cab, I'm in a hurry."

Earl pointed up toward the station depot. "There's a cabstand up at the light. Ask for Dan Jackson, he's a friend of ours."

"O.K., fine, I'll do that." He smiled. "Hold it a minute. Here I am taking your last cigarette and everything and I don't even know your names. I'm Driscoll, Jack Driscoll." He stuck his hand out.

Earl shook it first. "Mine's Earl Edge."

"I'm Coley. Coley Simms."

"Well, that's better." His cigarette was out and he triggered it out of the white bone holder. "I'll see you boys around. Take care of yourselves, now." With that he turned and walked toward the blue cabstand light in the distance.

They watched him pass into the darkness, and then out of it, and then into it again. The train was beginning to move. Coley said, "You reckon he came from Detroit?"

"I don't know, but I bet you anything he's some kind of shark. You see those long hands on him? And asking about the St. Louis Cafe like that."

The train was picking up speed fast.

Coley raised his voice over the sound of the couplings. "He ain't been having much luck lately if he can't afford no cigarettes."

Earl shouted back. "Come on. Let's get the sacks. We're going to mess around and lose this coal."

The train passed, made the big turn out beyond Spider Hill, and straightened out for the 110 flat miles to Savannah.

After picking up a big wheelbarrow-wheeled wagon and ten 100-pound crokersacks at Earl's house, they loaded up almost eight hundred pounds of coal and took it to Clyde Peevy's. Clyde complained that it was too hot to buy coal in July but agreed to take it all for $4.50. He still wanted them to consider working for him as a lookout.

Nine blocks away Jack Driscoll sat in a dry concrete culvert sucking on his empty cigarette holder. The sweet smell of July peaches from the farmer's market drifted over him, and he tried to stop thinking of the hunger that was pulsing in his stomach and making his head ache. Instead he thought about the lies he had told the boys, of riding in refrigerator cars, about coming from Detroit, and about being an officer at Fort Jackson instead of a mess hall corporal.

He wondered why he had had to lie about everything. From Newark to Columbia had been two full days in the fertilizer car. That had been long enough. But nothing was ever really enough for Jack. If it was two days, he had to make it seven. If it was one hundred dollars, he had to make it five hundred. And standing there on the railroad path with a quarter, three dimes, and one nickel in his pocket, no job, no cigarettes, and holes in his twenty-nine-cent socks as big as silver dollars, he had had to pretend he was taking a taxi to the clean sheets and cool rooms of the Jewel Hotel. He shook his head sadly and swore to himself that he was going to quit lying.

As he sat in the dusty culvert tapping his fingers on his knees in time with the music coming from the Dixie Belle Beer Garden across the street, Jack began thinking about his last day in Columbia. It had been his discharge day two years before, and with his twelve hundred dollars mustering-out pay he had been planning on going home to Newark to buy a poolroom with his old high school buddy, Oscar Robbins. He had already bought his train ticket, but at the last minute he was unable to resist a final game of poker at Mason Richards' St. Louis Cafe.

Jack had played well but he lost steadily. Knowing he shouldn't, but figuring his luck had to change because his cards were so good, he invested another two hundred dollars. He kept losing. He wanted to go and he wanted to stay. He won a small pot, then lost two big ones. He invested again. His straights lost to flushes, his flushes to higher flushes, and on the final hand his three tens and two kings lost to three queens and a pair of fours. Mason was the big winner. And when he had smiled and peeled off his sunglasses to buy the players a drink, Jack had wanted to drag him across the table and choke him.

Jack squeezed his left fist in his right hand and cracked the knuckles. He hadn't figured out what Mason had done until just two weeks before, when he was working as a night clerk and bellhop at the Brightwater Hotel in Newark. That night a heavy loser in a big pot-limit game on the third floor jumped up cursing, drew a gun on the dealer, and tore his sunglasses off. The glasses were infrared and the cards were marked.

The minute the glasses were held up, Jack realized Mason had used the same trick. He was furious. Downstairs in the deserted 4 A.M. lobby he popped a deck of cards together in a double cut and began slamming down poker hands on the potted palm stand which stood before the big mirrored column in the center of the room. No wonder the cards had been so close. No wonder he'd won only the small pots. He kicked the lion's claw foot of the table, dragged in the cards, and began stacking the deck. If he had arrived in Newark with his twelve hundred dollars it would have all been different. It would have been Jack's and Oscar's, not just Oscar's alone. He dealt slowly, watching his hand action in the mirror. He fed himself aces back to back and then a king. He longed to be dealing across the table into Mason's grinning face. He paired the king and eased himself a third ace from the bottom of the deck. It would be like shooting a fish in a barrel.

Later he lay awake with a cold cloth over his eyes to keep out the bright sunlight and thought about what he would say to Mason if he saw him again. Maybe he'd smile and wink. "Hello, Mason. You remember me." Or maybe he'd play it straight and simply sit down opposite him and nod. "Hello, Mason. When you quit wearing the shades?" As he thought more and more about Mason he began thinking about going back to Columbia. The big-time poker games in Newark were too big for him, the small-time men's-room games too small. He felt locked out and locked in. He had $2.85, no car, he owed Oscar $65, and he had used up his next week's salary in advances. Newark was a dead-end town, and even though it was only July he dreaded going through another Jersey winter. In Columbia he wouldn't have to buy an overcoat.

Jack heard the spraying water and the whirling brushes of a street-cleaning truck coming down the street. He shifted away from the culvert opening to keep from getting wet. After the truck had passed he turned his suit coat inside out, folded it into a pillow, and, lying down next to the inch-wide stream of gutter water, he fell asleep.

Chapter 11

Early the next morning Jack got up quickly to avoid being seen coming out of the culvert. The night's sleep had refreshed him, but his appetite had increased. At the Moon Mullins Cafe he tried to avoid looking at the big menu that was chalked in white above the back bar, as he ordered a glass of water and a cup of coffee. The coffee made a brown heavy stain on his slow throbbing hunger, and he wished he could have one of the glazed or jelly-filled doughnuts pyramided before him. Leaving the Moon Mullins, he went to the Greyhound bus station, shaved, changed his shirt, found a newspaper, and started looking through the classified ads under the column GRILL HELP WANTED.

Jack moistened his fingers and pressed his long hair down behind his ears as he walked up the block to the Casablanca Restaurant, a big orange-colored one-story building on the corner of Dogwood and Lee Streets. Scalloped red neon ringed the base of the roof on all four sides, and hanging in the two big plate glass windows looking out over the traffic circle of Moss Hill were a series of nine smiling neon pigs spelling out BAR-B-QUE and leaping into a big neon pot. He paused before the big glass door, took two deep breaths to conceal his hunger, and entered. After an intense interview with the proprietor and the proprietor's wife, which lasted until nine o'clock, he had the job on the grill and the sandwich board.

By nine-thirty Jack had eaten six fried eggs, a half pound of crisp fried Canadian bacon, five slices of toast, a full quart of freshly squeezed orange juice, and four cups of the best coffee he thought he had ever had. He lit a cigarette that the owner had given him and smiled into the shiny chrome behind the wide grill. The reflection of his starched white apron snugged tightly around his thin waist pleased him and, cocking his tall chef's hat to one side, he fanned an imaginary deck of cards and began dealing.

Wilson Wade Hampton Peeler, the owner of the Casablanca, was slightly over fifty and had grown up in the Bottom with Lonnie, Doc, M.L., and Holly Yates. Wilson was short and stout, with a full head of sandy hair that he parted carefully and smoothly to the right. His boyish hair and fatigued eyes, a result of the long split-shift hours he worked, gave people a confused and changing picture of him. If two customers were to come in within fifteen minutes of each other, the first might say, "Hey there, Wilson, you looking great. Must be living right. Must be doing something right."

Wilson would get himself set up with that. Then another fellow would come in and whisper, "Come here, Wilson." Wilson would leave the cash register and lean over the counter, thinking he was going to hear a new joke. "Wilson, you in any kind of trouble? You look like you ain't had a lick of sleep in a month. No lie, boy, why don't you take off a few days?"

Wilson worked from seven in the morning until the lunch crowd left at two. He then went home and listened to the radio and rested his feet until five. He returned at five-thirty for the dinner business and stayed until closing at midnight. Every dish that was served when he was on duty had to meet with his close personal inspection and approval, and every customer that presented his check at the cash register had to answer to the smiling Wilson. "Did you enjoy the food?"

The customer would usually answer "Yes."

Wilson would fumble with the change or count it out slowly enough to get in his big question. "And how did you like the sauce?"

All sandwiches at the Casablanca were covered with Wilson's stinging barbecue sauce and served with a knife and fork. If a customer wanted a ham sandwich or a grilled cheese and insisted that no sauce be spread over it, Wilson would come smiling out from behind the cash register or out of the kitchen and say, "Just try it. That's all I'm asking you to do. Just try it. Believe me, you'll thank me later."

"Listen, Wilson, save yourself some steps, just give me a ham sandwich. You hear that? Just a ham sandwich with nothing on it. And don't go drenching it with that goddamn sauce. I got a bad stomach."

After the customer had left, Wilson would shake his head and mutter, "They just don't know what's good."

It had taken Wilson eleven years to perfect his barbecue sauce, and he lived in fear of it being copied. To protect it he never showed the secret of the mixing and the blending to his cooks or even to his wife, Sophie. He also refused to

have curb service or outgoing orders. But with all the pre-
cautions he took, he still worried that some local restaurant
might steal his recipe. Every other week he would get in his
Chrysler and drive out to Holly Yates', The Bearcat
Drive-In, Ed White's, and three or four other barbecue
places along the Two-Notch Road and the Charleston
Highway to check the different barbecues.

The years of worrying and rushing and the long fourteen-
and fifteen-hour days had taken their toll on Wilson, and
while he would work the first eight hours with a firm step
and an occasional Spanish flourish when replacing the linen
on the center tables, the last three hours found him limping
and trying to keep on the duckboards as much as possible.
Every night at closing time he would soak his feet in hot
salts while Sophie checked the register, counted up the
money, and turned off the neon signs and the parking
lights.

Sophie Wade Hampton Peeler, a dark-eyed and heavy-
set Capricorn, considered her marriage to Wilson, who was
a Leo, very fortunate and happy. Twenty-four years before, Wilson had hired her from the kitchen of Holly Yates'
first luncheonette, knowing she could bring her customers
along. Holly had offered her a raise and a part of the business to keep her, but Sophie had had plans of her own. At
the Casablanca she had worked her way up from cook to
waitress to cash-register girl, and two years after leaving
Holly's she had become Wilson's wife.

Jack liked the tightly planned kitchen at the Casablanca.
He liked the spring in the new duckboards, the walk-in ice-

box, and the perfect temperature control on the French-fry pots and the big grill. He soon grew accustomed to the shine of the chrome behind the grill, the heft and the feel of the French-fry baskets, and the fine tool-steel spring of his spatula and grill fork. At first it was hard pouring the barbecue sauce over the filets, the tenderloins, and the double cuts of baby lamb chops as Wilson insisted, but after a few days he didn't mind.

The dinner rush was over, and he and Wilson were in the kitchen. Sophie had finished her marketing and gone to a Cary Grant movie at the Palace. Wilson said, "I got to call the linen man in the morning. How you fixed on aprons?"

"I'm all set." Jack nodded toward the front. "How's the counter look?"

"Couple coffee drinkers, that's all." Wilson shoved himself up on the sandwich counter and watched Jack mash out hamburgers and interleaf them with waxed paper.

In his long experience with cooks, Wilson had learned how to spot the drifters and the heavy drinkers. He also prided himself on being able to watch a man move on the grill or on the long counter and predict almost to the day how long he would stay. But Jack was different; he was a mystery; he was unlike any cook Wilson had ever worked before. He was fast and smart and he knew his way around a kitchen, and Wilson liked and trusted him. But there was a smoothness and a flair to his motions that made Wilson feel that Jack's days at the Casablanca were numbered. Wilson often thought that a long black Cadillac or a Chrysler Imperial with northern license plates would pull up in front of the Casablanca and Jack would climb in the back seat and drive off. Or two Federal Bureau of Investigation men would walk in one day around first dark and he would untie his apron, dry his hands, and walk out between them.

"Tell me something, Jack. You ain't always been a cook, have you?"

"Well, I've done a couple other things, but I guess cooking is the closest thing to me."

Wilson tamped a cigarette on the order counter and lit it. "If you take my advice, boy, you'll stay with cooking. You got a nice move and you know how to take hold. I swear if I don't believe you could go a long way in this field." He pulled his apron up so he could cross his legs. "The way I see it is any man can fry a steak or a couple chops or section up a chicken and drop him in the deep fry. That's what I call a cook, a grill cook; some folks just call them fryers. But when you stop to think about the great chefs, how they come up with new salads and fancy baking and brand new dishes, well, that's something else and I believe you'd go along with me on that, wouldn't you, Jack?"

"Yessir."

"Now you take those French fellows. They keep a soup cooking or a sauce simmering for two and three weeks. That's right, two and three weeks, and each day it gets better and each day they add themselves a little something extra to it. Some little pinch of this or a dab of that, those little secret ingredients. Well, you figure it out for yourself. You take a soup that's been worked on like that for a few weeks, there ain't no one around that can copy that recipe. Chances are the chef himself don't know what all he put in there." He drew on his cigarette and let the smoke trickle out. He thought of France.

Wilson Peeler, except for going to Charlotte, North Carolina, to pick up some produce, had never been out of the State of South Carolina. "You know one day when I find me a cashier I can trust and a cook I can get along with"— he shot a quick look at Jack—"I'm going to take me a trip over there to Paris, France. That's my ambition, boy. What I'd like to do is just sort of drift around and pick up what I could about French cooking. I wouldn't go messing with the tourists and that crowd. No, I'd want to get off by myself. Maybe I could even pick up some of the language. I wouldn't go wearing those loud-ass Hawaiian shirts, either, like a lot of them do and just get drunk and go to all those leg shows and whore houses. I'd just mosey along on the back roads and sniff around the small restaurants." He closed his eyes and let the smoke trickle from his mouth and his nose. "Yessir, I'd get me down there in the south of France, that's where they really cook up a storm. Leave the old lady at home, she could go up to Irmo and visit her mother and sister. I'd want to take plenty of time. That's the kind of thing you don't want to rush. I'd be trying to discover me some recipes that I could bring back and introduce here in Columbia. You know, Jack, if I found something, you know like a special kind of soup or a great main dish, I might even trade my barbecue sauce recipe for it. You know something? I bet those French would be hogs about that sauce."

He didn't want any answer. His eyes were still closed. Jack was afraid he would burn himself with his cigarette, and he watched it carefully.

Wilson spoke softly. He sounded as if he were speaking downwind and the words were to a great green plain. "France . . . France . . . Paris, France. . . ." He kept his eyes closed and in the same voice asked, "What's another town in France, Jack?"

Jack said, "Calais."

"Calais . . . Calais. . . . There's a nice name too. . . . Calais. . . . You know any more?"

"Bordeaux."

"Paris . . . Calais . . . Bordeaux . . . Bordeaux. . . . Those are fine names, that's the kind of sounds we need on our menu. Bordeaux, Bordeaux. Got any more?"

"Normandy."

"Normandy, oh, that's nice too. I've heard of that one. Wasn't there a battle there or something?" He rubbed his cigarette out in a Maxwell House Coffee can top. "You know those French names, they do something to you. No doubt about it, they got a much better sound than ours. Now you take a name like Irmo. What in the hell kind of name is that? And Ballantine's Landing and Green Pond and Four Holes. There just ain't no comparing them. Yeah, that crowd over there, they know how to live. And they know how to cook. And just as sure as I'm sitting here on this sandwich counter, I'm going to get my ass over there. And I don't mean in no ten more years, I mean soon." Wilson slammed his open palms on the wooden counter. "That's what I'm going to do, Jack. You hear?"

"Yessir, sounds good to me."

"That's just what I'm going to do. Get me a cook I can work with, get me a cashier, get some French records, and . . ."

A customer shouted for the cashier. Wilson had been sitting on the sandwich counter too long, and the edge had cut off the circulation in his feet. When he slid down from

the counter, they were sound asleep. The pain was fierce
and he reached for the back of Jack's stool.

"Cashier! Where's that cashier?" came from the front.

"Jesus, it's like a thousand needles." Wilson limped
quickly toward the swinging doors. "I'm coming. I'm coming."

Chapter 12

It was almost midnight and Earl and Coley were behind the Casablanca, going through the garbage cans looking for whiskey bottles. Their bicycles were lying in the tall grass, and the chrome of the wheel rims and the handle bars glistened in the neon.

Coley turned his flashlight off and wiped coffee grounds from his hands on the sides of his overall pants. "Ugh, I hate this. I'm wrecking these pants. Why can't they separate the damn garbage!"

"Don't make so much noise. Old Peeler'll think we're breaking in." Earl kept his light shaded with his hand and picked four bottles out. He lowered them carefully into a crokersack he had tied to his belt.

Suddenly the bolt lock on the kitchen door sounded, and the door opened. A voice half shouted, "Mr. Peeler, I'm going out for a smoke."

Earl closed the lid, dropped his bag, and ran toward the bicycles. Coley was right behind him. They dropped down in the tall grass and crawled around to watch the door.

A tall figure stood in the doorway, then moved toward

the side of the building away from the smell of the garbage cans. After throwing back his wrap-around apron and pulling out a package of cigarettes, he sat down on a stack of Pepsi-Cola and Orange Crush crates.

Earl punched Coley's arm. "Hey, look, it's that fellow from the fertilizer car."

"Yeah. Come on, let's go see him."

Jack stood up when he saw them coming. "Well, if it ain't my friends from the Atlantic Coast Line. Sit down, take the load off your feet. How about a cigarette?" They took cigarettes and Jack lit them quickly with his bone lighter. "What brings you round here this time of night? Ain't no coal back here."

Coley sat in the short weeds. "Bottles, Jack. We get them out of the garbage."

"What they worth?"

"Penny for halves and two cents for pints."

Earl said, "Movie money, that's about all."

"You find any?"

Earl balanced an Orange Crush crate on one end and sat down. "Couple dozen so far. Not too good. Do better right after a week end."

Jack said, "Hell, that's no fun plowing through them chicken bones and slop. Tell you what, from now on I'll set them aside for you. How's that sound?"

Coley said, "Sounds fine."

Earl drew in on his cigarette. He pushed the smoke into his nose and then let it out slowly. "Me and Coley sure didn't figure you for a grill cook."

Jack smiled in the dark. "What did you figure me for?"

Coley said, "Some kind of shark, maybe a pool hustler."

Earl said, "You play much pool, Jack?"

"Naw, I never made the grade there, but I'll turn a card now and then."

Earl said, "It's poker, then! Right?"

"Yeah, you might say that. I'll sit in on a game once in a while."

Coley propped himself up on his elbow and watched the smoke from his cigarette turn bright pink under the flashing neon. "How you like working for old Wilson?"

Jack rubbed his wrists and began flexing his fingers. "Not bad. Not bad at all. He puts out good food, I'll say that for him. And he's sure got him a following on his barbecue. This town must be barbecue crazy."

Earl dropped his cigarette into an empty beer bottle. "It's all in that sauce. When people want barbecue, they come here. When they want hamburgers they go out to Holly Yates'."

Jack stood up and stretched. "I got to check out. I got something on the stove."

Coley said, "You reckon there's any bottles inside?"

"There ought to be a few. You boys sit tight and I'll bring them out."

Jack returned carrying two bags. One held eight half pints and five pints; the other, four pork barbecues and two R.C. Colas. "There's a bottle opener in the bag."

Coley said, "Damn, Jack, thanks. This is great."

Earl unwrapped his first barbecue. "God, I'm starved. Thanks, Jack."

Jack laughed. "Sit back and take your time. No one's going to bother you. Put the bottles in the crate when you're finished. O.K.?"

Coley had his mouth full. "Good deal."

JULY

Earl was sprawled over his living room couch, reading the new *Jungle Jim* comic book, when a disc jockey on Station WXOY announced that he was dedicating a medley of Hank Williams' records to Holly Yates, who had just returned from a twenty-day bass and rockfish trip on the Santee River. Before the first chorus of "Cold, Cold Heart" was half over, Earl was down the steps, on his bike, and heading for Coley's.

At Holly Yates' Cooper Ridge Road place, the Fourth of July Special of fried chicken, French fries, lettuce and tomato, hot rolls, and coffee for fifty-four cents had been extended for two weeks, and American flags, skyrockets, and red, white, and blue firecrackers were still painted on the plate glass windows. They went inside and, sitting in one of the side booths, ordered small Cokes and told the waitress they wanted to see Holly.

Holly had six restaurants in town, but the Cooper Ridge Drive-In was his biggest. The walls were covered with pictures of him shaking hands with Hollywood movie stars and famous band leaders and singers, or standing and grinning in the center of some big civic ground-breaking ceremony.

There was a jukebox station in each of the eighteen red leatherette booths that horseshoed around the room and five more on the long fountain counter. The twenty-three stations fed into an enormous bubbling Wurlitzer jukebox that held two hundred records. One third was modern and light classic, one third was western and old-fashioned, and one third was straight hillbilly. The lunch crowd played the modern and the light classic, but at night and far into the morning the hillbilly ran three and four to one against the others.

With six restaurants, each with seven to twelve curb boys, three to four cooks and four to six waitresses plus cashiers, stock boys, delivery boys, and clean-up boys, Holly was always having a problem with help. Someone was always getting married, divorced, leaving town, running off with someone else's wife or husband or best friend, or getting drunk or getting locked up. When they were in jail Holly bailed them out, when drunk he sobered them up, when in trouble or sick he gave them his lawyer or his doctor; he never took them off the payroll. In return Holly's help was loyal. They stole a little but Holly knew this and they knew that Holly knew it, so they never stole much. It was a good relationship, and when the unions would come around and try to organize them they would just laugh and say they were already organized.

Holly came out of the kitchen drying his hands and took a Corona-Corona out of the cigar case. "Hello, Earl, Coley. Be right over."

Holly Yates had been born and raised a block from the Cooper River, and he had been the leader of the old drugstore gang that had included M.L., Doc, Lonnie, and Wilson Peeler. He was short and barrel-chested with dark curly hair and clear blue eyes. When he was younger he had won the state-wide jitterbug contest at the Township Auditorium.

Holly slid into the booth next to Earl. His hands and face were brown from fishing. "What you boys doing these days?"

Earl said, "Oh, been selling a little iron and a few bottles, not much else. We're trying to get up money to buy a car."

Holly touched his finger tips together. He had a diamond

ring on his right little finger, a ruby on his left. "You hitting them coal cars?"

Coley said, "Once in a while, but they been coming through pretty fast lately."

Holly smiled. "Man, we used to hang under that Cherry Street bridge and drop down on them like bobcats on a bo' hog. I got on one one night and it speeded up and I couldn't get off till we got to Orangeburg."

Earl said, "Holly, we need jobs, we need them bad. You think you could use us?"

Holly called Mildred, the waitress, over. "Give me a slice of apple pie with a cut of cheese. And let me have a cup of hot chocolate. How 'bout you fellows? It's on the house."

They ordered hamburgers and malted milk shakes.

"Sure I can use you. They got a revivalist coming in next week. Love, Sonny Love, that's what he calls himself. And I'm going to need me some good boys."

"We'd really put out for you, Holly. I swear we would. Ain't that right, Coley?"

"We'd do it, Holly."

Holly finished off half of his pie and cheese with one stroke of the fork. "All right, Coley. I'll put you on the curb. You can swing that. Herman, out there, he can break you in. Earl, I want you on the grill. Preach is going to need some help. You think you can handle that?"

"I know I can, Holly. What you paying?"

Holly pointed his fork at Coley. "You'll be getting twenty-five dollars a week, and you can triple that if you hustle them tips. Earl, I'll start you at fifty and if you shape up I'll raise you to sixty. Course you know I can't use you when school starts. They're getting rougher than a cob on that."

Earl's straw made a sucking sound on the bottom of the milk shake glass. "That's fine with us. When do we start?"

"Tomorrow. You want another hamburger?"

Coley nodded. "They sure are good."

Earl said, "The best in the South, ain't that right, Holly?"

It was the right question. Holly was a nonstop talker on the subject of hamburgers. He dabbed his mouth with a napkin. "You take that hamburger and I don't care what you think you could do to it, there ain't no way in this world of you making it any better. No way. I use the finest meat there is, the finest tomatoes, lettuce, and onions there are. And I fry that piece of meat in the finest grease money can buy."

He stirred the whipped cream in his hot chocolate. "These damn chain operations spreading 'cross the country, they're the ones that're ruining the hamburger business. Most of them come from up North to begin with, so what in the hell they know about cooking? Putting out those little precooked, frozen patties and warming them up and turning them loose for fifteen cents. Hell, any fool right off the street can tell you the minute you freeze and unfreeze hamburger you ain't got nothing. If I caught one of my cooks freezing a piece of meat I'd have him out of here so fast his ass would be spinning like a flywheel. I say folks are tired of that low quality. They're tired of getting that big motion and that instant service and that hot bun with nothing inside. They want a piece of meat they can get their teeth into. Hell, you slip that little two-ounce patty out of one of those fifteen centers and throw it across the room and it will sail. I ain't lying, that's how thin it is."

Holly thought about this for a minute and leaned in close. He was talking slower now, biting off each word. He was mad. "And it ain't only thin, hell no. That ain't the half of it. They stretch that meat out with flour and oatmeal until it's white, then they add in that damn beef blood and color it back to red. Some of that stuff's so soft with filler it won't even hold together. Now I ask you, if that ain't a helluva way to treat the public."

The waitress served the hamburgers and Holly shucked the cellophane off his Corona-Corona cigar. "I got me a mind to take out a full page ad in the *Record* and expose those low-life bastards, that crowd at the Instant Shop and that other monkey out there that calls himself Bite Quick. Hell, they don't know what the word beef means. Hot damn, maybe I'll do that. Maybe I will."

Earl started to speak, but Holly held up his hand and pointed at Coley. He was winding down. "I'm going to tell you something, boy. I'm selling quality here and I'm selling speed. You talk to any of the boys and you ask them what's the main thing I raise holy hell about. They'll tell you it's being slow on that curb. I want to look out there and see you move when you hear those horns or see those lights flash. Ain't nothing a customer hates more than seeing a sorry curb boy."

Coley said, "I'll move, Holly."

Earl said, "What hours is Fleetwood working?"

"Three to one. Same shift as you and Preach. Why you ask?"

"No reason, I just wanted to know."

Holly looked close at Earl. "I know Fleet ain't the easiest man in the world to work with but there ain't no reason why you can't get along. He stays on the fountain and you stay in the back." Holly stood up. "You boys got your health cards?"

Earl shook his head.

"Well, come on, get out of here and get them. That's all I need now is to get messed up with that Board of Health crowd."

The interview was over.

Chapter 13

It was 2:45 the next day when Earl and Coley pulled their bicycles into the back of Holly's parking lot. Herman Spires saw them and came back. Herman was a short, wiry colored boy. He was a Business Administration student from Benedict College and had been Holly's curb boy captain for two years. "Hey, Earl. Hey, Coley."

Coley said, "You hear about us coming to work?"

"Yeah, you on the curb, right?"

"Right. Earl's on the grill."

Herman grinned. "Give me the old curb any day, rain or shine. Man, you can operate out here." He snapped his fingers twice. "I mean op-er-ate." One of his cars blew. "Gotta go. See you later."

As they pushed their bicycles over to the rack a loud horn blasted. A white convertible Ford with a straight exhaust came racing at them. They were trapped. Earl dropped his bike and jumped. Coley tripped over his front wheel but scrambled to the side of the building as the driver slammed his brakes on. It was Fleetwood Driggers. He got out of the car laughing. "Talk about something funny, you shoulda seen the looks on you all's faces. Man, you got to be quicker than that!"

Coley shouted, "You're out of your goddamn head! You crazy or something?"

Earl looked at Fleetwood. "Only thing funny is your stupid face."

"Don't get smart, shrimps, or I'll knock your heads together. I thought it was funny as hell. Best laugh I've had all week. Why don't we try it again tomorrow?"

Fleetwood got back in his car, gunned the engine, doubled clutched it, and roared off to the employees' parking area.

Earl picked up his bike and checked to see if the handle bars had slipped. "What a jerk. He gives me a red-hot pain."

Fleetwood Driggers was Holly's main-shift fountain man. He couldn't cook because he couldn't stand the grease heat long enough, but he had good soda-fountain hands and a nice smile. Customers liked him. They never tipped him but they liked him. He was big and heavy set, six feet two or three, plus a big blond pompadour, plus his soda-fountain cap which stuck up another four inches. His face was long and thin like a greyhound's, and his ears were smoothed down flat at the sides of his head as if he'd been raised at top speed or in a high wind. He had a fast name and everyone called him Fleet, which made it that much faster.

With the exception of Blue, who worked on garbage and mop and ran errands, Preacher Watts was the only colored man on the inside at Holly's. All of the curb boys except Coley were colored, but Agnes the cashier, the five inside waitresses, and Fleetwood were all white.

Preach was just between dark brown and blue-black, and

JULY
he had a razor welt that looked as if someone had laid a
ruler from the tip of his left ear to the edge of his chin and
carefully followed it. His hands were much lighter than his
face, and his front four teeth, two upper and two lower,
were framed in bright yellow gold. He was tall enough to
reach the back of the grill without straining, and he had
long fine fingers that were calloused with toaster and grill
burns. Preach knew how to use the callouses and could pick
up a toasted barbecue from a flat-bed toaster with his bare
hand without catching his breath. He was thin for a fry
cook. He kept that way by never eating anything fried.
Whenever he got hungry he'd go outside and sit in his 1937
Terraplane and send in his order. Everything had to be
broiled or baked, and for lunch he always had a salad or
cottage cheese and fruit.

Preach was in his last year at the Bible College, and during his breaks and meals he'd sit out in his car and study.
Once in a while a member from the congregation where he
was apprenticing would come into the kitchen with a problem. Preach would take him off behind the dirty laundry or
out by the barbecue pit and they would talk it over.

Coley sat on the curb boys' bench outside the order window and took his turn hopping cars. One of the older boys,
Jason, showed him how to remember cars by their taillights,
and Herman taught him how to scatter change on his tip
tray. At first Coley was embarrassed about using it, but
Herman soon convinced him it was the only way to make
money.

Herman believed in giving the customer all of his change
in dimes. "You take a fellow who's with his girl friend, and
he starts picking at eight or nine thin dimes. Now he's really

163

got to work to round them all up. He's bound to get rattled."

Coley said, "I've been holding my tray sorta loose too. That way they can't put any pressure on it."

"Now you're talking. But don't let them get it near that window sill. They'll just block it there and scoop all your money out."

Preach broke Earl in on the big grill, and in a few hours he was handling small orders by himself. In two days he could cook anything from a hamburger to a fried chicken dinner, and during slow spells Preach was able to take a few breaks and catch up on his homework.

Sometimes during a lull, Holly would send Fleetwood back into the kitchen to help. Fleet hated the kitchen and anyone connected with it, but Holly would insist that he go back and help get ready for the after-the-movie rush. Fleet would complain that he couldn't stand the heat, but Holly would laugh and slap him on his back. "Go on, boy, get in there and give them a hand. We're all just one big happy family here. I like to think that any man I got can double on any job at any time. What if an emergency came up? Figure it that way."

Fleet would come back and work near the door where he could feel the air conditioner from the front. Preach would let him slice tomatoes or strip lettuce to keep him out of the way. After a few minutes on the board slicing tomatoes, Fleet would stick his thumb and forefinger in his eyes and pinch his nose. He'd make sure Holly saw him and he'd shake his head slowly. It worked every time and Holly would come back. "You all right, Fleet?"

Fleet would pretend not to hear him until Holly repeated

the question. Then he'd say, "All I got to do is close my eyes and there that monkey is."

Holly would reach up and pat his shoulder. "You better get out of here and get some air, boy."

Fleet would start untying his kitchen apron, which was always spotless. If Holly was in earshot he would say, "Man, I don't see how you boys stand this grease heat, it must be two hundred right now." Then he'd put on his short white soda-fountain jacket with FLEET printed over the left breast pocket and his stiff white overseas-type cap with HOLLY's on the front, crease his pompadour forward and up and light a cigarette. If Holly were still present he would say, "Ain't no heat worse than grease heat unless it's steam heat. How come it don't bother you none?"

Preach would say something like, "I guess we used to it."

But one night Holly walked off. Fleet made sure he was out of hearing range and then looked at Preach. He screwed up his long pale face and tried to look intelligent with his jaw and his steel-blue eyes. "Preach, you a college man. Tell me something, right or wrong. Can a nigger stand more heat than a white man?"

Earl said, "It don't bother me, Fleet. Maybe it bothers you 'cause you got weak blood."

"I didn't ask you anything, runt. I asked that question to the Preacher."

Preach said, "I don't know, Fleet. I never gave it much thought."

"Well, I think you better start thinking about it. Next time I ask you, I want me a straight answer."

The soda fountain was one world at Holly's and the kitchen was another. Fountain boys could sit at the counter or in the booths during their breaks, but the cooks were always so greasy and streaked with ketchup and mustard that they had to go out back and sit by the barbecue pit.

Preach came in from his supper break carrying two volumes of philosophy on his empty tray. "Earl, you know anything about Immanuel Kant?"

"No."

"How about Frederick Hegel?"

"Him either."

"Which one you want to hear about first?"

"Give me the first one."

Preach put his hands in his pockets under his apron and began walking back and forth on the duckboards while Earl skinned the big double grill down with his spatula. "Well, first off you spell him K-A-N-T and you have to go for that long "a"—Kant. Immanuel Kant. Yessir, that was one fine man. Fine. He was born over there in Germany. Lot of the philosophy men came out of Germany. Looks like they got it in their blood."

Preach kept walking back and forth on the boards, talking about Kant's philosophy. Every few minutes Earl said "I understand" or nodded his head, but most of the time he was grinning at his reflection in the big triple pop-up toaster. Preach might as well have been talking Chinese.

Earl finished cleaning the grill and began slicing tomatoes, trying to see how thin he could get them. The tomatoes were firm and the bread knife was sharp. He sliced them thinner and thinner until they were so thin they rolled up like carrot curls.

Preach finished up by saying, "Well, that's enough of him for tonight. You get too much thrown at you and you can't swallow it. Now I'll tell you a little bit about Mr. Hegel, and tomorrow we'll come back and visit Mr. Kant again." He laughed as if he knew Earl hadn't understood a word. "Boy, when I get through with you those high school teachers are going to think you some form of genius."

Coley and Herman were on the curb boys' bench, spitting at a Dixie cup. Coley spat. "What's your biggest tip, Herm?"

"Oh, I get a deuce every now and then. A drunk gave me a five one night, but I think he thought it was a one." Herman kept spitting short. "You got over your shies yet?"

Coley nodded.

"Good. Keep staring them cats down. Give them the old cheap eye. Catch 'em right and you can make 'em think they're taking money right out of your pocket."

A tan Chrysler pulled into the last car stall.

Herman said, "You want it?"

"O.K."

Coley went out to the car. Wilson Peeler smiled up. "Hello, Coley. When did you start here?"

"Hello, Mr. Peeler. Couple days ago." He handed Wilson the menu.

Wilson read it carefully, checking to see if there were any new specials or if Holly had dropped his prices on anything. "How's the barbecue?"

"Ain't as good as yours, but it'll pass. Why don't you have a hamburger?"

"No, I got my jaw all set for a barbecue right now. Make sure it's sliced, though. I don't like the way Holly handles his minced. And give me a bottle of Schlitz."

Coley wrote the order out and put it on the spike in the kitchen window.

Holly called him inside. "Ain't that Wilson Peeler's Chrysler out there?"

"Yessir."

"I thought so. He order a barbecue?"

"That's it. Barbecue and a bottle of Schlitz."

Holly looked out at the car. "You can set your watch by him. He comes sniffing around here every two weeks right on schedule." He speared up two pieces of sliced barbecue that were steeping in barbecue sauce and carried them over to the sink. He turned on the hot water.

The steam rose from the scalding water, and in a minute the brown barbecue pork looked like strips of pale gray sponge. Holly placed the meat between two slices of a bun, flipped in a pickle chip, and put the sandwich in the flat-bed toaster. "He'll like this."

Coley served the barbecue and beer and came back to the window. Holly had sent Herman out to his Lincoln Continental to get his race track binoculars, and he stood behind the Venetian blinds watching Wilson peel the top part of the bun back.

Holly laughed. "He's got the top off. Now he's smelling it. Wonder what he smells? He's closed the bun and he's smiling. Now, oh-oh, he's tasting it. He's smiling again. I think he swallowed it. Oh, sweet Jesus, he's taking another bite." Holly was laughing so hard he couldn't hold the glasses still. He handed them to Agnes. "What's he doing now?"

"He must be liking it; he's eating it right fast."

Holly took the glasses back. "God damn, he ate the whole thing. Wonder if he wants another one. Maybe I've invented something. Oh, God, I can't stand it." He sat down. "Hey, Coley, run out and tell him that that barbecue is with my compliments. Try and get him to eat another one. Make him pay you for that beer, though."

Wilson tipped Coley fifty cents and began backing out of the lot. Holly picked up the public address microphone. "Hey, Wilson!"

Wilson stopped and looked toward Holly.

"How'd you like my new barbecue sauce? I'm going to start featuring it next week. You reckon I can get fifty cents for it?"

Wilson smiled and drove off.

At the drugstore Doc was polishing glasses. He looked up as Wilson came in. "Hello, Doc."

"Well, if it isn't the Peeler himself. Hello, Wilson."

Lonnie was leaning on the end of the fountain drinking a beer. "Hello, Wilson, how's the boy?"

"Hi, Lon."

M.L. came out of the bathroom in the back. "Wilson! Boy, you been a stranger lately. How you been?"

"Pretty good. Busy. Real busy."

M.L. said, "You looking real good. Let me buy you a beer."

"O.K., good idea."

Doc opened four beers and set them on the counter. "These are on the house."

M.L. held up his bottle of Budweiser. "To Wilson. Here's looking at you."

They drank.

Doc said, "How's your feet been?"

"Pretty quiet lately. I think that Absorbine Junior did the trick."

"You're keeping plenty of powder on them, aren't you?"

"Half a can a day. I probably smell like a Savannah whore house."

Lonnie patted him on the back. "Wilson, it's nice seeing you. It's been a month since you been around. You shouldn't do that to your old buddies. I swear, you shouldn't."

M.L. said, "Yeah, we got to keep the old gang together. These young bucks are trying to crowd us out. Holly came by yesterday, said he caught fifty bass down at the Santee. He's looking good, too."

Wilson took a swallow of beer. "Holly just tried to pull a fast one on me." He told them about the barbecue sandwich.

Doc laughed. "Hell, why don't you forget Holly's sauce? He's got about as much chance of making barbecue like you as me and Lonnie here. Say, I hear you got yourself a new cook."

"Yeah, boy named Driscoll. Jack Driscoll, comes from Newark. He was stationed here at the Fort."

Doc said, "Any good?"

"The best. Good cook, and he don't mind putting in a few extra hours. You don't find that kind around any more."

Doc lit his cigar. "You said a mouthful there. Any day I get one minute over eight hours out of Bo-Bo I'm lucky."

M.L. said, "Open up another round there, Doc. This is on me."

Wilson said, "O.K. One more, then I got to be getting in."

M.L. shifted over so he could look at Wilson and Doc at the same time. "I tell you it's a crying shame. A crying shame, the way you boys like to fish and both of you strapped here with jobs on your back. I tell you it makes you stop and think. You know none of us are getting any younger."

Wilson finished his first beer and reached for his second. "He's right, Doc. Stone right. We're both killing ourselves."

Doc nodded. "The help's so sorry, that's the problem. I been trying to get me a boy in here to train for two years now, so I could take some time off. I keep coming up with zero. Nothing."

Wilson smiled. "I'm keeping me a close eye on this Driscoll boy. I still ain't forgotten that trip to France I been promising myself."

Doc laughed and winked at M.L. "The day you go to France is going to be about one day after Judgment Day."

Wilson said, "You ain't saying I ain't going?"

"I'm saying you been talking about that trip for twenty years. You're not going to no France. You're going to talk about it till your jaw drops off, but you'll be lucky if you get out of Richland County."

Wilson sprinkled salt on the back of his hand and licked it off. "You just wait, Doc. You just wait. One of these days, I ain't saying tomorrow or the next day, but one of these days I'm going to be on that Silver Meteor heading out of here for New York City. And after that, it's going to be Paris, France."

Doc said, "Twenty years is a long time to plan a trip, Wilson. You got to admit that."

Lonnie said, "Don't mind him, Peel. He's just jealous." He put his arm around Wilson's shoulders. "Boy, I bet you'd have yourself a time over there in Paris! I hear some of them night clubs don't ever close."

"I wouldn't be going over there for that, Lon."

"I know, Wilson, but you'd sure as hell have to walk by them. I hear some of them places will grab you, quick like, and snatch you inside. Oooooo, man! What I wouldn't give to put me in a little time over there."

Chapter 14

It was around midnight and Preach and Earl were in the middle of the after-the-movie rush. The big grill was almost full, and Earl had two three-basket French-fry pots going on potatoes and chicken. They were even with the orders and all of the supplies were stocked and ready. Suddenly Holly came rushing through the door shouting. "Jesus Christ, you ought to see them! You ought to see them! It's unbelievable. Sonny Love got over nine thousand and every damn one of them's headed this way."

Agnes paled. "Nine thousand?"

Holly said, "Nine-o-o-o. Nine thousand. And they'll be here in ten minutes."

Fleetwood screamed like a turkey. "We'll be swamped. I can't handle no crowd like that. I just can't do it."

Holly stood panting in the doorway between the kitchen and the fountain. "I ain't worrying about you. I can give you a hand. What I'm worried about is the kitchen." He snapped his fingers at Fleet and pointed for a Coke. "How about it, Preach? You want to start frying ahead?"

Preach was cutting up onions; Earl was slicing tomatoes.

"No, let 'em come. Earl and me can handle them. You better get us up some more buns and meat, though."

Holly moved over to the sandwich board and patted him on the back. "Listen, you say the word and I'll close the place down. I ain't ruining my good help for no crowd like that. It just ain't worth it."

Earl said, "How 'bout a bonus or something extra if we can hold them?"

Holly smiled. "That's a promise. I'll take care of you, don't worry about that."

Fleet opened the door. "Holly, how in the hell you 'spect me to get up enough ice? I'm already low on syrup. How about me, Holly? What am I going to do when they start ordering milk shakes? I'll get so far behind they'll walk out."

Preach laughed. "Don't worry, Fleet. That crowd's not going to be ordering no milk shakes. That's a Pepsi-Cola and hamburger crowd."

Fleetwood didn't like the way Holly was giving all his attention to the kitchen. He stomped back to the fountain and began noisily checking and filling his syrup stations. He shouted out, "Agnes! Give Blue the storehouse keys. Have him get me up four simple syrups and about a dozen gallons of Pepsi syrup."

Agnes was ten feet away. "Do you have to yell like that?"

"Damn right I do. If that stuff ain't here we're in trouble, and I mean real trouble. And tell him to crank up that ice maker, we're going to need another three hundred pounds at least. I knew I should have stayed home tonight. Who in the hell is Sonny Love, anyway?"

Before Agnes could tell him, they were in the driveway

and blowing their horns and flashing their lights for service. The revival had been from nine until midnight, and they had been singing, praying, shouting, and rolling. Now they were hungry. In ten minutes every parking space was filled and the cars were backed up to the street for service. In each car there were four, five, as many as eight people.

Preach was right about it being a Pepsi-Cola crowd, but he was wrong about it being a hamburger crowd. They ordered hamburgers, hundreds of hamburgers, but they also ordered chickens, steaks, and barbecues. At twelve-thirty Earl and Preach were working at top speed. Orders were stacked a foot deep on the icepick spike in the window, but they couldn't touch them until they had room. There was no room on the big grill. There was no room on the long sandwich board. There was no room anywhere. At 12:45 Earl counted quickly: sixty hamburgers, forty barbecues, twenty-eight fried chickens, and fourteen steaks. Preach took over the incoming and outgoing orders and the finishing work on the sandwich board. Earl fried. All eight of the three-basket Fry-O-Laters were full and going, the big grill was packed solid with hamburgers, and every broiler had four and five steaks hissing and flashing grease fires.

Preach kept saying, "Don't rush, boy. Don't fight 'em. I got everything under control. Just fry. You see an empty space on the grill, fill her up. I'll keep track. Don't worry." Preach laughed. "If we get in real trouble we can always get old Fleetwood back here to help us out."

But Earl worried: the ten curb boys were screaming at the window, and the four waitresses were pounding on the order bell and begging for their orders.

Holly was on his high wooden stool next to Agnes. From there he could check the incoming and outgoing orders, help Agnes, supervise and serve the curb boys, and keep an eye on the fountain. It was too hot to open the kitchen door, but he could see Preach and Earl through the twin glass portholes. He was speaking on the public address microphone to the curb boys, soft talking and trying to steady Agnes, and looking back to the kitchen and shouting, "Get it out. Come on, Preach, Earl, get it out."

Coley loped up to the window with an empty tray and banged it down on the long shelf. "I'm still looking for three chickens, two chocolate shakes, and a Dr. Pepper." He leaned against the window. His feet were tired and his wrists were sore from carrying and hanging the heavy trays. "They ain't tipping, Holly."

Holly put the shakes and the Dr. Pepper on the tray and totaled the bill. "Three dollars and thirty-five. Try smiling at them." He turned away, shouting, "You girls, don't crowd round Agnes like that! How many times I got to tell you to stay in line?"

Coley pulled his tray out and moved away from the window.

Herman came up. "Man, I ain't stopped to draw a clean breath. How you doing?"

"They ain't tipping a dime."

Herman swung the heavy tray up on one hand and carried it level with his right ear. "They're turkeys, all right. No doubt about that. You try telling them you're a Sonny Love fan?"

"No, I didn't think of that."

"Well, hell, man, use your brains. Tell 'em you're giving your tips to Sonny Love. I had one poor bastard who passed up an extra order of French fries and gave me the quarter."

JULY

As Coley hooked the tray onto the window of a 1947 Chevrolet and snugged the rubber washer up against the door he saw the flashing lights of a Nash Ambassador with a $7.60 bill. He arranged four dimes and four quarters in his shirt pocket. If they gave him a ten-dollar bill he would give them a one-dollar bill back and the dollar-forty in change.

The driver spoke. "Son, them were mighty fine chickens. You tell Mr. Holly Yates we shore enjoyed them." He turned to the couple in the back seat. "That right, Emily, Fred?"

Emily said, "We didn't leave hardly enough for the cat to eat. It was delicious. You tell Mr. Yates we're from Lakeville, and that was the best fried chicken we ever set in our mouths."

Sydney, the driver, said, "And you tell him we compliment him on his fine service."

Coley touched his tip tray in his back pocket, thinking they might leave him a dollar.

Sydney said, "What's the damage?"

"Seven-sixty, sir."

"All right, here it is. Fred, I'll get this and you and me will settle up when we get home." He handed Coley a ten-dollar bill.

Coley took the ten and handed him back a one. "Sorry, but I got to give you the rest in change."

"That's all right, son."

Coley poured the change into his tip tray and held it up. Sydney nodded at the tray. "What's that?"

"What, sir?"

"That little thing you put my money in?"

Coley gritted his teeth. "My tip tray, sir."

177

"Tip tray?"

"Yessir, that's what they call them."

"Tip tray! Well, I'll be dogged. Why, son, what do you think you're doing? That's my money you got there. I ain't obliged to give you no tip."

Fred spoke up. "Let me say a word here, Sydney. I've run into this before." He sat forward. Coley could see half of his face in the white light of the parking light. He was very pale. "Son, I hope you don't think the apostles carried tip trays round when they passed out the loaves and the fishes to the multitudes."

Coley couldn't think of an answer. A black Buick was flashing its lights for him and he wanted to leave.

Fred continued. His hands were resting on the back of the seat. They seemed whiter than his face. "Well, they didn't, son. Here, I'm going to give you a little something to study." He handed Coley three pieces of paper. They were information tracts on healing and the Sonny Love Message to the world. "Now I want you to read these and I want you to study them carefully."

Sydney touched Coley's hand. "Son, no hard feelings, but I think you ought to listen to what brother Fred just said. It just ain't right to want a man to pay more than he owes, and it ain't right for a fine-looking boy like yourself to be expecting it. You read over these facts. Then you ought to be considering going down and seeing Sonny Love while he's here in town. You ain't too young for Jesus, son."

He smiled up again at Coley and pressing the tip tray down on the window sill with his left hand he scooped the $1.40 out with one smooth motion of his right.

Coley held the tracts in his hand. He didn't know what

to say or do. He pulled out his curb money, and as if the tracts were money, he folded them around the thick roll. Sydney took the Nash out of gear and started the engine. "Watch your feet, son. Good night now."

Coley shoved the thick roll of money and tracts into his pocket and picked up his tray. The Nash backed up and swung around into the driveway. Holly's neon reflected on the phosphorescent red sign on the back bumper, turning it bright orange, and as the car moved into the darkness the words I RECOMMEND THE LORD TO YOU framed with red taillights on each side shined out into the darkness of the southbound Cooper Ridge Road.

In the kitchen the French-fry pots were bubbling white as the fresh-cut potatoes and the breaded chicken were scalded and fried in the 380-degree Crisco. Earl looked at the room thermometer on the refrigerator. It was 110 degrees and climbing. He and Preach were too busy to speak, and the only sounds were the steel on steel of Earl's spatula turning and lifting the hamburgers and skinning back the heavy grease, the crunching sound of Preach handling lettuce, and the steady chop-slip, chop-slip of sandwiches being cut and slid onto paper plates. The fat at the back of the grill drained down the keyhole like water down a drain. The duckboards began to get slippery. Flour and cracker meal from the chicken batter rose in the heavy grease-filled air, and Earl's hands and arms were white with flour and sticky with eggs. Preach went through a case of lettuce in less than an hour.

Up front the jukebox was on full blast and everyone was running and shouting. Fleetwood's razor-thin voice cut through the noise. "I'm almost out of Pepsi syrup. Agnes, goddammit, can't you hear me? I need Pepsi syrup."

Holly shouted, "Blue says we're out. Give 'em Root beer. They won't know the difference." He came back to the kitchen doorway. "Preach, you need any help?"

Preach smiled down at the sandwich board. His fingers were flying. "No, we're set. Tell you what, you can screen these orders out for me. We can't be taking no more orders for omelettes and Western sandwiches. They just too much trouble."

"Jesus Christ, did you take any?"

"A couple; now we can't. Look for yourself. Can't even squeeze in another hamburger, let alone get messed up with an omelette leaking all over the grill."

Holly picked up the public address microphone. "All right out there! Listen a minute! There will be no more orders for omelettes or Western sandwiches. You hear that? No more Western sandwiches and no more omelettes. We're too busy for them. Everything else is fine. We got hamburgers, chicken. We got steaks and we got some nice fresh-sliced and minced barbecue. But no more omelettes or Westerns. I thank you."

At one o'clock the rush had reached its peak and was holding on. The exhaust fan slowed down in the heavy air and couldn't pull the smoke and the heat out of the kitchen fast enough. The temperature was 118 degrees, and Earl had to throw salt on the duckboards to keep from slipping. Holly opened the back door and turned on the twenty-four-inch Tornado fan. The smoke thinned out, but the heat around the grill and the fry pots held at 118 degrees. Sweat was running down Preach's nose and ears into the barbecue and the lettuce cups, and he couldn't stop it.

Earl tried to work back from the grill but he was too short and couldn't reach the back rows. The heat was getting to him. The walls seemed to be covered with well-done hamburgers. He began working too close to the frypots. He was taking too many chances. He began to get delirious. His head felt light and he had cold flashes at the back of his neck; he felt like dancing. He was working too close to the fires. Instead of using the long broiler fork for pulling out steaks, he held on to his grill spatula and went in under the flames.

The orders were still stacked up in the window. Horns were blowing. Fleet and Holly were arguing about ice and screaming at the curb boys to pick up the orders and keep the window clear. The order bell kept ringing. Holly smoked his black cigar faster and faster and kept shouting. The girls in the front were wild-eyed and frantic, slamming their open palms on the partition glass and begging for hamburgers, chickens, steaks, barbecues, anything that was ready.

Earl wanted to stop and check supplies. It was his job to keep Preach supplied on the board. If he could only leave the grill for a minute and check the supplies. If he could only leave the grill and dance. He had a tremendous urge to dance. The heat was making his ears ache and he could taste the heavy grease on the back of his teeth; it tasted good. His socks were soaked and his deep-ridged tennis shoes were as slick as beef liver. Everything began to shift in the room. He was getting dizzy. He wondered where the monkey would come from. He stared at the big black grill, now brown with hamburgers, well-done to the right, medium to the left, and rare in the middle. "Keep your eyes on the rares, the well-dones will take care of themselves." Little faces began appearing in the hamburgers. Sixty little faces, all bright and clear. The well-dones looked older than the rares. He figured that was as it should be. The mediums were all grinning. He began tapping his spatula on the edge of the grill and doing a little delirious dance on the salt-covered duckboards.

Preach touched Earl's spatula with his bread knife. "Heat got you? Hey, boy, heat got you? Tell me, you see the monkey?"

Earl said, "I think so." He did a double shuffle and went down on one knee. The monkey rose up from the well-done hamburgers, turned into a gorilla, and wrapped him in his smothering arms. The next thing Earl knew Preach was shoving ice chips into his mouth. The gorilla made a gargling sound in his ear, laughed, turned back into the thin little monkey and vaulted back up on the grill. He ran across the grill, stepping lightly from the mediums to the well-dones, and dived into the bubbling 380-degree grease. Earl felt better. The first noise he heard was Fleet shouting, "I'm all out of Dr. Pepper syrup. Where in the hell is that goddamn Blue? Blue, damn your black soul, where are you?"

Preach was slapping Earl's face. "Hey! Hey! You all right?

Earl sat up. "I'm fine now." He picked up his spatula from the floor. "Anyone see me?"

"No, no one 'cept me." Preach turned over six rare hamburgers with his bread knife. "Boy, you gave me a real scare there. If I had to work this here with Fleet or Holly I wouldn't have made it."

The compliment brought Earl around sharp and clear, and he turned over seven mediums with a nice rolling wrist motion that Preach had taught him.

Preach smiled and pulled down another handful of orders. "Here we go." He shifted back to the sandwich board.

Earl began talking out loud in case the monkey started climbing out of the grease again. "Bar-be-cue, sliced, thirty-five cents, with a side of potato salad and three pickle chips, one chicken-in-the-rough, a piece of breast, a piece of thigh, a leg, and a tender wing. A lettuce cup, two slices of tomato, a dab of mayonnaise, and a serving of salt and pepper. Two large and generous handfuls of French fried potatoes and here you are, sir, for only one dollar and twenty-five cents. Cost you a dollar fifty at Ed White's, and he gives you two wings and no thigh. Now ain't that nice?" He laughed. "How we doing, Preach? I feel fine now."

Preach looked at Earl to make sure he was all right. "Don't say ain't. We doing fine, boy. We got everything under control."

Earl picked up the next order. Four bacon, lettuce, and tomato sandwiches on whole wheat toast. "You see this?"

Preach looked. "Send it back. We can't handle it."

Earl kept his little singsong going. "No, Preach. Let me handle it. I got a little something I been wanting to try out." He threaded twenty-four slices of bacon onto a skewer fork and lowered it into the deep bubbling fat.

Preach said, "Man, that isn't going to taste like nothing."

"I know, but look how fast she cooks." It was done. It was crisp and seared and had shrunk down to one tenth its size.

Preach punched the whole wheat bread down in the toaster. "Normally I wouldn't let you send it out. But seeing that it's for Sonny Love and his crowd, it won't do no harm. I bet that crowd don't know bacon from pork liver."

Preach finished up the bacon sandwiches. "We need some tomatoes."

Earl shook the potatoes onto seven orders of chicken-in-the-rough, hooked the empty frying basket to the lip of the Fry-O-Later, and quickly went to the refrigerator and put as many tomatoes in his apron as he could carry.

Preach grabbed them and rolled them out onto the sandwich board. He began slicing. He didn't seem to be hurrying but he was efficient, and every time he moved a whole tomato collapsed into ten or eleven slices. In less than two minutes, with a beautiful fanning motion, he had sliced the entire bunch.

"God, Preach, I didn't know you were that fast."

Preach laughed. "I can move right well when I have to. Next time we get a break I'll show you how to do it."

A few empty spaces began to appear on the back of the grill. It was three o'clock. The rush was over.

Preach said, "I got to have me a break. O.K.?"

"Fine with me. You must be pretty tired."

"No, nothing like that. I been thinking about that Immanuel Kant, and I'll be dogged if that rascal hasn't got me stumped. I thought I had him a few nights back. But I messed around and let him slip away." He took off his apron and wiped his head with the inside of it. "I won't be long."

When Preach came back from his break he was laughing. "That Sonny Love crowd is as bad as the Jehovah's Witnesses. They don't tip a dime."

"How'd Coley do?"

"Pretty sorry. Even Herman didn't make it. And that rascal can get a tip out of a stone."

Earl shut the grill and the fry pots down, and they began cleaning up. Fleetwood drifted into the kitchen. He was fanning himself with his little soda-fountain cap. "What a night! Jesus, what a night! What does that Sonny Love do to them?" He put both hands in the small of his back and stretched. "My damn back is broke. I bet I scooped up a hundred gallons of ice cream." He sat down on the high stool at the end of the sandwich board. "Christ, doesn't it ever get cool in here?"

Preach was at the sandwich board, cleaning out his condiment containers.

Fleetwood said loudly, "Hey, Preach, how 'bout if you fry me a steak?"

Preach didn't want any trouble. He was too tired to argue. "Sure thing, Fleet." He reached over and turned on the grill burners. "You sure you want it fried? I can broil it for you. No trouble at all. Make it more tender."

Fleet looked him in the eye and said, "Listen, Dark Meat, if I wanted it broiled I'd of said so."

Earl reached in the refrigerator and pulled out a gristly steak. Preach had been saving it for Blue's dog, and it had been in the back of the refrigerator for weeks. It was darker than the other steaks, almost black, and the edges were curled up as if it had already been partially fried. Earl tossed it out on the center of the grill where it was the hottest.

Fleet got up from the stool. "What kind of steak is that? It looks like a damn tire shoe."

Preach slid a big T bone out. "How's that?"

"That's O.K."

Preach put the steak on the side of the grill and began salting it down. He speared the curved dog steak with his fork and dropped it in the garbage. "You like anything else, Fleet?"

"Yeah, gimme some onion rings."

Earl said, "Aw, hell, Fleet, eat some potatoes. We haven't got any onion rings ready and you know it."

Fleet didn't look at Earl. He was watching for Preach's reaction. He spoke slowly. "I don't want no potatoes."

Preach laid his grill fork on the sandwich board. "Give him the rings, Earl. I'll make up the batter."

Chapter 15

Wednesday was Earl and Coley's day off. After going by two used car lots and not finding anything cheap enough that would run, they went to the drugstore. Earl asked M.L. if he'd seen Lonnie. M.L. was fluffing his hair forward, covering part of his bald spot. "He ain't been around. I don't know where he is."

Doc was on the telephone, frowning and shaking his head. "Mrs. Osborne, I'm sorry. I'm sorry as I can be but I can't do a blessed thing about it right now. I'm all alone here. If it hurts, call Doc Tyler." He closed his eyes while Mrs. Osborne talked. "Well then, call Drysdale. Bo-Bo's off today and I can't leave here for a minute." He shook his head and looked down at the four empty banana split dishes before him. "Tell you what, if someone comes by heading your way I'll send some up. Yes, I understand. Listen, I got to take care of some customers now."

He hung up the telephone and, grabbing the ice cream scoop, he lunged at the vanilla. He spoke to M.L. "You know where Tyler is? Down at the Santee. The bass are damn near jumping in the boats." The ice cream was hard and he had to use both hands on the scoop. "Everybody in town is down there, and here I am stuck in this goddamn soda shop." He handed Earl the scoop. "Here, make up four splits for that crowd back there. I got to fill this prescription. Make yourself a soda when you're finished."

"One for Coley too?"

"Yeah, one for Coley too."

When Doc came out of the back licking a gummed label for Mrs. Osborne's package, Earl and Coley were sucking on chocolate sodas with eight scoops of ice cream jammed into the tall glasses. Doc said, "That old lady's going to bury me yet."

M.L. said, "Tell her to go on down and see Sonny Love. Maybe he can straighten her out."

Doc turned the overhead fan on high. "Hell, she's too lazy to even stand in the healing line."

Coley's mouth was full of ice cream. "Does Sonny Love really cure people, Doc?"

"Depends on what you're talking about."

Coley swallowed. "I mean like cancer and heart trouble and kidneys and lights and all, things like that."

Earl said, "And bone breaks. He can't go fixing no bone breaks, can he?"

"Naw, he can't do nothing there." Doc opened a carton of Camels and began stacking them in the cigarette rack. "I guess he might be able to clear up a few head colds now and then. But I sure as hell wouldn't want him prodding around my prostate or trying to talk no stone down for me."

M.L. said, "Why don't you boys go down there and take a look for yourself? Ain't no admission. I imagine he passes the plate a few times but that ain't ever bothered you before."

Doc said, "Might be an education for you."

Earl said, "That ain't a bad idea. I've never been to one of those things. How about it, Cole?"

"Suits me."

M.L. said, "Let us know how you make out."

For four days and four nights Columbia and Richland County had twisted in torment under the shoutings of Sonny Love. No sin was too small, none too large. Dancing, loud clothes, loud talk, Sunday movies, Sunday radio, all were shouted out and damned as if they had been chiseled in brimstone above the gates of hell.

The big air-conditioned tent at the foot of the Bluff Road sucked the movies, the ball games, and the honkytonks dry. Beer and whiskey sales dropped and three poolrooms shut their doors. The town was deserted from eight until midnight, and, while the tent would seat only eight thousand, another four to five thousand stood silently in Jack Dawson's pasture behind the tent, listening to the voice of Sonny Love from the public address boxes hung in the chinaberry trees. Both radio stations carried the entire program and the commercials were whispered and sandwiched in only when Sonny was busy wiping the streaming sweat from his face or when the music was turned on during the many collections.

Ten thousand pledges were taken and ten thousand souls were saved. Rumors spread that people had seen a halo appear over Sonny's right hand, the hand they said he had the healing power of life in, and that every diseased person he had touched was cured for life. It was announced that in one night he had absolutely saved three patients in their last stages of cancer. One claimed that she had awakened in the morning and found three cancers, two the size of good-sized walnuts and one the size of a small lemon, lying on the pillow next to her; said they looked like cinders.

It was almost dark when Earl and Coley got off the bus at the Bluff Road and started across the field toward the big tent. Loud-speakers were blaring out "Throw Out the Lifeline" at full volume, and red dust from the parking lot rose and sifted and settled in the suffocating swamp heat. They worked their way through the crowd into the tent. Coley's mouth dropped open as he stared straight up. "Jesus, look how high she goes!"

Earl said, "This place must of cost a fortune. It must be a hundred feet high. Hey, they got it air-conditioned."

They sat down about halfway to the platform at the front. The healing line had already formed around the inside of the tent and was pulsing and flowing like a cold snake on a warm road.

Earl nudged Coley. "Let's get in the line. We can tell him we got the cramps."

Coley grinned. "I'll tell him we need a hundred dollars."

"Look at that one. Boy, what you reckon he's got?" A fat man wearing a baseball cap backwards and a suit vest over a pair of overalls was standing with a tall man who was bent so far over he looked as if he were looking for something on the ground.

"Probably a hernia or something."

A small, shrill lady in a green print dress, wearing black ankle socks and tennis shoes, turned around. "You boys better mind your tongues in here."

When she turned back around, Earl crossed his eyes and pulled the corners of his mouth down.

JULY

At eight o'clock sharp the music changed to "Love
Lifted Me," and Sonny Love stepped forward. Behind him
were forty-two empty chairs. He motioned to the wings,
and forty-two ministers from the Pentacostal and Holiness
churches of the three counties around Columbia filed up
onto the platform and took their seats. They had closed
their churches during the month of the revival, and taking
a small percentage of Sonny Love's collections they had in-
structed their congregations to be with Sonny every night
he was in town.

Sonny Love was big. He had a big head and a full, heavy
pelt of black hair outlining his red face. He had a deep
voice, and when he announced that he was going to take off
his coat and get down to business for the Lord the audience
laughed. Earl and Coley found themselves laughing along
with the crowd. Sonny took off his coat and unbuttoned his
sleeves. The ministers took off theirs and the background
behind him turned shirt-sleeve white. Sonny gripped the
microphone and stepped forward.

Earl said, "Man! Look at the size of those wrists."

Coley nodded. "You don't get that sitting around reading
no Bible."

A heavy hand settled on each of their shoulders and a
huge face leaned in between them. "They don't allow no
talking in here when *he's* speaking. I hear one more word
and I'm throwing you both out."

They didn't look around.

Sonny's voice got louder, then softer. It began to break
and tremble. He pushed his sleeves back over his fire-red
arms. He paused. "Love, that's what he was talking about.
Love, that's all. That's all that sweet man was talking
about."

And then, so softly they could barely hear him, "Love, love. That's all he had on his mind."

The woman next to Coley began picking at his sleeve. Coley jerked away. "Leave me alone." He leaned forward out of the way as she started trembling.

Sonny dropped to one knee, then the other. He caressed the microphone almost to the floor. The black cord lay wilted around him. "Love . . . love . . . love. . . . That's all . . . he . . . was . . . trying . . . to say."

The audience rocked slowly to the delicate balance that he brought them to. Their eyes were closed. Their dry fingers lightly touched their knees; their feet lightly touched the floor. The air-conditioner pumps seemed to key in with the rhythm, and the tent expanded with the half breaths, the long sighs, and the "Sweet Jesus" of the eight thousand. Outside, the four thousand in the pasture sank sobbing to their knees, staring at the public address boxes in the chinaberry trees.

Sonny rocked them sweetly, gently, carefully. He could talk no more. He wept before them, and his crystal tears glistened on the microphone. He tried to break through his heavy sobs but couldn't. "Sw . . . sw. . . ." He smiled, wiped his eyes on the inside of his shirt sleeve, and shook his head. Then again "Sw. . . ." It came through. "Sweet Jesus. . . . Sweet, Sweet Jesus." He collapsed forward, sobbing; his head and elbows rested on the floor; his face was buried in his arms. The crowd whispered "Sweet Jesus" back with their eyes closed. They began to weep.

Suddenly Sonny leaped to his feet and, in a voice that made the filter screens on the air conditioners vibrate, he screamed, "BUT WE KILLED HIM! WE KILLED HIM! WE KILLED THAT SWEET MAN! WE

KILLED THE SON OF GOD!" His face looked black. His hair was wild. His chest expanded and he was bigger. "LOOK AROUND YOU. LOOK AROUND YOU. I'M TALKING ABOUT YOU!" He thrust an accusing finger at the audience. "I'M TALKING ABOUT YOU." He thrust again. And again. Six times, seven times, eight times.

Each time the crowd recoiled and groaned. Sonny stomped down on the floor and crossed the stage in long stalking steps. He held the microphone before him rigidly, and with the other hand he thrust the long and avenging finger into the quivering crowd. "I'M TALKING ABOUT *ALL OF YOU.*"

Back and forth, back and forth across the wide stage, before the forty-two ministers of the gospel, before the eight thousand seated sinners he raced and stomped and cried and bellowed. He held the black cord in his right hand and whipped it behind him like a gigantic tail. The ministers took up the chant: "SWEET JESUS. SWEET JESUS. SWEET JESUS." The fever rose higher and higher. The crowd twisted in their seats, unable to stand the rising pressure, unable to stop it.

"KILLED HIM. KILLED HIM. KILLED THAT SWEET, SWEET MAN JEEEEEEEEEE-SUS."

The woman next to Coley shrieked and grabbed his arm. He couldn't pull away. She rose up shaking, carrying him with her. Coley pushed his elbow into her ribs and twisted loose.

Sonny stopped in the middle of the platform and, throwing his head back and raising his arms, he paused. His shadow on the seventy-foot tent wall behind him was an enormous cross. He waited, breathed in, firmed his jaw, and in a voice that made the canvas tent expand he roared,

"AND WHAT ARE *YOU* AND WHAT ARE *YOU*
GOING TO BE DOING ABOUT IT *NOW?*"

The audience gave forth with its loudest, longest, lowest
groan and then it cracked. Shrieks and screams came from
everywhere, and the rising cry of "SWEET JESUS" rattled the aluminum struts in their junctions at the top.

Men rose, women rose; wives led husbands, husbands led
wives. Whole rows rose as one. Backsliders, backbiters, liars
and hypocrites, drunks, reformed drunks, whores, relapsed
whores, all pushed their way to the wide sawdust path and
lined up for Jesus. They were crying, sobbing, laughing,
singing. Several got loose and began rolling on the floor.
The others smiled and cried and made room for them. The
attendants put on the record "Come to Jesus." Dogs barked
in the distance.

The music was loud. "Come to Jesus. Come to Jesus."
And they came. They came. They came. Like late-Septem-
ber Elberta peaches, orange yellow and soft and full of
juice. Too heavy for the limb, too ripe for shipping. They
came. Sonny blessed each one and sent them back to the
Salvation Tent, where the attendants took their Love Offerings and put them on the mailing list for Sonny's book, *The
Healing Life and the New Way.*

The seats around Earl and Coley were empty. Earl whispered, "You still want to go up for that hundred dollars?"

"Hell, no! Let's get out of here."

The four thousand in the pasture gathered around the
chinaberry trees, the telephone poles, and the tallest men.
Some clung and wept on the condensers and the casements
of the air conditioners sticking out from the tent, and three
men and two women began rolling in the patch of field peas
lighted by the lights of a watermelon truck, while over a

hundred gathered around them singing and clapping hands. A tall drunk with a small, hairless head, dressed in white coveralls, stood in confusion at the edge of the field. He had been waiting for a bus and had been attracted by the crowd. A roller, thinking he was one of Sonny's leaders, raced to him and pitched forward in the dirt. The drunk backed off but it was too late; others had followed. In a minute he had gathered a group of rollers. When he saw he was trapped, he stood still and watched. A curly-haired woman with bright orange-red lipstick and a black dress on scratched at his foot. He kicked her away. Suddenly she began convulsing and horseshoeing back and forth.

Someone shouted, "She's been taken hold of! She's chunking out the demons!"

The woman spun around and began bubbling and making strange gargling noises.

"It's the tongues. It's the tongues. It's the tongues of the unknown."

A short man in overall pants and a T shirt with *Fort Jackson* and *God Bless America* in red and blue across the front tugged at the drunk's sleeve. "What's she saying? What's she saying?"

"How the hell would I know? It's Greek to me."

The short man whispered quickly, "The tongue's in Greek. It's coming through in Greek."

"Wish we had a Greek to tell us what she's saying."

"Must be something mighty powerful. Look at her roll."

Earl and Coley were outside the tent. Coley whistled. "Look how that old beetle scratched me up."

"God Almighty! I was really scared there for a minute."

Coley tucked his shirt in. "You weren't by yourself."

Chapter 16

Doc poured a bottle of Budweiser into a sixteen-ounce Dixie cup for M.L. It was Sunday and there was a hundred dollar fine for selling beer. From a distance the Law would think M.L. was drinking an extra-large Coke or a milk shake to go.

"Slow tonight, ain't it?"

Doc rang up M.L.'s money. "They're all down there with that Sonny Love. My beer business has dropped like a stone. Hell, I don't know what to buy, what to stock, what to put on ice, nothing."

M.L. wiped the beer foam from his top lip. "What burns me up is the money Love's bleeding out of this town. Calls them Love Offerings. You know he don't have to declare a dime of that to the tax men, not a goddamn dime, and I mean he's raking it in in washtubs. By the time that bastard moves out there won't be enough cash left to buy seed."

"It's a crime, that's what it is." Doc opened a bottle for himself and filled another milk shake container.

"You hear how T. Tommy Denny gave up his golf championship?"

Doc shook his head.

"Love converted him and the damn fool took the pledge on no Sunday golf. They had the final match set for last Sunday and he forfeited. It's all in the paper."

"Jesus Christ."

Suddenly M.L. handed Doc his beer. "Somebody's coming."

Doc put both beers in the bottom of the fountain sink. If the Law came he planned on tipping them over and turning the hot water on. Someone with heel cleats on his shoes was marching down the sidewalk whistling "The Church in the Wildwood." He came into the light of the front window. It was Lonnie Register.

M.L. shook his head slowly. "Jesus wept."

Doc put the beers back on the counter. "Hello, Lon. You gave us a scare there for a minute."

Lonnie smiled and nodded. "Hello, Doc. Hello, M.L."

M.L. said, "Say, you look kinda funny. You feeling all right?"

Lonnie beamed. "I feel fine. Ain't had a drop in nine days and nine nights. And that's a fact. And what's more, when you see me nine months from now I'm going to tell you the same thing. I've changed my whole perspective on things, Martin."

"Bullshit."

"Give me an Orange Crush, Doc."

Doc said, "I thought Sonny said you boys weren't allowed any soft drinks."

"Naw, he ain't said that. That's all those rumors running around. He ain't said nothing like that at all." He reached for a package of peanut buttered cheese crackers. "I'm heading up to Holly's to see Earl and Coley." Lonnie lipped the top of his bottle and took a long drink. "Them boys been worrying me about my car all summer, and now I want to get rid of it."

M.L. said, "Why now?"

"Personal reasons. Let's just say I want to spend more time on my work and with my family and less time out in the back yard."

M.L. said, "I don't want to butt in, Lonnie, and you know it. But why don't you kind of wait a spell before you do that? Those boys can wait. Just let it sort of drift for a while, and then see how you feel about it."

"My mind's made up, M.L. I don't need that car. I don't need it any more than I need that beer you're fixing to pour down there."

"Yeah, but things might change."

"I ain't going to let them. No sir. I ain't going to give them a chance to change."

Doc shook his head. "You're making a mistake, Lonnie."

"No, Doc, I got a strong feeling on this."

M.L. said, "It's your car, Lon."

Lonnie finished his drink and opened the door. "Why don't you boys take off tonight and go down and see Sonny Love? You ought to at least hear what he's got to say."

M.L. shook his head. "It ain't right, Doc. It ain't. A nice fellow like Lonnie getting all messed up like that."

Doc scraped a piece of cup wax from his teeth. "He doesn't have a chance."

"Let me try something out." M.L. picked up the phone and called Holly's. He asked for Earl.

"Earl, this is M. L. Anderson. Now I want you to listen

and listen close. Lonnie's heading up to see you and Coley right this minute and he says he wants to sell you his car. . . . I know, I know. But you gotta go along with what I'm telling you. Lonnie ain't right. Sonny Love's got him hooked. If you buy that car now, it would be like buying it from some looney out at the insane asylum, and I mean that. . . . Now listen, Earl, I'm a good deal older than you and I know what I'm talking about. . . . That's fine, boy. I knew you'd see it my way."

M.L. hung the phone up. "It's O.K., Earl won't buy it."

Doc opened two more Budweisers. "Well, at least the kids in this town haven't lost their minds."

Earl left the phone booth and raced after Coley. He saw him crossing the yard near the barbecue pit carrying a full tray of empty beer bottles. "Hey, Coley! Coley! Wait up. Boy, do I have the news. Do I have the news! Lonnie wants to sell the Hudson."

"No lie?"

"He's on his way here right now. How much money you got?"

"Twenty-one, maybe twenty-two. Hell, we got seventy at home. Let's go get it."

"No, there ain't time. Listen, there's one problem. I told M.L. we wouldn't buy it."

"What're you talking about?"

"Oh, he sounded all serious and all, said Sonny Love converted Lonnie and he ain't right. I just couldn't say no to him."

Coley said, "Screw M.L. What does he have to do with it, anyway? If Lonnie's selling, I say grab it."

Earl looked up the driveway. "We'll ask Lonnie if he really wants to sell it. He's a grown man, he doesn't need M.L. to look after him."

Coley put his tray down on the curb. "Here he comes now. Jesus, let's don't mess up."

Earl waved to Lonnie. "Let him do the talking, Coley."

Lonnie crossed the yard.

Earl said, "Hello, Lonnie."

Coley said, "Hello, Lonnie."

"Evening, boys. Looks like you got a busy night."

Coley said, "Oh, we ain't busy now. We're both on our breaks."

"Well, I came to talk about the Hudson." Lonnie looked toward the neon-lighted building. "Any place we can sit down around here?"

They led him between a line of parked cars out to the barbecue pit. It was dark there, and the smell of cooked pork and hickory ash was heavy. They sat down on the bench, with Lonnie in the middle. Earl wanted to smoke but he knew he was too nervous to light a cigarette. Coley sat still, gazing at the deep pit, and waited for Lonnie to speak.

Lonnie cleared his throat as if he were about to make a long speech. "It's a good car, boys. Mighty good. You know the care I've taken with it. I don't have to tell you about that."

Earl wanted to agree but he was afraid it might drive the price up.

"I put a lot of hours on that engine and a lot of time on that transmission." Lonnie paused again and repeated slowly, "A lot of time. A lot of time."

Earl said, "Lon, you sure you want to sell it?"

Coley took a breath and added, "Maybe you'll miss it."

"No, my mind's set. I know what I want to do." Lonnie gripped Earl's left knee and Coley's right. "You boys want that Hudson and I want to get shed of it. Now let's come to some kind of terms."

Earl said, "O.K., Lon."

Lonnie said, "Now if I said two hundred dollars, which would be about what I could get from a dealer and about what she's worth, you boys might think that was too high. Then again if I said fifty dollars you'd probably say that was too low."

Earl said nothing. Coley laced his fingers together between his knees and squeezed tight.

"So what if we say a flat seventy-five?"

Earl said. "Great! That's great! Perfect price! That way we can put some new stuff on her if she needs it."

Lonnie smiled. "That car don't need anything. It's ready right now."

Coley jumped up. "I'll go get a piece of Holly's stationery. We'll make it legal. Preach can draw it up for us."

Lonnie said, "No, no. Ain't no need in all that. You got my word. That's all you need. Bring your money down in the morning." He cocked his wrist watch to catch the light. "I got to be catching a bus."

Earl said, "We'll be there at seven-thirty, O.K.?"

"Naw, make it around ten. I want to put the wheels on and the seats in and get the registration and all ready."

Coley said, "And we got your word it's a deal, right?"

Lonnie shook Coley's hand, then Earl's. "It's a deal. Hold her in the road, now."

As Lonnie crossed the parking lot Earl grabbed Coley's hand in a silent fierce handshake. Coley gripped hard and they slapped each other on the shoulder with their free left hands, two times, three times, four times. "Seventy-five dollars, Coley! Holy Moley! How about that! It really happened! We got it! We got it! It's ours!"

Coley was talking so fast he could barely understand himself. "It's worth two-fifty easy, Earl, easy. He ain't driven it at all. I tell you we could turn around and sell it to Longanberry's or Zuck's for two hundred and fifty dollars right now, with no strain. That's one of the best cars Hudson ever built, and Lonnie's taken care of it like it was made out of pure gold."

They were too excited to stand still. They walked toward the order window. Both were talking at once.

"Jesus, I still can't believe it." Earl grinned and pounded Coley on the back. "Seventy-five dollars, that's perfect, perfect, and he was dying to sell it."

Coley sparred at Earl and hit him on his shoulder. He danced out and faked two lefts. "M.L. was crazy. Crazy as hell."

Earl ducked under Coley's left and they clinched. "Oh, man, Coley, our troubles are over. From now on it's all gravy. Gravy! Man, oh, man! Our own car!"

Slinging their arms around each other's shoulders, they let out a long, wild rebel yell and then another.

Holly stuck his head out the window. "What in the hell's going on? Earl, get your ass back in that kitchen."

In the morning the car was ready. The wheels and hub caps had been put on and the car looked as if it had just been Simonized. Lonnie had the hood up and was busy adjusting the carburetor setting. "You boys are getting a mighty fine machine here. Migh-ty fine. Listen at that compression. That engine's clean enough to sit in your living room."

Coley was afraid something might go wrong at the last minute. "Sounds great, Lonnie. It really does."

Lonnie gave them the registration ticket and the bill of sale and Earl counted out the seventy-five dollars. They shook hands and Lonnie handed Earl a set of keys. "Take good care of her, boys." He reached in and, after picking a fleck of dust from the dashboard, he patted the steering wheel. "O.K., she's all yours."

Earl drove fifteen blocks and Coley drove fifteen. The radio worked on all stations. The heater came on fast, and the three-toned horn sounded deeper than Dan's. They crossed town and headed out the Cooper Ridge Road. Earl climbed over the seat and sat in the back with his feet up on the front seat. "Oh, man! What a ride! What a ride! She rides better than Loganberry's Buick."

"Hey, watch those feet. You're getting it all dirty."

Earl sat up and leaned forward. "Let's see what she'll do."

Coley pushed on the accelerator. The indicator moved to 55.

"Come on, let her out."

Coley said, "This is fast enough. If we get a speeding ticket we're through."

Earl sat back and stretched out on the seat. "Oh, Lordy Lord! She's really ours. Seventy-five moldy dollars, what a deal!"

Coley turned the wheel loose. "Look here, Earl. Look at that front end. Look how she holds the road. He's really got her balanced."

At the drugstore Earl took his handkerchief and started

polishing the grille and the front bumper. "We need a couple chamois cloths and some chrome polish."

The Hudson was a black 1940 four-door Special with great leaded areas on top where it had been repaired from a wreck. Coley whistled. "Boy, she's seen some rough days. Look at that leading. Wonder how many times she's been rolled."

"Jesus Christ, you complaining already?"

Coley said, "I'm not complaining. She's heavy. Nice and solid. She'll be great on long trips."

Earl squatted down so he could see under the drugstore awning. It was two thirty. "Come on, we got to get going."

Coley turned into Holly's driveway and stopped in front of the curb boys' bench.

Herman was sitting down counting change. "Whose car?"

Coley said, "Ours, just bought it."

Herman stuck his head in the window. "Looks pretty sharp. Lemme hear the motor."

Coley flicked the switch on and started up.

"Sounds good, sounds real good. What she cost you?"

Earl leaned over to watch Herman's face. "A hundred and seventy-five."

Herman whistled. "That's a lot of money. But she sounds like she's got a lot of juice. Yeah, you all got yourselves a real car there."

Chapter 17

Fleetwood Drigger's best move was on banana splits. Customers came in just to see him work.

Most fountain men follow the classic pattern of slicing bananas for banana splits. They peel the banana, lay it flat on the board so the hump is on top, and then press the knife straight down. But Fleetwood had a one-handed method that no one could copy. First, with the banana in his left hand, he would nick it on the side; he claimed this let the air in. Then he would make his slice. Then, without touching it with his right hand, he would squeeze the banana in some mysterious way so that it would come sliding out of the peel into the split dish perfectly halved and ready for the ice cream and the fruits and syrups. Whenever anyone else tried this, they would either go in too deep on the incision and cut their hand or else not deep enough, and when the banana was squeezed it would come oozing out along the top like thick mustard.

The supper rush ended at nine, and Fleetwood was working on four banana splits for a group of summer school students from the University. Earl and Preach were standing in the doorway cooling off in the air-conditioner draft. It was Wednesday and Coley was off, but Holly hadn't been able to get a relief for Earl and had told him he would get an extra day's pay.

Fleet finished the four splits and lined up five more glass trays on the back of the ice cream holes. As he began slicing bananas he looked up and caught Earl and Preach watching him in the mirror. Suddenly he was red-faced and furious. He slammed down his knife, screaming, "Holly! Holly! Goddammit, I quit. I quit, you hear?"

Holly came down from his high stool. He was eating and daubing a napkin at his lips. "What's the matter, boy?"

Fleet shouted, "Look!" He pointed at the mirror. "They dogging me. They stand there watching me. I can't work with them bastards watching my every move. They studying me and stealing my ideas. I ain't going to do it, you hear? I'm leaving here! I'm going over to Ed White's."

Holly put his hand up on Fleet's wide tight shoulder. "Come on, boy." He took him out into the yard. When they came back Fleet had calmed down. Holly stuck his head in the kitchen. "Preach, you and Earl come on outside. I want to see you a minute."

They sat on the barbecue pit bench facing the low hickory fire. Holly spoke slowly. "I'm going to put it to you men straight. If Fleet leaves and goes to Ed White's, I lose the high school and the University trade. They come down here to time him and then they go out and bet him against the boys at White's and the Bearcat and God knows where else. Now you see why I got to pamper him so? You think I like to work with all that hollering and shouting going on? You think I like to put up with that crap?"

Preach said, "I see what you're up against."

"So I want you boys to go back in there and apologize to him. I know it's tough, but you see how it is. I want you to do it for Old Holly." He paused. "Old Holly would appreciate it."

They said they would.

Holly shook Preach's hand. As he squeezed Earl's, Earl said, "How about that ten-dollar raise you promised me? How's that look now?"

"O.K. as of tonight." He turned to Preach. "And that goes for you too."

Preach spoke. "That's mighty nice, Holly. Mighty nice. I could use that extra money." He pulled out a package of Juicy Fruit chewing gum and, after giving Earl a slice, he slowly unwrapped his. "What if someone was to beat old Fleet on the fountain?"

Holly said, "If I saw someone do it I'd snap him up and fire that loudmouth so fast he wouldn't know whether to walk or run."

After the Sonny Love crowd rush had ended and Holly had closed up, Fleetwood came back to the kitchen. Preach was filling up the condiment line for the breakfast cook and Earl was putting the last soapstone touches on the grill. Everyone else was gone. Fleet sat up on the sandwich board. "I suppose it's too late for bacon and eggs?"

Earl said, "You're damn right it is."

Fleet smiled softly. "Well, what if I said I wanted me some bacon and eggs and I wanted you to fix them for me?"

Preach was at the refrigerator. He was staying as far away from Fleetwood as he could. No one answered. Fleet tapped Earl on the shoulder; Earl stopped scrubbing on the grill. He leaned on the soapstone and stared down at the gray and brown grill.

Fleet tapped him on the shoulder again. "How about the eggs?"

Fleetwood was too big to fight, but Earl had the soapstone in his right hand and the rat-tailed knife sharpener was hanging on the edge of the counter. He gripped the stone, trembling. "Fleet, why don't you forget the bacon, just have the eggs."

"How's that again?"

Earl raised the soapstone. "You can suck the eggs, you rotten son of a bitch, that's what."

Fleet got down from the sandwich board slowly. Earl jumped back and unhooked the knife sharpener. Fleetwood took a long step forward. His eyebrows leveled. "I'm going to make you eat that brickbat."

Preach shouted, "Hold it, Fleetwood!"

Earl looked over, figuring Preach had a meat cleaver or a grill fork. He had nothing in his hands except two heads of lettuce.

Fleetwood smiled. He began pulling his little clip-on necktie off. "You're the one I really want."

Preach's voice dropped back down to his soft, mellow range. He put the lettuce in the refrigerator and closed the door. "I ain't no fighting man, Fleetwood. You know that."

Earl shoved the sharpener into his back pocket. He still held the heavy soapstone in his right hand. "We can both take him, Preach. We can kill the son of a bitch."

Fleet jerked around. "Shut up, you little snot, or I'll drown you in that grease." He turned back to Preach. He was a head taller than Preach and about forty pounds heavier. "I been waiting for you too long now. What were you telling Holly, you black bastard?"

"You want to know?"

"Damn right I want to know. And I'm finding out before we leave this kitchen."

"All right, I'll tell you." Preach began walking back and forth on the duckboards. He spoke slowly. "The way I see it, Fleetwood, you and me are going to have to butt heads sooner or later. I been trying to avoid it. I been trying real hard, but it don't do no good."

Fleetwood pushed himself back on the counter and put his feet on the sandwich board. "Take your time, Preach. Take plenty of time."

Preach stopped. He looked at Fleetwood's feet. "Now why you want to go put your feet on my board like that? You know that's not right." He walked to the refrigerator and back. "There's only one thing I can do, Fleetwood. I got to straighten you out."

Fleetwood laughed.

Preach kept walking. He spoke even slower now, as if his voice were carrying and he was listening for the echo. "Fleetwood, Holly Yates tells me all about this bookmaking around town on your soda jerking speed. He tells me that all the high school and University boys say you are the fastest thing going." He continued walking. "He tells me how it's you who keeps this place filled up with that school trade."

"Preach, if you got something to say, say it. I ain't going to sit up here and listen to you all night."

"O.K. I'll get to the point right now. Holly Yates told me that if someone beat you on the fountain he'd hire him in a minute and fire you."

Earl had put the soapstone down. He kept his hand on

the knife sharpener in his back pocket. "That's what he said, Fleetwood. I swear to God, that's what he said. I was sitting right there on the bench when he said it."

Fleetwood said, "Hell, that ain't no news, he told me the same thing. I know all about that. Come on, I had enough of this, let's go outside."

Preach held up his hand. "Hold it. Listen, Fleetwood, you were right about me watching you in the mirror. You were right about that. But you were wrong about the reasons. I wasn't trying to learn anything or copy your style. I was just checking it. You want to know why I'm not studying or copying your style?"

"Yeah, Blue Gum, tell me all about it."

"Thing is, Fleetwood, you just don't have no style. You got a lot of big movements, but you don't have no style. You move a lot of air around and you spin a lot of wheels, but you don't get too much done. I'll tell you something else. The reason you been beating the other soda boys is 'cause they just worse than you. That's all. First time you run up against any competition, church is going to be out."

"Don't hand me that. Those boys have timed me with a race track watch. I'm the fastest man around, with Spartanburg and Charleston thrown in."

Preach shook his head. "You look good, no doubt about that. But you're slow. I know a man in town that's about forty per cent faster than you and he hasn't jerked a fountain in five years."

"Who's that?"

Earl sat up on the high stool. He hung the sharpener on the sandwich board. He knew who Preach was going to say. His hands and arms were trembling. He held them around his knees and closed his eyes, hoping that Preach would drag it out slowly so he could wallow in every juicy second of it.

Preach stopped walking. "You looking at him."

"Don't make me laugh."

"No, I'm not going to make you laugh. All I'm going to do is straighten you out, like I said I was. Now listen at this. What if I would take a job at Mr. Ed White's for a few days. Just a few days, mind you. Just enough time to let the boys make a lot of bets on you, and then you lose. Why you'd be out of here faster than a turkey going through the corn."

Fleet lit a cigarette. "You mean you'd go over to White's, just to get me fired?"

"I would. I wouldn't like to do it, but you don't give me much choice. You see, Fleetwood, you just don't happen to be a reasonable man. If you were reasonable you wouldn't be there with your feet on my sandwich board threatening me."

Fleet's lips parted in a nasty knife-edge grin, and he reached over and ground his cigarette out in the middle of Earl's clean grill. "That ain't very reasonable either, is it?"

Preach's expression didn't change. "No, that's pretty low-life too."

Fleetwood raised up from the sandwich board. "Nigger, let's cut this crap out. I want you outside."

"You don't want me to show you how slow you are?"

Fleetwood paused. "You mean you want to race me now? We're closed."

"Would you rather I show you up tomorrow when the school crowd gets here? Normally, I work better in front of a crowd. It wouldn't be too good if I was to beat you right here on your own fountain." Preach smiled. "You might even wind up back here in all this grease heat."

Fleetwood jumped down from the board. He rushed to the front and turned on the lights. "O.K., Dark Meat, what you want to make?" He looked over his clean fountain. He knew every inch of it: where everything was, how the taps worked, which syrup dispensers were slow, which fast, everything.

Preach sat down at the counter and pulled his railroad watch and chain out of his pocket. "Fleet, you go first. Write down what you want to make. Make four or five things, make more if you like."

Fleetwood looked suspicious. "I don't trust you. Who's keeping time?"

Earl said, "I'll hold the watch."

Fleet whipped his apron on. "Like hell you will."

Preach hung his watch over the menu holder on the counter. "No need to trust anyone. You begin when you want to. When you finish, that's your time."

Fleetwood picked up a piece of soap. He made a list of what he was going to make on the mirror: two chocolate sundaes, four strawberry sodas, eighteen small Cokes, and seven banana splits.

Earl said, "You better cut that down. Holly'll have a fit if he finds out you wasted all that ice cream."

Preach said, "No, that's O.K."

Fleetwood said, "I'll wait till three-thirty sharp."

He put on his short white jacket and cap and brushed the side of his hair away from his face and up into his tall pompadour. He looked coldly at Preach. "Listen, this doesn't mean you ain't getting your ass cut when we're through.

The minute you're done here we go outside. You understand? You too, runt. You ain't out of this either." He dried his hands on his apron and looked over his long gleaming fountain. "Say, how 'bout a little side bet?"

Preach said, "O.K. with me."

Fleetwood tossed his wallet on the counter. "There's fifty-eight dollars in there. How much you want?"

Earl said, "I want ten." He laid his only ten-dollar bill on the wallet.

Preach said, "I got the rest."

There were fifteen seconds to go. Fleetwood said, "It's your funeral." As the second hand touched sixty, he flung open the vanilla, strawberry, and chocolate ice cream holes. He went to work on the sundaes. At 3:32 and ten seconds the chocolate sundaes were finished, lined up on the counter, and he was squirting strawberry syrup into the four tall soda glasses. At 3:35 and five seconds the sodas were finished and standing next to the sundaes. Fleetwood triggered eighteen six-ounce Dixie cups from the cup dispenser, picked up five in his left hand, and began filling them with cracked ice.

Earl sat on a bar stool directly in front of him. He kept one eye on the watch and one eye on Fleetwood's flying hands. His movements were shorter than Earl had remembered. There seemed to be a new jerky quality about his rhythm, but Earl knew his speed had increased since they had watched him. Fleetwood slid five Cokes out on the counter. He picked up five more empties. He had big hands; he could hold seven empty cups when he wanted to, but when he worked from the ice container to the Coke dispenser he preferred five. Preach sat next to Earl, smoking slowly. Fleetwood finished the eighteen Cokes and had them lined up on the counter at 3:38 and twenty seconds. He slid seven banana split dishes out on top of the fountain, pulled seven bananas out of the back bar compartment, and began nicking, slicing, and squeezing. Preach let the smoke out carefully, sighed, and left the counter.

At 3:44 and forty-five seconds Fleetwood threw up his hands and shouted, "Done!" The entire order had taken fourteen minutes and forty-five seconds. Fleetwood picked up one of the eighteen Cokes and began drinking it. His uniform was spotless and his hands were clean and dry. He came out from behind the fountain, took off his hat, pushed his hair back, and sat next to Earl.

Preach drank one of the Cokes and watched the sweep second hand lift the minute hand toward four o'clock. "That was the fastest I ever seen you work, Fleet. You looked real good. O.K. if I start at ten of?"

Fleetwood lit a cigarette. "Listen, don't start brown-nosing me now. The minute you finish we're going outside."

There was one minute to go. Preach looked tired. He began walking back and forth on the duckboards behind the fountain as if he were in his kitchen. He didn't look at the watch until he had walked back and forth four times. When he looked up the second hand had five seconds to go.

He started slow, much slower than Fleetwood. Fleetwood saw it and began grinning. It was a strange grin, like a long zipper being opened and then slowly closed. By the time Preach had finished the sodas he had lost a full minute.

Earl was scared. He knew his ten dollars was gone. He wished he had kept the sharpener in his pocket. He wanted to be close to the kitchen so he could rush in and get the grill fork that was hanging by the door.

Preach picked up only three Coke cups at a time. But he picked them up cleaner than Fleetwood and he worked the dispenser faster. He gained a half minute of the time he had lost on the sundaes and sodas and went into the seven banana splits forty seconds behind Fleetwood's time. He was moving fast but he was too far behind. Earl was ready to jump for the door.

And then it happened. Suddenly Preach found himself; everything began to fit into place. The old Preach that Earl had watched fan the tomato slices during the Sonny Love rush came to the surface, flashed there, caught fire, and stayed there. His motions shortened. He speeded up. The ice cream scoop was flying as he crouched close over the banana split boats and swayed from the vanilla to the chocolate to the strawberry ice cream holes. When he dipped and ejected into the dishes it was a solid, continuous movement. No elbows, no knees, no pivots; just wrists and hands and head. The ice cream was ready. The bananas were sliced and placed. He spooned the fruit, poured the syrups, and sprinkled the nuts. His left hand was full of maraschino cherries; in his right was the whipped cream cylinder. Each split was quickly topped with three shots of whipped cream, one for each ice cream flavor, and each was capped with a bright-red long-stemmed cherry. He was finished.

Fleetwood had taken six minutes and twenty-five seconds to do seven banana splits. Preacher Watts did them in four minutes flat. He took his watch from the menu holder and slid it across the counter. "That does it, Fleet."

Earl screamed, "Hot damn, son of a bitch!" He ran down

the counter spinning the bar stools and doing his delirious dance again. When he got to Fleetwood he pounded him on the back as if he were an old friend. He vaulted up on top of the counter, did a rapid heel dance, and let out a rebel yell that made the beer glasses rattle.

Preach had won by one full minute and forty-seven seconds. He took the victory quietly. "Fleetwood, you ought to have that chocolate valve checked. It's sticking." He took off his apron and pointed to Fleetwood's wallet on the counter. "You want to do the honors?"

Earl grinned. "Yeah. Fifty-eight of them, Fleetwood."

Fleetwood didn't say a word. His face was the color of his hair. He took all of his money out of his wallet and counted out fifty-eight dollars on the counter. All he had left were his Social Security card, his Board of Health approval, and three plastic-covered pictures of himself. "I suppose you're going to tell Holly first thing in the morning?"

Earl said, "You bet your sweet ass we are."

Preach handed Earl twenty dollars and slipped the rest into his own wallet. "I'll let you know, Fleet. I haven't decided yet. You better be going on home now. You look tired."

Earl was still sitting on top of the counter. He was worn out; the dancing had finished him off. He thought he would eat one of the chocolate sundaes to pick up his energy, but he changed his mind. He reached for another Coke. Fleetwood hung up his soda-fountain jacket and cap and opened the front door. He turned back to say something but couldn't think of anything.

A last wave of strength swept over Earl. "Hey, Fleet, they got great bacon and eggs at Ed White's. They might even make you up some onion rings."

Fleetwood closed the door and started across the yard.

Earl cupped his hands to his mouth. He shouted so his voice would carry through the venetian blinds and the window. "If they say onion rings are à la carte, tell them to go to hell."

Preach sat at the counter next to Earl, drinking a Coke. They stared over the sundaes, the sodas, the Cokes, and the fourteen banana splits into the fountain mirror.

"Preach, how 'bout if I bring Coley along when you tell Holly? He hates Fleetwood's guts too."

Preach sipped his Coke.

"Preach, we're going to get rid of him, ain't we?"

"Don't say ain't, boy." He picked up another Coke. There were thirty-one left on the counter. "Why don't you go home now, Earl? You going to be dead tonight."

"Whoa, now, I want to know when you're going to tell Holly. I want to be there for that. Besides, we got to clean this mess up."

Preach was quiet for a long time. The ice in the Cokes had melted, and the long-stemmed cherries were slowly sinking into the soft ice cream. Earl ate the strawberries from the banana splits. "Wonder what your Immanuel Kant would say to do about a first-class bastard like Fleetwood Driggers?"

Preach's face lit up like one of the banana splits. "Boy, I tell you, you're getting smarter every day. I swear you are. I was just figuring what he would do if he was sitting here with all the cards I'm holding and looking in that mirror."

Earl pounced. "He'd say, ram it to him. That's what he'd say, ram it to him."

Preach looked serious. "No, he wouldn't say that. And you ought to know better. He was more profound than that. But I tell you what. I know exactly what that rascal would say."

Earl cradled his chin in his hands and closed his eyes. He smiled. "Tell me slow."

"I suspect he'd get out his old Categorical Imperative. That's that theory on right and wrong I was telling you about." Preach finished his Coke and rattled the ice in the bottom of the cup. "Then he'd rub his whiskers a little bit and then he'd say, 'Let's let him sweat.' "

As the eleven o'clock sun inched up over the sweet gum and chinaberry trees along Mulberry, the Hudson's shadow shrank until it barely covered Earl and Coley sitting on the drugstore curb. Earl had the rubber balls in each hand. He squeezed the left one, then the right one.

"Come on, Earl. Let me have 'em now."

"Not through. One hundred and twenty-eight, one hundred and twenty-nine, one hundred and thirty."

"You're doing it too long. Buck says only a hundred. A hundred is plenty. Come on, I gotta got to the store for Ma."

Earl strained. "Leave me alone. One hundred and forty-seven, one hundred and forty-eight, one hundred and forty-nine, one hundred and fifty. Whew! O.K., take 'em."

"God, they're hot as fire." Coley leaned forward and began squeezing and counting.

Earl's head was in the sun, and he slid forward into the shade.

Coley finished and leaned back rubbing his sore wrists. "M.L. told me Jack Dempsey used to pick up a calf every day before breakfast. And when that calf became a full-grown bull he could still pick him up."

Earl said, "I don't believe that. I don't care who said it. Who in the hell can pick up a full-grown bull? They must weigh a ton."

"I'm just saying what M.L. told me. Said he read it somewhere. Said Dempsey could kill a bull if he hit him in the head with his right."

Earl measured his right wrist with his left hand. It seemed bigger. "Wonder if he ever did?"

Coley hooked his thumbs inside the top of his pants and stretched out. "You know what would make a great fight? Jack Dempsey and Joe Louis. I mean if you could fix it so they were both the same age and all. Man, that would be a fight to end all fights."

Earl leafed his fingers together and squeezed hard, watching his wrist veins bulge. "Dempsey would take him."

"Now, how in the hell can you sit there and say that?"

"He was a better fighter! Anyone will tell you that." Earl gazed across Mulberry to the telephone wires that touched the tops of the chinaberry trees. Shreds of yellow and red paper were clinging to the struts, and strings of an old box kite caught in the wires near the transformer on the corner. There was no breeze and the paper hung motionless. "You know, if Sugar Ray Robinson had Louis's weight, he could take either one of them."

"A two-hundred-and-seven-pound Sugar Ray Robinson! Man, he could kill anybody. Now you're talking about a fight. Jack Dempsey against a two-hundred-and-seven-pound Sugar Ray. Man, that would be the fight of the century. Hell, that would probably be the greatest fight in history."

Earl stared back at the old kite. There were more bits of yellow than red. "Yeah, Buck told me Sugar Ray, pound for pound, is the greatest fighter that ever put on a jock. If he came in at two-o-seven he would really be something."

Coley pulled out his grocery list. "I'd better get this stuff for Ma."

"O.K., I'll wait for you here."

Coley made a U turn and drove across the street to the A & P store. Earl sat down next to M.L. on the bench and picked the lint from a sour ball. "You're still sore 'bout us buying that car, ain't you?"

M.L. lowered his paper. "Yeah, boy. I kinda figured you were a man of your word. Guess I just figured wrong."

"But he really wanted to sell it. I swear he did. We asked him. Go on, ask Coley, ask Lonnie, if you don't believe me."

"Next time I'll know better." M.L. glanced at the Hudson and then back at Earl. "But, you know something? I don't think I'm as sore about it as I was."

Earl balanced the heel of his left shoe on the toe of his right. "How come?"

"Because I've been sitting here for two weeks now listening at that engine and hearing that transmission whine when you catch second." He folded the paper to the movie page. "I figure everybody's getting just exactly what they deserve out of that deal. Things seem to be leveling out."

Earl wagged his left foot slowly. "You ain't saying Coley and me got a lemon?"

M.L. scanned the page. "If I were you, I wouldn't be planning any cross-country trips."

Coley came back and they sat in the Hudson's back seat reading comic books, waiting until it was time to go to Holly's. Coley glanced up. A man was standing at the front-door window looking in at the dashboard. He backed up and, squatting down on the fringe of dead grass between the mailbox and the curb, he began rolling a Bull Durham cigarette. He was wearing a dark glare-blue suit with long black shoes and socks. Sitting low and straight on his head was a brand new high-crown straw hat with a thin red band running around it. He kept watching the car as if he had something important to say.

Coley folded his funny book. "He's been squatting there going on five minutes. I been timing him."

Earl was reading *The Human Torch*. He didn't look up. "Ask him what he wants."

"You're closer. You ask him."

"God Almighty, can't you do anything?" Earl sat up, reached over, and dropped *The Human Torch* face down on the front seat. He squinted out. "Anything you want to know about her?"

The man got up slowly and came over to the car door. He was short, but he had a long stride. "This here your car?"

"Yessir, we own it."

The man had a long, sad, tubelike face. He shook his head. "You know your chassis is out of line? I think she's sprung."

Coley leaned over Earl. "How you know that?"

The man drew carefully on his curved cigarette and spoke through the smoke. "I can tell by the shadow she throws on the ground."

Earl laughed. "You 'spect us to believe that?"

The man put one hand on the roof. "Son, I don't care if you believe that or not. But I'm going to tell you one thing, and you better dern sight believe it."

There was no anger in his voice, only a deep studied seriousness. It was as if he knew a great deal about cars, about Earl, about Coley, and about life.

He drummed his fingers on the roof of the car. "I'm telling you, I know cars. I know Hudsons. Before God, I know Hudsons, and I'm telling you to take what I tell you as cold gospel."

Earl figured he was a Pentacostal preacher by his fierce stare and the way his voice rose. He found himself being drawn toward and almost hypnotized by the fine black points in the center of the man's eyes.

"Yessir, before God, this is one of them. This is one of them, all right." He slammed his open palm on the steel roof. "This is a death car! That's what it is! If I've seen one, I've seen a dozen. You get shed of it, you hear? 'Cause if you don't, it's going to bury you." He paused and almost whispered, "This here car's going to be you boys' casket."

On the way to Holly's, Coley said, "Hey, she's heating up. Jumped fifteen points since I left the house."

Earl could still see the burning eyes and the straw hat of the stranger. "Probably needs water. Come on, hurry up! We're going to be late."

Holly stuck his head in the kitchen door. "Earl, go round up Coley. I got to talk to you."

Earl found Coley drinking a large Coke and looking at the water pump on the Hudson. "Holly wants to see us."

"O.K. Boy, this is going to cost some dough. She's leaking like a sieve."

Holly motioned them over to a booth. "I got some bad news for you boys. Hog came by. You just missed him. Said I had to get rid of both of you. Some bastard turned you in for being underage."

Earl said, "Damn! Hog probably did it himself."

Holly said, "That's how I figure it."

Coley finished his Coke. "How much time we got?"

"Couple more days till I can get replacements. I'll pay you for the week, though. Boys, I'm really sorry about this."

Coley said, "Beats me how we're old enough to get a driver's permit and too young to hang a tray. It don't make sense."

Holly shook his head. "Hell, you can drive a car in this state if you can see over the dash. Election's coming, everybody's scratching around trying to look like they're doing something. But don't worry, I'll get you back in as soon as they ease up."

Agnes called Holly to the telephone.

He stood up. "Sorry, boys."

Coley said, "Well, that cooks our goose. How much money we got?"

"Nine bucks plus this week's pay: a hundred, a hundred and five, that ain't bad."

Coley sucked on the ice from his Coke. "Well, we need thirty dollars for the car right now. The water pump's shot and the radiator's got to be cleaned out."

"Thirty?"

"Yeah, thirty. Twenty for a radiator cleaning and a stupid pump costs eleven."

"Damn, that's a lot of money. Are you sure?"

"I'm positive."

Earl untied his loose apron, looped it and the string around his waist twice, and tied it tight. "I've got to get back in the kitchen. We'll work it out."

Coley stared at his Dixie cup. "Yeah."

Chapter 18

Coley had been right about the water pump costing eleven dollars, but he'd been wrong about the radiator. At the S & H Radiator Shop, Ed Levis told them that spending twenty dollars on a flush job would be like throwing money down the drain. The radiator was shot. A new one cost $61.60.

Earl felt sick. "Can't you plug her up? They can't be very big holes, it just started leaking last week."

"There's no way, boys." Ed was a tall, dark, serious man. "The pipes are rotted out. There's no metal left to put patches on."

Coley said, "How come it went so fast?"

"Age, son, age. Cars get old, like everything else."

"And you don't have no secondhand ones?"

"No, 'fraid not, they just ain't around. Let me tell you something, your best bet's going to be a new one. I mean that. Then you can stop worrying about it."

Earl said, "Yeah, but sixty-one sixty, that's a lot of money."

"Not in the long run it ain't." He opened his Flat Rate

224

Manual and spun it around. "I'll give you a good deal. Here, look for yourself, sixty-one sixty, that's the wholesale price. I won't charge you for the labor and the hoses."

On Wednesday Holly hired replacements and paid Earl and Coley the full week's salary. Eleven dollars went to Gus for the water pump and $61.60 was counted out on the greasy counter of the S & H Radiator Shop.

With the new water pump and the radiator in the Hudson, the engine cooled down and ran smoother. It started easier and had more power. But to Coley the car still felt strange. He raced the engine and crouched down near the gear shift base.

Earl said, "Now what in the hell you think you're doing?"

"Something's loose, I keep hearing something."

"Well, if anything else happens, we're screwed. Come on, let's go swimming. I'm about to roast."

Coley parked at the Little Eddy but kept the engine on. "She still sounds funny. Can't you hear it? It's down there deep. You gotta listen close."

Earl tossed his clothes over the headlight and the hood. "You worry too much. Come on, let's hit it!" He scrambled on top of the highest rock and, crouching down as if he were aiming a machine gun, he began firing at the Hudson and Coley and the thick bushes on the bank. He shouted, "You ain't taking me alive, coppers! Come and get me!"

Coley raised his hand and fired one shot. Earl's mouth dropped open; he belched, crossed his eyes, and clutching his stomach he did a dead man's dive into the muddy water.

It happened on Harris Street near the insane asylum. Coley was driving. He stopped for a red light and shifted into neutral. When the light turned yellow he started across the wide intersection, put the car in second, and began picking up speed. Suddenly, an explosion rocked and bounced the car to a stop. A cloud of black smoke puffed out through the ventilators and came seeping up through the floor boards. The engine froze.

Coley dashed around the front, jerked open the hood, and began fanning the smoke away with his cap. "Oh, no!" A jagged hole was in the engine block. They had thrown a rod. "We're ruined." His eyes were full and brimming over. He wiped them with the back of his hand, but the tears kept coming.

Earl slammed his hands on the fender. "God Almighty. I can't take any more. I just can't." He kept staring at the smoking hole. The thick engine smoke made him retch and his eyes were stinging. He leaned on the fender, feeling sick and broke and beaten. The big, blocked shadow of the insane asylum wall lay across the road, and he found himself wanting to cry and go in through the main gate and tell whoever it was there that decided if you were crazy or not all about it: about all of the money, the work, the sweat, the grease, the grime, and the dirt, and now about the busted engine block and the fact that they had \$4.26 between them. Maybe Dan and M.L. were right, they should never have bought it. Maybe the stranger who said he knew Hudsons and who had called it a death car was the one who was really right.

They sat down on the curb, watching the black oil smoke sliding across the street and vanishing into the box hedges along the asylum wall. A man driving an A-Model Ford slowed down and stopped, shook his head, and drove on. Earl's lips were trembling. He had goose flesh on his arms and he was shaking all over. "I'm for selling it."

"No one will buy it like this."

"Then we can sell it for junk. Let's call the yard and get it over with."

"O.K. with me. We sure as hell can't buy no engine."

A small kid came up, pushing a skate scooter. "What happened?"

Earl said, "Go away."

The kid pushed off, then turned and, with a thumb in each of his ears, he wiggled his fingers.

Coley broke a cigarette in two and gave Earl half. "You know this is going to sound stupid. But if we put a new block in there ain't much else that can go wrong."

Earl held up five fingers. "Transmission, rear end, carburetor. Rat's ass, Coley, that's crazy."

"Yeah, but they don't cost too much. Once you put in a new engine the rest is easy."

"I'm for selling."

"Me too."

They sat and smoked and spat and talked. Despite all of the Hudson's problems, it was theirs. It was paid for and they knew what parts they had put in and they knew they were getting close to a point where nothing else could go wrong. They also knew that the girls who would be sitting on the Columbia High School steps in six weeks when school started wouldn't know a transmission hum or a rear-end whine from a two-hundred-dollar overdrive.

"Credit!" Gus screamed. He couldn't believe it. "You want credit for an engine? You must be clean out of your minds."

Coley lied, "But we're both working every day, Gus. You know that. We could pay it off in a few weeks." Gus had asked $125 for a rebuilt engine.

Gus's voice was high and shrill. "How do I know you won't join the Marines or some other damn fool outfit? That's what Jethro did to me. Got into me for a hundred and fifty dollars, then joined up. That money's gone." His voice rose even higher. "Gone, you hear? Gone. I'll never get it back, and I'm stuck here with that goddamn coffee-pot Hupmobile. You want to buy a Hupmobile? No, hell, no, you don't! Nobody does." The thought of the dark, rat-colored Hupmobile, now marked down to $110, sitting in the back of the station made him sad. His voice thickened and dropped. "You know the government says I can't touch Jethro? Even when he gets out, I can't do a thing."

Earl forgot their troubles for a minute and thought of the wooden piston jammed into the Hupmobile's block. He grinned as he put a nickel in the Coke machine.

Gus moistened his lips and glared at him. "What you laughing at? You were in on that swindle, weren't you?"

Earl shrugged his shoulders and closed his eyes as he took a drink. "All I told Jethro was that the government cancels all your debts when you sign up."

Coley giggled.

Gus whirled around. His flushed face matched the red of the Coca-Cola machine. "So you were both in on it! I might have known Jethro didn't have sense enough to do it alone."

Coley couldn't stop giggling.

Gus shouted, "You listen at me! You ain't getting a

nickel's worth of credit, and I want that Hudson out of my yard this second."

Earl said, "Aw, come on, Gus, leave it here till tomorrow. We'll get the money."

"Where?"

"We got ways."

"O.K. One day. I'll give you one day. But if it ain't out of here by tomorrow I'm calling the sheriff."

Earl was wearing a white shirt with a red clip-on bowtie under a brown-and-white plaid winter jacket when he met Coley at the drugstore the next morning. Coley had on the blue serge suit he had graduated from junior high school in. It fit across the chest and around the waist, but it was too short at the wrists and ankles.

Coley leafed through the new *Mandrake the Magician* comic book on the counter. "You want a Pepsi?"

"O.K., let's split one. We got to start cutting corners."

While Bo-Bo was opening the Pepsi-Cola and watching Earl in the mirror, Coley coughed to hide the cellophane noise and pulled two bags of salted peanuts from the bottom of the rack.

In the back booth they opened the telephone book to the loan office listings in the yellow pages. Coley said, "How 'bout old Mason-Dixon Finance?"

"Naw, they'd remember us from Dan. Read the others."

Coley had his finger on the list. "Acme Finance, Acorn Loans, Ashley Loan Company, Better Deal, Inc., Carolina Loans and Discount, Drake's Fast Loans, E. Z. Loan Co., Foster Finance."

"Let's try E. Z. Loan, that sounds pretty good."

"Reckon they'll believe we're eighteen?"

Earl combed his greasy hair smooth and pushed his pompadour forward carefully. He put a cigarette in his mouth and frowned. "What do you think?"

Coley said, "About what?"

"Me, stupid. Don't I look older?"

"You look the same to me."

Earl jutted his jaw down to make his face longer and tried to look thoughtful. "How about now?"

"You look like you're going to vomit."

"Aw, go to hell."

On the bus ride uptown Coley scraped a message on the brown portion of a steel Schlitz Beer sign in front of him. It read: "Gus Haskell is a turd." He finished the "d" and signed his initials.

Earl sat with his elbow jammed onto the thin window ledge and his chin jammed into the heel of his hand, staring out at the glaring streets. He sat up, tucked his shirt in tight, and straightened his tie. "Sign mine too."

They got off the bus at Pine Street and went into the lobby of the Piedmont Building. Coley said, "Your hair's all sticking up in back."

Earl felt the top of his head. "It's dried out. I got to go fix it."

Earl squinted into the full-length mirror by the urinal in the men's room. He cocked his left fist high and his right low. "All right, Haskell, this is it. I've carried you for thirteen rounds." He faked a left, another left, bobbed up, and backed off grinning. "Yeah, you're ready now."

He weaved up from a crouch, slammed in with two quick combinations and a low right hook to the belt line.

JULY

Gus hunched over, holding his stomach. Earl grinned and, crouching for leverage, exploded up with a left uppercut and a straight powerful right. "Pow!" It was over and he pulled out his comb. He wet his hair, combed it down flat in back, and tucked the edges of the pompadour forward. Water dribbled behind his ears. He dried it off with toilet paper.

At the E. Z. Loan Company, Ted Harrison, the manager, pushed an ash tray toward Earl and Coley. "So you need a little money to tide you over?"

Earl said, "Yessir, a hundred and twenty-five dollars."

"Well, let me see here, now. Maybe we just might be able to work a little something out."

They agreed that the Hudson would act as collateral and the payments would be on a weekly basis rather than the normal monthlies. Ted explained about the interest and the insurance, but neither Earl nor Coley understood.

Earl agreed to put the loan in his name, and he began signing forms. He signed a yellow sheet, a red one; then a long two-part green one and finally a small orange card saying that he was eighteen and free from all other debts. When all of the papers were signed and stamped with the day's date, Ted counted out the money and handed him a plastic calendar with the weekly payment days circled.

Coley slapped Earl on the back. "Great going! He really thought you were eighteen."

Earl said, "You see me giving him that old James Cagney frown?"

At the bus stop on the corner of Broad and Pine, a Drake Bible School student was holding a Bible session before a

231

small crowd. He kept asking for questions but none came. As the Woodland Hills bus appeared on the next block, Earl said, "I got a question."

The student smiled. "Yes, son?"

"How come Jesus didn't know he was Jesus till he was thirty-three years old?"

The man smiled. "That's a good question, and I'd like to tell you about it."

The bus doors opened and they got on with the crowd.

A woman with a white scarf over her pin curlers sat down in front of them and turned around. She had a loud voice that kept getting louder. "Ain't right you sassing a man of the Lord like that. Think you're smart and fast, don't you? Well, if you was mine I'd whale the living lights out of you."

Earl looked up and read the bus advertisements.

The woman jabbed her thumb at him. "You mind what I say. You hear?"

PART III

August

Chapter 19

It was August; the black tar streets were soft and sticky, and the kids who were going barefoot had to cross them in a hurry. Downtown was almost deserted. The clothing stores on Broad Street hung amber sheets of vinyl in the windows to protect the dresses and suits from the searing sun. People were too hot to shop and the proprietors were too poor to close. Even the nights seemed hotter.

On the second of August Hog caught Earl speeding down Mulberry, and the fine was fifteen dollars. Two days later Coley was driving and watching Gladys Hightower switch across Pope Street near Cherry instead of watching a new Cadillac pulling out in front of him. When he finally stopped he had chewed off $110 worth of left rear fender and trunk. The Hudson lost one headlight and the bumper was badly bent.

At the E. Z. Loan Company, Ted Harrison shook his head, agreeing that the bill for $110 for the Cadillac was outrageous and that there ought to be a law against companies building cars with parts that expensive.

Earl signed a white sheet which explained how he was

reborrowing to pay off the old principal and the old interest. The payments leaped from $12.00 a week to $20.60.
After Ted counted $110 out onto the slick table he pressed
a buzzer and said he wanted them to meet someone. An ex-
All-Southern tackle from the University, who they had
heard had broken a Georgia man's jaw, stooped through
the door. He crossed the room in three strides. When he
shook their hands he was very careful. He seemed awkward
and shy and didn't say anything except "I'm pleased to
meet you."

Coley slumped down on the bus stop bench and stretched
out until his feet were resting on the curb. "This is our last
Kool."

Earl had his cap pulled down over his eyes and nose and
was staring through the tiny ventilation holes. "Maybe we
can still get those carpenter helper jobs."

"Naw, that ad's gone." Coley sat up. "Hey, here comes
Cowboy. He's going to kill himself on that wheel yet."

Cowboy came riding down the sidewalk, angling for the
drugstore yard. He slammed his brakes on, leaned the bicycle to one side, and spun around in a three-quarter circle.
The dust flew and he pushed his kickstand down and non-
chalantly began dusting his hat off. "Hey, Earl, Coley.
What you all doing these days?"

Earl said, "Not much, Cowboy."

Coley said, "Got an extra?"

"Sure." He tossed Coley a rolled paper.

Earl tapped Coley on the shoulder. "Hey! Save me a
drag on that cigarette. Damn you, it's all gone."

"I asked you if you wanted to finish it."

"Like hell you did."

Trigger came loping up with his head down and his tongue out. He had been a full block behind Cowboy. Trigger was a long dog with short legs, a hound's face, and small ears. He had a white, spiky terrier's coat, but brown hound spots covered his left side, his right eye, both front legs, and the last three inches of his long tail. The hair behind his ears had thinned and the skin was crusted with red mange. Two weeks of sulphur and axle grease had stopped the mange from spreading, but the smell had gotten so bad that Cowboy's mother had chased him out of the kitchen and forced him to sleep under the house.

Trigger whined and lay down with his nose on Cowboy's foot.

Cowboy frowned and squatted. "What's bothering you, Trig? Let me have a look? Hey you all, give me a hand here." Cowboy pushed Trigger onto his back and held him still. The dog's wagging tail swept the clay dust back and forth, and he looked up at Earl and Coley.

"Hold him, Coley. Goddamn ticks. Look at 'em. No wonder he's so sorry looking."

Coley said, "Easy, boy, easy. God, must be a hundred. Where'd he get them?"

Cowboy nodded across Bee Street. "That damn dog of Lonnie's, that's where. He ain't never washed him. I try to keep him away from Trig, but they keep sneaking off together." He lit a cigarette and smoked it down quickly to a red ash. Coley held Trigger's back legs apart while Earl shouldered his front legs out of the way and patted him. Cowboy drew hard on the cigarette and flicked the gray ash off.

Trigger's tail trembled and curled up tight and thin under him as he watched the cigarette. His ears flattened smoothly. His heavy-lidded eyes became slits and shifted from Cowboy to Earl, from Cowboy to Coley, and back to Cowboy. He seemed to be shrinking and holding his breath.

"Steady now, Trig." Cowboy parted the long fine hair between Trigger's legs and began singeing the brown ticks off. He lined up twenty-one dead ticks on the curb. "That's enough for now. I'll give him a bath tonight and get the rest with kerosene. The cigarette's making him nervous."

Coley let Trigger up and rassled his head. "I'd be nervous too."

Cowboy said, "Thanks, fellows, sure appreciate that."

Earl said, "Don't mention it. You got a couple extra cigarettes? We just ran out."

"Yeah, go on, take four. I'm trying to cut down." Cowboy swung his leg over his bicycle. "Take it easy now. Let's ride, Trig."

Coley spread the classified ads out on the car hood. "Hot damn, here's a new one. Listen at this. 'Wanted. Ice cream machine cleaners until September. Part-time night work. No experience necessary. A dollar-fifty per hour and company benefits.'"

Earl said, "Man, that sounds all right. Let's call them."

On their applications at the Piedmont Dairies they said they were sixteen and had had experience with heavy machinery.

Earl pointed at the big pipes running across the ceiling as the plant superintendent showed them the ice-cream-making equipment and the steam-cleaning procedure. "That's all ammonia cooling, ain't it?"

The superintendent said, "Yeah, how'd you know that?"

"Oh, I worked with my dad on one of them at the Morgan Dairies. We worked on their drain system, too."

"I guess you boys will do fine. Little bit of experience like that comes in handy. But you understand this ain't no long-range deal. Come September we got to let you go. We cut back to one shift when the heat breaks."

Coley said, "O.K. with us, we got to get back to school anyway."

They were given a key to the back door and a locker for their clothes. The shift was from midnight until three in the morning and the job was to take the ice-cream-making machinery apart, steam-clean it, rinse it with boiling water, let it dry on the duckboards, and then reassemble it. They worked stripped to the waist and wore black rubber boots that came to their knees, goggles, and heavy asbestos gloves. When they hosed the machinery down with steam, the temperature in the white-tiled room rose to 120 degrees, but they could cool off inside the freezing room, which stayed at a flat 40 degrees below zero. The superintendent told them that they could eat as much ice cream as they wanted as long as it didn't interfere with their work, and he had shown them where the chocolate syrup, the frozen strawberries, and the canned pecans and black walnuts were stored.

On the second night they sat in the air conditioning of the superintendent's office waiting for the machine parts to dry. Their goggles were shoved back on their heads as if they had just come out of combat, and their black and dripping boots were propped up on the glass-topped desk. In their laps were huge sundaes of soft vanilla ice cream with pecans and strawberries swimming in a flood of Hershey's chocolate syrup.

Earl balanced a final strawberry on top of a huge spoonful and opened his mouth as if he were yawning.

Coley added two more spoons of crushed walnuts and sat back and crossed his boots. "Boy, this is really the life. Damn, Earl. You're going to choke yourself."

It was almost midnight and Coley coasted down the long Hickory Street hill with the engine off, trying to save gas. Earl had his feet up on the dashboard. He was squeezing his rubber exercise balls. "Ninety-eight, ninety-nine, a hundred. Whew! Boy, if we keep this up we're really going to be in shape."

After the four days at the dairy their stomachs looked like honeydew melons. Earl had gained five pounds, Coley had gained four and a half. Coley pulled in behind the ice cream plant. The voltmeter needle was trembling on discharge. The battery was dying and the gas gauge was on one-sixteenth full. He hit the gauge with the heel of his hand to see if it was sticking and gazed out at the twelve delivery trucks lined up before the Texaco pump in the middle of the yard. "Let's try the key on the gas pump."

"It won't work."

"Well, we can try it, can't we?"

Earl jammed the dairy key into the lock. "Not even close."

Coley tried the Hudson keys. "Damn!" He rattled the lock. "I'll bet there's a thousand gallons in that tank."

Earl lifted up the gas tank cap cover on one of the delivery trucks. "Here's the ticket." He unscrewed the cap and flipped it up in the air like a silver dollar.

Coley blew down the gas tank sleeve. "Great! All we need now is some hose. We've got enough money for that."

At the Spruce Street Pharmacy they bought a shower hose without the head for twenty-nine cents.

Coley drove back slowly. The gas gauge was fluttering on empty and the lights were getting dim. "Let's take a little from each one. That way they won't spot it."

"Good idea."

In two nights they had siphoned fifteen gallons from the trucks. The Hudson's gas gauge needle rested solidly on three-quarters full. Coley said, "You know what? I bet we could take two gallons and those tanks would still register full." They were in the manager's office eating ice cream sundaes and smoking Kools.

Earl said, "Sure, 'full' can mean anything. Look at the Hudson, and that's a damn good gas gauge. I'll bet she varies three gallons."

Coley swallowed and sat forward. "Twenty-four gallons a crack. Hell, we can sell what we can't use."

The next night they arrived at the dairy with a ten-gallon service station can and three five-gallon steel buckets. They siphoned two gallons from each of the twelve trucks and loaded the car. The station can could be capped and carried in the trunk, but the three buckets had to be set on the back floor boards. Earl said, "These buckets are stupid."

"Come on, one night won't hurt. We can get some cans at the Army Surplus tomorrow."

"Well, you'd better damn sight drive slow. That stuff's going to be splashing like crazy."

At three-thirty Coley stopped at the foot of the Dogwood Street hill. "You ready?"

Earl was sitting in the back with the buckets. He had brought along some wood chips and he began shimming the buckets up so the gas wouldn't slop out. "O.K., but take it easy."

Coley kept the car in low and began crawling up the

long, steep hill. The headlights were dim and the green dashboard light was sinking. He touched the clutch and gunned the engine.

"Damn, Coley! Cut it out! Don't jerk!"

"The lights are going!"

"Cut them off! Hell, it's all over my hands and everything. Rat's ass!"

Coley climbed the hill with the lights off. When they leveled off at Lee Street he took the car out of gear and raced the engine, hoping the battery would pick up enough charge to get them home. Earl had pulled the wood chips out. The buckets were riding flat. Gasoline was on his shoes and hands and it covered the floor boards. He was drying his hands on the bottom of his T shirt. "Come on, Coley! What in the hell you stopping for?"

"Shut up a minute, will you?" Coley raced the engine until the windows rattled. "I'm trying to get some juice up."

"You don't need lights! Let's get going!"

Suddenly a motorcycle engine popped loudly and a low growling siren turned over once. A flashlight came on and the beam skimmed over the car, stopping directly in Coley's face. The patrolman began laughing. Coley tried staring through the three-cell flashlight beam. "That you, Roy?"

Roy laughed again and flicked the light off. "What you doing creeping up that hill with no lights?"

"Aw, we need a new battery." Coley kept the engine running, and twisting around he put both elbows in the window, hoping Roy wouldn't look in the back.

Roy said, "I figured that when I saw you gunning her. That's going to cost you a pretty penny."

He shined the light on Earl's face. "That you, Edge?"

Earl grinned. "Yessir." He didn't know whether to sit forward so Roy couldn't see the buckets or sit back so he wouldn't smell the gasoline on him.

Roy stepped to the back door. His light moved across the line of buckets. "Jesus, you all carrying moon?"

Coley said, "Hell, no. We ain't got no moon. Them's minnows, redbreast bait."

"No lie. Where'd you get them?"

"Hall's Creek, out back of the Drive-In."

Roy counted the buckets with his flashlight beam. "How come so many buckets?"

Coley said, "We want them fresh, Roy. Humphries won't buy 'em dead. He'll sell 'em dead but he won't buy 'em."

Roy was satisfied. He turned his light off and leaned on the window frame. "How's your maw?"

"She's fine, everybody's fine."

"That's good. Listen, how about if you put in a good word for me with Helen. Tell her I caught you speeding and I didn't arrest you, O.K.? You know, make it sound like you should have been arrested and all, and what a lucky break it was that I came by."

"All right."

"You be sure and tell me what you tell her, though, so I can back your story up. She's sharp as a razor. If she catches me in a lie, I'm done." Roy laughed and lit a cigarette.

Earl's heart rose; it seemed to fill his whole body. He closed his eyes and braced for the explosion.

Roy continued, "Yeah, we'll have us a little fun with her. Tell her I caught you right here on this hill. That way, it'll be easy to remember." He paused. "I guess you heard about me getting rid of this Harley-Davidson. This is my last month on her. Pretty soon, now, I'll be pushing a new Ford around."

Earl's eyes were fixed on the glowing cigarette. If it dropped or sparked, everything would blow.

"You know a lot of the boys down at the station prefer a motorcycle to a car. Funny, ain't it, how one fellow will swear by a motorcycle, and then the next one will swear by a car. I'll take a car any time. You go splashing through the sleet and all in about February and that's what I call cold duty."

He stopped talking and, with the cigarette still glowing in his mouth, shined the light back on the buckets. "They shore are quiet."

Coley said, "Water's getting stale. Guess they're beginning to get tired."

Roy let the light come up Earl's body, stopping on his face. "You still on probation?"

" 'Fraid so."

"Well, you stick with old Coley here, he'll keep you out of trouble." He frogged him on the arm. "Ain't that right, boy?"

"That's right, Roy."

Roy swept his light down the porches on the block. "I got to be checking in." He started to leave but stopped. "I smell gas."

He turned his light off so he could smell better. "Great God, what's that gas smell? This car's leaking."

Coley moaned, "It's the carburetor petcock. The damn spring won't hold."

Roy paused. He seemed to be staring at the buckets. Earl wanted to fan the fumes away, but he couldn't think of any way except blowing. Roy was shaking his head, and Earl was sure he had figured that it was gasoline and was wondering how he could arrest them and still keep on the good side of Helen.

"Boys"—Roy took a long, deep, red-hot pull on his cigarette—"you take my advice. You get rid of this car. You get yourselves a little six-cylinder job. Get a Ford, or a Chevvy. Hell, better still, you go get yourselves a little Willys. Now there's a car for you. Tell me something: how much you get on a gallon of gas?"

Coley didn't want to encourage him. "Fifteen, maybe twenty miles."

"Well, with a Willys you'll get thirty. Maybe more out on the open road." He lit another cigarette, and leaning in over Coley he took a look at the buckets with the burning match.

Earl tightened up and pushed back so hard on the seat he heard the cushion springs groan. He closed his eyes again. He wanted to hold his hands over his face. The funny book character, the Human Torch, leaped before him, and he saw himself suddenly burning like 117 pounds of cotton soaked in turpentine and shooting up through the steel roof into the night, only to arch shortly and drop brightly into the gutter, where the flames would reveal the last of his features and he would gasp and moan near the sewage drain; and after looking at the ruined Hudson and calling Roy Jarvis a dumb lousy bastard for lighting a match, he would sputter and die with his head pointed toward the lights of Wilson Peeler's Casablanca and his feet toward the University of South Carolina.

Roy discussed the carburetor on the Willys. He discussed the front end on the Willys, the short wheelbase on the Willys, and the over-all economy of the Willys. He compared the Willys to the Hudson, the Willys to the Ford, and the Willys to any car they could name. They didn't name any.

Finally, after another cigarette, another burning match, and another long look at the minnows to make sure they were all right, Roy said, "Well, I guess you want to get this stuff over to Humphries. Tell him I might go up to the lake this Sunday. If I do I'll be coming by for some shiners. And listen, you think about that Willys, you hear? Hey, and keep them lights on."

Coley said, "O.K., Roy. See you around."

"So long, Roy." Earl sat back exhausted.

Roy turned on his siren, made a hard foot-dragging turn, and went wailing back down the dark hill toward Haygood Street.

Coley drove slowly. He kept the lights on, having decided that it would be better to ruin the battery than be stopped again. He was soaking wet and too weary to talk. When he cut the engine in Earl's yard, he leaned on the wheel and let out a long, low sigh.

Earl said, "I think I ate too much ice cream. I don't feel too good."

"Me neither. What a night."

Because of their late hours at the dairy, they never met anyone except the superintendent who hired them and the secretary who paid them on Saturdays. All of their instructions and suggestions were posted on the bulletin board. On Friday night, under the heading "Night Cleaners," they found two messages: "Use more steam in corners of vats" and "Hang up clothes and hoses."

That night they took twenty-four gallons of gas and

stored it in a fifty-five-gallon Coca-Cola barrel under Earl's house. On Saturday they added twenty-four more gallons.

The following Monday the bulletin board under "Night Cleaners" was empty, but in the ice-cream-making room there was a note for them fastened with a rubber band to the steam hose nozzle. It was typed in capitals on a stiff three-by-five index card: "ATTENTTION MACHINE CLEANERS: QUIT MESSING WITH TRUCK GAS OR IT IS YOUR ASS. (Signed C. Jaffrey truck foreman.)" Attention had four "t's" in it.

Chapter 20

Jack Driscoll's telephone rang at six-thirty. It was Sophie. She was crying. "I'm sorry, Jack, but it's Wilson. His feet are worse. The doctor's here now and he had to give him a shot for the pain."

Jack rubbed his eyes and raised up on his elbow. "I thought they were getting better."

"So did he. Oh, Jack, he can hardly move around. His toes look like sausages and he can't even get his socks on. What are we going to do?"

"You stay with him. I'll go open up."

"But you can't handle the front and the kitchen."

"Don't worry about it, now. You just stay there. I'll call you later."

Jack dressed quickly, tightened his belt, and pushed his hair back. Maybe Wilson would be in bed or on crutches and he could take over as manager. Ever since his first week he had known that he'd never get up enough money for a poker stake on his salary. He'd thought of quitting and making money some other way, of even moving on and forgetting Mason Richards. But maybe this was the big break he had been waiting for. Wilson would have to give him a raise or a partnership or something.

At the Casablanca Jack took the orders, cooked them, and served them. During the breakfast rush he put twenty dollars in bills and coins in a cigar box on the counter near the register and as he served he quickly told the customers about Wilson and asked them to make their own change.

At ten-thirty, he had time to call Sophie. "How's Wilson doing?"

"He seems a little better. The shot eased the pain but his feet are still as red as fire. How'd you make out?"

Jack said, "Pretty good, but I'm going to need some help getting ready for lunch."

"All right, I'll leave in a few minutes. Lonnie's come over. He says he can stay with Wilson."

Sophie went into the bedroom. Wilson was in a pair of bright orange pajamas with the pants rolled up above his knees. He was sitting straight up in a ladderback chair with his feet in a pan of green liquid. Lonnie sat opposite him on a hassock, eating boiled peanuts out of a paper bag. The bag was wet and he was holding it on the bottom.

Sophie was wearing a black hair net over clip-pin curlers. "Boys, I'm going in and help out on the lunch crowd. Is there anything you want? Honey, let me put a pillow in behind you."

"I don't want no pillow! And listen, you stay on that counter until I call you. I don't want Jack alone like this any more."

"But Wilson."

"No buts. You do like I say."

Lonnie said, "I'll take care of him, Soph. Don't worry so."

She brushed her hair out quickly and checked her purse. "Well, you sure I can't get you something? Let me put those peanuts in a bowl for you."

Lonnie said, "Naw, this is O.K. You go on now. Everything's under control here."

Sophie kissed Wilson on the forehead and left.

Lonnie said, "You want the radio on? How 'bout the paper?"

"No, I don't want anything."

"Here, try a couple of these." He offered his boiled peanuts, but Wilson shook his head and stared down at his pulsing feet. He was frantic at the idea of Jack having to run the Casablanca by himself and he kept trying to figure out how he had managed during the breakfast rush; frying and watching the eggs would be the problem. The soreness in his feet had let up, but he knew that if he walked across the room the pain would come charging back. What was going to happen to him? What would happen to the Casablanca?

The doctor's warning thundered in his ears and he felt depressed and helpless. "I'm worried, Lon."

"I know you are, good buddy." Lonnie put his peanuts down on the coffee table. "But take me, for example. Smell my breath, Wilson. Smell it." He crouched over him and exhaled. "Like a baby's, ain't it?"

"I guess so."

"Two weeks ago it was like sticking your head under a buzzard's wing. I ain't lying. But not any more. No sirree, Bob. And look at those hands." He held them out. "Steady as stones. And that ain't no medical doctor's work, no sir. That's prayer and faith and Sonny Love."

Wilson slammed his hands on the armrest and shouted,

AUGUST

"Will you shut up a damn minute! You done told me about that Jesus shouter before, and I'm up to my craw with him."

Lonnie cleared his throat. "But Wilson, all I'm trying to do is get you to take a look on the bright side. This is a brand new chance for you. Lord, there's all kinds of things you can be doing besides working twenty hours a day in that café. It's the same thing I went through, the identical same thing." Lonnie inched his hassock closer. "From the day I got shed of the Hudson, from the day I handed over those registration papers, I been feeling better about everything. Here I am fifty years of age and I'm just getting started knowing my own wife. I tell you, it makes you stop and think. I swear it does. She's a talker, all right, but you stop and analyze it for yourself, and you see where she's been talking for twenty-five years and I wasn't hearing a word she was saying. She was just trying to get through to me, that's all. Bless her old heart."

Wilson frowned. "Come on, Lonnie, I told you I ain't studying no faith healing. Now just lay off."

Sophie had just finished wiping down the back bar and was starting to fill up the cigarette racks when Jack came out of the kitchen. It was almost eleven o'clock and he had been working for fifteen hours. Sophie said, "You must be worn out."

A customer was drinking a bottle of Atlantic ale and leaning on the jukebox listening to Roy Acuff sing "The Wabash Cannonball."

Jack poured himself a cup of coffee. "I'm all right. How you doing?"

"Worried. I'm worried sick about Wilson. I just don't know what I'm going to do with him. I been after him for

251

years to have those feet looked at, but he's so mule-headed I couldn't make a dent."

"It's a damn shame he didn't listen to you."

Sophie's heavy eyebrows seemed to hold her face in a tired weary frown. "He had to do everything, everything. He wouldn't stay in the kitchen and he wouldn't stay in behind the counter. You know, I had a feeling something like this was going to happen." She put the fresh cigarettes on the bottom of the rack and the old ones on top. Her voice was lower now. "I just thank my stars you came along. I don't know what we'd have done if it hadn't been for you."

Jack opened a packaged slice of raisin cake, carefully catching the crumbs in the cellophane wrapper. "You keep going from the duckboards to the tile and it will get you. It's got to." He bit into the cake. "You know I had me a buddy in the Army had himself the same trouble. Only he was worse off. Got so he couldn't walk on anything but the ducks. Got real bad, had to keep changing socks all day; five and six times, and I mean white socks, white cotton socks, no colors and no wools. He had him those little pads with holes in them at his heels and under his toes and some kind of little special thing under the balls of his feet. Special shoes, special socks, special powders, I don't know what all he didn't have that wasn't special, and I mean none of it did him a lick of good. I tell you when a cook's feet goes, he goes with them."

Jack stared at the sugar in the bottom of his cup, wondering why he had told this lie. He himself had had athlete's foot in the Army and had used powders and white socks, but there had never been a buddy with bad feet.

He shook his head and tried to think about Wilson.

"Maybe we could sit him up here on a stool behind the register. He wouldn't be walking then. He could keep a pan of one of those foot baths right under the counter."

Sophie said, "No use even thinking about that. If Wilson Peeler couldn't be out there to see the food fixed up and wasn't able to look in the booths and ask about it, he would go slap out of his mind."

"But he could ask them if they liked it at the register. He could do that. He does that anyway."

"No, it wouldn't be the same." She crumbled the Philip Morris cartons into the trash basket. "Wilson's got to see it. He's got to see people eating it. It makes him feel good."

At four-thirty the next day Wilson came limping in. He was wearing a new pair of white tennis shoes with razor slashes at the sides. He said hello to Sophie and nodded for Jack to join him in the kitchen. He looked slower and older as he pushed himself up on the sandwich board counter. "How'd it go today?"

"Pretty good. We managed all right."

Wilson looked around the kitchen. "You got a cigarette?" Jack gave him a Camel and lit it. He nodded at the white shoes.

"How those easy walkers feel?"

"I guess they're all right." Wilson took a deep drag on his cigarette. "Well, boy, I got two doctors' opinions today and they're both the same. They want me off my feet." He exhaled the smoke at his feet and touched his toes together. The bright steel eyelets of the new tennis shoes glistened in the fluorescent lighting. "Four hours, four hours a day, that's all I can put in. Any more than that and I'm winding up flat on my back."

Jack said, "Aw, you'll get better. Give it a couple weeks.

Doctors like to scare you like that. I had these bad tonsils one time."

Wilson interrupted. "No, boy, I'll never cut another sixteen-hour day and I might as well be facing it. They ain't talking about no few weeks either. They mean from here on out." He nodded at the storage bin. "Hand me that roaster pan. I got to break you in on making up my barbecue sauce."

Jack's fingers tingled as he pulled the pan down. A panic flooded over him; no one, not even Sophie, knew the barbecue sauce recipe. He knew he was set. Why wait? Why not ask Wilson for some money as a loan? As Wilson opened the vinegar bottle and arranged the condiments on the sandwich board, Jack tried to frame what he should say. He knew he had to ask right away. In another day Wilson might be too sick to talk, or Sophie or the doctors might be around, or he might even get well and just forget about everything.

Wilson's face was composed, resigned, almost serene. "First we take our vinegar and our mayonnaise and our mustard and we . . ."

Jack watched closely, memorizing the ingredients, the amounts, and the blending as if he were counting cards and figuring odds in a poker game. With three or four hundred dollars he could sit down opposite Mason and be comfortable. Maybe five would be better. He could bluff better with five and Mason wouldn't be able to raise him out of the game.

Wilson tasted the sauce and smacked his lips. "Perfect. Think you can do it?"

"Maybe. I'd better see you do it again, though. It gets pretty tricky right there at the end."

Wilson slid the pan into the icebox. "O.K. We'll make up a batch tomorrow, and then we're going to have to sit down and discuss something more permanent for you around here."

Jack said, "I don't know, sir. I wish you wouldn't be counting on me so. There's something I have to tend to back home."

Wilson winced. "Lord, I hope it ain't nothing that can't wait. I can't afford to go losing you now."

"Well, it's . . ." Jack pretended he was embarrassed.

"Come on, boy, tell me about it."

Jack blurted, "Well, sir, the truth is my old man's in the hospital in Newark and he let his insurance lapse and he's broke and I promised I'd go up there and sort of help out."

"If I gave you a couple hundred, could you wire it to him?"

"No sir, I'm afraid not. It's more like five hundred."

Wilson slapped his wallet on the sandwich board. "Well, hell, here's five hundred dollars right now. Shape I'm in if you pulled out for Newark I'd be up the old creek."

The breakfast rush was over and Wilson had left for the doctor's office. Sophie was behind the cash register painting her fingernails with a bright orange polish she had bought at a sale at Woolworth's and going over her marketing list. Jack sat down at the counter. "How about a hand of Gin?"

Sophie pushed the cards out and looked at their Gin Rummy scores. "Let's see, I owe you twenty-eight—thirty-two—thirty-seven cents." She fanned her fingers through the air. "You deal. I'm not dry yet."

Jack shuffled the cards over and over again. His fingers felt thin and fast. He cut the deck with one hand and in the same rolling motion slipped off a bottom card. Each time through the deck he stacked a card until he had twenty lined up the way he wanted them. "Wilson looked better today."

"Didn't he, though. It must be those treatments." Sophie blew on her fingernails. "He's sleeping like a stone."

Jack dealt. Sophie slid her cards to the edge of the counter to avoid using her fingernails. With each card she picked up he watched the pupils of her eyes. He remembered Dillard Moses telling him, "Look at the eyes, son. That's the secret. You got to forget the hands and fingers and nervous tics. Lot of these fancy boys will set you up with something like that, then suck you into a big pot and cross you like a snake. Watch the pupils. They're just like a woman. When things are bad they close up and get hard. When they're good they open up and get soft."

Sophie's large brown eyes said "Gin" before she did.

"Gin! Gin, Lord, Gin on my first ten cards! That's the first time I've ever done that!"

Jack raked the cards in as she marked the score down. He was pleased with his touch and his reading. "Boy, that's really one for the books."

At the St. Louis Cafe a five-piece band finished a fast introduction to "Night and Day" and the saxophone-playing leader began singing in a high bouncy voice. Jack leaned on the bar, drinking a draft beer and chewing on a pig's foot and looking the room over. The bandstand, the band, and the blue neon tubing scalloped around the walls were new, but everything else seemed the same. The Fire Department sign near the door announced that the room capacity was

460, and through the swinging kitchen doors he counted three cooks.

He finished his beer and pushed the glass back for a refill. "Is Mason in?"

The bartender slipped a paper coaster under a fresh beer. "Sure, he's around. Probably in the back."

The song ended and a few people applauded.

"They got a game going tonight?"

The bartender smiled. "Does a goat stink?"

Jack laughed and tipped him a dollar. "I got a better question. Is it open?"

"Thanks." He tucked the bill into his shirt pocket. "Wide open, if you can stand the freight. Go on back."

Jack knocked once on the back room door and entered. Five men were playing stud poker; Mason Richards was dealing. Mason started when he saw him but he smiled quickly. He had small squinting eyes that Jack knew would be impossible to read and a thin lip mustache that didn't break in the middle. The deep shadows above and below his eyes made him look as if he were wearing a mask, and when he smiled, his teeth that were bunched forward gave him a raccoonlike look. "Well, if it isn't Corporal Driscoll. Or was it sergeant? Driscoll, Driscoll—" He snapped his fingers. "Jack Driscoll, right?"

"Right. It was corporal."

Mason tapped his green visor. "How's that for a memory?" He introduced Jack around the table.

Holly Yates and Mason's lawyer, Bevo McNally, were on each side of Mason. Ed Hornsby, the big bootlegger from Spartanburg, was next to Holly and next to him was Johnny Castros, the owner of the Dixie Bee Cafe. Mason slid a captain's chair that had been painted green and spongespackled with gold in between himself and Bevo. "Give him some chips. A little fresh meat might pick this game up."

Jack took six fifty-dollar bills out of his wallet, creased them together, and tossed them to the middle of the table. Bevo was banker. He pushed out two stacks of ten-dollar red chips and one small stack of fifty-dollar blues. He had big hands that Jack figured would span more than seven half dollars. On his wrists he wore black leather wristbands and his fingernails were lacquered with a clear polish.

Mason's table was six-sided and standard with spills and troughs for chips and bills and bottle holes for beer. The thick pool-table green covering kept the light from bouncing. Beyond the bright two-hundred-watt cone from the green fan shade, the room was dark and silent. Mason said, "You from New York, that right?"

"Newark."

"Now I remember." Mason won a two-hundred-dollar pot and the deal went to Johnny.

Jack said, "What's the ante?"

"Ten dollars, only ten. Pot limit." Johnny dealt quickly, each card falling exactly where he wanted.

Jack caught a pair of treys on his third card and folded. On the next hand he checked kings and sevens to Bevo and lost forty dollars. Bevo had three tens.

Jack played two hands of no-stay and then he got the deal. He squeezed the deck tight, blocked it, and rubbed his finger down the edge. The cards were hot. They were fifty-dollar Bee Brand strippers from a mail order house in Chicago that sold exclusively to magicians. Each high card had its own dimension. The aces were the slimmest, the kings next, and down the deck to the nines. The rest of the pack was standard. Jack sighed and smiled behind his teeth. He was playing with amateurs.

For an hour Jack played cozy and took no chances. He soon saw that Bevo could read the cards as well as Mason. By the time he had dealt four times he knew the deck. He could, by shuffling and working the high cards into his left hand and the lows into his right, stack the deck and control the table.

Jack dealt and called the cards. "Down and dirty." Six cards slid into place.

The second card was up. "A five. . . .

"A little three. . . .

"A queen. . . .

"And a jack. . . .

"Another three. . . .

"And a jack for the dealer.

"Queen bets."

Ed Hornsby said, "Only twenty." Ed played in his undershirt. He was heavy and hairy. On his right forearm was a tattooed eagle clutching an American flag. On his left bicep in red and blue was the simple inscription: *Death Before Dishonor.*

Holly flipped in two reds and took a sip from his beer.

Mason said, "O.K. with me."

Jack picked up four red chips. He had jacks back to back. "Twenty to me and I'm going to sweeten it twenty more."

Mason laughed. "This meat's got a little juice in him."

Bevo said, "I'm in."

Johnny sucked on his pipe and folded.

Ed stayed in for one more card.

Holly played quietly. He paid for two more cards and then dropped out when Mason bumped the pot fifty dollars with threes and sevens showing.

Jack had wired his two jacks with a third and had two nines. The pairs of jacks and nines showing scared Bevo out, leaving only Mason. Jack knew he had him and checked. The suck worked and Mason pushed six one-hundred-dollar white chips forward, hoping to drive Jack out. Jack was ready. He slid his whole stack of chips to the center of the table and began counting.

Mason turned his cards down. "Take it."

Jack dragged the nineteen-hundred-dollar pot.

By two o'clock Jack had $2,500. Ed Hornsby and Holly Yates were the big losers. Holly began complaining. Jack watched his game, wondering if he would know a hot deck if he saw one. He telegraphed his good hands by spinning his ruby-stoned ring on his little finger, and the pupils of his eyes swelled up and softened when his cards were running together. When the last card locked to a flush or three of a kind, he looked like a man in love. He played frantically, plunging in to buy a pot with a five-hundred-dollar last bet, and then folding the next hand and sitting back looking insulted and as if the ten-dollar ante had been stolen from him.

The game circled, with Mason and Bevo winning steadily. Jack let Bevo suck him into a trap once, and he invested another three hundred dollars in a heart flush of Mason's. His stack of chips went up to twenty-four hundred dollars, down to nine hundred, and then slowly up to fifteen hundred. He was waiting for the deal. When the deal came around to him he asked for a new deck. He cut the federal tax stamp with his fingernail and skinned the cellophane from the package. He tossed the double jokers behind him on the floor and began riffling the new deck in a fast butterfly motion. They were the same mail order strippers, and as he laced the high and low cards together they felt like old friends. He dealt himself aces back to back, and fed Mason a pair of nines.

Everyone stayed in for the fourth card. Mason had a nine and two eights showing and a nine in the hole. Jack had his ace in the hole buried under two tens and another ace. There was an ace and another ten showing. Jack bet fifty dollars on the last card. Bevo, Johnny, Ed, and Holly dumped their hands in the middle and the bet went to Mason. He saw it and raised it five hundred more. Jack slowly counted out five one-hundred-dollar white chips and stacked them up. He knew the first card in the deck was a nine, Mason's nine. The next card was a king and the third his ace. He would have to deal seconds. With his left hand he pushed forward the fire white chips. In the same motion he flipped Mason his nine and skinned back the king. Passing his right thumb over the deck, he made a clean strip on the ace of clubs and dropped it down. He had aces and tens showing. He checked to Mason.

Mason pushed forward ten one hundred-dollar white chips to drive him out. "It's going to cost you a big one to see it."

Jack counted out ten white chips and then his last ten blues. "And I'm bumping you five hundred." He had two hundred dollars left in his wallet and he laid it on the table, hoping Mason would think he had more.

Mason drummed his fingers on the table. His eyes moved from Jack's cards to his wallet to his eyes. "I got to play my hunch." He pushed a five-hundred-dollar stack to the middle. "I'm calling your five." He slid another stack out. "And five more back at you."

Jack's heart dropped. He counted out his four fifty-dollar bills. "I'm light three hundred. I'll have to sign for it."

"Not in my game, you don't." Mason reached for the pot. "Next time don't try playing poker with Coca-Cola caps. You need money around here, man."

"Hold it! Hold it! How about Wilson Peeler's word? That ought to be good enough. I work for him, he'll back me up. Call him up, he's home right now."

Holly said, "You the new cook he's been talking about?"

"Right."

"Well, hell, I hate seeing you suck wind with a hand like that." Holly pushed three white chips forward. "Give me a note." Jack signed the beer pad and tore the page out.

Mason looked drawn; his eyes were darker. "O.K., boys, read 'em and weep. Full house, nines high."

Jack touched his ace of clubs to the edge of his hole ace. He flipped over the ace of hearts. "Not good enough, Mason. Bullets and tens." He dragged in the $4,400 pot and pushed Holly his three white chips. "Thanks on that. I won't forget it."

"Don't mention it." Holly tore the note in half. "Tough luck there, Mason."

Mason pushed his seat back. "Well, you can't win them all. Deal me out this time, I got to go to the head."

At four o'clock the game ended. Jack had won $5,060. After Bevo changed the chips to bills he crammed the big roll into his front pocket. "Not a bad night's work."

Mason smiled. "We'll get you next time, Hot Shot. Be sure and bring it all back."

Holly yawned. "I'm heading in. You fellows keep loose now. Nice meeting you, Jack. Hope you can cook like you play poker."

"Take care, Holly. Thanks again." Jack stretched his arms and legs out in a long straight line and arched his back as if he were laying out a half gainer. His shoulders and the back of his neck were tired and stiff from the tension. His eyes stung. "You still get cabs out here?"

Mason turned the poker light off. "Yeah, they park out front. Come up to the bar, I'll buy you a beer."

"No, thanks, I'll take a rain check. I want to get some sleep."

"O.K., Driscoll. See you around."

Jack headed across the parking lot toward a waiting cab, whacking the roll of money in his pocket with his palm and then the back of his hand. He smiled, thinking how he had fed Mason's own strippers back to him and what a great story it would make at Oscar's. His best move had been dealing the third ace; that had taken the nerve. He had dealt it fast and clean with no slipped card sound, and he knew he could do it again and again and again.

He stopped. Someone was following him. He looked back. He listened, but no sound came except the wind and the faint creaking of a metal Tube Rose Snuff sign rocking back and forth. Crossing the road quickly, he opened the cab door. Footsteps rushed toward him; he whirled around. Three men were on him at once. The biggest one grabbed him in a bear hug. The others pounded him in the face and stomach. He felt the air rush from his lungs and heard the dull watery sound of his ribs cracking.

The hot pain in his chest relaxed and he began drifting down. He could see through a small white opening. One man was shaking and slapping his face; another was talking. "Mason wants you out of town! You hear that? Tonight! You hear that?"

Jack wanted to say he'd go if they would turn him loose, but there was no air to speak with. The white opening was closing.

Jack lay at the side of the railroad tracks for an hour before he regained consciousness. He twisted his hips, hoping he would feel the bulk of the $5,060, but it was gone. There was no feeling in his chest, and when he swallowed the pain made him gasp. He began worrying if his heart had been damaged or his lungs punctured. He tried to imagine what the newspapers would have said if he had been found dead. The only lines he could think of were: "Jack Driscoll, about 30, formerly of Newark, New Jersey, found mysteriously dead on the Atlantic Coast Line tracks. Mr. Driscoll's survivors are unknown. Funeral arrangements at this date are unarranged." He lay still, looking at the green railroad signal lights, hoping to draw some comfort from the fact that he was still alive. None came. Two blocks away at the station depot he saw the blue light of the cabstand. He stood up and, leaning on a fire plug to catch his breath, he decided he could make it.

Dan Jackson was sitting in his Chrysler at the side of the station. He had just come back from a $2.50 trip to the Bearcat Drive-In out on the Bluff Road. His night's earnings came to $14.25 and he was trying to decide whether he should buy new vinyl seat covers from Gus or four new Cadillac hubcaps. It was the kind of decision he enjoyed making, and he began humming along with a blue-grass song on the radio from WLW in Cincinnati.

At first Dan thought the man propped up against the telephone pole was Lonnie, but then he saw that he was too tall and that he was wearing a suit. After spotting him with his twin searchlights, he helped him across the road and led him to the Chrysler. He thought about his upholstery and checked to see if the man was bleeding. "If I put you in my car you won't go getting sick on me, will you?"

"No, I'll keep my head out the window." Jack saw the sign on the back window. "You Earl and Coley's friend?"

"Yeah, we're pretty close buddies." Dan eased Jack into the front seat. "I'll run you out to the hospital."

"No, I don't want to go there." Mason's warning was spinning in Jack's head and when he breathed deeply through his mouth, trying to keep from getting sick, his ribs pounded. He had to get someplace where he could think. "Listen, I've been cleaned out. How about dropping me off where the kids live?"

"Mister, I ain't looking for no fare, but you got to go to the hospital. You look terrible."

"No, you do like I tell you. I'll be O.K."

Dan pulled up behind the Hudson parked in front of Earl's house. "There's their old piece of Hudson. You sure you going to make it now?"

"I'm O.K. Thanks for the lift."

"That's all right, glad to do it."

Jack leaned on the Hudson. He felt better just touching something familiar. The back door was locked. Slowly he circled the car, trying the others. They were all locked. He was feeling weaker and he decided to rest. Flattening himself down carefully, he slid under the low running board.

He moved away from the front wheels and lay under the drive shaft. He had to turn his face to one side to keep his nose from touching the bottom of the oil pan. As he lay still trying to breathe lightly to ease the pain, a faint dripping touched him and he realized he was getting wet. He was almost asleep. Reaching up he touched oil. The universal joint and the gasket around the transmission were leaking. He shifted to one side, and as he drifted off he wondered how many quarts of oil the Hudson was using and if it needed a ring job. Maybe it even needed a new transmission.

Chapter 21

At six-fifteen Cowboy knocked on the Edges' front door. It was Friday, and he wore his brown ten-gallon hat and boots and a dark blue cowboy suit. Trigger had followed him over his route and lay on the bottom step, snapping at flies and trying to catch his breath. Leroy came yawning and muttering to the screen door. He was in his shorts. "What in the hell you want?"

"Morning, Mr. Edge."

Leroy unlatched the door and leaned on the jamb. He pushed his hair back and squinted. "I asked you what you wanted."

Cowboy looked over Leroy's shoulder. "Ain't Earl up yet?"

"Hell, no, he ain't. And I'm not either."

Cowboy creased the front of his tall hat and stuck his jaw out. "There's a fellow out there under Earl and Coley's Hudson."

Leroy squatted down. "No lie?" He tried to see under the car, but the bottom part of the Hudson was hidden by the tall weeds.

Cowboy said, "No sir. I looked at him. He's sleeping."

"Probably some drunk. He'll roll out when the sun gets at him. Didn't Trigger see him?"

Trigger lay with his front paws crossed and his back legs splayed out like a half chicken.

"No sir, Trig's been having trouble with his nose lately. It's been dry as a gourd. He's been having a bad year."

Leroy yawned and looked at the clear sky. He took a long breath of cool air as if it would be the last he would get for the rest of the day. "Trigger ain't the only one."

Earl came to the screen door with his overall pants and tennis shoes on. "What's going on?"

Leroy nodded at Cowboy and went back to bed.

Earl got down on his hands and knees and looked under the Hudson. "God Almighty, it's Jack. It's Jack Driscoll."

Trigger began whining.

"Keep him quiet, Cowboy. Dad will raise hell if he starts barking."

"Hush up, Trigger." Trigger growled low and began wagging his tail.

Earl crawled under the car. "Wake up, Jack! Wake up! It's me, Earl."

Jack opened his eyes. "I'm hurt, boy, hurt bad. Come on, help me out." Earl and Cowboy pulled and slid him from under the car. Trigger tried to lick his face.

Earl said, "Jesus, how'd you get so greasy?"

"Your transmission's leaking. Get me in that back seat."

"Listen, Jack, we can take you inside the house. I'll get the Doc."

"No, I don't want no doctor. I'll feel better in the car."

Earl unlocked the door and they helped Jack in. He lay

down carefully. "That's better. Much better. Is your friend safe?"

Earl nodded. "This is Cowboy Strickland. Don't worry about him. Cowboy, Jack Driscoll."

Cowboy leaned over the front seat and shook Jack's hand.

Earl said, "Ain't you running late, Cowboy?"

Cowboy checked his Roy Rogers watch and whistled. "I got to be going." He snapped his fingers for Trigger, who was lying in the shade alongside the car. "Come on, boy. We're ridin'." He tested his right fist in his left palm and frowned. "If you need any help come round to the back of the house. I'll be home in another hour. Try not to wake up Ma." He rose up on his left pedal and started up the hill. Trigger tried walking fast, but when he couldn't keep up he began trotting.

Earl said, "What happened?"

"I'll tell you about it later. Take me someplace where I can lay down. I got to do some thinking."

"O.K., let me get a shirt."

Earl stopped at the refrigerator and loaded his pockets with hard-boiled eggs and oranges. He poured some salt into a piece of waxed paper, folded it, put it into his back pocket, and returned to Jack. "Here, suck one of these. It'll make you feel better."

The battery was almost dead. He let the car roll down the hill in second gear with the clutch out until it was moving fast enough to start. The engine fired and caught and they headed for Coley's.

Jack tossed the dry orange into the street. "Christ, kid, that gear box sounds like it's going to fall out."

Coley hung over the front seat facing Jack, as Earl headed for the Little Eddy. "Man, they really worked you over! You got a lump up aside your head as big as a golf ball. How 'bout your teeth, you lose any?"

"No, they stayed in."

Earl slowed down as they crossed the gullies on Stewart Street to keep from bouncing Jack. Jack told them about the $5,060 and how Mason's men had told him to get out of town. "Those boys play rough."

Coley said, "You ain't going to be leaving, are you?"

"Hell, no! I'm staying out of sight till I shape up. Then I'm going back and fix that bastard's butt right. Listen, get me to a phone. I gotta tell Wilson something."

Earl eased into the Spur gas station on Monroe Street. Jack called Wilson at home. In a straight grave voice he told him his father was dying and that he was going to have to go to Newark after all. Wilson asked him if he needed any more money, but Jack couldn't figure any way of getting it. He was in too much pain to walk into the Casablanca, and if he sent Earl or Coley in it would look suspicious.

At the Little Eddy, Earl and Coley pulled the back seat out on the ground for Jack to lie on and headed back to town for supplies. They bought a sleeping bag from a pawnshop on Franklin Street and then with Jack's key they went to his rooming house on Lee Street and picked up his toothbrush and shaving set, four decks of cards, and some more clothes. They drove to Holly's, bought two hamburgers, a milk shake, and two packs of Camels, and started back to the river.

"Listen, Jack." Earl was unwrapping a hamburger for him. "How about if I bring the Doc out? He can fix you up in no time. I know he can."

Jack was too long for the seat, and he lay on his back with his feet on the ground and his knees up in the air. "What am I going to be paying any doctor with? Boy, I ain't got a dime to my name. They cleaned me out." He ate the hamburgers slowly and swallowed carefully, trying to keep his chest from hurting.

Ten feet away the river current sighed against the red clay bank. An orange crate floated downstream, and in the middle of the river a crow sat on a rock watching them.

Coley squatted down. "Jack, you could pay the Doc later. He wouldn't mind. And he wouldn't be charging too much. He's really a pharmacist."

Earl said, "He'd keep his mouth shut too."

Later that night, by the light of the headlights, Doc taped Jack's ribs. Coley sat in the car gunning the engine so they could use the generator and save the battery. The accelerator pedal kept sticking and he kept reaching down to free it. Earl stood at the edge of the bright lights, shooing the flying ants away.

Doc spat out, "Goddammit. Keep them off me. Keep them off or I'm going to stop."

Earl moved in close and fanned his comic book faster and faster, scattering the green ants. Jack was standing up and holding onto the car hood while Doc slowly wound the wide tape around his chest.

"Scissors, Earl. Come on boy, move." He cut through the tape. "O.K., take 'em now." Doc finished up. "Well, that's it. That's it, and it's a pretty damn good job what with the conditions and all." He raised his voice. "O.K., Coley, turn your lights off. That's what's drawing these ants."

Coley cut the lights but left the engine racing. Jack said,

"How soon can I get back to work?"

"Depends on what you do."

"Grill cook."

"Well, let's say four or five days. But you're going to have to take it easy then. No bending and no twisting around. And no more fights."

"O.K., Doc. I'll take it easy."

Doc said, "All right, boys, let's get out of here. I got to close up." He climbed in the car and lit his cigar.

Earl gave Jack his last pack of cigarettes. "We got to check in at the plant."

"Don't go worrying about me. I'll be fine."

"O.K. We'll bring you out some grub in the morning."

Coley kept the Hudson in low gear as he drove up the Little Eddy path.

Doc said, "That big fellow from E. Z. Loan came by yesterday. He had Hog along with him. How much you in to them for?"

Earl's socks had slid down into his shoes. He tugged them up. "Plenty."

Doc said, "The Hudson?"

Coley nodded. "Yessir. It's eating us up. We had to buy a new block."

"Well, that E. Z. man didn't look like much of a talker. What you plan on doing?"

Earl said, "We got something cooking."

They left Doc off at the drugstore and went on to work.

Coley stripped his T shirt off and pulled on his rubber boots. "God, Earl, what if that man from E. Z. starts coming by our houses?"

"He ain't going to bother you. I'm the one that signed them stupid papers. Maybe we can borrow from some other place."

"We're in too deep now."

Earl snugged his goggles tight and headed for the time clock. "If we could just get up one payment, they'd leave us alone."

A new pink vacation list covered the "Night Cleaner" corner of the bulletin board.

Coley read down it. "Wait a minute!" He slapped the board. "Look at this." C. Jaffrey's vacation was due to start in three days.

Earl flipped a pinball machine slug in the air. "Great! All we need's a couple barrels."

That night Earl lay awake. Dogs were howling at the full moon, and in the Cherry Street drain ditch two cats with tails as thick as bottle brushes were arched up and crying like babies.

The 100-degree heat had made everyone in the Bottom nervous; no one was sleeping. Children were crying and Woodrow Frizzell at the corner was drunk and cursing his wife. "Keep it up! Keep it up! If you don't like it here you can pack your damn rags and git."

Lurlene shrieked, "Will you hush up! You done shouted at me so much you've probably given me a cancer."

The cats burst into a fight, and in the distance a police siren sounded.

Earl propped his feet up on the bedstead. He stuck the tendon above his left heel in between the first two toes of his right foot.

Their money problems began galloping by. Where was it going to come from? Where? That was the question. Where? When? How? Jesus, how? What if C. Jaffrey didn't go on vacation? What if he worked straight through and got paid twice? A lot of men do that. Maybe they could go to his house at night and talk to him in his garage. Tell him about the gas. Offer to split the profits with him. He could hear Coley's rapid, high-pitched voice in the dark garage. "Please, Mr. C. Jaffrey, just think about it. That's all we're asking you to do. Just think about it. We'd be taking all the risk." No, that wouldn't work.

He wrenched around, trying to think of something else. He had to get some sleep. He kept seeing the bill from E. Z. Loan and the black six-volt Delco battery in Gus's window. He heard and felt the grinding transmission of the Hudson and saw Jack waiting for them, wolfing down two hamburgers at thirty-five cents each, a double milk shake for thirty, and looking around for more. He saw the white card on the steam nozzle: "ATTENTTION MACHINE CLEANERS: QUIT MESSING WITH TRUCK GAS OR IT IS YOUR ASS." He saw a stack of fifty-five-gallon barrels. They were rising up over the housetops, higher than the telephone poles, higher than the trees, into the clouds. They would need fifty, a hundred, two hundred barrels; it was all crazy, crazy, crazy.

Earl spun around panting and mopped his streaming face with the edge of the sheet. He slipped on his pants and went out to the front porch. The crickets sounded furious at the heat and were scraping away louder than the locusts. At Woodrow Frizzell's a radio was playing.

Earl sat down on the top step and began picking at the yellow paint on the post. A tiredness oozed over him and he thought of Dan's friend Small Loans. He wondered what had happened to him. The paint had blistered in the heat and he pulled away a long soft ribbon. What had he done after they had repossessed his car? How had he gotten to work? Where was he now?

Saturday was payday, and after Earl and Coley had given Gus seventeen dollars for a new battery they went to Holly's and bought Jack a fried chicken dinner, which was on special for fifty-nine cents, and two packs of Camels. They had decided to go fishing and on the way to the Little Eddy they stopped by the farmer's market on Franklin Street and bought fifty cents worth of bee bait.

Two hundred yards north of the Little Eddy, Cedar Creek flowed into the Cooper River. It was a small, slow-moving black water stream winding through moss-hung sweet gums and tall gray cypress trees. While Jack was eating and reading the morning paper, Earl and Coley took their tackle and headed upstream. They skirted around the wild grape leaves and the green cane, hoping the mosquitoes would stay quiet, and worked their way through the swamp fern and elephant ears toward the redbreast hole. A cottonmouth moccasin sunning himself on a branch heard them and dropped heavily into the water. He surfaced and in a slow series of figure S's moved downstream.

Coley whistled. "Wish I had me a rifle. He must be eight feet long."

"Hope he didn't scare the fish away." Earl opened the cigar box and began sorting the bees.

A few had hatched, but they were still too moist for flying and were crawling around bumping into one another. They were too old and tough for bait and he shook them into the vines. With his knife he sliced the thin membrane covering the cells of the sleeping larvae which remained. They had faint black heads and yellow bodies and were perfect for redbreast bait. He whacked the strip of hive against his hand and they came spilling out.

Coley snapped redbreast leaders onto the lines and aimed the rods at a patch of sky to check the alignment of the ferules. "How the bees look?"

"Perfect. Only a couple black ones."

A loud splash sounded down the creek.

Coley said, "Hot damn! It must be bass! They're feeding." He yanked the redbreast leader off, snapped on a fly-casting spinner, and tied on a Yellow Sally.

The splash came again.

"They sound like hogs!" He tugged his cap bill down and ducked his head as he plowed through the spider web ladders that stretched across the narrow path.

Earl eased himself out on the uprooted oak tree that crossed the redbreast hole. He fastened three cleats of lead above the hook and bit down hard on the small wings until they were secure. He spat the lead taste out. After baiting the hook heavy with six bees, he slid the rod forward and lowered the line deep. The line grew tight and the rod jiggled at the very end. At the edge of the bank the water bubbled through the sunken limbs of the tree and he could feel the rhythm of the current. Coley, hidden by the cane-brake and the vines, was fishing a big bend downstream. When he cast long out beyond a thin sand bar, Earl could see the Yellow Sally splash and the trail of the long leader.

The light wind died, the water calmed, and the sun rolled up over the lower branches of the sweet gums. Earl set his pole in a fork in the branches and, stretching out on the tree trunk, he watched the water. Gray and brown water bugs swam and skidded near the bank. Dragonflies, green and gold and tipped with blue, dove and touched, and mud puppies, looking more like tiny moles than fish, scuttled in the shallows sending the mud dust flying.

A dragonfly lit on the tip of his pole and another one carefully examined his line. The fish weren't biting. He shifted on the rough bark and spat out at the line. He checked his bait, then lowered it back. The woods around him were too wet for rabbits, but high in the trees the red fox squirrels leaped across the swaying branches, making their chickling, chattering sound. He leaned back on a thick limb and watched Coley wade out to the bright sand bar.

Coley was good with the fly rod. He was better than Doc. He could work his lure under trees and vines, barrel roll it around corners, and lay it on lily pads and let it trickle off. The sun outlined his hands, and as he folded the line in with a steady, riffling move they seemed transparent and in slow motion. He worked the area fast, making shorter and shorter casts. He stopped. He raised his thumb and forefinger in a circle. He had had a strike.

Earl waved back. Coley moved to his left to get squarely in the sun. He stood motionless, keeping the rod low to avoid making a shadow, and started a slow pass by the deep end of the sand bar. The water was shallow; he could see the fish but the fish couldn't see him. He brought the line in, whipped it back, and cast again. This time long, almost to the bank. He brought the line in slowly. The fox squirrels were quiet. The only noise was the bubbling water and the faint rustling of the leaves. The Sally trailed slowly across the bar, a thin shadow against the bright white sand.

Suddenly the sand bar exploded. A blue-black flash broke straight up and began spinning. It turned white, then blue, then black again. At the top of the leap it stopped, froze, and opened its bulldog mouth.

Coley screamed, "Jeeee-sus! Bass!" The rod hairpinned and strained as the bass drove toward the bank. Coley tried to work him away from the roots but could do nothing but hold on. The fish churned and broke back, cartwheeling and rolling toward the sand bar.

Earl rushed over, shouting, "You got him! You got him!"

Coley gave him line as he ran. He was scared it would break. "Oh, God, we need a net."

The bass ran thirty feet, then wheeled around to tear the hook out.

Coley pleaded, "Stay in there, Sally."

The bass jumped again, skidded against the bank, and slammed back down. Coley shouted, "He's getting stronger. He's going to snap it!"

Earl said, "Jesus, if we only had a net." He began cutting a willow branch.

Coley wound the line around his left fist slowly, gaining five or six feet of line.

The water churned again. The fish made a short strong lunge and backed up. The rod cracked near the handle. Coley was drenched in sweat. "Please, Lord. Please don't let it break."

The fish crashed through the shallow water. His black back came out. He turned over twice, winding up the line. His stomach flashed, then his back again. Coley moved forward. He took in the line fast. The bass was in deep water. Coley had gained most of the line back. "One second, Lord. One second."

He dropped the pole, grabbed the line with both hands, and worked close. He pulled again. The fish stopped and stared at him. There were only four feet of line left, but he was still too strong to be taken. Coley took a slow loop around his left fist and eased his baseball cap off.

He knew the fish was going to jump. The bass fanned his tail slowly, gathering his strength. He seemed to be coiling. Then with one convulsive move he leaped straight up. His big mouth flashed red and he jerked from side to side, trying to snatch the Yellow Sally loose. Coley moved quickly and took another loop of line. The bass came crashing down. Coley was on him. He crammed his cap and fist into the center of the big mouth. The teeth tore his arm but he drove it in deep. The bass slammed back and forth in tight horseshoes, trying to spin. Coley held on working his quick fingers, then his hand, through the gill plate and out the gills. He locked his hands together and screamed, "You're mine! You're mine! Jesus, look at him!"

Earl had a pronged stick ready. "God, he's great, Coley! Hang on!"

Coley dragged the fish up on the bank and Earl worked the stick through the other gill plate and out the mouth.

Coley freed his bleeding hand. "Look at him! Look at those shoulders, he's built like a man."

Earl lifted the fish up. "He weighs nine pounds easy."

Coley waved his cap in a wild circle. "Nine pounds of bass on a Yellow Sally! Lordy Lord Lord! Look at him! Let's show Jack."

"God damn! What a fish!" Jack was sitting on the car seat dealing poker hands onto the Hudson's running board.

Coley took the fish scale out of the glove compartment and hooked it under the gill bone. "Wow, eight pounds and one ounce! Ain't he something! Check those shoulders."

Earl said, "He had to ram his fist in his mouth to land him."

Jack raked the cards in. "He's the biggest I've ever seen. You better get that hand tended to, though."

Earl slid under the wheel. "Come on, Coley. Doc will fix it up. Boy, he's going to drop his teeth when he sees that fish."

Doc shouted, "God God! That's a bass! Where in the hell you catch him?" He rushed out from behind the counter. "Will you study the size of that mouth! You could put two oil cans in there and have room left over for a pack of cigarettes."

"Cedar Creek, right near the sand bar." Coley held the bass higher. "You should have seen him, Doc. He almost pulled me in. Wait till you see what he done to the rod."

Doc washed Coley's cuts with alcohol. Coley howled, whipping and snapping his hand. "Jesus, Doc! I'm burning up!"

"You'll be all right in a minute." He painted the cuts with orange-colored Merthiolate. "And you took him on a Sally. Damn if that don't beat anything I've ever heard. I always knew there were bass in that creek." Doc held the fish up. "Eight pounds one ounce. I'll be dog! Let me keep him in the ice cream hole for you; I want M.L. and Claude Henry to have a look."

Coley said, "O.K., I'll pick him up tomorrow."

After supper Earl and Coley sat on the Hudson's fenders watching Jack deal bottoms and seconds onto the hood. He made a double cut with his left hand and began dealing face-up hands of royal flushes. Earl said, "Man, that's what I want to learn."

The light faded and the fox fire in the river bushes turned a shiny silver green.

It had gotten too dark for cards. Jack lay on his sleeping bag with his knees raised and crossed. Coley sat on the fender with his leg hooked over the headlight. "You want to listen to the radio?"

Jack lit his cigarette and folded his hands behind his head. "No, I'd like something a little different. Don't you boys know something from school, some story or poetry? Yeah, poetry, you know any of that?"

They began laughing.

"What's so funny?"

Coley said, "We had to memorize some in school last year."

Earl sniggered. "Yeah and this kid Henry Erby started doing it, only he stutters."

Coley laughed, "Old Earl here squeezed two whole lines out before he bogged down."

Jack said, "What'd you learn?"

Earl dropped down in the pile of leaves they had used for the whiskey barrel. "'The Raven' by Edgar Allan Poe. You know it?"

"No, don't believe I do. Let me hear it."

"Hell, I can't do it. Hit it for him, Cole."

"O.K." Coley started at top speed and whipped through the first verse with the words running together. Then he slowed down, breathed deeply, and moaned the second out toward the river.

Earl lay spread-eagled in the leaves.

Coley had forgotten the third verse, but he plunged ahead in a slow, rich voice that sounded as if it had an extra egg in it to the lines he remembered. He cupped his hands over the ventilator slots on the car hood and made a deep hollow sound. " 'Sorrow for the lost Lenore— Quoth the Raven nevermore.' "

Jack flipped his glowing cigarette toward the river. "Boy, that really rubs up against you. He must have been some kind of poet."

Coley slid down the fender and sat on the running board. "There's a picture of him in the principal's office. All you have to do is look at his face and you can tell what he went through. Jack, he's considered the greatest poet that ever drew breath."

Jack said, "He's something, all right. You know any more?"

"No, that's all." They were quiet.

Earl spoke. "You know any poems, Jack."

Jack laughed and then stopped when his ribs began hurting. "I know a line of poetry, one line. How about that for a man pushing thirty? Oh, I know a psalm or two, but you can't count that."

Earl said, "Let's hear it."

Jack cleared his throat. " 'When your landlord would no longer take your notes in lieu of rent I saw you walking.' "

The birds had settled in their nesting places and lightning bugs were flashing. Coley said, "Is that all?"

"That's it, that's all I got. Fellow up in New Jersey said it came over from the Chinese or the Japanese way back there."

Earl snapped a dry twig and chewed on the end. It tasted

of pine gum. "What does 'lieu' mean?"

" 'Instead' I guess."

"That's what I figured."

Coley had his hands up against the ventilator slots and was rumbling, " 'Quoth the raven, nevermore.' " An owl whispered by, and across the black water the night fog began rolling in.

Chapter 22

Earl began scratching himself under his arms and between his legs. "I think I got red bugs."

"Well, stay over there. I sure don't want them. Probably got them from those leaves." Coley slowed down at Haygood to let a dog cross the road.

They had left Jack off at his room and were heading for the dairy with seven ten-gallon Army Surplus cans and two lengths of garden hose packed in the trunk. As they pulled into the parking lot Earl saw that Coley was grinning. "What's so funny?"

"Nothing." Coley hooked his chin over the steering wheel and began screwing and unscrewing the gear shift knob.

"What's eating you, anyway?"

Coley started to speak but stopped. A single giggle popped out. And then another. "You know something? We got about as much chance of getting out of this mess as a snowball in hell." He sniggered out loud. "The minute we get two dimes ahead we'll probably blow out all four tires."

Earl was scratching. "And you figure that's pretty funny."

Coley laughed. "I think it's funny as hell when you add in all this stupid gasoline and all the barrels we're going to need."

"Boy, you got about as much sense as a piss-ant. Come on."

Inside the locker room Coley skinned his shirt off and put on his asbestos-lined gloves and his black rubber boots. Earl was wearing the Y.M.C.A. T shirt he had won for swimming forty yards underwater. He decided to keep it on, hoping the hot steam would kill the red bugs. They slogged down the hall, checked the bulletin board, and headed for the ice-cream-making room.

Earl cocked his goggles up on his forehead and checked the steam pressure while Coley started pulling the long hoses from their reels. Coley sang out, "Looka here! Damn!"

Taped to the nozzle of the hose was another three-by-five card from C. Jaffrey. "ATTENTTION MACHINE CLEANERS —DO NOT TRY ANYTHING FUNNY WHILE I'M GONE."

Earl snatched his gloves off and threw them on the floor. "Dammit, dammit, dammit. If that ain't the damn limit."

They sat down on the floor and lit cigarettes. Coley said, "Boy, I was counting on at least one or two loads."

"Me too. Rat's ass! And after all that planning. What in the hell are we going to do?"

They sat leaning against the wall, smoking and staring at the ice-cream-smeared machinery. Coley stood up. "Well, come on, let's get this over with."

The three-to-eleven shift had been making chocolate ice

cream. Brown spots and streaks clung and dripped down the white tiled walls. It covered the bottoms and the sides of the eighty-gallon stainless-steel mixing vats, and warm icicles of it dripped slowly from the mouths of the three ice cream makers onto the duckboards.

Earl opened the steam valve and began spraying the deep vats. The chocolate melted fast and began flowing. He could taste the rich cocoa and butter smell. High-pressure live steam hissed and billowed and rose up above them, covering the eight-inch ammonia pipes crisscrossing the ceiling. The steam cloud dropped lower and lower until it was touching their heads, and as it began condensing on the ice-cold pipes heavy drops of water rained down on them.

After finishing the vats, they stripped the ice cream makers down and laid the heavy valves and screws on the duckboards. Coley hosed the parts with boiling water as Earl played the steam over the walls.

Suddenly a blast thundered and shook the building. Coley snatched his goggles off. The steam junction had blown at the valve; a screaming whistle filled the room, and live steam at 550 degrees was shooting to the ceiling under 250 pounds of pressure.

Earl's goggles were fogged up; he couldn't see. He had both hands on the steam hose and was afraid to let go. The geyser was three feet wide and sounded like a train whistle. Coley grabbed him by the belt and jerked him to the wall. They were cut off from the hallway door, and he pushed him into the freezing room.

Earl peeled his goggles off. "Whew! We could have been scalded."

Coley cranked the safety valve down. The porthole glass in the door was fogged over and the two-way thermometer had shot up to 145 degrees. He tightened the valve. "Look at her climb! That stuff will take the meat right off the bone."

"Man, I'm glad you saw it!" Earl's nose stung in the icy air and he began breathing through his mouth. His T shirt had been soaked by the steam and, as it cooled, traces of frost were appearing on the red-and-blue blocked Y.M.C.A. letters. He rubbed his hands in his armpits and with short, fast half steps walked around the room trying to keep warm. Bags of ice cream mix and sugar and dairy cans of milk were stacked to the ceiling. Along the far wall five-gallon containers of ice cream were ready for the Saturday trucks. Each container was marked and coded and each had the truck driver's name on it.

Coley tried to look through the porthole, but the steam cloud was still solid. The double thermometer read 152 degrees in the ice-cream-making room and 35 below zero in the freezing room. His teeth were chattering, and the fine red fuzz on his chest was frost-covered and white. Shoving his fists in his pockets, he began doing side-straddle hops. He spotted a steel box and, hopping over, he kicked it open. The toolbox was filled with steamfitting tools, wrenches, screwdrivers and an eighteen-piece socket set. He squatted down and stacked up seven crescent wrenches. "It's prewar stuff made in Germany." He held up a thread-cutter. His hands were trembling with the cold and the skin felt sticky on the knurled handle. "That's fifteen dollars right there."

Earl slapped and rubbed his arms and began stamping his feet on the floor. The cold made his ears ring. "Good deal! We can unload them on Gus." His breath smoked out. He picked up a hammer and a steel chisel and began whacking away on a square, frosty block next to them. "What the hell's this? Cement?" The chisel went through and a corner chip fell off. It felt slippery and he rubbed it in his hands to thaw it out. He tasted it. It was butter. "Taste it."

Coley sucked on the butter and spat it out. Their eyes met in the dimly lighted freezing room. They didn't have to speak. Earl tried to lift the cube and had to go down into a deep crouch to get it up. They slid it over to the weighing scales; it weighed 58 pounds.

Earl rubbed his freezing arms. "This is great! We can sell all we can haul to Doc and Nick." He began counting. "God Almighty, they're everywhere. They must buy it by the ton. And it ain't coded or nothing. We got it now, Cole, we really got it. They'll never miss it. Boy, this is perfect, perfect."

Coley hunched forward with his hands deep in his pockets. His eyelashes were white with frost and his lips were so stiff he had to speak slowly. "Ain't no way on earth they can keep track of all this butter. No way."

Earl's face was numb with cold. He felt as if he'd just stepped out of a dentist's chair and his jaw was filled with novocain. He took his right shoe off and began rubbing his toes. "I think the cold killed those damn red bugs."

When the steam disappeared and the temperature had dropped down to 115 degrees they went back inside the ice-cream-making room. They rinsed the machine parts down with hot water, reassembled the makers, leaned the duck-boards up to dry, and left a note on the bulletin board that the steam valve was broken. After hanging up the hoses and their boots they spread a copy of the Columbia *Record* across the back seat of the Hudson and began loading the butter. They laid four cubes side by side and covered them with thick slabs of dry ice.

Coley drove toward the drugstore. "Car feels good with that load. How much you reckon we should ask for it?"

Earl put his feet up on the dashboard. "They get around ninety cents at the store. Let's try fifty. We can always back off from there. Fifty times two hundred and thirty pounds, that's a hundred and fifteen dollars. How 'bout that for one haul?"

"Beats the flying hell out of gasoline. We can pay E. Z. off and everything."

At four-fifteen Coley parked in front of the drugstore and lit a Kool. They had decided to sell the neighborhood houses until the drugstore and the Double Dip opened.

The first customer was Cowboy. He coasted out of the alley by his house and steered toward the Hudson. He rode his bicycle sideways with one hand on the ruby-studded saddlebags behind him and the other lightly touching the handle-bar grip. It was Saturday, and he was wearing his white Collection Day suit with his Battle of the Alamo kerchief. He shoved his kickstand down and moseyed over with his long, slow, rolling John Wayne stride. He walked as if it was downhill and kept his hands a foot out from his body as if he was afraid of soiling his white leather gloves. "Hello, Earl. Hello, Coley."

"Hello, Cowboy."

"Morning, Cowboy," Earl said. "Is your mother up?"

It was an hour before dawn but Cowboy was already squinting. He loosened his drawstring and slid his hat to the back of his head. "She's still asleep. Why you want to know?"

"Go wake her up. Tell her we got fresh butter. All she wants, real cheap."

Coley took his pocket fish scale from the glove compartment, hung a five-gallon bucket onto it, and hooked the scale over the window frame.

Cowboy frowned toward the sun as if to draw it up. "Where'd you get it?"

"Never mind about that. Go tell her."

"O.K., Earl." Cowboy trotted up the street, holding his hands high to his chest, and took the nine steps to the porch in two long strides. In a minute his mother and her sister appeared in the doorway. They were wearing identical tea-rose pink nightgowns and hair nets. Cowboy came loping back with a flat frying pan. "They want a dollar's worth."

By seven-thirty they had had five customers, and Thelma Register said she would take ten pounds at forty cents a pound if they came back after she unloaded her refrigerator. By eight-fifteen the dry ice was gone. The butter had changed from the frozen white color to a bright shiny yellow.

Coley said, "It's melting. We need more ice."

"Don't worry about it. Doc'll be here any minute now."

"I'm going to see if Mrs. Hall wants some."

Earl said, "Try Murdock's and Elrods. And tell 'em to bring their pots and pans."

Mrs. Hall called across her back fence to Mrs. Kelly and Gertrude Haygoode. Mrs. Kelly got on the phone and called Claude Henry Hutto's wife Sally. Mrs. Duvall and Lurlene Frizzell came down to the corner carrying roasting pans and five-quart stewing pots. Earl was kept busy cutting and weighing the butter and collecting the money.

He jammed the dollar bills in his back pockets and made change from his front. The sun cleared the scrub oaks along Mulberry; it was getting hot. The butter was cutting easier.

When Cowboy came back from his route, Coley borrowed his bicycle to ride up Bee and try more houses. "Hey, there's Bo-Bo. Wonder where Doc is?"

Earl dried his hands on the back of his pants. "I'll go see. Give us a hand, Cowboy."

"O.K." Cowboy pulled out his nine-inch deerfoot-handled, Tennessee throwing knife that he carried in a secret compartment in his right boot and began cutting and weighing.

Earl raced over to the drugstore. "Hey, Bo-Bo. When's the Doc coming in? Me and Coley got some butter."

Bo-Bo began loading dirty glasses into the sink. "He went fishing last night. Doc Boykin's going to be on prescriptions."

Earl knew the Doc would be gone at least a week, maybe two. "Listen Bo-Bo, I got a good chance for you to save Doc a lot of money sitting out in that car." Earl explained.

Bo-Bo didn't look up.

"Bo-Bo, you ain't going to stand there, letting a deal like this slide through your fingers, are you? That butter will cost you ninety cents a pound at the A and P. We'll let you have it for forty. You just can't say no to that. Think about it."

Bo-Bo poured soap over the glasses. "You ain't letting me have nothing, Earl Edge. Doc left me in charge here, and I ain't getting mixed up in nothing shady."

"You saying there's something shady going on, Bo?"

"All I know is that when someone comes around the minute you open up saying he's got two hundred pounds of butter he wants to get rid of for half price, something's wrong."

"O.K., Bo-Bo, maybe you can't buy it. Tell you what. How about letting us put it in your freezers till the Doc gets back? That way he can have the final say."

Bo-Bo pulled three onions out of the storage bin under the counter and began peeling them. "No dice, Earl."

Earl kicked his foot into the wooden molding at the base of the counter. "God damn you, Bo-Bo. If you had snake's brains you'd be a genius. Doc's going to throw a living fit when he hears this."

Bo-Bo began chopping the onions. "Leave me alone, Earl. I got work to do."

Earl leaned over the counter. "Listen, you rabbit-faced shit for brains, I'm telling Doc about this. If he doesn't kick your ass, me and Coley are. You hear that?"

"O.K., Earl, I'll make a note of that."

Earl slammed the screen door. Outside in the blinding sun he jerked his cap down and kicked a Dixie cup into the street. He spun around, went back inside, slapped a nickel on the counter, and telephoned Nick.

At the Hudson, customers were lined up with pots and pans and serving trays in front of Cowboy. Most of them were on his paper route, and as he cut and weighed and made the change he asked each of them how his delivery service had been. He wanted to know if his throwing their paper on the porch had disturbed them and if they wanted him to slip the paper behind the screen door slat or under the wooden door.

Trigger crawled out from under his porch, yawning and walking stiff-legged until he got his bearings. He had slept through Cowboy's delivery. In front of the Hudson he stopped, wagged his tail slowly, and began arching his back to stretch. He picked up the smell of butter and began sniffing around the car. A hound from down Mulberry and Lonnie's Midnight saw him and loped over. All three dogs began whining and scratching on the wheels and the doors. Trigger got down low and crawled under; the others followed.

A small terrier and a big bushy red chow trotted up. The terrier quickly scratched himself under but the chow was too big, and he began barking and skinning his back on the low running board.

Suddenly they began fighting. A whimpering howl shot out from under the car. It was Trigger. Cowboy slapped his hat on top of the car, whipped on his leather gloves, and jerked him out by a rear leg. The others kept fighting and howling and whopping themselves up against the oil pan and the drive shaft. Midnight was too big to move in the narrow space and after he had been bitten by the smaller, faster dogs he came whining and crawling out sideways. Trigger sniveled and whined to get back under.

Cowboy shouted, "Will you shut up now! I'm tired of listening at you!"

Earl told Nick he would sell him some butter for half the store price and that he was driving by the Double Dip in a few minutes. Buck said he would buy ten pounds. He called Holly's but the line was busy.

He raced back to the car. Cowboy was swamped with two-pound buyers, dogs, flies, and kids on bicycles. His hat was on the car roof and he had taken a cube of butter and placed it on a newspaper on top of the engine hood. He grinned at Earl. "I can get at it better up here."

The butter was melting faster than it was selling. It flowed over the hood, into the ventilator slots, into the radiator grille, down the fenders, and was puddling on the running board. Earl started to cuss him out but when he saw that the three cubes in the back seat were melting even faster, he decided Cowboy was right. He got down on his knees and elbows; butter was dripping through the cracks in the floor boards. The dogs had stopped fighting and were lying on their sides licking at it, while black horseflies and green blowflies were crawling at the edge of the spreading pool.

Coley rode up. Earl told him about the Doc, and they decided to try and sell everything to Nick. They slid the butter from the hood into a bucket and left it for Cowboy to sell. Coley gunned the engine to drive the dogs out. The butter was melting faster.

"Take off, Coley. It's going down like the *Titanic*."

Coley swung around the corner at Bee and began picking up speed. A deep knock from the transmission made the gear shift jump and the car shake. "Oh, God, listen at that." He eased off on the gas.

Earl said, "Keep her running! Keep her running! Jesus, what next!"

At the Double Dip, Nick was pouring nickels and dimes into the cash register drawer. "You sounded like you were in a hurry, Earl. What's the trouble?"

Earl swallowed hard, trying to catch his breath. "No trouble, Nick." He watched Nick study his face.

"Like I said, Earl, I don't have much call for butter any more. I swear I don't. You know, it's funny." He stopped and smiled. "A year ago, when I switched over to oleomargarine, I thought I'd get some trouble from my customers.

But you know something? I never did. Not one complaint.
How much you got?"

Earl hesitated. "We're saving sixty pounds for Buck.
That leaves about a hundred and ten. Let you have it for
sixty dollars."

Nick rubbed his mustache, looking as if he was watching the last bet in a big poker game. "I'll give you twenty-
five."

"Hell, Nick, we're getting fifty cents a pound. Make it
forty."

"Thirty. Take it or leave it."

Earl borrowed a big cookie tray and went out to the car.
"Shit house mouse! I had to pretend we were saving sixty
pounds for Buck and I still only got thirty dollars. Give me
a hand."

Coley was jiggling the gas pedal with his foot. "I can't,
the gas is sticking. If she cuts off we're dead."

As he slipped the second cube into the ice cream hole,
Nick snapped his fingers. "Damn, Earl, I'm sorry. I'm really
sorry. I don't have enough to pay you. I ain't been to the
bank yet. Listen, I tell you what, can you come back later
today?"

"How late?"

"In the afternoon. I have to go by the bank and get some
cash. Tell you what, make it around nine tonight. That
way I'll have all the day's money and there won't be any
chance of a slip-up."

Coley kept working the gas pedal and watched the leaking butter form a puddle around a Dr. Pepper cup in the
gutter. The temperature on the thermometer under the
Double Dip awning read 99 degrees. He was drenched with
sweat. The transmission pounded louder and he kept pray-

ing it wouldn't jump out. He heard someone shouting, "Coley! Coley! Coley!"

It was Cowboy, riding his bicycle as hard as he could and waving his white hat. Trigger had filled up on butter and was half running and half walking. He ran slow and low to the ground, stopping to catch his breath, checking to see if he was sick, and then running a few more yards trying to catch up. Cowboy braked hard and gasped and frowned as if he were in great pain. He had to wait a minute before he could talk. "I was all set to cold cock him, Coley, I swear I was."

"What you talking about?"

"That A and P fellow Channing. I was going to slide up like I was asking for a light." He stepped on his kickstand and backed away from the Hudson. "Then finish him off with the old long right." He reached back as if he were picking up a heavy stone and traced a nine-foot haymaker through the air. He had to take two steps to keep on balance and complete the follow-through. "He kept shouting how we were cutting in on his business. Boy, he'd of dropped like a sack of seed."

"For Christ's sake, Cowboy! What in the hell are you talking about?"

"He called the Law and told them about the butter and all about your selling it and how I was in on it and everything."

"Jesus!" Coley jumped out. The Hudson sputtered and almost died. He slid back in and pumped the gas. The engine coughed, held, and then speeded up. He pounded on the horn. He was frantic. He waved for Earl to come out.

Cowboy shouted, above the roaring engine and the horn, "I told him you were going to Olympia! Pretty good, huh?" Trigger had sneaked over to the Dr. Pepper cup and was lapping the butter up. Cowboy whirled and screamed, "Damn your hide! Quit messing with that butter! You going to be running around here shittin' like a goose."

Earl came racing out. Coley told him about the A & P man. "Oh, God, we gotta move. Little Eddy! Go there! We gotta wash her out."

Coley slammed the car into reverse. Cowboy shouted, "Hey, here's you all's money. I collected eight dollars and forty cents."

"Keep it, Cowboy. You earned it."

Coley crossed Broad with the transmission pounding like an air hammer and headed down Monroe.

Earl said, "Slow down! The damn stuff's splashing."

Coley turned into the Bottom. The streets were all clay.

At Pickett Street a siren sounded. Coley looked around. It was a black Ford. It was the Law. His red warning light was on. "Oh, my God!"

Earl groaned. "Jesus."

Coley jammed the gas down to the floor, sending the red dust flying. He turned left at Cedar Street. The Hudson's shock absorbers and coil suspension were better than the Ford's for riding over the clay gullies, but Coley knew the minute they got on pavement they wouldn't have a chance.

The siren wailed again and stayed on. It was closer. Earl pulled his T shirt up over his face. He didn't want the Law to see him until the last possible minute. He had to have time to think. He peeked through the neck hole out the back window. The Ford was bouncing like a fast grounder. "Come on, Coley! Open her up!"

"I am, I am." Coley held the Hudson on a flat sixty. They were nearing Maple Street. He had both hands on the wheel, holding it at the bottom, to secure himself to the seat on the bounces. A hundred yards ahead lay a foot-deep gully the rain had washed out. He shouted, "Hang on!"

Earl pushed both hands against the ceiling to keep from being driven through the roof. They hit the gully going sixty. The car leaped in the air and slammed down, bouncing. Earl thought his back had broken in two places along with his wrists, his arms, and his elbows. The radio jarred on. The Hudson skidded but held the road. Earl looked back. "He's stopping for it! Hit Colored Town. We can lose him!"

Colored Town was the moonshine drivers' favorite place for losing the Law. It was a low gray maze of shacks and shanties standing in knee-deep weeds. Zigzag alleys squirreled and curled through it, cutting it into a hundred pieces and leading nowhere. It lay dead ahead.

Coley pushed the Hudson to sixty-five. At Rose Avenue he hit the brakes, turned hard, and double clutched down to low gear. They were on Elbow Alley, a one-lane dirt path that ran like a mad dog between Pickett and Spruce. The Hudson bounced and rocked between the tar paper and corrugated steel shacks. Coley slowed to ten miles per hour, weaving through a beehive of wash pots, bicycle frames, car shells, and trash piles.

Earl kept looking out the back window. "He's gone! He's gone! Keep going!"

Coley ran the corkscrew whiskey pattern Earl had shown him on his bike: up Easy Street to No Name, down No Name to Joe Louis, around the Blossom Inn over to Lancy. He plowed through a cinder dump and stopped on Sweetwater one hundred feet from Spruce Street, which ran straight to the river.

AUGUST

"Great driving!"

The radio was on, and the Aristocratic Pigs from Greenville were singing:

> Ballantine Sausage,
> Folks all like it so,
> Sister, Dad, and Brother,
> Also Little Joe.

Coley said, "Go take a look."

Earl jumped out and raced to the corner.

They were parked by the side of a long shotgun house
that had been painted a rat's-skin gray as high as a tall man
could reach. The stairs, the fence, and porch rails had been
torn up for firewood. In the front yard three colored kids
were sword-fighting with mop handles and umbrellas
stripped of their spokes and cloth, while across the alley
two men in overall pants and undershirts were on Fred
Flood's store gallery arguing. A goat walked by.

The street was clear. "O.K., Coley. Haul ass."

Coley steered the car down the steep Spruce Street path
between the pokeberry bushes and the blackberries. They
were near the canebrake. The river was in sight. An announcer from Spartanburg was reading the cotton and hog
market.

He slowed down and shifted to low and began plowing
through the sand bed. The car stopped. He pushed the accelerator down, and the wheels began spinning. Suddenly
the wheels touched firm ground. The car leaped forward.
Coley released the accelerator. It had jammed on the floor.
He froze. The engine roared.

Earl dove for the accelerator and pulled up. It tore away
from the floor board. They shot down the path through the

299

canebrake. The river was fifty feet away. It was all mud, all downhill. Earl shouted, "Brakes! Brakes! Hit the brakes!"

Coley slammed the brakes and grabbed the emergency handle. The car was sliding through the mud; the radio was on full blast. He forced the gears into reverse and cut the switch. The engine stopped, the wheels locked, but the car kept slipping.

Earl yelled, "Hop out! Hop out! Grab her!"

They jumped out. Each grabbed a doorpost. They pushed back. The Hudson kept sliding, taking them with it.

"Dig in, Coley. Dig in." Earl leaned hard into the doorpost and growled, "We can hold her."

Coley strained. "I am. I am."

Both front doors were open. Earl dug his collarbone into the post. He watched Coley straining. He had never realized how thin his arms were. The car slowed down until it was barely moving. They were five feet from the edge of the water. The radio was still on.

"We got her, Cole. We got her now."

There were tears in Earl's eyes. His collarbone and back felt as if they were on fire, and he knew he couldn't hold on much longer. He ground his teeth together and dug the sides of his shoes into the soft wet clay. The car kept moving, slowly. The grille was on the edge of the bank.

"Almost, Earl. Almost. One more time."

Their eyes met. They gathered what strength they had left and leaned into the door posts as hard as they could. The car shivered and stopped. The grille was hanging over the water.

Earl said, "That's it. Now hang on."

The announcer began talking about a statue of Jesus Christ that glowed in the dark. It was seventeen inches high and for a limited time it was being made available locally for only $6.90. You were to simply write the words "Jesus Christ" on a postcard and send it in to Station WXOY.

Earl's mind cleared. He remembered the trick of chocking the wheels with the back seat. If he could get the back door open and pull the seat out, he knew it would hold until he could go for help.

The announcer said, "And now, ladies and gentlemen, I want you all to sit back and hear a little of that smooth singing of Mr. Merle Travis."

Slowly Earl reached for the back door handle. He didn't want to relax his grip on the doorpost. He strained backwards. His hand closed on the handle. He turned it carefully.

Coley spoke. He seemed to be suffocating. "Earl. The bank's going."

"Where?"

"Right here."

Earl was rigid. One hand was on the doorpost, the other on the handle. He heard the dropping sounds of clods of clay. The car quivered. It lurched forward, groaning. They grabbed the posts tight and dug in deep. They held on. They pushed. It was no use. There was no place to stand. They slid backwards, staring terrified into each other's eyes. They were staring and gripping the posts when the car splashed in. Merle Travis from Nashville, Tennessee, was on the second chorus of "Smoke, Smoke, Smoke That Cigarette." The Hudson floated for a minute, with Earl holding one post, Coley the other. Then it pointed its grille at the open sky as if to say farewell, made a deep gurgling sound, and sank.

The water was fourteen feet deep at the Little Eddy, and

Earl and Coley went down with the Hudson, holding onto the doorposts. Coley surfaced first, then Earl. They swam in and clawed their way up the mud bank. Earl lay face down in the deep tire marks trying to catch his breath. His body ached all over. But the tears in his eyes weren't because of his hands, his shoulders, or his back. They were for their 1940 Hudson that was quietly digging its own grave in the silt bottom of the Cooper River.

Coley raised up and tapped Earl's shoulder. "You got the money?"

Earl shoved his hands in his pockets without rolling over. It was still there. He nodded. He'd lost his baseball cap.

Coley lay flat on his back with his arms spread out, as if he were being crucified. He was beginning to smile. It was the same grin Earl had seen on his face on the way to the dairy. He stopped grinning. He began giggling. He giggled again, quickly, nervously. It became a shrill birdlike noise, and he couldn't stop it.

Earl wiped the mud from his face with his sleeve. He wanted to tell Coley to shut his dumb mouth, but then he realized that he too was smiling. He tried to hold it back; it broke through. He was grinning and crying at the same time. He looked at Coley stretched out in the mud and began to laugh. He wheezed and coughed and snorted as he tried to say, "We didn't have—we didn't have—we didn't have a goddamn Chinaman's chance."

They laughed and laughed and laughed.

They sounded like dogs, and hogs, and screaming wild Richland County guinea hens. They sounded as if they had seen and heard the funniest, wildest thing in the world, and that they would never be able to stop. Their laughter shot up over the mud they had slid through, over the sand they

302

had stuck in, back through the canebrake, through the pokeberry bushes and the blackberries, all the way up to Bee Street. It came echoing back. It echoed back from the tin cans, the beer bottles, the deserted car shells, the broken bicycle frames, the rotting tires and oil drums, and all the JESUS SAVES and REPENT YOU SINNERS painted on the backs of Burma-Shave signs. It echoed back from all the kerosene lamps and the black wash pots, the sagging overall-hung clotheslines, the skinny hounds and weary cats, the mail order bedspreads and the Metropolitan Life Insurance calendars and Sears Roebuck catalogues filling the lives that filled the rows of rat-colored shotgun houses lining the streets of the Black Bottom section of Columbia.

They stood up. They kept laughing. They had to sit back down. They stood up again. And finally, with tears of laughter mixed with tears of loss and river mud and butter, they looped their arms around each other's shoulders and stumbled back through the canebrake toward the drugstore.

They had laughed while the Hudson sat on the river bottom and the last bubbles of trapped air from the glove compartment and the engine block broke on the muddy surface. They had laughed almost all of the way back to Bee Street. But as their clothes began to dry they quit and walked silently with their hands deep in their pockets.

The only sound was the squish-squish of their wet shoes.

They sat at the railroad bank and watched the five-forty Orange Blossom Special go by and then the six-fifty slow freight. They didn't count the cars on the long freight. Coley didn't want to go home for supper; Earl wasn't hungry. The final slice of the Coca-Cola red sun sank and the cotton mill whistle blew eight long times.

Earl turned over on his stomach so his back could dry, and cradling his chin in his hands he gazed down the shiny tracks. "You feel like working?"

A lizard flashed by and, stopping on a brown crosstie, turned himself brown, then streaked for the dry briers in the drain ditch. Coley felt his shoes. They were still wet. "I don't want to ride no bus."

"Me neither. You want to quit?"

"Yeah, but we get paid tomorrow."

"O.K. One more day; then we'll tell them to ram it."

Chapter 23

Lonnie and Thelma were in the living room, sitting before the cinder-and-ash-filled fireplace. Thelma said, "Honey, you want another Orange Crush?" It was 98 degrees.

"No thanks, I'm still swallowing that supper."

"I got that recipe from Maude. Didn't that celery give it a nice taste, though? I remember Momma had a dish almost exactly like that. Now what in the world did she call it? Oh, I can't think of it now, but we used to have it all the time. Daddy used to lap it up. He'd come back for seconds and thirds. So did Henry. Joe liked it too. Momma didn't take to it though. Funny, ain't it? Funny how you can cook and cook and then you just can't eat. Maude said the very same thing. Said she made up some okra and corn and tomatoes for Leroy and Earl the other day, and they sat down and ate like hogs, and all she could do was just dab at it."

"Is that right."

"Hand me the fan, sweetie. Lord, this heat is going to kill me yet."

Lonnie got up and took the cardboard fan from the S & H Radiator Shop off the mantelpiece.

"You know what I'd just love, Lonnie?"

"What's that?"

"For you to slip on your shoes and us go get on the bus and go up to the movies. I bet there's something good showing at the Magnolia. We ain't done that in a long time. I bet it's cool in there."

"Honey, I'm tired, you know that. I been painting ceilings all day. My arms are about to drop right off."

"I understand. Well, we'll go next week. I'll keep checking the papers. I'll pick us out a good one. Is that all right with you?"

"O.K."

Thelma began fanning herself. "You know I was telling you about that dish Momma made; well, it wasn't exactly like Momma's. Momma didn't put any bell peppers in hers and she used sweet potatoes instead of Irish. Maybe we'll have it again when this heat breaks. How does that sound?"

Lonnie didn't answer.

"I asked you something."

"I'm sorry, sugar foot. I had something on my mind. Ask me again."

"When you want me to cook that stew for you again?"

"Any time, any time."

Lonnie had been thinking about the Hudson. He pulled his watch chain out and began fingering his feeler gauge on the end.

Thelma smiled and sat back, rocking. She was pleased with the new Lonnie. She spread her knees to let the air get at her legs and fanned herself with the red and blue fan. "This heat. This heat. You sure you don't want another Orange Crush? I got a crate in today, so don't be shy."

It was eight o'clock. Lonnie had already had six. "No, not now. Maybe later."

"How about some peanuts? There're some fresh boileds in the kitchen. They might sharpen you up for another Orange. Oh, Lonnie, I'm so glad you ain't out back messing with that old car and swilling that nasty beer. Lord, you used to sit over there and smell like a trash pile." She fanned herself under her neck. "But not any more."

Lonnie's thoughts turned over. If he had some boiled peanuts he would then drink another Orange Crush, maybe two. "You say you bought another crate?"

"Sure did."

"They put twenty-four in a crate, don't they?"

"That's right, twenty-four. That'll last you till Monday; then I'll get you another. You go through a crate pretty fast. Don't worry, honey, we ain't going to run out."

He thought of the soft drink and beer box at the drugstore. On one end Doc had Cokes, Pepsis, R.C. Colas, Dr. Peppers, and Orange Crushes; once in a while he would stock two or three Nehi Grapes. On the other end was the beer and the ale. Miller's was on the end, then Budweiser, then Schlitz. Pabst Blue Ribbon was on the side and the rest of the box was filled with Atlantic ale and beer and Champagne Velvet. He'd never liked Champagne Velvet; it had a sweet taste. Lonnie preferred Miller High Life. Once in a while he would try a Budweiser or a Schlitz, but he always came back to Miller's.

Thelma sighed. "This heat. This heat. Won't it ever let up? I been hot as a stove all week. There ain't a drop of air in this house." Small beads of perspiration dotted her upper lip. Her short hair was wet and she kept lifting it from the back of her neck and sighing. Every few minutes she would raise one of her arms and fan underneath. "It must be one hundred and five right this second."

A faint tickle touched the back of Lonnie's throat. It was a new sensation, but it was old. He couldn't help thinking about Miller High Life. He could see the clear bottle, the gold-yellow liquid, and the cross-shaped back label. He could feel the tickle growing and moving up his throat. It settled above and behind his back molars. It seemed to be pulsing. Lonnie shook his head, sucked his teeth dry, and went to the kitchen. He opened an Orange Crush and returned to the living room.

Thelma fanned and smiled at him. "Honey, you really love them, don't you?"

Lonnie nodded and took a drink. They were just too sweet. It was almost like eating candy. Beer wasn't sweet. It was different. It was colder and it held its cold longer. It had a deep brown taste that reminded him of dark cellars. There weren't any women in Lonnie's idea of what beer tasted like. There were men there, only men. They were sitting around having a good time telling stories about hunting and fishing and about cars. But there was something else he couldn't put his finger on. Maybe it was the malt smell? Maybe it was the sudden malt smell that shot up when the cap came off too fast and you had to scramble to keep from losing any. Lonnie took a sip of the Orange.

Thelma leaned over and fanned him. "There, sweetie, how does that feel?"

He felt trapped and wretched. He didn't want to lie and he didn't want to tell the truth. Maybe there was some middle ground. He could go for a walk or a movie. Maybe he could go over to the Edges' and see the Hudson.

Thelma sat back and fanned under her arms again. "Whew, I just don't see how I'm going to get through this week. That stove heats things up so. Honey, I was just thinking. What if we had a cold supper for the next few nights. You wouldn't mind that so, would you? That stove is just too much for me in this heat. I swear it is. I could make us up a nice tuna fish salad with fresh tomatoes and some cucumbers and . . ."

"Sounds fine." It really didn't sound fine at all. Lonnie hated salads for supper and he knew Thelma knew it.

"Honey, did I ever tell you about the time my daddy brought the preacher home for dinner and Momma had to catch and kill the chickens? Lord, if that wasn't something."

"I think you told me about that last week."

"It's a nice story, ain't it?"

"Yes."

"Alma says I'm real good at telling stories. Said I got a real flair for it. Says I got a nice way with people. Wasn't that nice of her to say that?"

Lonnie nodded.

"Remember when I told you how we had only two Dominecker hens, and Momma wasn't too sure she could catch them? Well, Aunt Rachel—that's Daddy's half sister, she's the one that married the soldier."

Lonnie looked over his black-stockinged feet at the gray hearth. He sipped at his Orange while Thelma described the catching, the cleaning, and the cooking of the chickens.

At one point in the story she stopped and, closing her eyes, she frowned. "No, wait a minute. It wasn't like that. I'm getting way ahead of myself." She backed up, came at it from another direction, and finally got to what Aunt Rachel said.

Lonnie smiled.

Thelma sighed. "How about getting me a nice glass of ice water? I'm about to die right here."

"O.K."

Thelma drank the water fast. She was excited. "Did I tell you about the time Momma spanked me for going inside the colored church?"

"I don't think so. Go on, I'll stop you if I've heard it." Thelma's story was old. Lonnie felt safe only half listening, for he knew he could answer any questions she might ask him about it later. His spirits were dropping and he rolled the Orange Crush bottle back and forth between his hands, thinking how everything had changed, with Wilson mad at him and Sonny Love on his way to Washington, D.C. He had no friends and no place to go.

He didn't want to hang around M.L. and the Doc at the drugstore, and there were too many drunks at the Silver Dipper. He had tried the S & H Radiator Shop but it was too noisy. Finally he began stopping by the Carolina Double Dip until Nick became a problem. He was a Greek Orthodox and he didn't understand about healing and the unknown tongues, and when he looked at Lonnie's copy of *The Healing Life and the New Way* he began laughing.

Then the day came when Lonnie was walking down Congress Street. He stopped on the 1600 block and looked through the window of the Christian Science Reading Room. He went in, hoping there would be a receptionist there, someone to introduce him around. But the Reading Room was just that; they were all readers. When he introduced himself to a man crouched over a magazine, the man raised his hand and pointed to the sign on the wall saying "Quiet Please."

Lonnie thumbed through the magazines and the periodicals and then left. A man on the far side of the room smiled and, following him outside, introduced himself. For the first few minutes they seemed to have a lot in common. Lonnie suggested they have a cup of coffee at the Dixie Bee across the street. After ordering coffee and a slice of marble cake, Lonnie began telling how he hadn't had a drink or smoked a cigarette in almost a month. The man said he believed in healing and that he was sorry he had missed Sonny Love. But as he was putting sugar in his coffee, Lonnie felt the conversation easing away from religion. The man began asking him a lot of personal questions. He did it smoothly and Lonnie hadn't minded. They ordered more coffee. The man announced that he was in the life insurance field and gave him his card. Lonnie felt cornered in the dark, high-sided booth but saw there was no way of escaping. He studied the card reading *Clayburn "Buddy" Morris, "Your Insurance Friend," 1419½ Congress Street.*

Clayburn had finally said, "Judging from what you tell me I don't believe you're adequately covered. A man like you ought to be able to plan ahead and have his fingers on exactly where he stands. Lonnie, I'm sure it would be a great comfort to you to know that in the event of your passing on your wife would be taken care of."

Thelma finished her story. "Did I tell you what Maude said today?"

"No."

"Says she's going to take that pattern I cut out of the *Record* and make herself a dress like mine. Course it ain't going to be the same color, but it's going to be the same style. She sure liked the way I made it up. Liked the shoulders, and the way I got it to fit in the back."

Lonnie's eyes were fixed on the cinders in the grate. He began thinking about the Hudson. Maybe he would go over to the Edges' after it was dark. He put the bottle down on the hearth and began rubbing his feeler gauge. Lonnie didn't know that the Hudson was sitting on the bottom of the Cooper River. He opened the gauge and fanned the steel blades out. He wouldn't let Maude invite him inside for iced tea. No, he'd sit on the steps and gradually he would turn the conversation to cars, the way Clayburn Morris had turned it to insurance. And when he got Leroy and Earl on cars it would be easy to bring up the Hudson.

Lonnie thumbed the ridge on the one-ten-thousandth-inch blade, thinking how nice it would be propping up the hood and leaning in over the fender again.

Thelma's voice cut through. "You know what Alma told me? She said, 'Thelma, I swear if I had the talent you have when it comes to making things like that, I'd get me a little money together and I'd open me up a shop.'"

Lonnie could hear his own voice rolling across the Edges' dark porch. "Listen, Earl, let me take a quick look at her while I'm here. Go get your flashlight. You'd be surprised how much gas you can save if she's timed right. I used to keep a pretty close watch on her. You can't hear it with the naked ear. Better still, Leroy, let me use your light, this won't take but a minute."

Lonnie clicked the Orange Crush bottle on his bottom teeth. He could feel his hands unscrewing the air filter and jiggling the carburetor. A warm, sure feeling tingled over him, and he decided to go over every point with a piece of sandpaper and then carefully measure the gaps. It was nice under the hood. The old oil and burnt grease mingled with the rubber smell from the radiator pipes. He leaned in over the battery and the water pump. He felt at home. "Hand me those long-nose pliers, Earl. Ask Leroy if you can borrow his socket set. Yeah, yeah, looks like she's carrying some grit. You been buying that cheap gas, ain't you?" He had a soft rag in his left hand, the pliers in his right, and above him on the hood support the wire caged mechanic's light glowed brightly. He dried his hands and shifted the light. "You got a small screwdriver? And get me a coffee can or something to put some parts in." Slowly Lonnie disassembled the carburetor and placed each part in a Chase & Sanborn Coffee can. Later he would trigger enough gas through the carburetor to wash the parts, then he would dry them off and carefully put them back together. He hunched up on top of the manifold to get in closer. Leroy was looking over his left shoulder; Earl his right.

Leroy said, "I thought she was firing funny. My truck's doing the same damn thing and burning gas like it's going out of style. How about it, Lon? When you get through could you take a quick look at her?"

"Be glad to, Leroy. I'll need some more rags. And get me a big glass of ice water."

Thelma fanned between her legs and up under her arms. "And Alma said, 'Thelma, you take a little dressmaking shop like that and you could make yourself a nice piece of change. And Lonnie's handy. He's as handy as they come. He could help out on repairs and on the heavy ironing. You'd be surprised how much that would save you.'"

Lonnie was still with the Hudson. He turned the light off and closed the hood. "Earl, you going to have to bring her by the house tomorrow. I want to check out the wiring. Looks to me like you got yourself an ignition leak. It's going to take some close looking to find it."

313

Earl said, "Anything you say, Lonnie."

"Listen, we're eating early at the house, so get it around there before dark."

"O.K., I'll be there."

Lonnie felt Leroy's hand on his shoulder as they walked back to the Ford pickup. Leroy opened the hood and hung the light on the brace. "The way I see it, it's the carburetor. I bet that thing was designed by a damn oil company."

Lonnie ignored him and peered in.

"O.K., Lonnie, I understand. I won't say another word. You just go ahead and do anything you want. Is that enough light for you? I got another one in the garage. I can hook her up in a minute."

"This is O.K., Leroy. Leave me alone for a minute."

"You're the boss, Lonnie."

Thelma got up and walked to the window. "God, it's so hot in here I thought the window was closed. There ain't a soul on the street. Probably all up at the Magnolia." She laid her hands on Lonnie's shoulders. "Sweetie, it would be hot helping me do that ironing. But we could be careful and watch our pennies and pretty soon we'd have that place air-conditioned. Then it would be real nice for you."

Lonnie leaned into Leroy's engine and began checking the wires to the plugs. "O.K., Leroy, crank her up. Let's hear how she sounds."

Lonnie began testing the plugs. One was bad, and one sounded as if it was about to go. "She's leaking oil, Roy. They fouling out. You need a ring job."

"Son of a bitch. I knew that would happen. Now where in the hell am I going to come up with sixty dollars?"

Lonnie looked back into the dark engine. "Maybe I could

do it for you, Roy. I ain't doing nothing these days in the evening. Course you got to pay for the parts and all."

"Oh, hell, yeah, Lonnie, I could afford that. But that's a big job. You'd be on it two or three nights."

Lonnie wedged the light in at the side of the engine block. "Might even take more than that."

He leaned down with a long-handled socket wrench and tightened the bad plug. "I'll just check your carburetor while I'm here. Then we got to call it a night." He stepped back and cleaned his hands.

"Lon, let me go inside and get you a beer. I got some Miller's in the box and it's so cold it's got ice floating in it."

"Sounds fine, Leroy. And bring me out a touch of salt."

"Sure thing."

Lonnie spoke aloud to the fireplace. "Fine. Fine."

Thelma smiled. "What's fine, honey?"

He stood up, put the Orange Crush on the mantelpiece, and slipped on his shoes. "I'm going out for a walk."

"Ain't you going to finish your Orange?"

"Maybe later, hon."

"All right, but you get back here early, you hear? You know you ain't been sleeping too good lately."

Exactly seven nights after Sonny Love had left on his pilgrimage to Washington, D.C., Lonnie leaned over the drugstore fountain. "Give me a cool one there, Doc. Yeah, Miller's. That one right there on the end. It looks like it's been in there a good while."

Doc joined Lonnie in his first beer, filled him in on all the news, and told him about the Hudson.

"Damn, they couldn't get her towed out?"

"You know the Little Eddy bank, Lon. What're you going to back a tow truck up to?"

"Yeah, I guess you're right. Damn, what a rotten shame." He nodded at the beer case for another Miller's. "I sure hate to hear that."

Doc opened two more bottles.

Chapter 24

Wilson beamed when Jack walked into the Casablanca. He shouted for Sophie and rushed out from behind the counter and shook his hand. "Boy, if you ain't a sight for sore eyes!"

Sophie came out of the kitchen wearing a tall chef's hat. "Land sakes. Where you been? We been worried crazy about you."

Wilson said, "Holly came by and told us about the game. Hell, we all figured you were long gone for good."

Jack opened his shirt and showed them the taping. He told them about the beating, Mason's warning, and how Earl and Coley had taken care of him.

Wilson said, "Well, I'll be goddamn! I never did trust that crowd out there. Bevo too. How about that!"

Sophie poured Jack a cup of coffee. "But we could have taken care of you. Lord, if you ain't the limit. How you feel now?"

"Oh, I'm O.K." He explained the telephone call and how he was embarrassed about the five hundred dollars.

"Don't you worry about that money. There's going to

be a lot more where that came from." Wilson pushed him the sugar across the counter. "I got some plans that are going to make us both rich."

Two couples came in and sat down in the front booth. Wilson folded a towel over his left arm. He was still wearing his tennis shoes. "We'll talk about it later."

Jack stacked three slices of Pullman bread up and sliced off the crusts for a baby club sandwich. "This old kitchen looks pretty good after laying out in those damp woods."

Wilson sat up on the order counter. He tightened the knots in his tennis shoestrings and pulled up his socks. "I didn't draw a clean breath while you were gone. I had to get me in some temporaries and oh, man, what a mess that was! One stole three hams the first night he was on. Snuck them out in the garbage. The other kept sipping on paregoric."

Jack breathed in through his teeth. "Oh, that stuff's bad."

Wilson smiled. "Now let me tell you the news. Old Holly's been after me for years to go into curb service and quit worrying about my sauce and, by God, all of a sudden it started making sense. I guess those couple bad days I had there with my feet kinda sharpened things up."

"You run six places like he does and you got to know what you're talking about."

"That sidewinder's got more ideas about curb service and expanding than Carter's got pills. Says we ought to make a big splash. Like sort of a *première*. Get a big truck with some music and some dancing girls and run it around town and just raise hell."

Jack said, "How 'bout some of those monkeys with electrical guitars? You know, that new equipment they got now. That's plenty loud."

"That'll do it. That'll bring 'em running."

Jack shook the potatoes in the French-fry basket. "Why don't we make a real night of it and rack old Mason's ass? I mean it. I could take a thousand dollars into that game and take his last dime."

"Now you're talking. Hell, I'll go all the way with you. Maybe Holly would want a piece."

"No, leave him out. This has got to be figured close and it's got to be kept quiet."

"Well, I'll bankroll you. Don't worry about that."

In the morning Jack drove Earl and Coley out on the Augusta Highway and rented an oversized, sixteen-wheel, flat-bed rig that had been used during the war to haul B-29 fuselages. Neither Earl nor Coley was tall enough to reach the brakes and handle the big steering wheel. When they returned to the Casablanca Jack told Wilson they were going to hire Lonnie to drive, paint a big sign, and decorate the truck bed with neon and strings of colored lights.

Wilson was in the kitchen taking a foot bath and reading a copy of the *Reader's Digest*. "Well, don't count on him. He's probably still sore at me for booting him out of here. Damn fool was coming in and trying to recruit people for that ass-hole healer."

Earl laughed. "He's all through with that! He was down at the drugstore last night drunker than a hoot owl."

Coley said, "Yeah, he was running around like he was Sonny Love and telling M.L. he could touch his head and make his hair grow back in."

Wilson put the *Digest* in his back pocket and reached for his towel. "That sounds like the old Lonnie."

After seeing an audition at the Veterans of America Night Club, Jack closed a contract with Abe Greene of the Talents Unlimited Enterprises at 1817½ Franklin Street for three guitar men and three dancing girls who called themselves the Georgia-Carolina Rockettes for three hundred dollars. It was set up in two installments: one hundred and fifty then and one hundred and fifty after the show was over.

That night Wilson placed a big sign in the front window announcing that the Casablanca would be closed all day Friday. Everything was set.

On Friday night at eight o'clock Jack walked into the St. Louis Cafe with two thousand dollars in one pocket and a pair of brass knuckles in the other. He didn't stop at the bar but went straight to the back room.

Holly saw him first. "Hello, Jack. How you been, boy?"

"Fine, Holly. Wilson said say hello."

Mason's eyes met Jack's. "Well, if it isn't our old buddy Driscoll. When did you get back in town?"

Cordell Mullins, the owner of the Fried-Rite Donut Company, and Holly moved over and made room for Jack opposite Mason.

"Couple nights back. You miss me?"

Mason smiled. "Sure we missed you. I been holding that seat open. Give him some chips, Bevo."

Mason's face was blank but Bevo, sitting next to Mason and across from Ed Hornsby, looked nervous. He fingered a stack of hundred-dollar whites and a stack of fifty-dollar blues. "How many, Jack?"

"Let's try a thousand."

Mason dealt.

Jack watched Mason's eyes stop for a split second as each hole card skidded to a stop and he read it. For a tall man, his hands were short and flat, his fingers stubby. They weren't hustler hands. They were too short to palm a card or deal seconds. They were even too small to hide an extra pair of buster dice in a crap game. Jack pulled his cards together and checked his hole card.

After three games Jack had the deal. He shuffled the Bicycle playing cards slowly, trying to figure out how they were marked. They all felt the same. They weren't strippers. He fanned the cards out across the table, pulled out a cigarette, and fitted it into his holder. As he lit it he saw that the wheel spokes on the bicycles were shaded and there was a slight difference in their lengths. The aces would have the longest spoke, the deuces the shortest. The suits were marked with the shading.

Mason said, "Come on, Driscoll. Call the game."

Jack pulled the cards together with a smooth stroke. He cut them once and pushed them to Holly for another cut. "Little hand of stud. Ten in the middle."

Jack won the hand and then lost four in a row. He won the next big pot and then got the deal again. He checked his watch. It was 9:45. The lights of the parking cars kept flashing by the edge of the roller shade. Friday was a big night for the St. Louis Cafe. Jack riffled a fast accordion pass and then a tight butterfly shuffle. He could feel everyone's eyes watching his flying fingers.

Holly said, "Let me see that again."

The cards whipped and crackled. He slapped them down hard, spun a single card into the air in a short boomerang, and caught it in position with the deck.

Holly said, "Whew! Where'd you learn that one?"

Jack smiled. "Oh, around, just around." He looked at Mason. "Mason, how 'bout a new deck? These don't feel right."

Mason said, "I don't like the way you're handling those cards, Driscoll. How don't they feel right?"

"Feel sticky, Mason. I guess they're old."

Mason pulled out a new deck. Jack examined the tax stamp and then the edges of the cellophane wrapping.

Mason glared at him. "And I don't like the way you're looking at them."

Bevo squeezed and twisted his left wristband. Perspiration was beading his upper lip.

Jack said, "How 'bout if I made a little side bet with you, Mason?"

"What kind of side bet?"

Jack pushed all of his chips to the center of the table and then laid his wallet with the extra thousand dollars on top. "There's nineteen hundred dollars there. You want to cover it? Better still, let Bevo here take half. He's in this thing too."

Ed Hornsby spoke. "What thing?"

Jack tapped the new pack on the table. "I'm betting these cards and most of them in that drawer are spooked."

Mason rose slowly. "I'll break your goddamn jaw. What in the hell you talking about?"

Ed pulled Mason down. "Let him finish."

Cordell pushed all of Mason's chips to the center of the

table. Holly reached over and raked in Bevo's. Bevo grabbed. "Hey, I ain't betting that on anything."

Holly said, "Sure you are, Bevo. You and Mason are in this until it's over."

Mason's eyes were hard and tight as he glared at Jack. "Boy, you ain't leaving this place alive."

Jack said, "Give me the cards, Ed."

Ed pulled out seven decks and tossed them on the table.

Jack opened the first deck of Bicycles. They were cold. He tossed them aside. The second deck was hot. "Here we go."

The men crowded close, their eyes moving from Jack's hands and cards to the faces of Mason and Bevo. Mason's face was flushed; Bevo was sweating. Jack showed them how they could read the deck by watching the spokes.

Mason said, "I didn't put those cards in the game."

Jack opened another hot deck of Bee Brands and explained how strippers worked.

Ed said, "Lord, how'd he get by the tax stamp?"

Jack said, "Simple, go around it. Take a razor blade and slice open the pack on the side. He reseals the cellophane with a regular clothes iron." Jack shucked the cellophane off and ran his fingernail into the glue flap on the side of the package. It opened easily. "That trick's forty years old."

Holly looked at Mason. "You crummy, rotten bastard."

Ed pushed all of the chips to Jack. "That's yours, Jack. You earned it. Right, boys?"

Holly said, "Yeah, we got a lot more coming than that. Something like four years' worth."

Cordell and Ed went to the corner of the room and began whispering. Mason sat still, quietly staring at the green cloth before him. Except for the whispering of Cordell and

Ed and the faint drumming of the pale fingers of Bevo Mc-Nally it was quiet in the room. Jack finished counting the chips. He had won $4,050.

Suddenly two shots came from the open field behind the café. They sounded like shotgun blasts. Jack checked his watch. It was exactly ten o'clock. Everything was on time. He let the roller shade up. Earl and Coley had started the fireworks. Roman candles were popping and bursting against the black night and the wild crackling sound of a huge amplifier being tuned pounded on the windows and the sides of the building. Mason was standing up. "What's that?"

Holly put his hand on his shoulder. "Keep your seat."

Jack stepped aside so Mason could see the Roman candles and skyrockets rising and bursting and settling slowly on the open field. "Mason, tonight's a big night for you and one you ain't going to forget for a long, long time." He wanted to say more but he didn't want to miss the noise and the fireworks. Greens and golds and reds were bursting and re-bursting high in the sky, and, near the truck that was now visible, great fans of sparklers and spinning, whirring firecrackers seemed to set the tall grass and the weeds on fire.

The Roman candles gave way to a sudden series of loud parachute sky bombs, and as the bright orange-red neon sputtered and came on, framing a gigantic red, blue, and gold sign announcing THE BARBECUE KING, the electric-guitar-playing trio, with more amplification than they had ever dreamed possible, filled the air with their wild and crashing chords. The fireworks stopped and the St. Louis Cafe crowd began gathering around the truck bed.

Ed counted the chips and stacked up packs of ten- and

twenty-dollar bills. Jack began stuffing them into his pockets. He smiled at Mason. "Ain't it funny, Mason? How you'll be gliding along just as smooth and pretty and nice. Like you got everything set and paid for, and nailed down, and everything's perfect. And then one day when you're least expecting it, something you done forgot all about will come sneaking up and grab you in the ass!"

He laughed, shook his head, and started for the door. Holly still had his hand on Mason's shoulder, and Cordell and Ed were holding Bevo lightly by his elbows.

Forty yards from the truck Jack stopped and watched the wildly lighted and incredible scene before him. The dancers were whipping back and forth between the guitar players and the growing crowd. At the other side, another and bigger crowd was pressing against the truck bed for Wilson Peeler's thirty-five-cent barbecue sandwich. Wilson sat under the blazing red neon, his white tennis shoes planted on each side of a twenty-gallon pot of sliced prime pork. To his left and behind him rose a great mound of cut buns and plates.

Sophie, in a new dress and a green-trimmed Casablanca cap on her head, sat next to him with half a beer carton for a cash box, opening and handing out beer and Dr. Peppers. She pushed the cans and the bottles out to the crowd and kept shouting that beer was only twenty-five cents and Dr. Pepper a nickel.

Earl was at the end with another pot, a mound of buns, and a stack of plates. Coley crouched next to him over a wooden box filled with beer and Pepsi-Colas and, like Sophie, had a carton for making change.

A sea of hands were waving dollar bills and the crowd was shouting for more and more barbecue. Wilson's hands flew like birds, from the cut buns to the sauce-drenched pork to the paper plates and back to the cut buns. His face was wreathed in a soft and satisfied smile. Wilson was happy. He had at last found himself. He knew that behind him were eight hundred pounds of prime pork steeping in the world's greatest sauce, that behind the pork were over twenty-five hundred cut barbecue buns, and behind that were seven stacks of paper plates four feet high, and that if he was called upon he could tell them to release the gates of Fort Jackson and he would personally feed the hungry dogfaces who had had the misfortune to have been born up North and had never known the joy of a perfect barbecue sandwich. Wilson was making twelve to fifteen sandwiches a minute, and as fast as he made them Sophie was there to hand out the beer and the Dr. Peppers and take the money. When the first twenty-gallon pot got low and began to shift, Wilson gripped it with his tennis shoes and plunged down until his head vanished.

And the crowd: "Ain't he something?"

"He's the king. He's the King of the Barbecue."

Wilson heard it all. He wanted to say, "Say it again," but he was too busy and they wouldn't hear him.

"Look at him go. You ever in all your life see a man make sandwiches so fast?"

"No, and I never tasted sauce like that."

"And don't he put plenty on? Oh, I like the way he puts it on."

"It's so good it hurts my gums."

"Oh, Lord, I got to have me several more."

"Hey, Mr. Barbecue King, you aim on coming out here every night?"

Sophie shouted, "You all come out to Wilson Peeler's

Casablanca on the corner of Dogwood and Lee. You can't miss it. Right at the foot of the hill. There it is right on the sign, read it. And we got curb service, every night."

Earl made barbecues; Coley served the drinks and collected the money. "Faster, Earl, Faster. We're way behind."

"I can't go any faster. Damn, I hope Jack's all right."

Lonnie sat in the truck cab racing the engine to keep the power up for the neon, the string of colored lights, and the electric guitars. He was eating a barbecue and drinking his third beer.

Jack rubbed his hands together and started across the field. He felt light and springy on the grass. He swung up on the truck, grinning at Earl and Coley.

Earl shouted above the noise, "What happened?"

Jack slapped both front pockets. "Cleaned him out." He patted Wilson on the back. "Move over." He pulled a stool up to the side and slid another twenty-gallon pot of barbecue forward.

Wilson said, "How'd you do?"

Jack leaned into Wilson's ear. "Won four-o-five-o and broke Mason's ass. Holly and the boys got him and Bevo. I'd sure hate to be in their shoes."

Wilson reached over and, with his right hand that was covered with sauce, shook Jack's hand. "Boy, you are something. I swear you are." He shouted, "Hey, Soph, Jack won four thousand and fifty dollars!"

Sophie shouted back, "That's your France trip, honey, right there."

Wilson tried to snap his fingers but they were too wet with sauce. "What a night! Great God, what a night!"

Jack was dipping pork and closing the buns. He dipped

327

faster. He shouted to the customers not to forget where the barbecue was coming from and to be sure and tell their friends. He liked the idea of Wilson in France and wondered how the French would receive him in his white tennis shoes. Maybe he could get a little sports car and drive through the South of France and visit the small towns. In the morning he would buy Wilson some French language records.

The music came to life again and this time so strong that the big truck bed began to vibrate. In the great aluminum pots the pork barbecue moved and sloshed against the sides. The stacked boxes of cut buns began shifting. Sophie was humming and tapping her can opener on the edge of the beer crate she sat on. Wilson was beating time with his shoe on the side of the pot. Jack looked out and saw the crowd begin to clap and rock to the simple beat. And then he realized, as he dipped and spread the dripping meat on the open buns and closed them and placed them on the paper plates, that he, too, like Wilson, like Sophie, like Earl and Coley, the long-sideburned musicians, the whirling dancers, and the great, surging, pork-filled crowd that now flowed around the entire truck and seemed to fill the very night itself, was moving to the deep and driving beat.

Chapter 25

As the news of the appearance of Wilson Peeler on the barbecue truck and the disappearance of Mason Richards began spreading, the size of Jack's winnings rose from four to
six to ten to twenty thousand dollars. It finally settled on
$36,500 and someone swore they had heard Jack say that
every penny would be plowed back into the remodeling of
the Casablanca. Even the newscaster at WXOY, with only
a sliver of the facts, made an official announcement. He said
Columbia needed a new prestige restaurant and that he, for
one, was going down to look in on Wilson Peeler's curb
service and "The New Casablanca."

"The New Casablanca," under Wilson and Jack's partnership, began to change. The parking lot was quickly
paved, colored lights were strung, and four public address
boxes were installed to carry the music of the jukebox out
to the waiting cars. Business doubled, and Wilson and Jack
hired four curb boys, another cook, two inside waitresses,
and a cash register girl for the day shift who was a graduate
of the Drake Bible School.

Wilson came strolling into the Casablanca during the lunch rush. He wore a new black-and-white-checked sports jacket, white slacks, white tennis shoes, and cocked above his grinning face was a Swiss Alpine hat with a bright red brush sticking straight up in the air. He stopped at the head of the counter, and, raising his left hand high, he let trail down a long green railroad ticket for the Silver Meteor to New York City.

Sophie came out from behind the counter, and after hugging him she stood before him holding his hands. "Oh, honey, I'm so glad. You're finally going. I just can't believe it."

Jack finished serving a hot roast beef platter and shook Wilson's hand. "You sure look good."

Wilson smiled. "The man at the ticket agency says on Air France they cook and serve authentic French cooking and champagne while you're in the air. I sure as hell don't want to miss seeing that. Wonder how they do it with all that jouncing around and all?"

"Those French are pretty tricky."

"They got to be, to come up with something like that. You really have to give them credit."

Jack said, "I wouldn't mind seeing that myself. But listen, you get yourself some rest. Don't you go over there and just hang around the kitchens. Get out and look around. There's a lot in France besides just cooking."

Wilson went over to the booths and began shaking hands with his customers.

"Staying two months, Morris. Maybe more. Maybe more if I take a notion. It's sort of a combination vacation and business trip.

"Hello, Woodrow. How do I look?"

"Fine, Wilson, you look fine. That's a sharp coat you got on there, what it cost you?"

"Forty-seven fifty up at Henderson's. Good fit, ain't it? I tell you, Woodrow, I feel like a new man in it. What do you think of the hat?"

"That's sharp too."

"Here, try it on!"

Woodrow Frizzell cocked his head to one side and peered into the thin mirror at the end of the booth. The mirror distorted his face and made the hat long and narrow. He kept raising up until he got a true image.

"Hell, I like that, Wilson. I really do. Looked pretty sporty at first but it shore feels nice. What they asking for a hat like that?"

"Four ninety-eight."

"I'll be dogged. Well, I'm shore as hell going to get me one of them. What you call them?"

"Swiss Yodeler or Swiss Climber, something like that. You just go in and talk to Dewitt. Tell him you want the hat he sold me. You can't miss it."

Wilson went to the next booth. "Hello, Calvin, Cedric. How you doing there, Mitchell?"

"Hello, Wilson."

"How's that sauce, Maurice?"

Wilson kept his Alpine hat on while he took his last foot bath. His luggage was packed and standing by the living room door and his tickets, samples of his barbecue sauce, and his passport were ready. He patted his feet dry. After dusting them with Dr. Scholl's foot powder he reached over and switched on his new French conversation record and picked up his nail clippers. Wiggling his toes to let the talcum sift in between them, he sat back with his left foot in his towel-covered lap. He smiled as he rounded and smoothed the edge on his big toenail, and in a slow, puzzled nasal tone he began following the French instructor. *"Bon jour, madame. Bon jour, monsieur. Bon jour ma-dem-a-selle."*

For Sophie, Pluto and Neptune movements placed Capricorn in a favorable position, and her monthly guide said, "The 20th will be a good day for following your innermost desires. This is the day you should visit your relatives and mend all family ties." She announced to Jack that in two days she was going home to Irmo, and she began showing him how the receipts and tax information were filed and how the marketing was set up.

Four days later Jack was making up the week's menu. "Damn, if you boys were only fifteen. It would all be so simple then."

Earl slid back into the corner of the booth. "Well, we ain't, and Hog knows it."

Coley was reading the list of hillbilly and modern songs on the jukebox station.

Jack shoved his pencil behind his ear. "Well, you can eat here. I won't charge you a dime for that."

Earl said, "We don't want no handouts, Jack."

"No one said you did. Hell, boy, straighten out. I owe you a lot more than I'm going to be able to pay you with a few hamburgers and a little moldy-ass curb job. Where you think I'd be if it wasn't for you all and that old Hudson?"

Coley dropped a nickel in the slot and punched a Spike Jones record. "Don't mind him, Jack. He's still got that river bottom on his mind."

"Well, maybe this will pick you up." Jack handed each of them an envelope. "Go on, open it."

Coley tore his open. A folded card dropped out saying, "Thanks. Jack." Inside the card was a brand new one-hundred-dollar bill. Earl had the same.

Coley said, "Jeeee-sus! A hundred apiece! Man, Earl, we got it now. Damn, thanks, Jack."

Earl grinned. "Wow! Holy Moley! Jack, we sure don't deserve this much! I mean it!"

Jack said, "The hell you don't."

A dusty whirlwind swept through the drugstore yard, and after picking up cigarette butts, Dixie cups, and Butterfinger wrappers it dumped them on Mrs. Gulley's lawn. Midnight was up to his shoulders in Doc's garbage can. The rushing whirlwind noise scared him and he jumped back. The can crashed down and he streaked off, carrying a chicken foot in his mouth.

Doc opened an accordion file of plastic-covered photographs of himself and the bass he had caught at the Santee River and laid them on the counter. Lonnie whistled. "That's some fish, Doc." He had his painter's cap pushed back on his head and he needed a shave.

"It ain't like Coley's but I got both fists in his mouth."

M.L. said, "Is he a bigmouth?"

"Damn right! You don't see smallmouths running around weighing no six pounds. I'm having this picture blown up to about four feet square and I'm putting it right in the middle of that mirror."

"Yeah, it'll look nice there." M.L. slid the beer box open. "You all drink much?"

"We didn't bring any back. I tell you, you get out in that

swamp and you don't suffer so in the morning. Must be the air." Doc was tan, and he rubbed his peeling forehead with the heel of his hand. "You know, a man could do a lot worse than living down there on that river. I swear I get down there and I don't have a trouble in the world."

M.L. said, "I guess you heard about Mason Richards."

"Yeah, I got it from Ed Hornsby. I almost fell out of the boat. You know, that son of a bitch Mason stung me for six hundred and seventy dollars one night before I even knew I was in the game."

Lonnie opened a bottle of Miller's and shook his head. "No more. No more. Not round here he ain't."

Doc said, "That Driscoll must really be an operator. I tell you, when I was setting that boy's ribs I kinda figured he was something a little special. Didn't bat an eye when I made him tighten up for the adhesive. Hell, I've seen bigger men than him go down on their knees and cry on that."

Lonnie sipped his beer. "I guess Wilson's in old Gay Paree right this minute. Wonder what he's doing."

M.L. said, "I swear, I never thought he'd make it."

Doc rubbed the counter down with a wet cloth. "He never would have if Driscoll hadn't shown up. That café would have buried him."

Lonnie said, "Makes you feel nice, don't it, hearing a story like that and seeing how everything worked out so good and all?" He aimed the top of his bottle at the ceiling fan and closed one eye. "Oh, I bet that old dog's having himself a time in Paris."

Earl and Coley parked their wheels in the bicycle rack, and picking up Doc's paper they headed for the back booth. "Here's one." Coley pointed. "Nineteen thirty-six

Ford, one owner, thirty thousand actual guaranteed miles, needs body work, a hundred and sixty dollars."

Earl closed his eyes and figured quickly. "Hell, that's only two thousand miles a year. That's got to be a lie."

Lonnie drifted back and slid into the booth opposite them. He scratched part of his beer label off and rolled the paper into a small ball. "I just can't feature that Hudson going down like that." He balanced the paper ball on the lip of the ash tray and began rolling another one. "I guess it would cost a fortune to drag her up. Course it wouldn't be too much trouble drying her out. I'd need new seats and maybe some new woodwork."

Coley kept his finger on an ad. "It can't be done, Lonnie. There just ain't no way."

Lonnie frowned. "Well, I got to be coming up with a car. I just got to get my hands on something."

Earl said, "Here's a 'thirty-six Ford for one-sixty."

"I don't want no Ford. Besides, I ain't laying out that kind of money."

Coley said, "How 'bout Jethro's Hup?"

Lonnie sipped his beer. "Nineteen twenty-six Hupmobile. Oh, oh, that's old. That's back there, all right. Wonder what Gus'll turn it loose for?"

Earl said, "He's down to seventy, but asking ain't getting."

Lonnie said, "Don't he know about that piston yet?"

Coley circled an ad for a 1938 Buick. "I don't think so."

"Well, hell, maybe I could skin him way down."

Earl said, "No maybe to it. I'll bet if you play it right he'll pay you to drag it away. But Lonnie, it ain't going to run a lick."

Lonnie took a long pull on his beer and then a short one.

"Oh, that don't matter so much. I just want something I can mess around with. I'll get her to run all right." He tapped the bottle on his bottom teeth. "Nineteen twenty-six Hup. Yeah, that wasn't a bad year for Hupmobiles. Not bad at all. Oh, they built them babies back there then. Good work. Good heavy work. No sir, they just don't build them like that any more."

M.L. came in from the bus stop bench in a hurry. "Come out here, Doc!"

Doc came to the door of the prescription room.

Lonnie raised up in his seat. "What's going on?"

"Claude Henry says the Law just caught Peevy. They're holding him uptown."

Doc said, "Jesus Christ."

"Damn!" Lonnie slammed his fist on the table. "Anyone with him?"

"No, all alone."

Lonnie got out of the booth. "Where'd they catch him?"

"Caught him at home. Broke in his back door and caught forty gallons in his sink before he could dump it."

Lonnie shook his head once. "That's going to be rough. They'll cream his ass for sure this time."

A motorcycle coughed and popped outside. It was Hog Wallace. He gunned the engine, cut it, and came in smiling. He had been in on the raid at Peevy's. Leaning on the fountain, he slapped his black leather gloves across his hand. "Well, Doc, M.L., Lonnie, I guess you boys heard the news. I told him myself we were going to get him. He had plenty warning."

Doc said, "You want something, Hog?"

"Yeah, give me an R.C. Cola."

Doc opened the bottle. "You wouldn't care to drink it outside, would you?"

"Don't get too smart, Doc." He looked back at Lonnie. "Too bad you weren't there. I'd have loved to drag your ass in on something beside D and D."

Lonnie stuck his finger in the top of his bottle and made a popping noise. "Go to hell, Hog."

Hog said, "Listen, you little ape, next time you even breathe out of line it's going to be ninety days. And I don't mean no painting."

Earl slipped into the back room, took a bottle of oil of mustard from the prescription shelf, and went out the rear of the store. He ran alongside Doc's Buick and came up behind Hog's Harley-Davidson. Hog was still facing Doc and had his back to the street. Earl emptied the bottle on Hog's saddle and ran around to the back door.

Hog was still talking. "Clyde Peevy will be coming out that Penitentiary gate a lot smarter man than when he went in. Next time, he'll be thinking twice before he gets tangled up with any more whiskey." He finished his drink and went outside.

Earl whispered to Lonnie what he had done, and they all followed Hog outside and stood under the awning.

Hog pulled on his gloves and centered his cap. He looked at Lonnie. "Don't forget what I told you." He swung up and came down on the crank. The engine fired and caught. Hog settled himself on the seat and throttled back and forth, pretending to clear the engine. He made the engine backfire and sputter and then revved it up high. Kicking the stand back he pushed off, shifted to second, and within a hundred yards was heading up Bee doing fifty. He almost made it to M.L.'s house. He braked suddenly and leaped off. The mustard had worked through to his skin. He tried to hunch himself forward so he wouldn't touch the cloth, but his pants were tighter than sausage casings. He glared back at the crowd watching him from the drugstore yard and then rode off slowly, standing up.

Earl grabbed Coley by the arm and pulled him back into the rear booth. "Boy, are we lucky! Are we lucky! We can get rid of E. Z. Loan and get a car and everything now."

"What're you talking about?"

"Listen, Coley, now this has really got to be secret. Me and Dad and Charley and Lonnie built an automatic still for Clyde up there on Pope Street, and it's all stocked up and just crying to be run."

Coley said, "Well, if you think you're sucking me into running any old still you got another think coming."

"Coley, dammit, this is an automatic. It won't take more than a couple hours. We just start her up, mix in the water, and then carry it out to O'Hara's. He'll buy every drop with no questions asked. I can guaran-damn-tee that."

"How you expect me to believe you after that last pile of bull you fed me? You must think I'm loony."

"Aw, come on, Cole. All we'd need is one run. Just one little old measly run. Look at this." He multiplied $5.50 a gallon times fifty on the newspaper margin. "Look, two hundred and seventy-five dollars for one night's work. Hell, in one night we'd be up to what we made at the dairy the whole time. I ain't lying." He added the $275 to the $200 they had. "Looka there. Four hundred and seventy-five dollars! Boy, we could buy a car and a half with that."

"This is crazy, Earl. What in the hell you know about running any old still?"

"I know plenty, and anyhow this one runs itself. You're going to come, right?"

"No, I ain't messing with any more whiskey. I suppose you think we could carry it out to O'Hara's on our wheels?"

"I can borrow Dad's truck. You know that."

"Well, I ain't going. You're probably lying anyway."

"Listen, I'll admit I lied last time, O.K.? But this is different." Earl drew a circle around the $475. "Four days from now and we'd be cruising around in a brand new car."

"I said no."

Chapter 26

At ten o'clock that night Earl and Coley jimmied the back window at 906 Pope Street and climbed in. Earl checked the windows. The black shades were still drawn and taped down tight. He turned the lights on.

Coley said, "Wow! Will you look at that!" He rubbed his hand down the seven-foot kettle. His face and red hair were lost in the copper reflection but his white T shirt and low-slung overall pants shimmered back, making him look wide and squat. "Boy, this is really something else. It's like a factory."

Earl looked in the mash vats. They were dry as dust. He jumped up on a scaffold crosspiece and, grabbing a higher piece, he chinned himself twice and then skinned the cat. He hung down backwards. "Look here. You could hang a car on it. This baby is built." He dropped down. "Come on, let's get started."

Earl knew that the more meal they used the better the whiskey would be and had decided to use his grandfather's recipe of sixty pounds of meal to every hundred pounds of sugar. They dragged the heavy bags from the storeroom and began loading one of the mash vats. When the vat was half full they filled the cooker with water and lit the boiler. The 180 needle jets of the Detroit burner flashed on with a low whooshing sound, and the water in the heater coil began boiling.

After they had filled the vat with boiling water they stretched the black tarpaulin over it to hold the heat in. Earl explained how they would wait three days for the mash to ferment and then begin the run. They would then light the burner and open the valve that fed the mash slurry through the preheater into the cooker.

"Jesus, Earl." They pushed their bicycles along the dark sidewalk behind the Governor's Mansion. "It really is easy. Anybody right off the street could run that thing."

"Didn't I tell you that?"

"Listen, you ain't holding nothing out on me, are you?"

"Hell, no, you got everything. I swear it."

A party was going on inside the Mansion, and black Cadillacs with low license plate numbers were lined up like hearses in the driveway. The sound of music came over the deep lawn.

"O.K., Coley, O.K., there is something else. We've got to wait three days for the mash to ferment, right?"

"Right."

"Well, why not go whole hog? I mean, why not make up two more batches? There's enough meal and sugar and we'd be getting triple the money. You just said yourself how simple it is."

Coley lifted his front wheel over the Spruce Street curb. "I guess we might as well. We've gone this far. But no getting in more supplies. We agree on that?"

"Agreed. Oh, man, we'll be able to get a car easy. And I mean a good car."

Each night, for the next two nights, they made up a vat of mash. By staggering the batches and allowing three days for fermentation, they planned to run the first run on the fourth night, the second on the fifth, and the third on the sixth.

It was the third night and Earl lay in bed with his flashlight spotted directly above him on the ceiling. Leroy and Maude were asleep. He could hear Leroy snoring. Slowly he counted the twenty-nine boards in the ceiling and the fourteen tongue-and-groove planks in the wall. The three nights of mixing sugar and meal and water had flown by. In less than twenty hours he would have to open the valve and light the burner. Turning the flashlight off, he wondered what it would be like. Would it smoke, or rock, or bubble? Would it leak steam, or backfire, or would the burner simply hiss smoothly and the whiskey come running out of the condenser like water from a drain? He had lied to Coley; he had never seen a still in operation. It was true he knew all the parts and the connections and he knew the mash mixture recipe, but he had never really seen one work. What if something went wrong. What? What could go wrong? A small voice behind his eyes cleared its throat and whispered that it might quietly simmer and then simply explode. Maybe it would be smart to check with Lonnie first. Lonnie would know what to if anything happened, and he would know exactly when to start the run. The voice stirred. "And by the way, good buddy, that's something else you don't know beans about. How you figuring on handling that?"

If they ran it too soon he knew the yield would be short and the taste strong. If it were too late, it would be weak and have a water bead like beer and taste like kerosene. Maybe O'Hara wouldn't buy it. He gripped the flashlight tight. Would it give off a certain smell? Would it be bubbling? Would it turn black or brown or red or green? How in the hell would he know when?

A light wind had blown up, and the hard August chinaberries sounded like hail as they dropped and rolled down the tin roof. Hadn't Leroy and Lonnie both said that the still would run itself? That it was one hundred per cent automatic and that there was nothing to do? Yes, he lied. He flashed the light on, then off, then on again. He began counting the knotholes in the ceiling. At nine he stopped. If the number was even he'd go ask Lonnie's advice; if it was odd he wouldn't. He counted; it was twenty-eight.

Earl pushed his bicycle along the drain ditch. Someone had broken the street light at the corner, and it was too dark to ride over the deep gullies and the big stones. At Bee Street the pavement began and he swung on and started pedaling.

He coasted down Lonnie's driveway into two bright mechanic's lights. Lonnie was wearing his greasy blue coveralls and no shirt. He was working on a dark four-door touring car. It was Jethro's Hupmobile. His big green toolbox, three empty Miller's bottles, and two full ones were standing on the wide rubber-coated running board. "Hello, Lon. When'd you get her?"

"Just a few hours ago." He had the head of the block off

and was crouched in close over the cylinder holes. "Don't stand too close. You'll get dust in her."

"You didn't pay Gus no seventy dollars, did you?"

The wooden piston had picked up moisture and expanded and frozen in the cylinder wall. Lonnie had been trying to work it loose. He dried his hands. "I'm going to have to take it out with a chisel."

"What'd you pay him?"

"Ten dollars."

"Ten! Wow, that's all right! How'd you swing it?"

Lonnie sipped his beer and looked over the long straight-eight engine. "I took the head off and chipped a little bit of the piston off. Then I called him over to take a look."

"Jesus, he must have had a stroke."

Lonnie's eyes were shining like dimes. He seemed to be speaking to the engine. "I told him I'd take it off his hands and give him ten dollars if he'd do the towing and he said O.K."

"That all he said?"

"That's all."

Lonnie covered the cylinder holes with a newspaper and emptied the tools from his pocket. "Course it's going to need a lot of work. But I'll tell you something: working on a machine like this is a downright pleasure. Here, take a look at this fuel pump." He moved the light over. "That's brass, solid brass. I mean they didn't fool around when they put this buggy together."

Lonnie opened another beer and sat on the running board. "How come you ain't in bed?"

"I'm in trouble, Lonnie. I need your help. Me and Coley mixed up a batch of mash at Clyde's place. We're going to run tomorrow night."

"Christ, boy! I hope you know what you're doing. They catch you in there and they'll put you both under the jail."

"We're just going to make one run. We've got to get that E. Z. loan paid off and we're thinking about another car."

"You ain't telling Leroy, are you?"

"You're the only one that knows. Lonnie, we mixed the batch Monday night around ten, and I ain't sure when to start cooking."

Lonnie rocked his beer back and forth. "I'd say a shade less than three days. In winter it's slower. We used to add a few pounds of yeast then and top her off with about an inch of bran to hold the heat in. But this is prime weather for working. Yeah, I'd say sixty-eight, maybe sixty-nine hours. Now don't be telling Leroy I told you this."

"Don't worry. But how do we know *exactly* when to run?"

"It'll be moving. That'll be enough for you to go on. There's a lot of ways of testing. Sugar levels and sacrometers and all, but that takes years to learn. You just wait till she starts moving, then slap her in the kettle. What kind of car you got in mind?"

"Zuck's got an ad for a 'thirty-eight Buick. Lonnie, this thing can't blow up on us, can it?"

Lonnie finished his beer and opened his last bottle. "No, don't worry about that. Just keep that mash flowing in and out and you got no problems." He moved his toolbox and lay back on the front fender. "Nineteen thirty-eight Buick, now that ain't a bad car. You know when I was driving for old Hoot Cooper I had me a nineteen thirty-four Buick. That thing would dig down and scratch. I kept the back end jacked up so high with heavy duty springs it looked like a jack rabbit with a sore ass when it wasn't loaded down with four or five hundred pounds of whiskey."

The cotton mill clock rang four times.

"Boy, you better get on home. And listen, you all watch yourselves on this and for God's sake keep it quiet."

Earl yawned. "O.K., Lonnie, thanks a lot."

"Don't mention it. If you pick up that Buick, how 'bout bringing her by? I'd like to take a look at her for you."

"O.K. Good night, Lonnie."

Lonnie finished his beer and turned his mechanic's light off. "Good night, Earl."

At seven o'clock Earl and Coley threw the tarpaulin back. The mash was rolling; it was time to start the run. The mash slurry was a greasy gray, almost beef-stew color. It was turning and coiling just as Lonnie had said it would. Bubbles swelled and popped and the sweet-sour terrible smell of fermentation poured over them.

"Whew!" Coley backed up. "It sure stinks."

"You can say that again."

Earl had told Leroy and Maude that he was staying at Coley's. Coley had told Harlis and Mary he was at Earl's.

Earl said, "I'm ready when you are."

"Let's go."

Earl fired the burner, and the 180 needle jets came on whistling.

After starting the force pump between the mash vat and the preheater, they opened the waste valve from the cooker to the fire hose and the downstairs toilet. The slurry made a wet, sucking, slapping noise as it was sucked into the still. The run had started. The preheated mash would cook in the kettle and pass out the hose as slop. The rising steam vapor would flow into the doubler for redistilling, then to the water-jacket-covered copper coil, where it would condense into whiskey and drain into the blending tub. The kettle whistled louder and lower than the Detroit burner, and the two noises sounded like a train engine warming up.

Earl's hands were wet and trembling. When he lit a Kool he had to hold the match with both hands. He moved from the mash vat to the blending tub to the burner, pretending he was inspecting the connections. The heat was rising. His cigarette was wet. He could hear his heart pounding. There was nothing to check or inspect or measure. There was nothing to do. He smoothed an imaginary bend out of the hose and squatted down to run a pencil into the end of the condenser coil. It was clear. The burner noise was higher; the cooker louder, lower. The kettle rocked. The rising noise scared him, and he felt his galloping heart moving up into his throat. Suddenly the cooker made a deep thumping noise. The room shook. Coley said, "Jesus! What's that?"

Earl froze. "I don't know."

They stood in the doorway. The fire hose was between them on the floor. The kettle belched again. They backed up toward the steps.

A faint whispering, hissing sound came from the condenser and a thin trail of white vapor rose to the ceiling.

Earl said, "I think she's coming through."

The vapor stopped and a single tear of raw corn whiskey formed on the tip of the coil. It quivered, then dropped loudly into the copper-lined Coca-Cola barrel.

Coley grinned and stepped forward. "It's whiskey."

Earl sighed and moved away from the door. Another

drop came and then another. They came faster and faster until they sounded like bee-bee shots in a ping-pong ball. Earl and Coley stood close and watched the rapid drops turn into a thin shining stream. The thumping noise at the cooker stopped. The only sounds were the whistling burner and the trickling corn.

Earl put his wet hand on Coley's wet shoulder. "Didn't I tell you it was going to be a snap?"

Downstairs the mash slop flowed from the fire hose into the toilet with a soft bubbling noise and was sucked down into the big sewage pipe under the street. The closed and taped windows kept the heat inside, and before the bottom of the blending tub was covered the room was scalding hot. They skinned down to their shorts. Coley stood at the sink, squeezing his finger to the tap, skeeting water on himself.

Earl's pompadour was plastered flat. He kept drying his hands on the back of his shorts. "Move over."

He stuck his head under the spigot and pushed his hair straight back.

Coley said, "How much longer?"

" 'Bout an hour. I'm roasting."

As the mash level in the vat dropped, the whiskey level in the blending tub rose. By midnight it was at the fifteen gallon mark.

At one-thirty the run ended. It had yielded almost twenty gallons. They cut the 180-proof corn to 90 proof by adding in twenty gallons of tap water and began siphoning from the blending tub into the five-gallon kegs. After they bunged eight kegs and carried them downstairs, they rolled them under the fence and into the cemetery.

Together they slid back three grave vaults. *Morris M. Herskovits 1868-1932* and *Meyer Blaustein 1890-1941* received three kegs each. *Sandra Katzenbach "a loving wife" 1870-1930* received two.

Later, they lay on the mattresses in the dark room, smoking and planning how they would spend the money.

Earl said, "Forty gallons times five-fifty. That's two hundred and twenty dollars. Not bad, not bad at all."

"And for only one night. Hell, we can pay E. Z. with Jack's money and put most of this on the car."

Earl stubbed his cigarette out on the floor. "And if we average forty gallons for the next two nights we're talking about six hundred dollars."

The house creaked and groaned as it cooled and the sour smell of mash slop began tapering off.

Coley pulled his sheet up over his legs. "Boy, we're going to smell like mash slop for a week."

Earl said, "I'm going to get me some new clothes and one of those Air Corps jackets."

"Me too. And a white scarf for the jacket; that's real sharp. And a fly rod and some good lines and a net, and I need me a couple sweaters. Maybe I'll get a generator and a light for the wheel too. They got one up at Sears for eight dollars."

"Let's go to sleep."

"O.K., good night."

They woke at six. After dressing and checking to make sure no one was watching they sneaked out to the garage where they had hidden their bikes and rode uptown.

At the Midtown Restaurant on Broad Street they ordered grits and eggs and bacon.

Coley yawned. "God, I'm sleepy."

"Drink some more water. I hear that helps."

Earl lit a cigarette but after the first puff he put it out.

Coley said, "When we seeing O'Hara?"

"How 'bout tonight?" Earl wiped his toast over the last traces of egg. "I'll call him now."

Earl told Tom O'Hara who he was and that he had found forty gallons of corn in the swamp up near Pontiac. O'Hara said he didn't like the idea of buying whiskey from minors but since he was Leroy's son he'd be willing to take it off his hands for two dollars a gallon. Earl told him he could get it taken off his hands in West Columbia and they would pay the going rate of five-fifty per gallon delivered, and if he wanted it he would have to pay that.

O'Hara said he would.

That night Earl borrowed Leroy's truck, telling him he wanted to go to a night ball game out in Blythewood. He and Coley loaded and secured the eight kegs to the truck bed and started off. On South Broad Earl brought the heavy truck to a full stop in front of the raised tracks of the Southern Railroad. He was afraid the kegs might crack together. He crept across the tracks in first, shifted to second, and headed out the Fairgrounds Road to Tom O'Hara's.

Tom O'Hara was a large fat man with small hands and feet, no hair, and a loud shrill voice. Two of his six sons, except for their wispy straw-colored hair, looked and sounded exactly like him. O'Hara operated a honky-tonk which was a long low room with ten booths, a dance floor, a jukebox, and a beer license. The ladies' room was inside, the men's outside. He sold beer, whiskey setups of ice cubes and soft drinks, Nabisco peanut-buttered cheese crackers, peanuts, pig's feet, boiled eggs, Stanback Headache Powders, and Sen Sen. He kept his corn whiskey out behind the men's toilet in a sweet potato mound.

O'Hara said he was still worried about buying from minors. "Guess it wouldn't do no good to ask for a better price?"

Earl shook his head.

O'Hara sent his oldest son, Boyd, out to get a keg. He pulled the bung out and daubed corn into his palm. He rubbed it briskly to get the heat up and cupped his hands over his nose. "Smells good, real good." He tipped the keg and poured out a dipperful. He tasted it and sucked it in and out of his brown teeth. "Prime! Prime! That's prime stuff, all right. Good mash mix, real good, and a good slow copper run. That's first-class whiskey, no doubt about that. I'd shore love to know who made it." He tasted it again. His tongue raced back and forth across his lips like a lizard over a trash pile. "Yeah, yeah. And they put a little age on her, too. That stuff's been sitting around for a year or my name ain't Tom O'Hara." He took another drink. "No rough edges, no echoes. Got her all smoothed down. Nice, real nice." He shouted to two of his sons sitting in a booth drinking beer and eating pistachio nuts. "Boyd, you and Norman unload this stuff. Come on now, get the lead out."

After he had checked the whiskey bead on each keg for low proof and each level for short measure, he counted out $220.

Earl said, "Mr. O'Hara, I'd appreciate it if you wouldn't let on anything about this. I mean I wouldn't want it to get back to Dad or anyone."

O'Hara pushed the money across the counter. "Son, that's the best stuff I've bought in two years. Don't think I don't appreciate it. If you go running into any more, you be sure and call old Tom first, you hear?"

Earl recounted the ten twenties and the two tens. "Yessir, we'll call."

Coley drove a few hundred yards before he burst out laughing. He stopped, cut the lights, and collapsed on the steering wheel. "You hear him? You hear him?" Tears were coming to his eyes. "He thinks we're professionals."

Earl spread the bills out on the dashboard. "I thought I'd croak when he kept licking at it."

Later that night the second batch ran fast and smooth. The run ended shortly after two o'clock, yielding ten full five-gallon kegs, and by three-thirty their work was done. The graves of Herskovits, Blaustein, and Katzenbach each received three kegs. The tomb of Herman Feldman, 1871–1939, received one.

Chapter 27

Coley divided the newspaper, giving Earl the comics and sports section and keeping the used-car ads for himself. They were at the Midtown Restaurant. After a breakfast of waffles, grits and eggs, and double orders of link sausages and a slow and careful reading of the car ads, they headed for the E. Z. Loan Company to pay off their entire balance.

By ten o'clock they were strolling through the low-priced Chevrolets and Fords at Loganberry's Used Car Lot. They checked a 1939 Chevrolet marked *A Steal at $150.*

Coley spat between his teeth. "They're all junk. Let's try something newer."

They began drifting toward the front of the lot and the more expensive cars. They sat in the big Airflow Chryslers, the Packard Clippers, and the DeSotos; they looked under the hoods of the long Buicks and smoothed their hands over the rich leather upholstery of the automatic-transmission Cadillacs. Earl slid in under the wheel of a flaming red Lincoln Continental convertible. He slammed the glove compartment door. "Listen at that, it's like a refrigerator."

Coley ran his hand over the dashboard. "Feel that. Feel that dash. Just run your hand over it."

The Lincoln was two years old and was priced at $4,100. Earl hunched forward and pumped the brakes. "Can't you just see old Ambrose's stupid face if we come cruising up to school in this baby? I'll bet the horn's something."

"Try it."

The four-tone horn sounded like a trumpet and trombone duet. Loganberry's manager shouted from his office, "All right, you kids, quit messing with that Lincoln!"

The last run on the third night went even faster; by midnight it was half over. The strong smell of cooking mash made the air feel dense, and the breathless room got hotter. As the heat rose they watched the blending tub and kept checking the fire hose in the toilet to make sure it was draining properly.

And then a faint tapping sound started in the feeder pipe. Coley said, "What's that?"

"I don't know."

The noise thickened and speeded up.

"It's getting worse."

"Christ, it's the pump. She's choking up." Earl lay on the floor and pounded on the pipe with a length of two-by-four. It jammed again and the noise came back louder. He lay near the burner and the cooker so he could reach the force pump valve. The heat was fierce. "Jesus, I can't stand it. How's it look?"

"She's moving. Here, move out, I'll try it."

Earl rolled out and Coley slid under and began pounding. "Turn the burner down! I'm roasting!"

"Can't, she'll lose steam! Keep hitting!"

"I am! How 'bout the fan?"

Earl plugged the big sixteen-inch fan in and turned it on Coley's head. "That's better. Come on, take over. I gotta rest."

Earl found a second piece of two-by-four and slid back under. The fan blew hard but the air was scalding. He gulped in the gas burner fumes and felt his throat and chest tighten.

Coley soaked the bed sheets in the sink. They wrapped them around their heads, lay back down, and kept pounding on the big four-inch valve. It got better; the noise stopped and the mash flowed smoothly. Then it got worse, much worse. They hit the pipe harder and faster until it coughed free and began flowing. Earl had to stop. He needed air. He felt dizzy and rolled out on his back to catch his breath. The heat waves rose up through the honeycomb of steam pipes like weary snakes, shrinking the still to a toy one minute, then stretching it up until it crowded the vaulting ceiling.

"Come on, Earl."

"All right, all right." He rolled back under.

They worked furiously. The mash was still flowing. They soaked the sheets again, but after a few minutes they were bone dry and felt as if they had just been ironed.

Earl felt a headache rising between his eyes. He wondered if the monkey that had visited him at Holly's was waiting for him and would soon come sliding down the scaffold. He kept glancing back at the condenser coil. The run had to be over soon.

Coley gasped, "I've had it."

Earl raised his heavy arm and hit the pump. "Few minutes more. There can't be much left."

They kept pounding.

The stream suddenly stopped. The mash was out; the run was over.

Earl turned the burner off and rolled out twice to the middle of the floor. He was too weak to stand up.

Coley lay under the feeder pipe, waiting for his strength to come back. The outline of his body was sweated to the floor and he stared at a single crack between the boards, wondering how much weight he had lost. He could feel Coach Rice grabbing the wings of his shoulder bones and telling him he was too light for B squad and pointing to the water bucket.

Earl rose and turned off the lights. He pulled the tape from the shades and opened the window.

Coley crawled over on his hands and knees. "I thought I was on fire there."

Earl said, "I almost passed out."

"Whew, thank God it's done."

They kneeled at the back window with their faces stuck out into the cool night air.

Earl sighed. "I don't know when I've been so tired." He lay his face on the ledge. "If I stand up I'll drop dead."

Coley closed his eyes. "You smell mash?"

"Sure, we'll probably smell it in our sleep."

"No, I mean different. It's really strong. Jeeee-sus! Look! Oh, God!"

Below them a white foam of mash slop was spreading across the back yard. In the moonlight it looked like soap-suds.

"It's us, Earl. We're leaking! Something's broke!"

Earl jumped. "The toilet!"

They raced downstairs. The toilet was clogged and was

gushing like a broken low-pressure water main. The bath-room and the back room were three inches deep, and the white slop was bubbling up over the fire hose and flowing thickly under the back door into the yard.

Earl leaned his head on the door jamb and raked his fin-gernails down the board. "Rat's ass! Rat's ass! We should have checked it."

Coley waded through the slop and waggled the flush handle back and forth. "Damn! Damn, what a stupid, crummy mess."

They went outside. The hard, sun-baked clay was hold-ing the slop like a porcelain tub. It covered the yard and was building up and frothing near the fence. Earl said, "Will you smell that!"

"It's going to stink worse when the sun hits it. Come on, let's get our clothes and get the hell out of here."

Earl felt the slop working through his tennis shoes and soaking his socks. "If we could only kill the smell."

Coley said, "How about Lysol? Bleach? Hell, what about flushing it down with straight water?"

"Flush it! It would go in the street. We'd have to dig a hole a mile deep."

Coley was whispering fast. "Aw, hell, Earl, I'm scared. I'm for clearing out."

Earl snapped his fingers. "Got it! Ammonia! That'd do it."

"But we'd need a barrel to do any good."

Earl said, "Listen, you stay here and load the whiskey. I'll get the truck and try Holly."

Coley hiked his jockey shorts up with his wrists. "Bull! You ride around while I'm working here with this smell spreading. That's great."

"Come on, Coley, we ain't got much time. Start stashing. I won't be long."

"Well, you better get back here fast or I'm hauling ass."

After picking up Leroy's truck Earl drove to Holly's. He told Preach the problem, paid him for sixteen gallons of household ammonia packed in four corrugated cartons, and headed back for Pope Street. He drove fast. He was too nervous to be tired and he felt better with the sixteen gallons of ammonia riding next to him. At the corner of Liberty and Harris he slowed down for the stop sign, shifted to second, and began picking up speed. The sudden beam of a flashlight and the rapid popping sound of a motorcycle engine hit him at the same time.

"All right, Edge, pull over."

Earl stopped. His heart rose, choking him and thundering in his throat. He gripped the wheel tightly and wanted to bang his head on the hard rubber. It was Hog Wallace.

"What in the hell you mean running that stop sign?"

Earl didn't answer. His feet were sticky and he could smell the mash slop on his shoes. His socks felt ice cold. He wondered how much Hog knew. Maybe the Law was already at Pope Street. Maybe they already had Coley and had sent Hog out to pick him up.

Hog played his flashlight spot over the empty truck bed and then into Earl's face. "You're up to something, boy. I can tell it."

Earl said nothing.

The light stopped on the cases of ammonia. "So. So, that's it. Carrying a little moon for Leroy. Well, I'll be damn." He circled the truck and opened the door. He pushed one of the cartons hard, then shook it. The eight half-gallon jars clunked together. Hog leaned in the pickup further,

AUGUST

sniffing and frowning. "Smells like sour mash." He smiled.
"That's it, all right. Not only hauling it, you been running
it, ain't you? Well, I finally nailed you, you little bastard. It
took a while but by God I've got you now. I'm going to put
you so far back in that cell block you're going to need a tele-
scope to see daylight."

Earl was afraid to speak. He was afraid to tell him it was
ammonia and afraid not to. If he told him it was he'd have
to explain what he was doing with it. Hog might put him
under the hot lights at the station house and sweat 906 Pope
Street out of him.

Hog shone his flashlight in Earl's face. "Look me in the
eye, Edge. You might as well tell me now. It'll save us both
a lot of trouble. Where you meeting Leroy?"

Earl didn't answer. He tried to push his left shoe off with
his right foot but the laces were too tight.

"O.K., wise guy, follow me down to the station and
don't try anything funny. No! Wait a minute. You go
ahead, I'll follow you." The Harley-Davidson roared. Hog
shouted, "O.K., Edge, let's go."

Earl drove slowly. He held his head high and stiff as he
switched feet on the gas pedal and untied the laces. The
right shoe came off, and he peeled the sock down and
jammed it in. The left shoe was easier. When he turned the
corner at Harris and Pine he tossed the shoes out the window and began rubbing his feet on the rubber floor mat,
hoping to drive the mash smell away.

Hog's motorcycle backfired and popped as he turned it
off and coasted up to the station house. "O.K., Edge, let's
check your belongings."

Earl reached up to the night clerk's desk and laid out the
car keys, his jackknife, his two rubber squeezing balls, three

Tootsie Rolls, two packs of matches, and almost a full package of Kools.

The clerk gave him back the candy, the Kools, and the matches. He looked at Earl's feet. "Don't you wear shoes?"

"No sir, not today."

Hog gave Earl a light shove. "O.K., Pete, give him a nice dark one. He's been giving me a lot of trouble."

Earl's feet felt sticky and cold on the cement as he followed Pete down the cell block. Lonnie's paint job was still glistening and fresh-looking, but the corridor was damp and smelled of rust and lime suphur. A thin icicle of fear inched up Earl's spine as Pete slid the steel door back.

Pete rapped his nightstick on the bars for attention. "Anyone in here know Edge?" The sound echoed twice. He lowered his voice. "What's that first name again?"

"Earl."

"Anyone here know Earl Edge?"

Someone cursed and rolled over heavily. A twangy Horse Creek Valley voice sang out, "Cut that racket out and get them infernal lights out of my eyes."

Another voice cut through. It sounded as if it was coming from a deep hole. "Which Edge?"

"I said Earl. Earl Edge."

"That Leroy's boy?"

Earl said, "Yessir."

"That's him."

"I know him. He can stay with me."

"O.K., Jesse. I guess you could use some company." He touched Earl's elbow and moved him forward. "Jesse don't sleep too good."

Pete left and Earl shook hands with Jesse. "Apple's the name, son, Jesse Apple. Me and Leroy used to play ball together." He nodded at the top bunk. "That's yours. You can sit here till he turns the light off."

Earl sat down and pushed up on the steel slat springs on his bunk. "Wow, that's really hard."

"You get used to it."

The forty-watt water-stained bulb above them gave off a greenish yellow light. They were in a corner cell with three concrete walls and a low ceiling. Only the door and the front wall were bars. The room was damper than the corridor; behind the toilet it was green with mold. Thick chicken-wire-reinforced plaster was hanging down in big chunks from the ceiling and the room had the strong gray smell of sour mop. The toilet had no seat.

"How you flush that?"

"They do it for you. All kinds of services around here."

Jesse was a dark intense man with a deep worried look around his eyes and mouth. He seemed to have been raised in the dark, for the dim caged light made him frown and cup his hand over his pale oyster-colored eyes. He had big, long, heavily veined, almost tortured-looking hands. Jesse's brown and gray hair smelled of Brilliantine and he parted it down the middle, combing it flat behind his ears the way the old ballplayers did when they were being photographed for Cooperstown. "How's Leroy doing?"

"Pretty good."

"He still driving that Ford?"

Earl offered Jesse a cigarette but he shook his head. "Yessir, he's still got it but he's been talking about trading it in." He flipped the match out through the bars and leaned back on the wall. "You know, this place ain't too bad."

Jesse said, "Son, I generally like to read from the Book about this time in the morning. Maybe you'd like it if I read aloud. That way we could both get a little something out of it. You see, I'm studying to be a minister."

"Yessir, I'd like that." Earl climbed up into the top bunk and pushed the itchy brown army blanket to the foot of the bed. He didn't want to hear Jesse read but he knew there was no way out of it. He wondered what had happened to Coley.

The light in the cell went out and the sudden darkness scared him. He wanted Jesse to keep talking. A high nasal voice from down the cell block sighed, then groaned, then sighed again. He seemed to be in great pain.

"Who's that?" Earl shivered; the fear came back stronger.

Jesse turned on a pencil flashlight. "That's Bob Ragsdale. They got him on bigamy. Couldn't leave the women alone. Had himself three wives. Now he's got two years and a case of insomnia. Can't sleep a lick."

Earl leaned over the bunk. He was too scared to go to sleep. He had to keep Jesse talking. "Three! Where'd he keep them?"

"Two in Georgia and one right here in town."

Earl thought of two more questions. "How'd they catch him?"

"Hepatitis. Came down with hepatitis and couldn't work for two months. I guess he just couldn't cover all his houses."

"Where'd they catch him?"

"Don't know. Boy, you know that must have been something hard to handle. Imagine having to keep on your toes like that. He probably wore himself out worrying."

A voice boomed from down the corridor. "Hey, Jess, how 'bout knocking it off?"

"Sorry, Herbert."

Jesse cleared his throat and lowered his voice. He read the twenty-third, the twenty-fourth, and the twenty-fifth Psalms. He had a low steady throbbing voice. He stopped after the twenty-fifth.

Bob Ragsdale sighed wearily again and tossed on his hard leaf springs.

Jesse turned his light off. "How'd you like my reading?"

"Nice, Mr. Apple. Nice. I like it. It's got a nice bite to it."

The darkness felt heavy and liquid around Earl, and he wished Jesse would keep his light on. He had to keep him awake. "Read some more, Mr. Apple. I really like it."

"Just call me Jesse. You're right, little Edge, it's got authority. That's what I put into her. You notice how I emphasize things a lot without having to shout?"

"Yessir, that's the main thing I like. Makes it easy to follow."

Jesse folded his pillow behind his head. "People like it better that way, I swear they do. You take some Jesus-shouting lint head up there loudmouthing everything he says. Hell, people can't follow that noise."

"You're really right, Mr. Apple. Why don't you read a little bit more? Here, let me hold the light for you."

"No, boy, that's enough reading for tonight."

Earl's feet were still gummy and cold from the mash. He tucked them under the blanket and leaned his chin on the edge of the bed frame. "When you getting out?"

"January."

"January! That's five months! They can't hold you here but ninety days. I know that for a fact."

"I'm pulling nine months here; then I go down to do seven to nine for the state."

"Months?"

"Years."

"Damn, Mr. Apple! What they get you for?"

"Manslaughter."

Earl's chin froze on the metal bed frame. His heart pumped hard, then seemed to stop, then began thudding against the thin cotton mattress. He didn't want to talk but he knew Jesse was waiting for him to say something. "You—" He paused and searched for another way of saying it. There wasn't any. "You—you kill somebody?"

"Yeah, that's what they tell me. I guess you want to hear about it, don't you."

Earl didn't answer.

"I had me this 'forty-seven Ford and Junior—that's my dead sister's son who I raised—he had a 'forty-seven Special." Jesse fell back into his slow psalm-reading voice. "I told him not to buy it in the first place, but he went ahead like a damn fool and got it anyway." Jesse sighed. " 'Bout a week after New Year's Eve he wanted to borrow my Ford. Said he had his in the garage and he wanted to go out to a square dance. Well, hell, I'd done made my plans for going to a revival meeting out at Ballantine's Landing." He stopped. "You listening, boy?"

"Yessir."

"Well, we got to arguing. I tell you, these boys your age coming up nowadays got about as much respect for their folks as a snake in a ditch. Anyhow, I don't take sass from no man, much less a boy I done broke my ass feeding, so I fropped him up aside the head. Next thing I see he's got his switchblade out and he's picking at his fingernails. But all the time he's picking I could tell he was just craving to take a swipe at me. At me! His own flesh and blood! Hell, I'd of given him the fool car if he hadn't started that. I was all set to back down. I swear I was."

Jesse hooked his fingers under Earl's springs and pulled down hard. Earl jumped as the bed jerked and rattled, and he grabbed onto the chain support with both hands.

Jesse's voice was louder now. "You take a boy like that and you grab ahold of him by the scruff of the neck and you ram him right down in the middle of religion and you hope something will stick. But not Junior, no sir. Him and gospel was like oil and water. They just wouldn't mix. I'd cram it down his throat and he'd just rare back and spit it out."

Jesse talked about his wife. He told how sorry she was. How she was always chasing after the motorcycle riders and how she had set a bad example for Junior. "If I told her once I told her a thousand times to shape up. I said, 'Damn you, you scroungy bitch, shape up and get this mess cleaned up or ship out.'"

A voice pleaded from down the corridor. "Jesse, for God's sake. Let that boy get some sleep."

Thinking about his wife made Jesse madder, and he wondered which motorcycle rider she was holding on to and which tourist camp they were heading for. He shouted out, "Go to hell, Herbert! What in the hell do you know about anything?"

Earl heard every word but at the same time he heard nothing. All he was aware of was the simple fact that he was alone with Jesse Apple and Jesse had killed his own dead sister's son for sassing him. He sat up slowly and braced his back against the wet wall. He grabbed his knees and raised his feet up high. He wished he had his shoes. If

Jesse came for him he would kick him in the face and start screaming. Herbert and Bob Ragsdale were awake; maybe they could help. But how?

Maybe Jesse would come at him some other way. Maybe he had a piece of metal he had filed away from the springs or a tin plate he had shaved down into a slim dagger. Earl's legs were tired, and he lowered them to save his strength. A slight scratching sounded. He jumped. "What's that?"

"That's rats. They come down the drain from the roof. Damn place ought to be condemned."

Earl took a deep breath. He tried to speak in a low steady voice. "Why don't you read some more? I wouldn't mind a few more psalms."

Jesse lit a cigarette. "Naw, I ain't studying no psalms now. Got too much on my mind. A man's a damn fool when it comes to women. Yancy, that's my brother-in-law from my first wife, he told me about her and I wouldn't listen. Told me I wouldn't be able to keep her out of them damn juke joints. Yessir, if I'd a listened to him I'd be a free man right this second."

He was quiet. Outside a diesel truck was pulling the hill in low gear.

"Never get married, boy. That's my advice. Take your money to a cat house, you'll be better off."

"Yessir."

"Listen at Bob Ragsdale down there. Finest fellow you'll ever want to meet. Look what they done to him. Why in the hell should he ever want to get out of here?"

"You're right, sir."

"And what do the wives do while we're in here rotting? Nothing! Not a good goddamn thing! Just sit on their tails listening to hillbilly music and go running off spraddle-

AUGUST

assed to the honky-tonks and drive-in movies behind the
first son of a bitch that's got a Harley-Davidson." He
cursed, slammed his cigarette against the wall, and pounded
the mattress with his fist. "I get so mad I want to tear this
damn place apart and every son of a bitching bastard in it."
He whirled over violently and grabbed Earl's springs.
"Jesus, I get mad!" He jerked down and wrenched from
side to side. He kicked his supporting chain.

Earl pressed back against the wall. The bed heaved and
rocked. The chain made a deep twanging sound, vibrating
the springs and the bars. He wanted to call for help, but he
was afraid Jesse would kill him before Pete could unlock
the door. Suddenly Jesse stopped and lay back panting. Earl
knew that his next move would be to climb up and grab
him. He bunched back and coiled tight, waiting; he decided
to shout "Murder!" rather than "Help!"

But Jesse didn't move. Instead he lay still and calmly lit a
cigarette. He smoked quietly for what seemed an hour and
then flipped his cigarette toward the toilet. It missed and lay
on the floor, slowly cooling and going out.

Earl was tired, very tired. The strain had exhausted him.
He had to have more strength to fight Jesse off. He decided
he would rest without sleeping. He would let himself rest to
the edge of sleep and then pull himself back. It was a bril-
liant idea. His head rocked to one side, his tight jaw slacked,
and a soft, wise, but weary smile slid across his face.

In a dream he saw that falling asleep had been a terrible
mistake. He pushed to get out, but he could get no leverage.
The walls were covered and dripping with oil, and a
strange yellow light filtered through. It was cold, colder
than the freezing room. It was hot, hotter than the Detroit
burner and the copper cooker. He tried to scream, but he

had no voice. There was no breath in his chest. No air in the room. He couldn't move.

The walls of oil changed to a bright blue sky. He was at the Little Eddy, sinking into the water and drifting down to the Hudson. He climbed in the back seat; two men were in the front. The current turned the thick pages of the *Human Torch* comic book, and carp and eel and maggot white river worms glided by. The driver turned around. It was Sonny Love. "Close the door, boy, we're driving to Jesus."

The other man was dressed in solid black and looked like the stranger who had warned Coley and him about the Hudson. He was reading loudly from the Bible and pounding on the dashboard with his fist.

Sonny gunned the engine, double clutched, and spun off with the tires screaming. He drove fast, weaving in and out of the tree stumps and water-logged crossties and orange crates that lined the muddy bottom. The river bottom raced by; Campbell's pork-and-bean and sardine cans, nail kegs and oilcans, cinnamon roll and candy wrappers, bicycle frames, automobile tires, bedsprings and inner tubes, Coca-Cola signs, Dr. Pepper bottles, and prophylactics all swirled and whirled around them. They seemed to be heading for Charleston.

There was something odd about the stranger. Earl grabbed the front seat with both hands and leaned forward to get a better look at him. It was Jesse Apple. Earl wanted to whisper to Sonny and warn him that Jesse was a killer, that he owed the state seven to nine years and that if it got dark enough he would kill them both. But Sonny was hunched way over the wheel and Earl couldn't reach him.

The valves were clattering, the engine strained. Earl held

on tighter, praying for Sonny to sit back. Hooded oily shapes drifted by and peered in. Black tree roots and phosphorescent-colored lizards clutched and clung to the windshield wipers. Sonny's voice boomed out. "Earl Edge, do you renounce all your sins and promise to live by the blessed word of Jesus for the rest of your mortal days?"

"Yessir."

Suddenly Jesse swung around and was reaching for Earl's throat. Earl leaped back. Sonny's voice was louder. "And accept his teachings and mend your sorry ways?"

"Yessir," he choked.

Jesse's hands were like an enormous posthole digger reaching for him. Earl pulled back and clawed at the window. Convulsing cottonmouth moccasins slipped and slid across the glass and he wrenched back to the other side of the seat. Jesse's hands were on him. Earl raised his feet and Jesse brushed them aside. Earl sat back, back. The promises he was making to Sonny were running together. "Yessir, yessir. I believe that. That too. Yessir."

The car skidded, spun around wildly. They rolled over and over. Jesse's thumbs were pressing on Earl's windpipe. Earl thrashed back and forth shouting, "Won't steal! Won't lie! Won't sell whiskey! No smoking! Yessir, I'll pray every time I get a chance! Only please, sir! Please get me out of here. Please!"

He screamed, "PLEASE, SONNY!" He was awake. His heart was racing, his throat was sore, his hands and chest were wet; he was rigid, unblinking, terrified.

He pulled his knees and cold feet up tight and whispered rapidly, "Please, Lord, please. Please get me out of here. I wasn't lying, I meant every word I said."

He threw his cigarettes at the toilet. He wanted to say,

"See there, Lord, see there. See, what did I tell you?" but decided the Lord might figure it wrong. He threw the matches after the cigarettes and lay back, telling himself over and over again that he had meant every word of every promise.

Coley climbed the stone fence at the corner so he could watch for Earl and the Law. He had stashed seven kegs and had two more to go. Two hours had passed, and he was furious. He was convinced that Leroy had refused to loan Earl the truck, and Earl was sitting in some diner eating a hamburger and trying to figure what to do next. Roosters were crowing in the south of town and lights were coming on in the small houses of the cotton mill workers that were on the seven to four shift. After he had loaded the last two kegs into the grave of Morris Blumenthal, 1870-1946, and slid the stone slab back into place, he secured the bottom plank on the fence.

In the yard the mash slop looked like a heavy frost. Another hour had passed, and it had run down the driveway and was flowing in the brick-lined drain ditch. The smell was stronger, much stronger. Coley pushed his bicycle across the street and sat down on a rusted car fender in the tall pokeweed and Johnson grass. He began worrying. If the truck had broken down, Earl could have taken a cab back. He had to be in trouble. More lights came on in the houses, and a morning newspaper boy rode by on a three-wheel heavy duty Schwinn bicycle. Maybe the Law had caught Earl and was sweating the still information out of him in the rick-rack room. He smiled; it would take more than hot lights and leather straps to crack Earl Edge. But maybe he had rolled the truck into a ditch. The pickup couldn't corner as fast as the Hudson, and Earl wasn't that good a driver. Maybe he was pinned under the truck somewhere. But where? Where had he gone?

The lights and radio came on at the same time at the house next to 906. The news announcer said that the temperature for Columbia and vicinity was going to be in the high nineties, the humidity sixty per cent. Octagon soap and Pillsbury flour were on sale at Sanderson's, and ground chuck was being featured at thirty-three cents a pound. Kelsey Miller, master of ceremonies of the Carolina Morning Show, announced that the next singer was Darling Darleen out of Wheeling, West Virginia, where she was known as the girl with a tear in her voice. Her first song was going to be "No Letter in the Mail Today." Darling Darleen's piercing Jew's-harp tone made Coley's bicycle spokes vibrate.

A low-slung brown and white hound loped down the middle of the street. Suddenly he veered off and followed the white trail of slop up the alley. He began a strange choppy bark, then came loping out, barked again, growled, and headed back down the middle of Pope.

The sun cleared the houses in the east. It looked like a bright, sugar-coated, candy orange slice and felt good on Coley's tired face. He closed his eyes and pointed his nose at it. He was convinced that Earl must have rolled the truck into a ditch and was either pinned under it or was limping back with blood streaming down his face. He tried to recall what ammonia smelled like. Maybe it was worse than the mash slop. What if someone called and complained about it? But maybe ammonia would act like a deodorant, would kill the smell and then vanish itself. He tried to remember the radio commercials about deodorants, but he began to doze. He caught himself and sat up straight. He tried to stay awake by listening to the words of a song being sung by two men and two women from Holly Hill, South Carolina, who called themselves the Holly Hill Sweet Singers.

It was a long sad song about a man sitting and smoking in his Ford parked in front of his house and waiting for his wife's boy friend to leave. He had been on the road selling something and he was tired. The name of the song was "I've Enjoyed About As Much of This As I Can Stand." Coley's eyes closed. Slowly his head dropped forward to his chest and he slept. The brown and white hound came back and stood in the middle of the street watching him. It was six-thirty.

A woman shouted. Coley jumped awake. The voice was coming from 908 Pope. "Hey, Emma!"

"Yeah!" came from 904 Pope.

"You see that stuff?"

"Yeah, I smelled it all night. Billy Joe says it's sour mash."

"You reckon they got a still in there?"

"No reckon to it. Billy Joe figures something must have broke for mash slop to come gushing out like that."

"Do tell. I kinda figured they had something in there. Place looked mighty suspicious to me. Well, maybe the sun will dry it up and there won't be no trouble."

"Yeah, in about a month. That stuff's two inches deep over here. Wish I had me a couple hogs. They'd lap it up and come right back looking for more." Emma laughed. She had a scratchy birdlike laugh. "I'll bet somebody's sweating."

"Ain't it the truth."

Coley knew there was no returning to the house. He

knew that when the sun hit the slop the smell would spread. It would either be the Law or the Board of Health. Somebody was bound to call someone.

A siren sounded in the distance. He pushed his bike off and slowly rode around the block. When he came back down Pope two cars of detectives and policemen were parked in front. Seven of the eight doors of the two cars were open: they had gone in in a hurry. Another car pulled up and out stepped four men armed with axes, crowbars, picks, and shovels. A fourth car pulled up and Tom Bennet got out yawning and dogtrotted up the brick-lined path.

Coley came down stiffly on his left pedal and started up Spruce. He was going to park up the hill and wave Earl off. Halfway up he saw Roy Jarvis coming down. Roy stopped.

Coley pulled his bike in close. "What's going on?"

Roy almost shouted. "Raid, big one. Caught one of the biggest stills in the state. Right here under our noses. I think the Sheriff's in there."

"How big?"

"Bigger than hell. I hear they made over a thousand gallons. Took it out in a moving van. Hey! They got Edge, that buddy of yours, up at the station."

"Jesus! What for?"

"Hog Wallace pulled him in on running a stop sign. Thought he was carrying moon, but it turned out to be ammonia. Boy, if that wasn't one dumb-ass piece of detecting I'll eat it."

"Is he in jail?"

"Hell, yeah. They had him in a cell all night. They'll let him out when the judge shows up. Boy, old Hog's ass is going to look like the inside of a hornet's nest when Monroe gets through chomping on it."

Chapter 28

The pigeons outside the cell-block window made a low curdling sound, and the smell of strong chicory-blended coffee came floating down the corridor.

Jesse snored.

Earl woke up freezing. He had kicked the blanket off during the night and it lay five feet below on the floor. He rubbed his feet with his hands and watched Jesse sleep.

Jesse was smaller than he remembered. The bunk was small but Jesse lay stretched out with plenty of room at the head and plenty at the foot. His face was brittle and old-looking, his long, almost transparent hands were the blue-white color of Blue John.

Earl knew he was too frail to be a strangler unless he'd used a piece of piano wire or a coat hanger. A fast man could handle him easy. Earl measured himself on the bunk. He was almost as tall. If they put him and Jesse in the ring with eight-ounce gloves and Jesse had no other weapons, he knew he could take him. He would move fast and back-pedal away from him. Jesse's legs would go first. Earl crouched on his knees and elbows and hung over the side of

374

the bed. He tightened his fists. He would keep circling and faking Jesse, wearing him down; then stalking, with long Sugar Ray Robinson shoulder-high lefts, waiting for the fatal opening.

Jesse could be faking. He was old, but he was tricky. He could be luring him in for a knee to the groin or some mystery punch. He had killed once; he could kill again. It would be long lefts, then quick short lefts, a fast combination, another, then back off with two ripping hooks, one high, one low. Jesse sagged. Earl smiled and the phantom two-ton bull-killing right sang in his head. He could feel it smashing and breaking the frail jaw of Jesse Apple. He rubbed the back of his right. He could feel the imprint of the whisker stubble.

Earl quietly lowered himself to get his blanket and cigarettes.

Jesse sat up and began combing his hair. "How'd the cigarettes get way over there?"

"Must have fell out." Breakfast was being served.

Jesse yawned. "Come on, sit here. How'd you sleep?" Jesse's bed smelled like toenails.

"Pretty good." Earl sat cross-legged like an Indian, with the blanket around his shoulders and arms and tucked under his feet. "That bed ain't too bad." He was hungry. He ate the hot corn bread and grits and fatback and drank two cups of the Luzianne coffee.

Jesse said, "Finish that coffee fast. That way you get another."

"They really treat you pretty good around here, don't they?"

Jesse barked a one-note laugh. "Sure, they treat you like kings."

The shadows of the bars moved across the ceiling and the coffee pot came around again. Bob Ragsdale was singing "If You Don't Love Me, I Wish You Would Leave Me Alone," and a trusty called Shim was soaking down the corridor with a mop.

Earl sipped his third cup of black coffee. "You know what? I dreamt about Bob Ragsdale and those three wives he had."

"That must have been something. How'd you make out?"

Suddenly, Earl heard voices coming toward them. "That sounds like my buddy."

Jesse said, "Use the mirror."

Earl pulled the clip-on mirror from the bed frame and held it out so he could see up the aisle. "It is! It's Coley!"

"Hi, Earl."

"Morning, Coley."

Jesse said, "Come on, Pete, let the kid in."

"Can't, Jess. No one's around to authorize it."

Earl gripped the bars close to Coley's hands. It reminded him of the movies.

Coley whispered fast. "It's all over. There's four cars down there and they're tearing everything up. God! I thought you'd been killed in a wreck or something."

"Hog caught me on Harris."

"Yeah, Roy told me."

"How you reckon they found out?"

Coley looked past Earl. He didn't want Jesse to hear. "Somebody must've phoned in. You can smell it a mile away, and the sun ain't even hit it yet. Hey, how come you didn't show Hog what you were carrying?"

"I figured they had us and I was stalling for time."

Coley was whispering so fast his words were running together. "Earl, the whole police force is there, even the Sheriff. God! Fingerprints! How about fingerprints? What about that? We should've worn gloves."

"Don't worry, they can't do a thing. They've got to catch you in the act. I know that for a fact."

"You ain't lying, are you, Earl?"

"No. Hell, no."

"Well I hope you know what you're talking about. How they treat you in here?"

"O.K." He sipped his coffee and watched Coley's eyes scan the cell block. "Coffee's good. Want a shot?"

"Sure. Say, where's your shoes?"

Earl squeezed the tin cup through the bars. "Hog picked up the smell and I had to get rid of them."

"I'm bushed." Coley sighed and lowered his voice. "I got everything stashed, every drop. Like to broke my back on those slabs." His teeth clinked on the cup lip. "We couldn't have done any good with the ammonia. The people next door smelled it last night."

Earl's lips touched the bar. "Listen, you know who my cellmate is?"

Coley moved to one side to look at Jesse and shook his head.

"It's Jesse Apple. Don't you remember him from the newspapers?"

"Nope, can't say that I do."

"Guess what he's in for?"

Coley took another look. "Insulting an officer? Resisting arrest?"

Earl made an "M" with his lips and whispered, "Manslaughter. Lean closer. Killed his own sister's boy. Got eight to ten years."

"Jeeee-sus, weren't you scared being with him?"

Earl smiled with the corners of his mouth. "Little bit at first. But I figured what the hell, he'd be a fool to try anything in here. Besides, I was pretty tired so I didn't pay him much mind."

Coley shifted to get a better look at Jesse. "What'd he do it with?"

"He didn't say. Tire iron or crowbar. I figure something heavy."

"Wait till everyone hears about this. You know, when the light catches him right he does look like a killer. Man, this is really something, Earl."

Coley handed the cup back and Earl pulled out his cigarettes. Coley struck a match. "He's got funny eyes, too. And that hair part in the middle is a dead giveaway. Ask him if he wants a cigarette."

Earl turned. "Want a smoke, Jesse?"

"What you smoking?"

Coley said, "Kools."

"Naw, I can't go that Menthol route. I got my own."

Coley leaned on the bars. "Roy says Judge Monroe's going to chew Hog's ass out for pulling you in like this. What're you saying about the ammonia?"

"I'm telling him I was carrying it out to Holly's Jackson Road place from Cooper Ridge. But you got to get out there and tell Holly to back me up. Listen, take a taxi. If they check him and he doesn't know what's going on, my ass is mud."

"O.K. You want me to go tell your dad? Maybe he can come down and vouch for you."

Earl tapped the cup on the horizontal bar. "No, don't tell him. He'd just get up there and talk too much. Monroe might trip him up."

"I better get going."

"Wait, you got to get my shoes before Hog starts checking around. I dropped them when I turned off Harris onto Pine. I crammed the socks down in the shoes."

"I'll find them." Coley took another look at Jesse. "So long, Mr. Apple."

"So long, son."

It was ten o'clock before Judge Monroe rapped his gavel on the block and adjusted his glasses. He read the report quickly and then listened to Earl's explanation of carrying the ammonia out to Holly Yates' Jackson Road place.

Hog said he must have made a mistake but he could have sworn he smelled sour mash. The judge drummed his fingers nervously during Hog's long account. He raised his hand, then slammed it down. "What in the thundering Sam Hill do you think sour mash smells like?" He glanced at Earl. "All right, Earl, you can go."

Earl kept a straight grave face. "Thank you, Your Honor." He pinched his shoulders back and went down the courtroom aisle with his arms barely moving. The oak doors closed behind him, and he began walking with a short tight stride toward the desk. His feet were still sticky.

Outside, he stood between the marble columns of the station house doors and lit a cigarette. He let it hang from the corner of his mouth and put the match in the other corner.

He took a long drag and then, after looking up Cedar and then down it as if he was expecting to be gunned down, he flipped the cigarette into the side of the building and headed for Leroy's pickup.

Coley was sitting in the dining room at Holly's house when a call came from Hog Wallace. They were eating buttermilk pancakes with apricot syrup and Canadian bacon.

Holly tapped his fork on his coffee cup saucer while Hog talked. Holly said, "I told Earl to bring it out to Jackson Road. I was running out and he had his dad's truck." He winked at Coley. "Now just what in the hell do you think he was doing? . . . Whiskey still? Are you clean out of your mind? That boy runs errands for me. . . . Lying? Why, you fat bastard. If you and the rest of that crowd down there would forget what the kids are doing and the damn jaywalkers, and get after some of these cheap bastards around town that's bringing in that horse meat from Argentina and calling it beef and poisoning the whole damn state, you might be worth something to the taxpayers. Instead, you . . ."

Hog interrupted. Holly laid his fork down carefully. He was mad. He waited until Hog was through.

"I don't have to listen to this crap from you. Now let me say something, old buddy. The next time you sit down in one of my places and have that big cheeseburger, I'm going to have a little surprise for you. You know what's going to be at the right side of your plate? A check, that's what." He hung up. "Boy, that takes one helluva lot of nerve. He said I was lying." Suddenly he laughed and cut through a stack of six pancakes with one stroke. "Now there's a real sap-sucker for you."

Coley flooded his pancakes with syrup and moved in close to his plate. "He is pretty stupid."

A cool wind was blowing up from the river that after-noon, and the drugstore awning was flapping when Earl and Coley pulled into the bicycle rack.

Doc said, "Hello, boys. What'll it be?"

Earl laid a twenty-dollar bill on the counter. "Two splits and two chocolate shakes."

Coley said, "Can I borrow your paper?"

"Sure thing."

Earl stepped on the weighing machine and dropped a penny in. He slapped his hand on the side. "Damn, Doc, this thing's busted. I weigh more than any old hundred and twelve pounds."

Doc stuck cherries on the banana splits and slid them and the shakes across the fountain. "Man checked it the other day. Said it was right on the button. Boy, you're lean as a cricket. You ain't got a lick of meat on you." He poured himself a glass of seltzer water. "Yeah, a hundred and twelve, that's about right."

Earl carried the splits and shakes to the back booth and slid in. Coley was reading the used-car ads. He circled one. "Listen at this: 'nineteen forty-one Mercury, thirty-two thousand miles, new engine, one owner. Two hundred and ninety dollars.' "

"Two-ninety, that ain't bad. Not bad at all."

Coley had his mouth full of ice cream. "We're short eighty-five dollars. Maybe we can jew him down."

"Short, hell. You ain't counting the cemetery money."

Coley swallowed. "I'm not counting that till we see it. Hog ain't no fool, you know."

Earl opened his mouth slowly and belched. "That's for Hog Wallace."

It was a week before Labor Day and the opening of school was only ten days away. The weather had turned cool, and hurricane warnings were up from Charleston to Cape Hatteras. The Yankees were in first place, DiMaggio was batting 346, and ground chuck was thirty-five cents a pound at Sanderson's. Earl and Coley were wearing their new Air Force A-2 jackets from the Army-Navy store zipped up over white silk scarves. Their baseball caps were pulled down low and square.

For five days they had ridden by 906 Pope. Each day Hog, who was now driving a Ford, was parked under a chestnut tree near the corner watching the house.

Coley braked hard and leaned his bicycle against the rough stone cemetery wall. "Hey, he's got on dark glasses today."

They chinned themselves and swung up on the six-foot-high wall and sat facing Hog. Earl said, "Boy, I bet he thinks he's another Charlie Chan."

"He looks like he's taking root."

The wind tumbled a Dixie cup down the drain ditch, and dead leaves were piling up at the sides of the grave vaults.

Earl popped his hands together. "Listen, pounds or no pounds, I'm still going out for football."

"Me too. Besides, who says weight's everything, anyway. We're sharp and we got speed to burn."

Earl lit two Kools and gave Coley one. "Damn right, and

382

we can practice handoffs and reverses and buttonhooks. We'll go out for halfbacks and they can use us as twin safeties."

Coley flicked his head and spat between his teeth out to the grave of Morris Blumenthal. "You realize we can almost spit on five hundred and twenty-five dollars?"

Earl laughed. "Wonder how much aging O'Hara'll figure on if it sits here much longer? Boy, if old Hog knew what he was guarding he'd have nine kinds of hemorrhage."

Coley tried to blow a smoke ring, but it drifted out in three pieces. "I wish he'd hurry up and get the hell out of here. I really got my jaw set for that Mercury."

Earl drew on his Kool and cupped it low in his hand. "He'll leave, Cole. He'll give up. One night he won't be here. One night. And that's all we need. That's all she's going to take."

A red dog carrying a Moon Pie wrapper in its mouth loped across the road, and the cotton mill whistle blew five long notes.